ÉMILE ZOLA was born in Paris in 1840, the son of a Venetian engineer and his French wife. He grew up in Aix-en-Provence, where he made friends with Paul Cézanne. After an undistinguished school career and a brief period of dire poverty in Paris, Zola joined the newly founded publishing firm of Hachette, which he left in 1866 to live by his pen. He had already published a novel and his first collection of short stories. Other novels and stories followed, until in 1871 Zola published the first volume of his Rougon-Macquart series, with the subtitle *Histoire naturelle et sociale d'une famille sous le Second Empire*, in which he sets out to illustrate the influence of heredity and environment on a wide range of characters and milieus. However, it was not until 1877 that his novel *L'Assommoir*, a study of alcoholism in the working classes, brought him wealth and fame. The last of the Rougon-Macquart series appeared in 1893 and his subsequent writing was far less successful, although he achieved fame of a different sort in his vigorous and influential intervention in the Dreyfus case. His marriage in 1870 had remained childless, but his extremely happy liaison in later life with Jeanne Rozerot, initially one of his domestic servants, gave him a son and a daughter. He died in 1902.

BRIAN NELSON is Emeritus Professor (French Studies and Translation Studies) at Monash University, Melbourne, and a Fellow of the Australian Academy of the Humanities. His publications include *The Cambridge Introduction to French Literature*, *The Cambridge Companion to Zola*, *Zola and the Bourgeoisie*, and translations of *Earth* (with Julie Rose), *The Fortune of the Rougons*, *The Belly of Paris*, *The Kill*, *Pot Luck*, *The Ladies' Paradise*, and *His Excellency Eugène Rougon* for Oxford World's Classics. His most recent work is *Émile Zola: A Very Short Introduction* (2020). He was awarded the New South Wales Premier's Prize for Translation in 2015.

JULIE ROSE is an internationally renowned translator, whose many translations range from Hugo's *Les Misérables*, Racine's *Phèdre*, and André Gortz's *Letter to D.* to André Schwarz-Bart's *The Morning Star*, Alexandre Dumas's *The Knight of Maison-Rouge*, and works by leading French thinkers such as Paul Virilio, Jacques Rancière, Chantal Thomas, and Hubert Damisch. She has previously translated (with Brian Nelson) Émile Zola's *Earth* for Oxford World's Classics, and won her most recent award for Philippe Paquet's biography, *Simon Leys. Navigator Between Worlds*. She was made a Chevalier de l'Ordre des Arts et des Lettres by the French government in 2016 and was elected an Honorary Fellow of the Australian Academy of the Humanities in 2019.

OXFORD WORLD'S CLASSICS

*For over 100 years Oxford World's Classics have brought
readers closer to the world's great literature. Now with over 700
titles—from the 4,000-year-old myths of Mesopotamia to the
twentieth century's greatest novels—the series makes available
lesser-known as well as celebrated writing.*

*The pocket-sized hardbacks of the early years contained
introductions by Virginia Woolf, T. S. Eliot, Graham Greene,
and other literary figures which enriched the experience of reading.
Today the series is recognized for its fine scholarship and
reliability in texts that span world literature, drama and poetry,
religion, philosophy and politics. Each edition includes perceptive
commentary and essential background information to meet the
changing needs of readers.*

OXFORD WORLD'S CLASSICS

ÉMILE ZOLA

Doctor Pascal

Translated by
JULIE ROSE

With an Introduction and Notes by
BRIAN NELSON

OXFORD
UNIVERSITY PRESS

OXFORD

UNIVERSITY PRESS

Great Clarendon Street, Oxford, OX2 6DP,
United Kingdom

Oxford University Press is a department of the University of Oxford.
It furthers the University's objective of excellence in research, scholarship,
and education by publishing worldwide. Oxford is a registered trade mark of
Oxford University Press in the UK and in certain other countries

First published as an Oxford World's Classics paperback 2020

Impression: 2

Published in the United States of America by Oxford University Press
198 Madison Avenue, New York, NY 10016, United States of America

British Library Cataloguing in Publication Data

Data available

Library of Congress Control Number: 2020009615

ISBN 978-0-19-874616-4

Printed and bound in Great Britain by
Clays Ltd, Elcograf S.p.A.

CONTENTS

INTRODUCTION

*Readers who do not wish to learn details of the plot will prefer
to read the Introduction as an Afterword*

ÉMILE ZOLA (1840–1902) occupies a distinctive place in the great
tradition of French (and European) critical-realist fiction. His main
achievement as a writer was his twenty-volume cycle of novels *Les
Rougon-Macquart* (1871–93), in which the fortunes of a family are
followed over several decades. The various family members spread
throughout all levels of society, and through their lives Zola examines
the changing social, sexual, and cultural landscape of the late nineteenth century, creating an epic sense of social transformation. The
Rougons represent the hunt for wealth and position, their members rising to commanding positions in the worlds of government
and finance; the Macquarts, the illegitimate branch, are the sub-
merged proletariat, with the exception of Lisa Macquart (*The Belly
of Paris/Le Ventre de Paris*, 1873); the Mourets, descended from
the Macquart line, are the bourgeois tradesmen and provincial
bourgeoisie. Zola is the quintessential novelist of modernity, understood as a time of tumultuous change. The motor of change was the
rapid growth of capitalism, with all that it entailed in terms of the
transformation of the city, new forms of social practice and economic organization, and heightened political pressures. Zola was
fascinated by change, and specifically by the emergence of a new
mass society.

The power of Zola's vision comes from his commitment to the
value of 'truth' in art. This was above all a moral commitment. The
novelist's emphasis on speaking the truth was based on his conviction
that the writer must play a social role: to represent the sorts of
things—industrialization, the growth of the city, the birth of consumer
culture, the workings of the financial system, the misdeeds of government, crime, poverty, prostitution—that affect ordinary people in
their daily lives. And he wrote about these things ironically and satir-
ically. Naturalist fiction represents a major assault on bourgeois
morality and institutions. It takes an unmitigated delight—while also
seeing the process as a serious duty—in revealing the vices, follies,

and corruption behind the respectable facade. The last line of *The Belly of Paris* is: 'Respectable people... What bastards!'

The commitment to truth corresponded to a new integrity of representation. Zola opened the novel up to entirely new areas: the realities of working-class life, class relations, sexuality and the body; and his work embodied a new freedom of expression in their depiction. In his sexual themes he ironically subverts the notion that the social supremacy of the bourgeoisie is a natural rather than a cultural phenomenon; the more searchingly he investigated the theme of middle-class adultery, the more he threatened to uncover the fragility and arbitrariness of the whole bourgeois social order. His new vision of the body, entailing a greater explicitness of description, is matched by his new vision of the working class, combining carnivalesque images with serious analysis of its sociopolitical condition. In *L'Assommoir* (1877) he describes the misery of the working-class slums behind the public splendour of the Empire, while in *Germinal* (1885) he shows how the power of mass working-class movements had become a radically new, and frightening, element in human history. The attacks Zola sustained throughout his career for his purported obsession with 'filth' were largely political in nature—attempts by the Establishment to discredit him. He was a reformist, not a revolutionary, and the denunciation of social injustice and hypocrisy embodied in his fiction is implicit, based on an aesthetic of 'objectivity'; but it is no less eloquent for that—Zola never stopped being a danger to the established order. It was entirely appropriate that in 1898 he crowned his literary career with a political act, a frontal attack on state power and its abuse: 'J'accuse...!', his famous open letter to the President of the Republic in defence of Alfred Dreyfus, the Jewish army officer falsely accused of treason.

Doctor Pascal

While *La Débâcle* (1892), the nineteenth novel of *Les Rougon-Macquart*, brought to a close the history of the Second Empire, *Doctor Pascal* (*Le Docteur Pascal*, 1893), the twentieth and final novel of the series, concludes the saga of the Rougon-Macquart family. Set in Plassans, the novel begins in 1872, after the fall of the Empire. Pascal Rougon, a doctor, first appears in *The Fortune of the Rougons* (1871) as the second son of Pierre and Félicité Rougon; his elder brother is Eugène

Rougon, his younger brother is Aristide (Saccard). He stands apart, to such an extent that he 'did not seem to belong to the family' (*The Fortune of the Rougons*, chapter 2). When he reappears twenty-two years later as the central figure of the novel that bears his name, it is as a heroic, almost messianic, old man, a kind of scientist-scholar, prophesying a glorious future. Devoted to medical research, he has spent his life studying genetics, chronicling and classifying the hereditary ills of his own family—the thirty descendants of his grandmother Adélaïde Fouque (Tante Dide). He keeps his files locked in a cupboard, along with a Family Tree he has painstakingly compiled. Additionally, he has developed a process of hypodermic injections which, he believes, will cure hereditary and nervous diseases. Pascal's young niece, Clotilde (daughter of Aristide), who lives with him, has acquired strong religious convictions under the influence of Martine, the doctor's pious old servant. Clotilde considers her uncle's work a vain, even sacrilegious, attempt to understand what can be known only by God, and begs him to destroy his manuscripts. The conflict between science and religious faith is the focus of the first half of the novel. Pascal responds to Clotilde's pleas:

I believe that the future of humanity lies in the progress of reason through science. I believe that the pursuit of truth through science is the divine ideal that man ought to set himself. I believe that all is illusion and vanity outside the treasure trove of truths slowly acquired and which will never again be lost. I believe that the sum of these truths, which are always growing in number, will end up giving man incalculable power—and serenity, if not happiness... Yes, I believe in the ultimate triumph of life. (p. 39)

Pascal shows his niece the genealogical tree, and, one by one, reads out his files and comments on them, rehearsing in a single sitting the narratives Zola took twenty years to produce: 'Ah! . . . There's a world, a society, a whole civilization in there, the whole of life is there, in all its manifestations, good and bad, hammered out in the forge fire that sweeps all along' (p. 97). Clotilde is won over, persuaded of the power of medical science and natural evolution.

Eventually, the doctor and his pupil begin an intimate and tender relationship, albeit incestuous. Pascal's mother, Félicité, is outraged that they live together out of wedlock. A financial crisis and burgeoning debts induce Pascal to send Clotilde away to Paris. He falls ill and dies before she can return. Félicité, desperate to keep the family skeletons hidden at any cost, burns her son's research papers. Clotilde, on her return, finds fragments of his work, as well as the Family Tree, and resolves to complete the project. Her and Pascal's child is born several months later, and the novel closes in semi-idyllic fashion— Nicholas White speaks of the 'euphoria' of the final pages[1]—by focusing on the hope for the future, and for the regeneration of the family, which is symbolized by the child.

The themes of *Doctor Pascal*, in particular its optimistic vision and the conflict it dramatizes between scientific materialism and religious faith, are best understood by placing the novel in the context not simply of Zola's original intentions for his novel series but also of the climate of ideas in France in the mid- and late nineteenth century.

Science and Literature

During the third quarter of the nineteenth century, France enjoyed a period of spectacular economic growth. Industrialization accelerated, while scientific discoveries were constantly converted into inventions and processes that began to transform everyday life. The transforming power of science seemed infinite. The cult of science underlay most nineteenth-century social theories, and predicated a universe governed by laws which, when grasped, would reveal the 'truth' about the nature of man and his place in the world. In philosophy the scientific method bred positivism, expounded by Auguste Comte (1798–1857) in his six-volume *Cours de philosophie positive* (1830–42). Comte believed that 'truth' was arrived at, not through metaphysical ideas derived from man's consciousness, but through the systematic analysis of observable phenomena; we can only know what we can observe. Positivism was thus virtually anti-religious, arguing that man must shed any belief in absolute supreme causes. It was deterministic in its application of science to society; society and the universe were connected, Comte held, through the inexorable workings of changeless natural laws. And it was optimistic in its view of what scientific method could achieve: Comte believed in 'social engineering', arguing that by applying scientific method to the study of man as a social animal, and thereby deducing the laws that govern

---

[1] Nicholas White, 'Family Histories and Family Plots', in Brian Nelson (ed.), *The Cambridge Companion to Zola* (Cambridge: Cambridge University Press, 2007), 19–38 (at 37).

the functioning of society, it would be possible to design appropriate policies to redress social ills.

Advances in all branches of the sciences seemed to confirm the potential of science to reveal the seamlessness of some overarching structure of connections. The search for a unitary pattern, a master key to an understanding of all social processes, was characteristic of much mid-nineteenth-century thought. Karl Marx offered his contemporaries the explanatory system of the class struggle as the key to human history. Charles Darwin (1809–82) became closely associated with Marx, for Marx's concept of the class struggle as the motor of human history was paralleled by Darwin's concept of the struggle for survival as the essential dynamic of human evolution. Darwin's ideas were popularized in France by the materialist philosopher and literary historian Hippolyte Taine (1828–93), who took the determinist view that major influences, which he termed 'race' (heredity), 'milieu' (environment), and 'moment' (historical context), were responsible for moulding the individual. Thus, in the middle decades of the nineteenth century, science not only acquired enormous intellectual prestige as the principal, or even the sole, model for the creation of true knowledge, but also became the basis of a kind of secular religion.

It was in this positivistic intellectual atmosphere that the young Zola found himself when he arrived in Paris from his native Provence in 1858. In 1862 he was taken on at the rapidly expanding publishing house of Hachette, where he became the head of the new publicity department. Working in this department provided him with a platform to develop a literary career, for it enabled him to learn about the publishing world and to meet many leading authors. These included Hippolyte Taine, the literary critic Charles Augustin Sainte-Beuve (1804–69), and Émile Littré (1801–81), a medical practitioner who was the leading propagandist of positivism during the Second Empire (1852–70). Converted from a youthful romantic idealism to realism in art and literature, Zola began promoting a 'scientific' view of literature. He was influenced by the realist novelist Honoré de Balzac (1799–1850); by the views on heredity and environment of Taine; by Prosper Lucas (1808–85), a medical theorist, author of an important treatise on natural heredity; and by the evolutionary theories of Darwin. Zola himself claimed to have based his writing methods largely on the physiologist Claude Bernard's *Introduction to the Study of Experimental Medicine* (*Introduction à l'étude de la médecine expérimentale*), which he had read soon after its appearance in 1865. In his essay *The Experimental Novel* (*Le Roman expérimental*, 1880), he argued that the 'truth' for which he aimed could only be attained through meticulous documentation and research. The work of the novelist, he wrote, represented a form of practical sociology, complementing the work of the scientist; their common purpose was to improve the world by promoting greater understanding of the laws that determine the material conditions of life. Clearly, literature cannot be equated with the laboratory in any properly scientific sense; however, as Linda Nochlin has written, in terms that are particularly pertinent to Zola: 'In making truth the aim of art—truth to the facts, to perceived and experienced reality—[the Realists'] outlook evinced the same forces that shaped the scientific attitude itself.'[2]

At the end of 1867, Zola published *Thérèse Raquin*, a melodramatic tale of adultery and murder. The critic Louis Ulbach denounced the novel as 'putrid literature'. Zola defended himself in a preface to the second edition (1868), in which he outlined his aim to produce a new, 'scientific' form of realism, which he called 'naturalism'. His purpose, he said, was to use a strictly experimental methodology to analyse the processes by which his characters (whom he calls 'temperaments') are completely dominated by their nerves and blood, are devoid of free will, and are drawn into every act of their lives by the inexorable laws of their physical nature. The epigraph to the novel was Taine's proclamation that 'vice and virtue are products like vitriol and sugar'. The novel was not only a great popular success, but also marked a crucial step in Zola's literary development. After its publication, he sent a plan to his publisher Albert Lacroix for a series of novels— which was to become *Les Rougon-Macquart*. Zola aimed to represent five 'worlds' (bourgeoisie, lower classes, commercial class, upper classes, and the marginal world of prostitutes, criminals, artists, and priests). His ambition, he said, was to emulate Balzac by producing an all-inclusive, multi-volume panorama of the contemporary world. Conceived initially as a sequence of ten novels, the project grew to twenty novels. The subtitle of the cycle, 'A Natural and Social History of a Family in the Second Empire', suggests Zola's interconnected aims: to use fiction as a vehicle for a great social chronicle; to use the symbolic possibilities of a family with tainted blood to

[2] Linda Nochlin, *Realism* (Harmondsworth: Penguin, 1971), 41.

represent a diseased society—the corrupt yet dynamic France of Louis Napoleon's Second Empire; and to demonstrate, in a way that would emulate contemporary scientific discourse, the determining influence on human behaviour of environment and heredity.

The Revolt Against Positivism

In late nineteenth-century France, two now-familiar Parisian monuments appeared, both with strong symbolic significance: the Eiffel Tower, erected in 1889 to celebrate the hundredth anniversary of the French Revolution and to coincide with the Universal Exhibition held that year to glorify science and material progress; and the Sacré-Cœur basilica on the summit of the Butte Montmartre, built between 1875 and 1914 as an expression of a will to spiritual renewal and, expressly, to expiate the sins of the city following its three-month takeover by the Commune of 1871, when the workers had persecuted priests and shot the Archbishop.

Much of the significant creative and discursive writing of the *fin de siècle* reflects the ideological strains of the period and, more narrowly, a powerful current of idealism: a sustained reaction against positivism and its claim that human reason could, through 'scientific method', come to know and understand everything. It became fashionable to speak of the 'bankruptcy' of science. Owen Chadwick writes:

In the 1880s passed over Western Europe one of those movements of mind that history perceives but cannot easily analyse or define. It was something to do with a reviving sense that the world holds mystery and that the prosaic explanations of the age after the romantics will not satisfy.[3]

The first collective manifestation of anti-positivist culture was the Decadent movement, which burst onto the French scene in 1884 with the publication of *Against Nature* (*A rebours*) by Joris-Karl Huysmans (1848–1907), and which was to become the dominant aesthetic of the *fin de siècle.* Huysmans began as a disciple of Zola, writing naturalist fiction (*Marthe*, 1876; *Married Life / En ménage*, 1881). *Against Nature* marked a deliberate break with naturalism and its materialist vision. The novel's anti-hero, a neurotic aristocrat named Des Esseintes,

---

[3] Owen Chadwick, *The Secularization of the European Mind in the Nineteenth Century* (Cambridge: Cambridge University Press, 1975), 239.

seeks to escape from the crass materialism of modern society by turning his back on it and withdrawing into a world of his own making.
He dedicates himself to realizing his own private fantasies and pleasures, attempting to create for himself an artificial paradise by living
life 'à rebours' ('back to front' or 'against nature'), thus carrying
to the point of psychopathology the vision of his master, Charles
Baudelaire (1821–67), who initiated the Decadent obsession with the
artificial and the perverse, arguing that the aim of literature and art
was not to imitate nature but to negate it.

The reader of *Against Nature* learns that the favourite writer of
Des Esseintes is the enigmatic poet Stéphane Mallarmé (1842–98),
the leader of the Symbolist movement. Just as Des Esseintes flees
modern life by withdrawing into a world of his own making, the
poetry (in both verse and prose) of Mallarmé is based on an aesthetic
ideal of self-containment. Central to Mallarmé's poetic principles is
his vision of a 'pure' work of art independent of the world outside
it—either the life of the author or the society in which the author
lives. He sought to develop a poetics that emphasized the patterns
created within the self-enclosed structure of a poem, by the words
composing it, rather than the referential function, however symbolic,
of those words. He was famed for his salons, weekly gatherings of
writers and intellectuals at his apartment in the Rue de Rome for
discussions of poetry, art, and philosophy.

Zola's naturalism began to be explicitly rejected by erstwhile
admirers. In 1886 Count Eugène-Melchior de Vogüé published a study
of the Russian novel, in which he made a famous plea for a novel free
from the shackles of naturalism, a novel which would deal with matters of the spirit as well as the flesh. With the publication of *Earth* in
1887 Zola's dark vision of a peasant world existing beyond all civilized values, and the prominence in his text of explicit sex and bodily
functions, brought to the fore once again the controversy that had
always informed critical responses to naturalism. *Earth* was greeted
with moral outrage. The most widely read expression of this outrage
was the so-called 'Manifesto of the Five'. Published on 18 August
1887 in *Le Figaro*, the day Zola finished his novel but while it was still
appearing in serial form, this 'Manifesto' (probably instigated, for
reasons of jealousy, by Zola's fellow novelists Edmond de Goncourt
and Alphonse Daudet) was a vicious attack on the novel and on Zola
personally. It was signed by five young authors claiming to represent

the younger generation of writers: Paul Bonnetain, J.-H. Rosny, Lucien Descaves, Paul Margueritte, and Gustave Guiches. Zola's 'violent penchant for obscenity', they wrote, was a symptom of his 'insatiable appetite for sales' and of his own psychological and physical dysfunction ('the illness of his loins'). In sum, *Earth* was nothing but 'a collection of scatological stories' in which the Master had sunk to the lowest depths of vulgarity. In similar vein, the well-known novelist Anatole France denounced the novel in *Le Temps* as 'the Georgics of Filth', while the influential Establishment critic Ferdinand Brunetière, writing in the *Revue des deux mondes*, took advantage of the manifesto to proclaim the naturalist movement bankrupt.

During the same decade, there was a remarkable revival of Catholic literature and a spate of conversions to Catholicism among the literary élite. Notable examples of these conversions were Huysmans, Léon Bloy (1846–1917), Paul Bourget (1852–1935), and Paul Claudel (1868–1955). As Richard Griffiths has written:

In the 1880's a Catholic Revival, though it would not have appeared so to the average man of the time, was only to be expected. Two centuries of unbelief (or, at best, deism) in intellectual circles, culminating in the positivist excesses of the Second Empire, could not but produce, eventually, a strong reaction; and that this reaction should take place primarily in the world of literature, where imagination and sensibility have so great a part to play, is not surprising.[4]

In his novel *The Disciple* (*Le Disciple*, 1889) Bourget, a former disciple of Taine, proclaimed the emptiness of positivist doctrines and the dangers of a life unsupported by absolute moral values. Positivism was further undermined by the writings of the philosopher Henri Bergson (1859–1941), who, in his *Time and Free Will* (*Essai sur les données immédiates de la conscience*, 1889) and his extremely popular public lectures at the Collège de France, stressed the existence within people of intuitive forces totally at odds with the mechanistic view of human behaviour embodied in positivism.

During this period there was, also, a growing mood of pessimism concerning the well-being of the nation. The psychological impact of France's calamitous military defeat at the hands of the Prussians in 1870, and the trauma of the Commune of 1871, when the workers of

---

[4] Richard Griffiths, *The Reactionary Revolution: The Catholic Revival in French Literature, 1870–1914* (London: Constable, 1966), 8.

Paris seized control of the city and declared its independence from the rest of France, should not be underestimated; nor indeed should the fears caused by the nation's declining birth rate ('depopulation'). Moral critics blamed the military disaster on demographic decline and moral degeneracy, while writers like the social psychologist Gustave Le Bon (1841–1931) began to develop theories of racial-historical decline, displacing the notion of degeneration from individual degenerates (cretins, criminals, the insane) to society (crowds, masses, cities). Le Bon saw in the crowd the unleashing of man's primitive instincts, a social regression, a symptom of moral and evolutionary decline. In a sense, degeneration theory is the dark side of Darwinian evolutionary theories of progress. Evolution, it was claimed, proceeds unevenly, and at any moment there are forces that pull us back down the evolutionary ladder.[5]

Pascal–Zola

Doctor Pascal embodies a defence by Zola of his naturalist project in the context of the shifting values of the *fin de siècle*, expressing his desire to participate polemically in the ideological struggles of his time. It also embodies a reflection by Zola on his activity as a writer. And it is a highly personal novel in a further sense, for it transposes intimate aspects of Zola's own life. Pascal may thus be seen as Zola's double in philosophical, writerly, and autobiographical terms.

'One could argue', writes Charles Bernheimer, 'about [the entire Rougon-Macquart series] that, if its method is naturalist, its subject is decadence, the corruption and degeneration of France under Louis Napoleon.'[6] Everything leads to the collapse of the Second Empire with the Franco-Prussian War, as described in *La Débâcle*. Moreover, Zola's vision in *Les Rougon-Macquart* is marked by the anxiety that accompanied modernization and rapid social change. The demons of modernity are figured in images of apocalyptic destruction or loss of control: the collapsing pithead in *Germinal*, the stock market crash in

---

[5] For a particularly illuminating discussion of contemporary discourses of decadence, see Daniel Pick, *Faces of Degeneration: A European Disorder, c.1848–c.1918* (Cambridge: Cambridge University Press, 1993).

[6] Charles Bernheimer, 'Decadent Naturalism/Naturalist Decadence', in *Decadent Subjects: The Idea of Decadence in Art, Literature, Philosophy, and Culture of the* Fin de Siècle *in Europe*, ed. T. Jefferson Kline and Naomi Schor (Baltimore: Johns Hopkins University Press, 2002), 59.

Money, the runaway locomotive in *La Bête humaine*. The railway in *La Bête humaine*, in bringing people together yet keeping them apart, symbolizes the disconnection inherent in modern society, of which the novel's psychopathic protagonist, Jacques Lantier, is an extreme, morbid example. In *Doctor Pascal*, Zola is intent, above all, on responding to those who saw in *Les Rougon-Macquart*, with its chronicles of greed, corruption, and murder, nothing but morbidity and darkness. He wanted to articulate the essential optimism of his work. It should be noted that during the 1880s his novels reveal the increasing prominence of mythic discourse in the representation of social reality. Just as he situates man within a total context of shaping influences, so he tends more and more to relate the personal and social action of his novels to a synthesizing world view. This view is essentially that of Darwinian evolution. Zola's conception of society is shaped by a biological model informed by the struggle between the life instinct and the death instinct: the forces of creation and destruction, degeneration and renewal. A myth of catastrophe is opposed by a myth of hope. This pattern of Eternal Return (visible throughout Zola's work, from the cemetery bursting with fecundity in *The Fortune of the Rougons* to the climactic images of germination in *Germinal* and *Earth*) had been given special emphasis in the eighteenth and nineteenth novels of the Rougon-Macquart series: *Money* (*L'Argent*, 1891) and *La Débâcle*. Zola wanted to make it understood that *Doctor Pascal* was written, as he noted in his preliminary notes for the novel, 'out of a love for life, out of admiration for its vital forces'.

Zola makes Pascal his double not only by expressing through him what he called, in his planning notes, 'the whole philosophical meaning' of *Les Rougon-Macquart* (that is, his optimism), but also by turning Pascal into an image (and symbolic affirmation) of himself as novelist. Pascal, the fictional character, is a surrogate of Zola, the naturalist writer. The idea of Pascal as an author, rather than a simple participant—one more pathological 'case'—in the narrative of the Rougon-Macquart family, is reinforced by the fact, as he explains to Clotilde, that he is free of the family's inherited characteristics by virtue of his 'innateness' (the term used in biology to describe the process whereby some individuals are totally unaffected by the hereditary transmission of genetic characteristics). Thus he is known by the people of Plassans as 'Doctor Pascal', not as 'Pascal Rougon'; he is able to stand outside the world of his family, like an author in relation

to the world of his characters. The effect of the metafictional dimension of *Doctor Pascal*—Pascal's outlining of the various narratives
that make up the preceding nineteen novels of the Rougon-Macquart
series, and his provision of supplementary details concerning the
various family members—is to create in the reader an awareness that
Doctor Pascal, and Zola's work generally, is not merely a defence of
scientific materialism (and a defence, in those terms, of the naturalist
project), nor simply a summarizing conclusion to *Les Rougon-Macquart*,
but a *narrative* construction, an *imaginative* work—'in short, it opens
up a reflection on the process of story-making and story-telling'.[7]

The Pascal–Zola equation also has a deeply personal dimension, to
which the myth of regenerative optimism is central. Only *The Bright
Side of Life* (*La Joie de vivre*, 1884) can be compared with *Doctor
Pascal* as autobiographical projection. By the time Zola wrote *Doctor
Pascal*, he had taken a mistress, Jeanne Rozerot, who had borne him
two children, Denise in September 1889 and Jacques in September
1891. (The Zolas were childless, but in 1859, five years before she met
Zola, his future wife Alexandrine had given birth to an illegitimate
daughter, whom she had given up to the Hôpital des Enfants-Trouvés
(Foundling Hospital). Eleven days later, the baby died.) The official,
printed dedication of *Doctor Pascal* reads:

To the memory of MY MOTHER and to MY DEAR WIFE I dedicate this
novel which is the summary and conclusion of my entire *œuvre*.

On 23 June 1893 Zola gave a copy of the novel to Jeanne, and on the
cover he had written:

To my beloved Jeanne, to my Clotilde, who has given me the royal feast of
her youth and taken thirty years off my life by giving me the gift of my
Denise and my Jacques, the two dear children for whom I wrote this book,
so that they might know, when they read it, how much I loved their mother
and how tenderly they should repay her for the happiness with which she
consoled me in my great sorrows.[8]

In May 1888, Zola's wife Alexandrine had hired Jeanne as her
lingère (embroideress and chambermaid). In late August, the Zolas
went on holiday to Royan, accompanied by Jeanne. On their return to

---

[7] Susan Harrow, *Zola, The Body Modern: Pressures and Prospects of Representation*
(Oxford: Legenda, 2010), 140.

[8] Quoted by Henri Mitterand in *Les Rougon-Macquart* (Paris: Gallimard, Bibliothèque
de la Pléiade, 1960–7), v, 1573.

Paris, Jeanne suddenly resigned her post. Zola installed her in an apartment in the Rue Saint-Lazare, not far from the Zolas' home in the Rue de Bruxelles. Zola and Jeanne became lovers in December. She was 21, he was 48. It was in the Rue Saint-Lazare that Denise and Jacques were born. Then, in November 1891, Alexandrine received an anonymous letter, telling her of the affair and the children, and giving her Jeanne's address. She was enraged. Zola, fearing 'a calamity', sent a telegram to his friend Henry Céard saying 'My wife is going completely mad' and asking him to tell Jeanne to vacate her apartment. When Alexandrine gained access to Jeanne's home, she vented her anger on the furniture, broke open a writing desk, and seized all of Zola's letters.[9] It is not difficult to see in Félicité's seizure of Pascal's manuscripts a reflection of the actions of Zola's wife.

She was deeply hurt. She felt betrayed. And she was distressed at the thought that close friends were privy to her husband's liaison, and that much gossip had circulated.[10] Slowly the crisis subsided, though deep tensions remained. A modus vivendi was developed, whereby Zola was able to share himself between two homes until the end of his days. Jeanne, Denise, and Jacques continued to live near the Zolas both in Paris and at Médan (they would spend the summer at a house first in the village of Cheverchemont, on the other side of the Seine, and then in Verneuil, which Zola could reach on his bicycle). Zola spent his nights and mornings with Alexandrine, but most afternoons would go to see Jeanne and the children. There were complications and constraints, but the arrangement—the double life—'worked'. Eventually, Alexandrine wanted to get to know the children, and once or twice a month, with Zola, took them out to the Tuileries, the Palais-Royal, the Champs-Élysées, or the Bois de Boulogne. After Zola's death in 1902 good relations were established between Alexandrine

---

[9] It was not until 2004 that the majority of Zola's letters to Jeanne were published: see Émile Zola, *Lettres à Jeanne Rozerot (1892–1902)*, ed. Brigitte Émile-Zola and Alain Pagès (Paris: Gallimard, 2004). Jeanne's letters to Zola were lost, perhaps destroyed by Alexandrine. For a well-informed (but inevitably fragmented) mini-biography of Jeanne, see Alain Pagès, 'The Story of Jeanne', *Bulletin of the Émile Zola Society*, 31–2 (2005), 3–15.

[10] The flavour of some of this gossip is reflected in the *Journal* of Edmond de Goncourt: '[Paul Alexis] confirms my suspicion that Zola now has a closet family (*petit ménage*). He confessed to him that his wife, though an excellent housekeeper, has many "refrigerating" characteristics, which has driven him in search of some "warmth" elsewhere. And he talks about how this elderly man of letters is feeling rejuvenated.' Edmond de Goncourt, *Journal: Mémoires de la vie littéraire* (Paris: Robert Laffont, 1989), iii, 350 (entry dated 21 November 1889).

and Jeanne. In 1906 Alexandrine began proceedings with the Conseil d'État to entitle Denise and Jacques to bear the name 'Émile-Zola'. Authorization was granted in May 1907.

Powerful currents of feeling flow through the portrayal in *Doctor Pascal* of the relationship between Pascal–Zola and Clotilde–Jeanne: pure happiness, 'the happiness with which she consoled me in my great sorrows' (as Alain Pagès notes, 'Zola was, in essence, an *unhappy* man'[11]); deep mutual affection; a feeling of rejuvenation (again, a biographical note: having adopted a strict diet, Zola was physically transformed in the late 1880s, losing fourteen kilos in six months); the joy of erotic gratification, described lyrically and at length; the expression of 'forbidden love' in the casting of the lovers as uncle and niece; but also a fear of ageing, a melancholic sense of the irremediable distance in age, and a growing awareness, as in *The Bright Side of Life* but in a different register, of death's shadow—a personal dimension that gives great poignancy to Pascal's statement of belief in 'the ultimate triumph of life'. Pascal dies on the very day after he receives word from Clotilde that she is pregnant; and the novel's conclusion celebrates a new life, Clotilde happily nursing their newborn son. Pascal's child is seen as a guarantee of continuity and renewal:

The child had come, perhaps the redeemer . . . [S]he, his mother, was already dreaming of the future. What would he be, when she had made him big and strong, by giving herself entirely? A scholar who would teach the world a bit of the eternal truth? A captain who would bring his country glory? Or, better still, one of those shepherds of men who quell passions and establish the reign of justice? (p. 294)

---

[11] Pagès, 'The Story of Jeanne', 10.

TRANSLATOR'S NOTE

Warning: the note below refers to details of the plot

THIS is the first major English translation of *Le Docteur Pascal* in seventy-three years—since the version done with brio by Vladimir Kean was published in the UK by Elek Books in 1957. Kean's was the third to appear. The first was by Zola's friend Ernest A. Vizetelly (1853–1922), published in the UK by Chatto & Windus in 1893, the same year the original appeared in France (with Charpentier). The second, published in the US by The Macmillan Company five years later in 1898, was done by a woman, Mary J. Serrano.

It's useful, though not essential (the point of a new translation being to be new), to look at earlier translations when they exist. Kean's has regrettably become a rare book. Vizetelly's of 1893 is just as rare these days, despite being reissued twice. Yet, for all the overwrought, florid ornateness of his language, Vizetelly's solutions are always illuminating, often deft. It's quite a leap from his generous extravagance to Serrano's spareness, but her version would inevitably have been done as a corrective. Though elegant, it is not always accurate, nor is it totally unabridged.

Both Serrano and Vizetelly cut sexual material from the text. Interestingly, Serrano does the first sex scene, with gusto, but shaves the second (there are only two, as such), and eliminates altogether Clotilde's letter announcing she is pregnant. Vizetelly cuts both scenes and excises and softens sexual references, but allows Clotilde to be (somewhat miraculously) pregnant by leaving the French word untranslated: '*Enceinte!*' Yet even Kean, cutting nothing and writing with such uninhibited modernity, can be censorious, as when he describes the doctor's 'sordid escapades with the first loose woman he met' in Marseilles, adding the adjectives 'sordid' and 'loose' and thereby providing a judgement Zola carefully refrains from making.

Translations, too, are of their time—and place. Vizetelly was working under legal constraint. From 1884 to 1903 Henry (1820–94) and his son Ernest, between them, published or translated almost every one of Zola's novels in the face of British parliamentary condemnation. Zola's novels were considered a grave threat to public morality, and

Henry Vizetelly was imprisoned for three months for obscenity for publication of Ernest's translation of *La Terre* as *The Soil* in 1888. In a display of shameless hypocrisy, *The Soil* was withdrawn from sale and others of the Vizetelly Zola translations were banned, but Zola's novels were allowed to continue circulating in the original, presumably for the benefit of the French-reading upper classes. Vizetelly was muzzled, though all excisions in *Doctor Pascal* were done with Zola's approval.

Zola said that this novel, which sums up and explains, via Pascal as mouthpiece, 'the characters that have passed through' the previous nineteen in the cycle, would 'refute' the charge he was a pornographer. He also wanted it to counter the charge of 'a lack of tenderheartedness', and said that Pascal would show 'that this is not so'. Readers might agree that this is the most tender-hearted, and intimate, and distressing, of the whole cycle. There are moments so harrowing and violent, I found them emotionally hard to do, just like Vizetelly, almost 130 years ago.

The overall challenge has been to get the register right, finding the right rhythm and consistency of tone. This is a complex work that shifts registers, not only from one chapter or scene to the next, but sometimes within a scene—as when Clotilde, in the hallucinatory banquet scene that is an emotional and erotic apotheosis, suddenly soars off into a pastiche of the Song of Songs, earnestly joined by Pascal. There are the scientific and medical disquisitions, where anachronisms need to be avoided; specialized terminologies of various kinds that need to be refreshed, while remaining historically accurate. There is the strenuously religious cast given to mission statements and creeds, the whole thundering sermon on heredity that pulses through the narrative, along with the aesthetically potent biblical fables and imagery.

There was the usual challenge of conveying Zola's stylistic eccentricities into readable English, unravelling the strings of clauses, flung together breathlessly with no, or few, conjunctions, while not straying too far from them; and there was the unusual challenge of orchestrating the incantatory, at times fetishistic, repetition of words and phrases, whole sentences, throughout the text, sometimes verbatim, sometimes, dizzyingly, with subtle rearrangements and changes.

So much in the book is vividly timeless: the powerful descriptions of nature, the weather, setting the mood and closely syncopated to the action; all the pungent verbs and fabulous muscular poetry of Zola's prose, with its indelible imagery rendering events. (The great prose poem of the family files, recited to Clotilde on 'the night of the storm', is written by Zola as one enormous continuous paragraph which I have broken up in order to make this important family history more comprehensible without, I hope, disturbing the momentum.)

And there are the things that are of their day. Usually, there is a taut and fertile tension between the two: the timeless and the epochal. Translating Clotilde is key here. She might once have been his life-size experiment in correcting heredity; she comes into her own as a complex being—one in whom Pascal's utopian fantasia of the forward march of humanity lives on in a sense of the rebirth of the Messiah every birth anticipates, but also the subject of her own beliefs and hopes, with the realist and the fantasist and mystic harmoniously combined. She is also, through most of the novel, a charge under Pascal's tutelage, expected to obey him and follow his wishes; and yet, she is an equal, his other mind, his other self, the artist and visionary who completes the man of science. The abiding opposition between science and religion is first expressed as a—friendly—contest between science and art. And Clotilde's ultimate embodiment of believing as an intransitive verb feels very modern, in fact contemporary, to me.

And so, I handled the use of various twinned terms, like submission, submissive; coquetry, coquettish; obedience, obedient, with greater subtlety than a literal translation would have offered. 'Dutiful', 'biddable', 'amenable', all perfectly correct synonyms for 'submissive', for instance, don't adhere to the stylistic repetition in the original, but benefit the rhythm of the English sentences in which they occur and suggest the ways in which submission manifests itself. When I do use the words 'submissive' or 'submission', they have greater weight. I've interpreted similar terms with equal flexibility, depending on mood and rhythm.

One other socially charged term of the kind needs to be explained. I initially used 'Master' as Clotilde's chosen term of address for her uncle, but finally opted to keep the French term 'Maître', as I do 'Monsieur' and 'Mademoiselle', for example. *Maître* and the feminine *maîtresse* are still used in France today to designate a teacher or mentor. Pascal is both, for Clotilde (as distinct from the servant, Martine, for whom he is a loved employer). Clotilde is his disciple—

not a *consœur*, that professional role is not available to her as a young woman of her time—but a disciple and indispensable assistant, who herself asserts her agency and status by preferring the term 'Maître', 'so affectionate, so tenderly reverential', we are told in the very first chapter, to Uncle or Godfather, 'which she found crass'. There are various forms of mastery and being mastered.

I'd like to thank Brian Nelson and Judith Luna for their impeccable editorial suggestions and advice. They have both contributed generously to this translation. Judith has been the guiding spirit of the Zola retranslation programme for Oxford World's Classics since 1998, and put a great deal of time and energy, even after retirement, into coaxing this Zola into better shape. Her insights and 'inside knowledge' have been invaluable. I'm also grateful to Rowena Anketell for her very fine and decisive work on the copy-editing.

SELECT BIBLIOGRAPHY

Le Docteur Pascal was serialized in *La Revue hebdomadaire* from 18 March to 17 June 1893. It was published in volume form by Charpentier on 17 June 1893. It is included in volume v of Henri Mitterand's superb scholarly edition of *Les Rougon-Macquart* in the 'Bibliothèque de la Pléiade', 5 vols (Paris: Gallimard, 1960–7), in volume xv of the Nouveau Monde edition of the *Œuvres complètes*, 21 vols (Paris, 2002–10), and in volume v of *Les Rougon-Macquart*, ed. Colette Becker et al., 5 vols (Paris: Robert Laffont, Collection Bouquins, 1992–3). Paperback editions exist in the following popular collections: Folio, ed. Henri Mitterand; Les Classiques de Poche, ed. Jean-Louis Cabanès.

Biographies of Zola in English

Brown, Frederick, *Zola: A Life* (New York: Farrar, Straus, Giroux, 1995; London: Macmillan, 1996).

Hemmings, F. W. J., *The Life and Times of Émile Zola* (London: Elek, 1977).

Studies of Zola and Naturalism in English

Baguley, David, *Naturalist Fiction: The Entropic Vision* (Cambridge: Cambridge University Press, 1990).

Baguley, David (ed.), *Critical Essays on Émile Zola* (Boston: G. K. Hall, 1986).

Harrow, Susan, *Zola, The Body Modern: Pressures and Prospects of Representation* (Oxford: Legenda, 2010).

Hemmings, F. W. J., *Émile Zola* (2nd edn, Oxford: Clarendon Press, 1966).

Lethbridge, Robert, and Keefe, Terry (eds), *Zola and the Craft of Fiction* (Leicester: Leicester University Press, 1990).

Nelson, Brian, *Emile Zola: A Very Short Introduction* (Oxford: Oxford University Press, 2020).

Nelson, Brian (ed.), *The Cambridge Companion to Zola* (Cambridge: Cambridge University Press, 2007).

Wilson, Angus, *Émile Zola: An Introductory Study of His Novels* (1953; London: Secker & Warburg, 1964).

Works in English on or concerning Doctor Pascal

Beizer, Janet, 'Remembering and Repeating the *Rougon-Macquart*: Clotilde's Story', *L'Esprit créateur*, 25/4 (Winter 1985), 51–8.

Butor, Michel, 'Zola's Blue Flame', *Yale French Studies*, 42 (1969), 9–25.

Duffy, Larry, *Flaubert, Zola, and the Incorporation of Disciplinary Knowledge* (Basingstoke: Palgrave Macmillan, 2015), *passim* but esp. 'Textual

Healing: *Le Docteur Pascal*'s Incorporation of Hypodermic Therapy', 194–217.

Mitterand, Henri, 'The Novel and Utopia: *Le Docteur Pascal*', in *Émile Zola: Fiction and Modernity*, trans. and ed. Monica Lebron and David Baguley (London: Émile Zola Society, 2000), 123–35.

Schalk, David L., 'Tying Up the Loose Ends of an Epoch: Zola's *Docteur Pascal*', French Historical Studies, 16/1 (Spring 1989), 202–16.

Schor, Naomi, *Zola's Crowds* (Baltimore: Johns Hopkins University, 1978).

White, Nicholas, 'Incest in *Les Rougon-Macquart*', in *The Family in Crisis in Late Nineteenth-Century French Fiction* (Cambridge: Cambridge University Press, 1999), 98–123.

Intellectual and Literary Background

Bernheimer, Charles, 'Decadent Naturalism/Naturalist Decadence', in *Decadent Subjects: The Idea of Decadence in Art, Literature, Philosophy, and Culture of the* Fin de Siècle *in Europe*, ed. T. Jefferson Kline and Naomi Schor (Baltimore: Johns Hopkins University Press, 2002), 56–103.

Birkett, Jennifer, *The Sins of the Fathers: Decadence in France 1870–1914* (London: Quartet Books, 1986).

Gilman, Sander L., and Chamberlin, J. Edward (eds.), *Degeneration: The Dark Side of Progress* (New York: Columbia University Press, 1985).

Griffiths, Richard, *The Reactionary Revolution: The Catholic Revival in French Literature, 1870–1914* (London: Constable, 1966).

Nye, Robert A., *Crime, Madness and Politics in Modern France: The Medical Concept of National Decline* (Princeton: Princeton University Press, 1984).

Pick, Daniel, 'Zola's Prognosis', in *Faces of Degeneration: A European Disorder, c.1848–c.1918* (Cambridge: Cambridge University Press, 1993), 74–96.

Pierrot, Jean, *The Decadent Imagination, 1880–1900*, trans. Derek Coltman (Chicago: University of Chicago Press, 1981).

Thiher, Allen, 'Zola's Collaborative Rivalry with Science', in *Fiction Rivals Science: The French Novel from Balzac to Proust* (Columbia, MO: University of Missouri Press, 2001), 125–66.

Further Reading in Oxford World's Classics

Zola, Émile, *L'Assommoir*, trans. Margaret Mauldon, ed. Robert Lethbridge.

Zola, Émile, *The Belly of Paris*, trans. Brian Nelson.

Zola, Émile, *La Bête humaine*, trans. Roger Pearson.

Zola, Émile, *The Bright Side of Life*, trans. Andrew Rothwell.

Zola, Émile, *The Conquest of Plassans*, trans. Helen Constantine, ed. Patrick McGuinness.

Zola, Émile, *La Débâcle*, trans. Elinor Dorday, ed. Robert Lethbridge.

Zola, Émile, *The Dream*, trans. Paul Gibbard.

Zola, Émile, *Earth*, trans. Brian Nelson and Julie Rose.

Zola, Émile, *The Fortune of the Rougons*, trans. Brian Nelson.

Zola, Émile, *Germinal*, trans. Peter Collier, ed. Robert Lethbridge.

Zola, Émile, *His Excellency Eugène Rougon*, trans. Brian Nelson.

Zola, Émile, *The Kill*, trans. Brian Nelson.

Zola, Émile, *The Ladies' Paradise*, trans. Brian Nelson.

Zola, Émile, *A Love Story*, trans. Helen Constantine, ed. Brian Nelson.

Zola, Émile, *The Masterpiece*, trans. Thomas Walton, revised by Roger Pearson.

Zola, Émile, *Money*, trans. Valerie Minogue.

Zola, Émile, *Nana*, trans. Helen Constantine, ed. Brian Nelson.

Zola, Émile, *Pot Luck*, trans. Brian Nelson.

Zola, Émile, *The Sin of Abbé Mouret*, trans. Valerie Minogue.

Zola, Émile, *Thérèse Raquin*, trans. Andrew Rothwell.

A CHRONOLOGY OF ÉMILE ZOLA

1840 (2 April) Born in Paris, the only child of Francesco Zola (b. 1795), an Italian engineer, and Émilie, née Aubert (b. 1819), the daughter of a glazier. The naturalist novelist was later proud that 'zolla' in Italian means 'clod of earth'

1843 Family moves to Aix-en-Provence

1847 (27 March) Death of father from pneumonia following a chill caught while supervising work on his scheme to supply Aix-en-Provence with drinking water

1852–8 Boarder at the Collège Bourbon at Aix. Friendship with Baptistin Baille and Paul Cézanne. Zola, not Cézanne, wins the school prize for drawing

1858 (February) Leaves Aix to settle in Paris with his mother (who had preceded him in December). Offered a place and bursary at the Lycée Saint-Louis. (November) Falls ill with 'brain fever' (typhoid) and convalescence is slow

1859 Fails his *baccalauréat* twice

1860 (Spring) Is found employment as a copy-clerk but abandons it after two months, preferring to eke out an existence as an impecunious writer in the Latin Quarter of Paris

1861 Cézanne follows Zola to Paris, where he meets Camille Pissarro, fails the entrance examination to the École des Beaux-Arts, and returns to Aix in September

1862 (February) Taken on by Hachette, the well-known publishing house, at first in the dispatch office and subsequently as head of the publicity department. (31 October) Naturalized as a French citizen. Cézanne returns to Paris and stays with Zola

1863 (31 January) First literary article published. (1 May) Manet's *Déjeuner sur l'herbe* exhibited at the Salon des Refusés, which Zola visits with Cézanne

1864 (October) *Tales for Ninon*

1865 *Claude's Confession*. A *succès de scandale* thanks to its bedroom scenes. Meets future wife Alexandrine-Gabrielle Meley (b. 1839), the illegitimate daughter of teenage parents who soon separated; Alexandrine's mother died in September 1849

1866   Resigns his position at Hachette (salary: 200 francs a month) and
        becomes a literary critic on the recently launched daily *L'Événement*
        (salary: 500 francs a month). Self-styled 'humble disciple' of Hippolyte
        Taine. Writes a series of provocative articles condemning the official
        Salon Selection Committee, expressing reservations about Courbet,
        and praising Manet and Monet. Begins to frequent the Café Guerbois
        in the Batignolles quarter of Paris, the meeting-place of the future
        Impressionists. Antoine Guillemet takes Zola to meet Manet. Summer
        months spent with Cézanne at Bennecourt on the Seine. (15 November)
        L'Événement suppressed by the authorities

1867   (November) *Thérèse Raquin*

1868   (April) Preface to second edition of *Thérèse Raquin*. (May) Manet's
        portrait of Zola exhibited at the Salon. (December) *Madeleine Férat*.
        Begins to plan for the Rougon-Macquart series of novels

1868–70 Working as journalist for a number of different newspapers

1870   (31 May) Marries Alexandrine in a registry office. (September)
        Moves temporarily to Marseilles because of the Franco-Prussian War

1871   Political reporter for *La Cloche* (in Paris) and *Le Sémaphore de
        Marseille*. (March) Returns to Paris. (October) Publishes *The For-
        tune of the Rougons*, the first of the twenty novels making up the
        Rougon-Macquart series

1872   *The Kill*

1873   (April) *The Belly of Paris*

1874   (May) *The Conquest of Plassans*. First independent Impressionist
        exhibition. (November) *Further Tales for Ninon*

1875   Begins to contribute articles to the Russian newspaper *Vestnik
        Evropy* (*European Herald*). (April) *The Sin of Abbé Mouret*

1876   (February) *His Excellency Eugène Rougon*. Second Impressionist
        exhibition

1877   (February) *L'Assommoir*

1878   Buys a house at Médan on the Seine, 40 kilometres west of Paris.
        (June) *A Love Story* (*Une page d'amour*)

1880   (March) *Nana*. (May) *Les Soirées de Médan* (an anthology of short
        stories by Zola and some of his naturalist 'disciples', including Mau-
        passant). (8 May) Death of Flaubert. (September) First of a series of
        articles for *Le Figaro*. (17 October) Death of his mother. (December)
        The Experimental Novel

1882   (April) *Pot Luck* (*Pot-Bouille*). (3 September) Death of Turgenev

1883 (13 February) Death of Wagner. (March) *The Ladies' Paradise (Au Bonheur des Dames)*. (30 April) Death of Manet

1884 (March) *The Bright Side of Life (La Joie de vivre)*. Preface to catalogue of Manet exhibition

1885 (March) *Germinal*. (12 May) Begins writing *The Masterpiece (L'Œuvre)*. (22 May) Death of Victor Hugo. (23 December) First instalment of *The Masterpiece* appears in *Le Gil Blas*

1886 (27 March) Final instalment of *The Masterpiece*, which is published in book form in April

1887 (18 August) Denounced as an onanistic pornographer in the *Manifesto of the Five* in *Le Figaro*. (November) *Earth*

1888 (October) *The Dream*. Jeanne Rozerot becomes his mistress

1889 (20 September) Birth of Denise, daughter of Zola and Jeanne

1890 (March) *La Bête humaine*

1891 (March) *Money*. (April) Elected President of the Société des Gens de Lettres. (25 September) Birth of Jacques, son of Zola and Jeanne

1892 (June) *La Débâcle*

1893 (July) *Doctor Pascal*, the last of the Rougon-Macquart novels. Fêted on visit to London

1894 (August) *Lourdes*, the first novel of the trilogy *Three Cities*. (22 December) Dreyfus found guilty by a court martial

1896 (May) *Rome*

1898 (13 January) 'J'accuse', his article in defence of Dreyfus, published in *L'Aurore*. (21 February) Found guilty of libelling the Minister of War and given the maximum sentence of one year's imprisonment and a fine of 3,000 francs. Appeal for retrial granted on a technicality. (March) *Paris*. (23 May) Retrial delayed. (18 July) Leaves for England instead of attending court

1899 (4 June) Returns to France. (October) *Fecundity*, the first of his *Four Gospels*

1901 (May) *Toil*, the second 'Gospel'

1902 (29 September) Dies of fumes from his bedroom fire, the chimney having been capped either by accident or anti-Dreyfusard design. Wife survives. (5 October) Public funeral

1903 (March) *Truth*, the third 'Gospel', published posthumously. *Justice* was to be the fourth

1908 (4 June) Remains transferred to the Panthéon

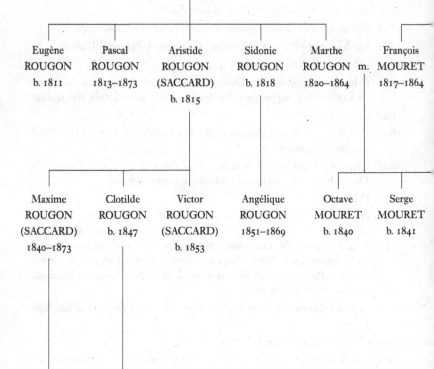

Adélaïde FOUQUE
(Tante DIDE)
1768–1873
m. ROUGON   Lover of MACQUART

Pierre ROUGON
1787–1870
m. Félicité PUECH

Eugène ROUGON b. 1811

Pascal ROUGON 1813–1873

Aristide ROUGON (SACCARD) b. 1815

Sidonie ROUGON b. 1818

Marthe ROUGON 1820–1864 m.

François MOURET 1817–1864

Maxime ROUGON (SACCARD) 1840–1873

Clotilde ROUGON b. 1847

Victor ROUGON (SACCARD) b. 1853

Angélique ROUGON 1851–1869

Octave MOURET b. 1840

Serge MOURET b. 1841

Charles ROUGON (SACCARD) 1857–1873

Child born in 1874 to Clotilde and Pascal ROUGON

FAMILY TREE OF THE ROUGON-MACQUART

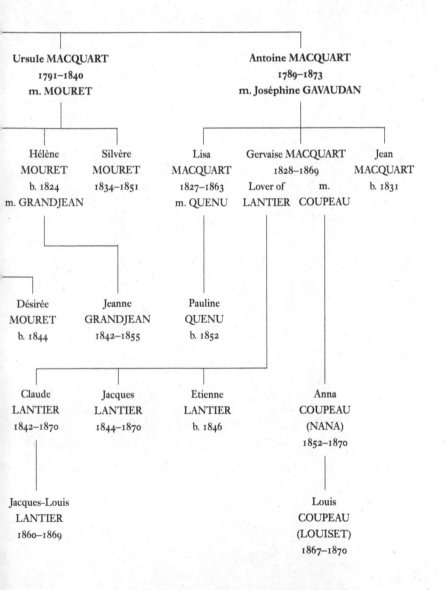

DOCTOR PASCAL

To the memory of MY MOTHER
and to MY DEAR WIFE
I dedicate this novel
which is the summary and conclusion
of my entire *œuvre*

1

In the heat of the torrid July afternoon, and with its shutters carefully shut, the room was perfectly still. From the three windows, only thin shafts of light came in through the cracks in the ageing wood; and, in the gloom, an incredibly soft luminescence bathed things with a diffuse and tender glow. It was relatively cool inside, away from the sweltering oppression that could be felt outdoors in the blast of sun setting the facade on fire.

Standing in front of the cupboard, which faced the windows, Doctor Pascal was looking for a note he'd come to get. Doors wide open, this enormous cupboard, in carved oak with strong and lovely ironwork, dating from the previous century, revealed on its shelves, deep inside its entrails, an extraordinary heap of papers, files, and manuscripts, piled up pell-mell and spilling over. For more than thirty years, the doctor had been tossing in everything he'd ever written, from brief notes to complete texts of his great works on heredity.* Searching through it was not always easy. But nothing if not patient, he rummaged around and gave a smile when he finally found it.

For a moment longer he stood there at the cupboard, reading the note, in a golden sunbeam streaming down from the middle window. In the brightness of the dawn-like light and despite his snow-white beard and hair, he looked solidly robust himself, even though he was nearing sixty; with his face so fresh, his features so fine, his eyes still limpid, altogether he looked so youthful that you would have taken him, standing there trim in his close-fitting maroon velvet jacket, for a young man with powdered locks.

'Here, Clotilde!' he said at last. 'Copy out this note. Ramond will never be able to decipher my terrible handwriting.'

He walked over and put the page down next to the young woman, who stood working at a tall desk in the recess of the right-hand window.

'All right, Maître!' she replied.

She didn't even turn round, so completely immersed was she in the pastel drawing she was just then slashing at with big strokes of her crayon. By her side, a vase bloomed with a spike of hollyhock of a peculiar violet, striped with yellow. But you could clearly see her small round head in profile, with her blonde hair cut short, and it was an exquisite and serious profile, the forehead straight, puckered in a frown of concentration, the eyes sky-blue, the nose fine, chin firm. Her bent neck especially was adorably young, milky-fresh, under the gold of her straggling curls. In her long black smock, she was very tall, narrow-waisted, and small-breasted, and as lithe and willowy as the divine figures of the Renaissance. Despite being twenty-five years old,* she was still girlish and barely looked eighteen.

'And', the doctor went on, 'will you tidy up the cupboard a bit. A person can't find a thing in there any more.'

'All right, Maître!' she repeated without lifting her head. 'In a minute!'

Pascal went and sat back at his desk, at the other end of the room, in front of the left-hand window; a simple blackwood table, also cluttered with papers and brochures of all kinds. And silence fell once more, the great peace that emanates from semi-darkness when it's sweltering outside. The room was vast, over thirty-two feet long by twenty wide, and had no other sizeable piece of furniture, apart from the cupboard, except two bookcases crammed with books. Antique chairs and armchairs trailed all over the place; while, as sole ornament, tacked up along the walls, which were covered in an old Empire wallpaper designed for salons and patterned with rosettes, there were pastel drawings of flowers in strange shades that you could only with difficulty make out. The decorative woodwork on the three double doors—the main door on the landing, the door leading to the doctor's bedroom at one end of the room, and the one leading to the young woman's at the other end—dated from the time of Louis XV, as did the cornice running around the smoke-stained ceiling.

An hour went by, without a sound, without a breath of air. Then, to distract himself, Pascal broke the band around a newspaper, *Le Temps*, which lay forgotten on his table, and let out a faint exclamation.

'Well, well! Your father's been made editor-in-chief of *L'Époque*,* the highly successful Republican newspaper that has been publishing the Tuileries papers!'*

The news must have been unexpected, since he gave a loud guffaw, both satisfied and saddened at once; and he went on in an undertone:

'Lord! You couldn't make it up if you tried... Life is amazing... Now that's what I call an interesting article.'

Clotilde did not respond, as though she were miles away and didn't hear what her uncle was saying. And he said nothing more, but grabbed the scissors after he'd read the article, cut it out, and glued it onto a sheet of paper, annotating it in his big uneven scrawl. Then he went back to the cupboard to file this new note. But he had to get a chair, as the top shelf was so high he couldn't reach it, tall as he was.

On this top shelf, a whole row of bulging files were lined up in orderly fashion, classified methodically. These were various documents, handwritten pages, official stamped papers, newspaper clippings, gathered into folders of stiff blue cardboard which each bore a name in capital letters. It was obvious that these documents were lovingly kept up to date, taken out endlessly, and carefully put back in place for, of the whole cupboard, this particular corner was the only one that was tidy.

When Pascal, standing on the chair, found the file he was looking for, one of the fattest folders with the name 'SACCARD'* written on it, he added the new note, then put the folder back under its letter of the alphabet. A moment later he forgot what he was doing and with some self-satisfaction righted a pile that was about to collapse. When he finally jumped down from the chair, he said:

'Are you listening? When you tidy up, Clotilde, don't touch the files up there.'

'All right, Maître!' she answered for the third time, docilely.

He started laughing again, with his air of native gaiety.

'It's out of bounds.'

'I know, Maître!'

He locked the cupboard again with a vigorous turn of the key, then threw the key to the back of a drawer in his worktable. The young woman was familiar enough with his research to put a bit of order into his manuscripts; and he was also happy to employ her as a secretary, getting her to copy out his notes whenever a colleague and friend, such as Doctor Ramond, asked him to pass on a document. But she wasn't a scientist, so he simply banned her from reading what he decided it was pointless for her to know.

Still, he was surprised in the end by how deeply absorbed in her work he sensed her to be.

'Cat got your tongue? You can't be *that* passionate about copying those flowers!'

This was yet another of the jobs he often gave her—doing drawings, watercolours, or pastels, which he would then add to his works as colour plates. For the past five years, he'd been conducting extremely interesting experiments on a set of hollyhocks, with a whole series of new shades obtained by artificial fertilization. To this kind of copying, she brought a meticulousness, an exactitude of line and colour, that was extraordinary; so much so that he always marvelled at such integrity, and would tell her she had 'a good little round noggin, neat and solid'.

But this time, when he came and looked over her shoulder, he let out a cry of comic fury.

'Ah! Get away with you! You're off in wonderland again! Will you please tear that up for me right away!'

She straightened up, cheeks red, eyes flashing with passion for her work, her thin fingers stained with pastel, the red and blue she'd pulverized.

'Oh, Maître!'

But in that 'Maître', a term so affectionate, so tenderly reverential, one that expressed complete surrender and that she preferred to the words 'Uncle' or 'Godfather', which she found crass, there passed for the first time a flicker of revolt, the claim of a human being coming into her own and asserting herself.

For nearly two hours, she had thrust aside the precise and scrupulous copying of the hollyhocks, and had just thrown down, on another sheet of paper, a whole cluster of imaginary flowers, dream flowers, extravagant and superb.* This sometimes happened with her, she would suddenly veer off, feel a need to escape into wild fantasies, in the middle of doing the most accurate of reproductions. She would indulge herself at once, always fall back to creating some extraordinary efflorescence, so spirited, so fantastic that she never repeated herself, inventing roses with bleeding hearts, weeping sulphur tears, lilies like crystal urns, even flowers of no known form shooting out starlight, leaving corollas floating like clouds. This particular day, on the page slashed with bold strokes of black crayon, it was a shower of pale stars, a whole stream of infinitely soft petals; while, in a corner, a nameless bloom, a chastely veiled bud was just starting to open.

'Yet another one you'll be tacking up for me there!' the doctor said, pointing to the wall, where other pastels just as strange were already lined up in a row. 'But what on earth does it represent, may I ask?'

She remained perfectly serious, and stepped back to get a better look at her work.

'I have no idea, but it's beautiful.'

At that moment, in stepped Martine, the only servant, who had become the real mistress of the house, having been in the doctor's service for nearly thirty years. Even though she was now over sixty she, too, was still young-looking, quiet and active as she was, in her everlasting black dress and her white coif, which made her look like a nun, especially with her pale calm little face and ash-coloured eyes that seemed to have been extinguished.

She said nothing, but simply went and sat on the floor by the foot of an armchair whose battered upholstery was letting the horsehair out through a tear; and, taking a needle and a ball of wool out of her pocket, she began sewing it up. For three days she'd been waiting for a moment to do this mending job, it had been haunting her.

'While you're at it, Martine,' cried Pascal jokingly, taking Clotilde's mutinous head in both hands, 'sew up this noggin for me, as well; it's sprung a leak.'

Martine lifted her pale eyes and gazed at her master with her usual look of adoration.

'Why does Monsieur say that?'

'Because, my dear girl, I believe you're the one, in all your devoutness, who's stuffed this good little round noggin, so neat and solid, with ideas about the next world.'

The two women exchanged a knowing look.

'Oh, Monsieur! Religion's never hurt anyone... And, anyway, when you don't have the same ideas, it's better not to go on about them, obviously.'

There was an embarrassed silence. This was the sole difference of opinion, one that sometimes caused rifts, between these three people otherwise so close-knit, living such a confined life. Martine had only been twenty-nine, a year older than the doctor, when she entered his household, back when he was just starting out in Plassans as a physician, in a bright little house in the new town. And thirteen years later, when Saccard, one of Pascal's brothers, sent his daughter Clotilde, then aged seven, down from Paris, after his wife died and he was about to marry again,* it was Martine who had brought the girl up, taking her to church and passing on some of the devout flame with which she had always burned. The doctor, who was broad-minded, let them indulge in the joy of believing, as he didn't feel he had a right to rule out for anyone the happiness faith offered. He contented himself with seeing to the girl's education later on, providing her with precise and sound notions on all things. For close to eighteen years they had lived together this way, all three of them, cloistered in La Souleiade, an estate located in a suburb of the town, fifteen minutes from the cathedral of Saint-Saturnin; and life had flown by, a happy life taken up with great hidden labours, yet a little disturbed by a malaise that was only growing—the increasingly violent clash of their beliefs.

Pascal paced up and down for a second, darkly. But he was not a man to mince words:

'You see, darling, this whole phantasmagoria of mystery is rotting your beautiful mind... Your good Lord didn't need you, I should have kept you all to myself, and you'd be better off.'

But Clotilde, shaking, her clear eyes staring boldly into his, stood up to him.

'You're the one, Maître, who'd be better off if your vision wasn't so blinkered... There's more to life than the things of this earth, why don't you want to see?'

Martine came to her aid, in her own words.

'It's all too true, Monsieur, that you who are a saint, as I tell anyone who'll listen, you ought to come with us to church... Surely God will save you. But the idea that you might not go straight to heaven, it makes me tremble all over.'

He stopped and faced the two of them, now in full rebellion, though they were usually so docile, at his feet, women lovingly won over by his gaiety and his goodness. He had already opened his mouth and was about to retort tartly, when the futility of the discussion leapt out at him.

'Look, just leave me in peace! I'd be better off going and getting on with work. Don't disturb me, whatever you do!'

With that, he went swiftly to his room, where he had set up a sort of laboratory, and locked himself in. The prohibition on entering was categorical. This was where he threw himself into manufacturing special preparations, which he never talked about to anyone. Almost immediately, the slow and regular sound of a pestle in a mortar could be heard.

'There you go,' said Clotilde with a smile. 'There he is at his devil's cookery, as Grandmother calls it.'

And she calmly went back to copying the spike of hollyhocks, filling in the drawing with mathematical precision and finding the right tone for the violet-coloured petals, striped with yellow, right down to the most subtly nuanced hues.

'Ah!' Martine murmured after a short while, sitting on the floor again, patching up the armchair. 'What a sorry thing it is for a saintly man like that to lose his soul, and just for the heck of it! Because, say what you like, I've known him for thirty years now, and he's never so much as hurt a fly. He's got a heart of gold, that man, he'd give you the shirt off his back... And easy-going with it, and always hale and hearty, always sunny, a real blessing! It's a crying shame he won't make his peace with the Lord. Wouldn't you say? We'll have to make him, Mademoiselle.'

Clotilde, surprised to hear Martine speak at such length, gave her word, looking grave.

'Without fail, Martine, I promise. We'll make him.'

Silence had again pervaded the room, when they heard the tinkling of the bell affixed to the front door downstairs. It had been put there to give warning in this house that was too big for the three people who lived in it. The maid seemed amazed and muttered under her breath: who could possibly have turned up in this heat? She got up, opened the door and leant over the banister, then reappeared.

'It's Madame Félicité.'

Old Madame Rougon stepped spryly in. Despite being in her eighties, she had just climbed the stairs as lightly as a girl; and she was still the same thin dark shrill cicada she had always been. Extremely elegant now, dressed in black silk, thanks to the slenderness of her figure she could still be mistaken, from behind, for a woman in love, some ambitious creature, chasing the object of her passion. Up close, her eyes had kept their fire in her dried-up face and she could smile a pretty smile, when she wanted to.

'Don't tell me it's you, Grandmother!' cried Clotilde, going to greet her. 'But it's hot enough to fry in this terrible sun!'

Félicité kissed her on the forehead and gave a laugh.

'Oh! The sun's my friend!'

She then trotted over to a window with brisk little steps and unbolted one of the shutters.

'Open up a bit in here, why don't you! It's too dismal, living in the dark like this. At my place, I let the sun in.'

Through the gap a jet of fiery light, a stream of dancing sparks, shot in. And under a sky the violet blue of a forest fire, you could see the vast parched countryside, looking dormant or dead in the obliterating furnace-like heat; while, to the right, above the pink rooftops, the spire of Saint-Saturnin rose, a golden tower, its arrises whitened to bone in the blinding glare.

'Yes,' Félicité went on, 'I'll probably run over to Les Tulettes* shortly and I wondered if you had Charles here, so I could take him with me... He's not here, I can see that. Some other time...'

But while she was offering this excuse for her visit, her prying eyes were darting round the room. Anyway, she didn't pursue it but started talking about her son Pascal, as she registered the rhythmic sound of the pestle that had kept up in the room next door.

'Ah! He's at his devil's cookery again! Don't bother him, I've nothing to say to him.'

Martine, who'd gone back to her armchair, nodded to declare she had no intention whatever of bothering her master; and there was another pause while Clotilde wiped her pastel-stained fingers on a cloth and Félicité began to pace up and down again with her little steps, inquisitively.

For nearly two years now old Madame Rougon had been a widow. Her husband, who had got so fat he no longer stirred, had ultimately succumbed, choking with indigestion, on 3 September 1870, the night of the very day he heard about the disastrous defeat at Sedan.* The collapse of the regime, one of whose founders he boasted of being, seemed to have struck him dead. Félicité thereafter pretended she no longer troubled herself with politics, living like a queen who had stepped down from the throne. No one was ignorant of the fact that in 1851 the Rougons had saved Plassans from anarchy, by ensuring that the *coup d'état* of 2 December was victorious there; or that, a few years later, they had conquered it again, defeating Legitimist and Republican candidates to hand the town over to a Bonapartist deputy. Right up until the war, the Empire had remained all-powerful there, so prestigious that it had won an overwhelming majority in the plebiscite.* But since the disasters, the town proper had turned Republican, the Saint-Marc quarter had gone back to its secret royalist intrigues, while the old quarter and the new town had sent to the Chamber of Deputies a liberal, vaguely tainted with Orléanism, a man more than ready to line up on the side of the Republic, as long

as it triumphed.* That was why Félicité, who was clearly a very intelligent woman, had stepped back and agreed to be no more now than
the dethroned queen of a deposed regime.

But that was still an eminent position, wreathed in a whole melancholy poetry. For eighteen years, she had reigned. The legend of her
two salons—the yellow salon, in which the *coup d'état* was planned,
and later the green salon, that neutral ground on which the conquest
of Plassans was sealed*—had been embellished with distance from
those vanished days. She was, after all, extremely rich. People also
found her extremely dignified in her fall from grace, never looking
back with regret or complaining, trailing along behind her, with her
eighty-something years, such a long train of furious appetites, abominable schemes and exorbitant gratifications, that she had finally
become revered. Her only pleasure, these days, was to enjoy her great
fortune and her past royalty in peace, and she had only one passion
left, which was to defend her history, expunging anything that, with
the passage of time, could tarnish it. In her pride, which fed off those
twin exploits* the townspeople still talked about, she kept watch with
jealous care, resolved to leave standing nothing but glorious records,
this legend that saw her hailed as a fallen monarch whenever she
walked through the town.

She went to the bedroom door and listened to the sound of the
pestle. Then her brow knitted with worry and she returned to Clotilde.

'My God, what's he making in there! You know he's doing himself
a lot of damage with this new drug of his. They tell me he nearly
killed one of his patients again, the other day.'

'Oh, Grandmother!' the girl cried.

But the old woman was launched.

'Yes, exactly! And that's not all they say, those old biddies. Go and
ask them, down in the faubourg. They'll tell you he grinds up dead
men's bones in the blood of newborns.'

This time, while even Martine protested, Clotilde took offence,
wounded in her affection.

'Oh, Grandmother! Don't go repeating such vile things! And Maître
who has such a good heart, who thinks only of everyone's happiness!'

When she saw them both riled, Félicité realized she'd overdone it
and returned to her wheedling.

'But, pussycat, I'm not the one saying these appalling things.
I'm just repeating the nonsense that's being spread about, so you can

see how wrong Pascal is not to take any notice of public opinion. He thinks he's found a new cure—nothing better! And I'll even agree that he's going to cure everyone, like he hopes to do. But why put on such mysterious airs, why not talk about it openly, why above all only try it out on that riff-raff in the old quarter and out in the sticks, instead of pulling off amazing cures among the quality in town—cures that would make his name? No, you see, puss, your uncle has never been able to behave like everyone else.'

She had adopted a pained tone, lowering her voice to lay bare this secret wound in her heart.

'Thank God, men of honour aren't in short supply in our family, my other sons have given me satisfaction enough! Isn't that so? Your uncle Eugène has risen high enough, a minister these last twelve years, almost emperor!* And your father himself has shifted enough millions, and been mixed up in enough great public works that have made a new city of Paris!* I say nothing of your brother Maxime, so rich, so distinguished, or of your cousins, Octave Mouret,* one of the conquerors of the new commerce, and our dear Abbé Mouret,* a saint that one! So, why does Pascal, who could have followed in the footsteps of every one of them, persist in living in his hole, like some old half-cracked eccentric?'

The girl rebelled further and placed an affectionate hand over the old woman's mouth to shut her up.

'No, no! Let me finish. I'm well aware Pascal's no dunce. He's done remarkable work, his submissions to the Académie de médecine have even earned him a reputation among learned men. But what does any of that amount to, beside the things I dreamt of for him? Yes! Having the whole upper-crust clientele of the town, a great fortune, being decorated, ending up with honours and a position worthy of the family... Ah! You see, puss, that's what I'm complaining about: he is not, and has never wanted to be, part of the family. My word! I used to say to him when he was a child: "Where on earth did you come from? You're not one of ours!" I myself have sacrificed everything to the family, I'd let myself be cut to ribbons if it meant the family was forever great and glorious!'

She straightened up her short frame and became quite tall, in her pride and pleasure in the one and only passion that had filled her life. But she had begun prowling around again, when she had a sudden shock, spotting, on the ground, the issue of *Le Temps* that the doctor had tossed there after cutting out the article to add to the Saccard file; and the sight of the space gaping in the middle of the page evidently spoke to her for, suddenly, she stopped pacing and dropped onto a chair, as if she'd finally found what she'd come looking for.

'Your father's been appointed editor of *L'Époque*,' she resumed abruptly.

'Yes,' said Clotilde serenely, 'Maître told me, it's in the paper.'

Félicité shot her a quizzical, anxious look, for this appointment of Saccard, this rallying to the Republic, was big news. After the fall of the Empire, he'd taken the risk of returning to France, despite his conviction as the director of the Banque universelle,* whose collapse had been followed by that of the regime. New power networks, a whole extraordinary plot, must have set him back on his feet. Not only had he obviously got his pardon, but more than that he was yet again handling a considerable amount of big business, embarked on mass-circulation journalism, back to creaming off his share of all the hush-monies. And the memory came flooding back of past quarrels between him and his brother Eugène Rougon, whom he had so often compromised and whom, by an ironic twist of fate, he may well have to protect now that the former minister of the Empire was no more than a simple deputy, resigned to the sole role of defending his fallen master with the same obstinacy his mother put into defending her family. She still meekly followed the orders of her eldest son, the high-flying eagle, even if he had been brought low; but Saccard was also close to her heart, no matter what he did, because of his indomitable need for success; and she was also proud of Maxime, Clotilde's brother, who had moved back after the war into his private mansion on the Avenue du Bois-de-Boulogne, where he'd eaten up the fortune his wife had left him,* before becoming prudent, with the wisdom of a man with diseased bone marrow, trying to outfox the paralysis that loomed.

'Editor of *L'Époque*,' she repeated. 'Your father's managed to wangle a real ministerial job. Oh, and I forgot to tell you, I wrote to your brother again to get him to come and see us. It'll distract him, do him good. Then there's the child, poor Charles...'

She did not insist, as this was another of the wounds from which her pride bled: Maxime, at the age of seventeen, had had a child, a son, with some maid,* and that child was now around fifteen, weak in the head, and living in Plassans, being passed from one to the other, a burden to all.

She waited another minute, hoping for a comment from Clotilde, a shift that would allow her to get to the point she was leading up to. When she saw the girl had lost interest and was tidying papers on her desk, she made up her mind, after casting a quick glance at Martine, who was continuing to stitch up the armchair as though deaf and dumb.

'So, your uncle cut out the article from *Le Temps*?'

Very calm, Clotilde smiled.

'Yes, Maître put it in his files. Ah, you wouldn't believe how many notes he's buried in there! Births, deaths, the tiniest things that happen in life, everything goes in. And there's the Family Tree,* too, as you're well aware, our famous Family Tree, which he keeps up to date!'

Old Madame Rougon's eyes flared. She stared hard at the young woman.

'Do you know anything about them, these files?'

'Oh, no, Grandmother! Maître never talks to me about them and he won't let me touch them.'

But old Madame Rougon didn't believe her.

'Come, now! You've got them right there, you must have read them.'

Very straightforwardly, with her calm directness, Clotilde answered, smiling once more:

'No! When Maître rules something out, it's because he has his reasons, and I don't do it.'

'Well then, my child,' Félicité exclaimed vehemently, yielding to her obsession, 'since Pascal's so fond of you and may well listen to you, you really ought to implore him to burn all that junk! What if he upped and died and people found the appalling things that are in there? We'd all be dishonoured!'

Ah! She saw those abominable files, at night, in her nightmares, setting out in letters of fire the true stories, the physiological defects of the family, the whole seamy side of its glory that she would have liked to bury once and for all, along with the ancestors already dead! She knew how the doctor had got the idea of putting those documents together when he first embarked on his great studies on heredity, how he'd been led to take his own family as an example, struck by the recurring cases he noted in it and which supported the laws he'd discovered. Wasn't it a perfectly natural field of observation, one right there in front of him, which he knew all about firsthand? And with the robust disinterestedness of a scientist, he had spent the last thirty years accumulating the most intimate information on his nearest and dearest, gathering and classifying everything, drawing up this Rougon-Macquart Family Tree, of which the voluminous files were merely a commentary, stuffed with proofs.

'Oh, yes!' old Madame Rougon went on ardently. 'On the fire, on the fire with all these old scribblings that'd sully our reputation!'

At that moment, the servant stood to leave the room, seeing the turn the conversation was taking, but Madame Rougon stopped her with an abrupt wave of the hand.

'No, Martine! Stay! You're not in the way, since you're part of the family now.' Then she turned her voice to a hiss and went on:

'A pack of falsehoods, all the lies our enemies once hurled at us in their rage at our triumph! Think about that a bit, child. Lies about all of us—about your father, your mother, your brother, about me, so many horrors!'

'Horrors, Grandmother? But how do you know that?'

The old woman was momentarily stumped.

'Oh! I suspect as much, that's all!... What family hasn't had its woes that could be misconstrued? Hasn't the mother of us all, that dear venerable Aunt Dide,* your great-grandmother—hasn't she been in the madhouse at Les Tulettes for the last twenty-one years? If God's done her the favour of letting her live to the ripe old age of a hundred and four, he's slapped her down cruelly by taking away her reason. Of course, there's no shame in that; only, what exasperates me, what we really don't need, is that people then say we're *all* mad... And, listen! Your great-uncle Macquart—didn't they spread awful rumours about him as well! Macquart once got up to some mischief, I'm not defending him. But, today, isn't he living a quiet life in his little place at Les Tulettes, a stone's throw from our poor mother, and looking after her as a good son should? And, look here, one last example! Your brother Maxime committed a terrible sin when he had that poor little Charles with a maid, and it's a fact that the sorry boy isn't right in the head. So what! How would you like it if people said your nephew was a degenerate, that he's a replica, three generations apart, of his great-great-grandmother, the dear woman we sometimes take him to see and whose company he so enjoys? No! That's it for families, if we're going to start dissecting everything, the nerves of this one here, the muscles of that one there! It's enough to put you off living!'

Clotilde had stood there, in her long black frock, listening closely. She had become grave again, arms hanging by her side, eyes on the ground. There was a pause and then she said slowly:

'It's science, Grandmother.'

'Science!' Félicité exploded, stamping her foot and trotting about again. 'A fine thing it is, their science, going against all that's sacred in this world! When they've torn everything down, a lot of progress they'll have made! They're killing respect, they're killing the family, they're killing the good Lord!'

'Oh, don't say that, Madame!' Martine wailed, cutting in, her narrow-minded devotion wounded. 'Don't say Monsieur's killing the good Lord!'

'Yes, my poor girl, he's killing Him, all right. And, don't you see: from the point of view of religion, it's a crime to let him damn himself like this. You don't love him, I swear! No, you don't love him, you two: you have the good fortune of believing, yet you're not doing a thing to set him back on the true path. Ah! Myself, in your place, I'd sooner chop that cupboard up with an axe and make a great big bonfire with all the affronts to the good Lord there are in it!'

She planted herself in front of the enormous cupboard and sized it up with her fiery eye, as if to storm it, to sack it, to destroy it utterly, quite as if she weren't a skinny dried-up old stick of eighty-odd. Then, with a wave of ironic disdain:

'Besides, for all his science, he doesn't know everything!'

Clotilde had remained completely engrossed in thought, eyes far away. She said in a hushed voice, forgetting the other two, talking to herself:

'It's true, he can't know everything... There's always something else, down there below the surface. That's what vexes me, it's what sometimes makes us argue: I just can't set the mystery aside the way he does: I worry about it, until it tortures me... Down there, all that desires and acts in the quivering dark, all the unknown forces...'

Her voice had gradually slowed, dropping to an indistinct murmur.

At that point, Martine, who had been looking grim for a moment, herself spoke up.

'What if it was true, though, Mademoiselle, that Monsieur was damning himself with all those filthy papers! Tell me, would we just let him go ahead? Me, you see, if he told me to go and throw myself off the terrace, I'd close my eyes and throw myself off, because I know he's always right. But when it comes to his salvation! Oh! If I could, I'd work at it in spite of him. Any way I could, yes! I'd force him. I can't bear the thought he won't be in heaven with us.'

'Now that's more like it, my girl,' Félicité applauded. 'You at least love your master with your head.'

Between the two of them, Clotilde still seemed irresolute. For her, belief didn't bend to the strict rule of dogma; religious feeling didn't materialize in hopes of a paradise, a place of delights, where you would meet your loved ones again. It was simply an inner need for a beyond, a certainty that the big wide world did not stop at sensation, that there was a whole unknown other world, which must be acknowledged. But her grandmother, so old, and the servant, so devoted, had shaken her in her anxious affection for her uncle. Did they actually love him more, in a truer and more enlightened way, these two, in wanting him to be without stain, free of his scholarly obsessions, pure enough to be among the chosen? Phrases from holy books came back to her, the constant battle waged against the spirit of evil, the glory of hard-won conversions. What if she set herself this sacred task, what if she were to save him after all, in spite of himself! Little by little her mind, readily attuned to adventurous exploits, was overcome with exaltation.

'Of course,' she said at last, 'I'd be very happy if he didn't rack his brains piling up those bits of paper, and he came with us to church.'

Seeing her close to yielding, Madame Rougon cried that they had to act, and Martine herself weighed in with all her real authority. They joined forces and began indoctrinating the young woman, lowering their voices as if hatching a plot from which a miraculous good would emerge, a divine joy with which the whole house would be embalmed. What a triumph if they were to reconcile the good doctor to God! And what sweet peace afterwards, living together in the heavenly communion of a shared faith!

'Well, what should I do?' Clotilde, asked, defeated, converted.

But at that moment, in the silence, the doctor's pestle started again louder than ever, pounding away with its regular rhythm. And Félicité, victorious, about to speak, checked herself and anxiously turned her head, glancing at the door of the adjacent room for a second. She lowered her voice:

'Do you know where the key to the cupboard is?'

Clotilde didn't answer, simply waved her hand to express her total repugnance at betraying her master in such a way.

'What a child you are! I swear I won't take anything, I won't even disturb anything. Only, you know, since we're on our own, and Pascal never reappears before dinner, we could just set our minds at rest about what's in there. Oh! Just a quick glance, my word of honour!'

The girl, unmoving, still did not consent.

'Then again, maybe I'm mistaken, probably none of the bad things I told you about are in there.'

That was the decisive move. Clotilde ran to the drawer to get the key and flung the cupboard door wide open herself.

'There, Grandmother! The files are up the top there.'

Martine, without a word, had gone and planted herself at the bedroom door, ears cocked, listening to the pestle, while Félicité, rooted to the spot with emotion, stared at the files. Finally, here they were, these terrible files, the source of the nightmare that was poisoning her life! She could see them, she would touch them, she would cart them away! And she drew herself up with a passionate thrust of her short legs.

'It's too high, puss,' she said. 'Help me, give them to me!'

'Oh, no, I can't do that, Grandmother! Get a chair.'

Félicité got a chair and nimbly hopped up on it. But she was still too short. With an extraordinary effort, she hitched herself up, managed to grow tall enough for her fingernails actually to touch the blue cardboard folders; and her fingers scrambled and curled, with claw-like scratchings. Suddenly, there was a loud bang: she had made a geological sample, a piece of marble that sat on a lower shelf, crash to the ground.

The pestle stopped immediately and Martine said in a choked voice:

'Look out, here he comes!'

But Félicité, desperate, did not hear and did not let go when Pascal stepped swiftly in. He had thought there'd been an accident, a fall, and he was thunderstruck at what he saw: his mother on the chair, her arm still in the air, while Martine had stepped away and Clotilde stood stock still, very pale, waiting, without averting her gaze. When he realized what was happening, he himself went as white as a sheet. A terrible anger boiled up inside him.

Old Madame Rougon, to make matters worse, was not remotely ruffled. As soon as she saw that the opportunity was lost, she jumped down from the chair, without making any allusion to the vile business he'd caught her at.

'Ah, there you are! I didn't want to disturb you. I came to give Clotilde a kiss, but here I've been prattling on for nearly two hours and now I must look sharp and hurry back. They're expecting me at home, they must be wondering what's happened to me. Au revoir, till Sunday!'

She took herself off, with perfect equanimity, after flashing a smile at her son, who remained respectfully mute before her. This was a stance he'd adopted a long time ago to avoid having it out with her, which he felt would necessarily be cruel and which he always dreaded. He knew her inside out and tried to forgive her for everything, with the broad tolerance of a scientist making allowances for heredity, the environment, and circumstances. And, after all, she was his mother, wasn't she? That alone would have been enough; for, in the midst of the alarming blows that his researches dealt the family, he maintained a great fondness for those closest to him.

When his mother was gone, his anger erupted and came beating down on Clotilde. He turned his eyes away from Martine and pinned them on the young woman, who had still not lowered her gaze but stood bravely accepting responsibility for her act.

'You! You!' he said at last.

He grabbed her arm and squeezed it, hard enough to make her yelp. But she continued to look him in the eye, without buckling before him, with all the indomitable will of her own personality, her own convictions. She was beautiful and irritating, so slim, so willowy, dressed in her black smock; and her exquisite blonde youthfulness, her straight forehead, her fine nose, her firm chin, took on a warlike charm in her revolt.

'You! I moulded you, you're my student, my friend, my other mind. I've given you a piece of my heart and my brain! Oh, yes! I should have kept you completely to myself, not let the best of you be taken from me by your blasted bloody Lord!'

'Oh, Monsieur, you're blaspheming!' cried Martine, who had come over to deflect some of his anger her way.

But he didn't even see her. Clotilde alone existed. And he seemed to be transfigured, lifted up by such a passion that, framed by his white hair and his white beard, his handsome face blazed with youth and with an immense wounded and exasperated tenderness. They gazed at each other a moment more, without giving in, staring into each other's eyes.

'You! You!' he repeated, in his trembling voice.

'Yes, me! Why, Maître, wouldn't I love *you* as much as you love *me*? And why, if I think you're in danger, wouldn't I try and save you? You worry so much about what I think, but what you really want is to force me to think like you!'

Never had she stood up to him like this before.

'But you're a girl, you know nothing!'

'No, I'm a soul, and you don't know any more than I do!'

He let go of her arm, made a vague sweeping gesture towards the sky, and an extraordinary silence fell, full of grave things, of the pointless discussion he didn't want to have. With a rough shove, he pushed past her and went and opened the shutter on the middle window, for the sun was going down and the room was filling with shadow. Then he came back.

But she needed air and space, so she went to stand at the open window. The shower of burning sparks had ceased and all that now descended from above was the last shudder of the sky, overheated and growing dim; and from the still burning earth, hot scents rose as evening breathed relief. Beyond the terrace, first came the railway track and the outbuildings of the station, whose main buildings could also be seen; then, crossing the vast arid plain, a line of trees signalled the course of the Viorne, beyond which rose the slopes of Sainte-Marthe, tiers of reddish dirt planted with olives, held up by drystone walls, and crowned by dark pine woods: a wide and desolate amphitheatre, sun-blasted, the colour of old baked brick, unfurling on high, against the sky, this fringe of dark foliage. On the left, the gorges of the Seilles opened up, a mass of yellow stones that had tumbled down among parcels of land the colour of blood and dominated by an immense ridge of rocks like the wall of a gigantic fortress; while, towards the right, just at the entrance to the valley the Viorne flowed through, the town of Plassans displayed its stacked roofs of faded pink tiles, the compact jumble of an old city, pierced by the tops of ancient elms, and over which reigned the high tower of Saint-Saturnin, solitary and serene at this time of day in the limpid gold of sunset.*

'My God!' said Clotilde, slowly. 'You would have to be pretty arrogant to think you could just take the whole world in your hand and know everything!'

Pascal had just got up on the chair to check that none of the files was missing. Then he picked up the piece of marble and put it back on the shelf; and when he'd locked the cupboard again, vigorously, he pocketed the key.

'Yes,' he said, 'to try and understand everything, and especially not to lose one's head over what one doesn't know, what one no doubt will never know!'

Martine went back to Clotilde to support her and show that the two of them had made common cause. And now the doctor saw *her*, too, felt them both to be united in the same determination to win. After years of stealthy forays, it was at last open warfare, with the scientist seeing those closest to him turn against his whole system of thought and threaten it with sabotage. There is no worse torment than having treachery at home, all around you, being encircled, dispossessed, destroyed by those you love and are loved by!

Then a terrible realization dawned on him.

'But you both love me still!'

He saw their eyes cloud with tears and he was overcome by an infinite sadness, in this incredibly calm end to a beautiful day. All his gaiety, all his goodness, which stemmed from his love of life, were convulsed by it.

'Ah, my darling, and you, my poor girl, you're doing this for my happiness, aren't you? Oh, dear! How unhappy we're going to be!'

2

THE next morning, Clotilde woke early, at six o'clock. She had gone to bed feeling angry with Pascal, they had been cool towards each other. And her first feeling was one of uneasiness, vague remorse, and an immediate need to make up, so as to remove the heavy weight on her heart that she felt settle there once again.

Quickly leaping out of bed, she went to half open the shutters on the room's two windows. Already high in the sky, the sun came in, slicing up the bedchamber with two gold bars. In the sleepy room, all clammy with the wholesome smell of youth, the bright morning brought with it little gleeful puffs of fresh air; while the girl, coming back and sitting on the edge of the bed, remained dreamy for a moment, clad simply in her shapeless chemise, which only made her look even slimmer, with her long tapered legs, her strong willowy body, and her rounded breasts, round neck, round supple arms; and the nape of her neck and her adorable shoulders were as pure as milk, like lustrous white silk, infinitely soft. For a long while, during the awkward age between the years of twelve to eighteen, she had looked too tall and gangly, climbing trees like a boy. Then, from the sexless young imp had emerged this gorgeous and charming creature.

Her eyes unseeing, she continued to gaze at the bedroom walls. Although La Souleiade dated back to the previous century, it had clearly been refurbished under the First Empire, for an old printed calico, showing busts of sphinxes inside spirals of oak crowns, had been hung for wallpaper. Once a bright red, the calico had turned pink, a vague pink that verged on orange. There were actual curtains on both windows and on the bed, but they had had to be cleaned, which made them even paler. And that faded crimson was truly exquisite, the colour of dawn, so delicately soft. As for the bed, hung with the same fabric, it had fallen into such decrepitude with age that it had been replaced by a different one, taken from a neighbouring room; this was another Empire bed, low and very wide, in solid mahogany trimmed with brasswork, and its four posts also bore sphinx busts similar to those on the calico wall hanging. The rest of the furniture was matching, too: a wardrobe with full-length doors and columns, a chest of drawers in white marble circled with a rim, a tall and monumental cheval-glass, a chaise longue with braced legs, and seats with very straight backs in the form of lyres. But a foot quilt, made from an old Louis XV silk skirt, brightened up the stately bed, which sat in the middle of the wainscotted wall, facing the windows; a whole heap of cushions made the hard chaise longue soft; and there were two whatnots and a table also adorned with old flower-brocaded silks, found at the bottom of an inbuilt cupboard.

Clotilde finally put on her stockings, slipped on a dressing gown of white cotton piqué and, thrusting her feet into her grey canvas mules, she ran to her dressing room, a room at the rear that looked out on to the other side of the house. She had had it hung simply with unbleached drill* with blue stripes; and the only things in it were pieces of furniture in varnished pine, the dressing table, two wardrobes, and some chairs. Yet it felt naturally and refinedly stylish, very feminine. That fastidiousness had sprung up in her at the same time as her beauty. Alongside the stubborn little tomboy she sometimes still was, she had become a responsive and tender-hearted young woman, a woman who loved to be loved. The truth was that she had grown up without restraint, never having learned anything more than to read and write, though later giving herself a quite broad education, helping her uncle. But there had been no fixed plan between them, she had simply become passionately interested in natural history, which had taught her all there was to know about the facts of life. And she kept her virginal modesty intact, like a fruit no hand had touched, doubtless thanks to her unconscious religious expectation of love, that deep womanly feeling that made her hold back the gift of her whole being, her annihilation in the man she would one day love.

She put her hair up and had a good wash, then, yielding to her impatience, she went back and gently opened the bedroom door and ventured on tiptoe, noiselessly, across the vast workroom. The shutters were still closed but she could see clearly enough not to bump into the furniture. When she had got to the other end of the room, to the door of the doctor's bedroom, she bent down and held her breath. Was he up already? What could he be doing? She heard him clearly padding about, probably getting dressed. She never entered this room, where he liked to hide certain research work, and it was always shut, like a tabernacle. Suddenly she was gripped with fear that he'd find her there if he pushed open the door; and she spun into serious turmoil, caught between the mutiny brought on by her pride and her desire to show her respect. For a moment her need to be reconciled with him became so strong that she was on the point of knocking. Then, as the sound of his footsteps came closer, she fled.

Until eight o'clock, Clotilde floundered about with growing impatience. Every minute, she looked at the clock on the mantelpiece in her room, an Empire clock of gilded bronze, with Love sitting against a stone gazing with a smile at sleeping Time. Usually she went downstairs at eight to breakfast, which she shared with the doctor, in the dining room. In the meantime, she threw herself into an elaborate grooming routine, did her hair, put on her shoes, put on a dress, a linen one, white with red spots. Then, with fifteen minutes still to spare, she did something she'd been wanting to do for some time and sat down to sew a small piece of lace, in imitation Chantilly, on her work smock, the black smock which she now found too tomboyish, not womanly enough. But on the stroke of eight, she dropped her work and raced downstairs.

'You'll be eating breakfast all on your own in the dining room,' Martine said quietly.

'Why is that?'

'Yes, Monsieur called me, and I handed him his egg through the gap in the door. He's at it again up there, with his mortar and pestle and his filter. We won't see him now before noon.'

Clotilde stood there distraught, her cheeks pale. She drank her milk standing, took her bread roll and followed the servant into the kitchen. All there was on the ground floor, besides the dining room and this kitchen, was an abandoned salon where they put the store of potatoes. In bygone days, when the doctor used to see patients at home, he would give his consultations there; but years ago they had taken the desk and the armchair up to his room. All that was left now was another small room that opened off the kitchen, the old servant's bedroom, which was spotlessly clean, with a chest of drawers in walnut wood and a bed like a nun's, hung with white curtains.

'Do you think he's gone back to making his spirits?' Clotilde asked.

'Heavens! What else can it be! You know very well he forgets to eat or drink when it takes him.'

At that, all the girl's frustration came out in a low lament.

'Oh, God! God!'

And while Martine went upstairs to do her room, she took a parasol from the stand in the hallway and went outside to eat her roll, disheartened, not knowing how on earth she would fill the time till noon.

It was already almost seventeen years since Doctor Pascal, having decided to leave his house in the new town, had bought La Souleiade for around twenty thousand francs. What he had wanted was to get away from it all, and also to give more space and more delight to the little girl his brother had just sent down to him from Paris. Sitting at the gates to the town on a plateau that dominated the plain, La Souleiade had once been part of a substantial old estate, but the original vast grounds had been whittled down to less than two hectares through successive sales, not to mention the building of the railway which had removed the last ploughable fields. The house itself had been half destroyed by a fire and only one of the two main buildings remained, a wing that was square, or four-sided, as they say in Provence, with a frontage of five windows and a roof covered in large pink tiles. And the doctor, who had bought the place completely furnished, had needed nothing more than to get the enclosure walls patched up and finished, to have peace and quiet in his own home.

Ordinarily, Clotilde loved the solitude passionately, loved this small realm she could circle in ten minutes but which still showed traces of its former glory. But that particular morning, she brought to it a barely contained fury. For a moment she walked out onto the terrace, at both ends of which hundred-year-old cypresses were planted, two enormous dark tapers that could be seen seven miles away. The slope then ran down all the way to the railway line, with drystone walls holding up the red earth, where the last of the vines were dead; and, on these sorts of giant steps, all that now grew were rows of puny olive and almond trees with tiny little leaves. The heat was already oppressive as she watched small lizards fleeing over the disjointed flagstones, between the fibrous tufts of caper bushes.

Then, as if irritated by the vast bowl of the sky, she crossed the orchard and the vegetable garden that Martine insisted on keeping up, despite her age, getting a man in only twice a week for the heavy labour; and she went up on the right into a pine grove, a small wood of pines, which was all that remained of the magnificent pine forest that had once covered the plateau. But here, too, she felt uneasy: the dry pine needles crackled under her feet, and the resin oozing from the branches was suffocating. So she continued along the enclosure wall, slipped past the front gate, which opened on to the Chemin des

Fenouillères, five minutes from the first houses of Plassans, and came out at last on the threshing floor, an immense area with a radius of sixty-five feet, which alone proved how large and important the domain had once been. Ah! This ancient ground, paved with round pebbles as in the days of the Romans; a sort of vast esplanade, covered in short dry grass just like spun gold, as if carpeted in thick-pile wool! What fine times she'd had there in days gone by, running and rolling around, or lying stretched out on her back for hours on end while the stars came out, deep in the boundless sky!

She opened up her parasol again and crossed the threshing floor, walking more slowly. Now she found herself on the left of the terrace, which meant she had done a complete circuit of the property. So she went behind the house again, under the cluster of enormous plane trees that cast dense shade over the back. The two windows of the doctor's room were on this side. And she looked up, for she had only drawn nearer in the sudden hope of seeing him at last. But the windows remained shut and she felt hurt by this as if it were a personal rebuff. Only then did she notice that she was still holding her bread roll, having forgotten to eat it; and she ducked under the trees and bit into it impatiently with her fine young teeth.

It was a delicious retreat, this ancient quincunx of plane trees, a lingering remnant of La Souleiade's past splendour. Under these giants, with their monstrous trunks, the light was almost dim, greenish, and exquisitely cool on scorching summer days. Once, a formal French garden had been laid out there, but all that remained of that were the borders of boxwood, which had obviously adapted to the shade, for the bushes had pushed up vigorously and were now as tall as trees. The main attraction of this shady nook was a fountain, which was actually a simple lead pipe embedded in a column shaft, from which a trickle of water ran perpetually, even during the worst droughts, as thick as a little finger. Further along, it fed into a large mossy pond, whose green stones were only cleaned once every three or four years. When all the wells of the district dried up, La Souleiade still had its spring, of which the great plane trees were surely the hundred-year-old offspring. Night and day, for centuries, this thin trickle of water, even and continuous, had been singing the same pure song, vibrating like crystal.

Clotilde wandered amongst the boxwood, which reached her shoulders, then went back inside to get a piece of embroidery and came back to sit at a stone table by the fountain. They had put a few garden chairs there, it was where they had coffee. And she affected not to look up from then on, as if absorbed in her work. Yet every so often she seemed to cast a glance, between the tree trunks, at the threshing floor, as blinding as a furnace in the fiery distance, with the sun blazing away over it. But in reality she was stealing a glance, through her long lashes, at the doctor's windows. Nothing appeared there, not even a shadow. And her sadness and resentment grew, at his abandoning her like this, at the contempt in which he seemed to hold her, after their quarrel of the day before. And she had got out of bed with such a strong desire to make peace then and there! Obviously he was in no such hurry, obviously he didn't love her, since he could go on living in anger. And little by little she grew sombre and reverted to thoughts of doing battle, determined once more never to yield again on anything.

At around eleven o'clock, before putting her lunch on the stove, Martine came and joined her, carrying the eternal stocking she knitted even while walking, whenever the house wasn't keeping her busy.

'You know he's still shut in up there, like a wolf, cooking up his funny food?'

Clotilde shrugged without taking her eyes off her embroidery.

'And, Mademoiselle, if I told you what people are saying! Madame Félicité was right, yesterday, when she said it's enough to make you blush... They had the nerve to tell me to my face, as sure as I'm standing here talking to you, that he killed old Boutin—you remember, that poor old man who had the falling sickness and dropped dead on a road somewhere.'

There was a pause. Seeing the young woman grow even more sombre, the servant went on, keeping her fingers furiously active all the while:

'Me, I wouldn't know, but it makes me mad, what he's cooking up... What about you, Mademoiselle? Do you approve of that kind of cookery?'

Clotilde promptly looked up, yielding to the flow of passion that was sweeping her away.

'Look, I don't want to know any more about it than you do, but I think he's heading for serious trouble... He doesn't love us any more.'

'Oh, yes he does, Mademoiselle! He loves us!'

'No, he doesn't, not the way we love him! If he loved us, he'd be here, with us, instead of up there, losing his soul, losing his happiness and ours, trying to save the world!'

The two women looked at each other for a moment, their eyes burning with tenderness, in their jealous rage. Then they went back to work, bathed in shadow, and didn't speak again.

Up in his room, Doctor Pascal was working with the serenity of perfect joy. He had hardly ever actually practised medicine, except for about a dozen years, starting with his return from Paris and ending the day he retreated to La Souleiade. Satisfied with the hundred-and-something thousand francs he'd made and wisely invested, he had done little else but devote himself to his favourite projects, maintaining a small practice of friends only, never refusing to go to a sick person's bedside, but never sending a bill either. Whenever people paid him, he would toss the money to the back of a drawer in his secretaire, regarding it as pocket money for his experiments and whims, a bonus coming on top of his annuities, whose total amount was quite enough for him. He scoffed at the bad reputation for eccentricity that his ways had earned him, and was only happy amidst his research on the subjects he felt passionate about. For many people it was a surprise to see that this scientist, whose lot of genius was marred by an overactive imagination, had stayed on in Plassans, that godforsaken town that didn't look as if it could offer him any of the necessary tools. But he had no trouble explaining the advantages he had found there, first and foremost a retreat of great calm, and then an unsuspected field of uninterrupted inquiry, into developments in heredity, his favourite field of research, in this remote country region where he knew every family and could follow phenomena kept hidden, over two or three generations. On top of that, he was close to the sea and had gone there practically every summer to study marine life, the infinite swarms in which life is born and propagated, deep in the vast waters. And lastly, in the hospital in Plassans there was a dissecting room, which he was practically the only person ever to use, a big, quiet, light-filled room where, for over twenty years, all the unclaimed corpses had passed under his scalpel. Besides, he was very unassuming, of a timidity that had long ago turned touchy, so he had been happy just to correspond with his old professors and a few new friends about the very remarkable reports he sometimes sent to the Académie de médecine. He lacked all militant ambition.

The thing that had led Doctor Pascal to focus specifically on the laws of heredity was, initially, work on gestation. As always, chance had played its part by providing him with a whole series of cadavers of pregnant women who'd died during a cholera epidemic. Later, he had kept an eye on deaths, completing the cycle, filling in the gaps, and reaching a point where he knew how an embryo formed, then how the foetus developed every day of its intrauterine life; and so he had compiled a list of the most concise and definitive observations. After that, the problem of conception, which was the basis of everything, had posed itself to him in all its irritating mystery. Why and how did a new life come into being? What were the laws of life governing this deluge of beings that made up the world? He didn't just stick to dead bodies, but extended his dissections to living humanity, struck by certain constant traits amongst his patients, and putting his own family especially under observation, it having become his main field of experiment, so precisely and completely did cases present themselves in it. Subsequently, as the facts piled up and were classified in his notes, he had attempted a general theory of heredity that could on its own explain them all.

This was a tough problem, one whose solution he had been refining for years. He had started from two principles, the principle of invention and the principle of imitation: heredity, or the reproduction of beings governed by resemblance; innateness, or the reproduction of beings governed by variation. With heredity, he had allowed only four types of hereditary transmission: direct inheritance—representation of the father and the mother in the offspring's physical and moral nature; indirect inheritance—representation of the collaterals, uncles and aunts, cousins, male and female; reversion inheritance—representation of the ancestors, one or two generations back; and lastly, influence inheritance—representation of earlier couples, for example of a female's first lover who has somehow virtually impregnated that female in relation to any future conception of hers, even when he is not the author of that conception. As for innateness, this produced a new, or apparently new, human being, in whom the physical and moral traits of the parents are mixed without leaving any apparent traces of either. Following on from this, and again taking up the two terms, heredity and innateness, he had subdivided these in turn, splitting heredity into two types: the favouring of either the father or of the mother by the offspring, the preference, or predominance, of one individual; or else a mix of both father and mother, such a mix being able to take one of three forms, the direct joining of parts, random distribution, or blending, going from the least good state to the

most perfect. With innateness, on the other hand, there was only one
possible type and that was combination—the chemical combination
that means that two bodies brought together can constitute a new
body completely different from those of which it is the product.*
That was a summing-up of a significant raft of observations, not only
in anthropology, but also in zoology, pomology, and horticulture. But
the difficulty began when, faced with these multiple facts furnished
by analysis, it came to synthesizing them and formulating a theory
that explained them all. There, he felt he was on the shaky ground of
hypothesis, which each new discovery transforms; and if he couldn't
stop himself from offering a solution, because of the human brain's
need for finality, he was open-minded enough to leave the problem
standing. He had thus gone from Darwin's gemmules and pangenesis,*
to Haeckel's perigenesis,* via Galton's stirps.* Then, he intuitively
picked up the theory that Weismann* later successfully advanced, and
focused on the notion of germ plasma, an extremely fine and complex
substance, part of which always remains in reserve in every new being
to ensure that it is transmitted, invariable, immutable, from generation to generation. This seemed to explain everything; but what an
infinite mystery it was still, this world of resemblances that are transmitted by spermotozoa and egg, where the human eye can make out
absolutely nothing, not even under a microscope of the highest mag-
nifying power! He was fully expecting his theory to be superseded
one day, too, and was only happy with it as a provisional explanation,
good enough for the current state of the issue, in this never-ending
investigation into life, whose very source, ejaculation, seems set to
escape our comprehension forever.

Oh, this heredity! What a subject of endless musings it was for
him! The surprising, the wonderful thing, wasn't it that resemblance
between parents and progeny was not comprehensive, mathematical?
With his own family, he had first of all drawn up a logically deduced
family tree, where the shares of influence, from generation to generation, were evenly distributed between father and mother. But almost
every time, the living reality belied the theory. Instead of resemblance,
heredity was merely the striving after resemblance, an effort thwarted
by circumstances and the environment. And he'd ended up with what
he called the hypothesis of cell abortion. Life is mere movement,
and so, since heredity was that movement transmitted, it followed
that cells, in multiplying from each other, pushed each other around,

crashed into each other and made a space for themselves, each striving after heredity—so that if during this struggle weaker cells died, what you got in the final result were significant disorders, totally different organs. Didn't innateness, the constant invention of nature he loathed, stem from this? Wasn't he himself so different from his parents only because of similar accidents? Or was it due to the latent heredity he had for a time believed in? Every family tree has roots that thrust down into humanity all the way back to the first man; no one starts out from a single ancestor, you can always resemble an earlier, unknown ancestor. Yet he had his doubts about atavism; his view was that, despite a remarkable example in his own family, resemblance must founder, after two or three generations, by reason of accidents and interventions, and the countless possible combinations. So what there was, then, was a perpetual becoming, a constant transformation in this effort communicated, this power transmitted, this shock that breathes life into matter and which is life itself. Many questions suggested themselves. Was there such a thing as physical and intellectual progress over the ages? Did the brain develop as it grappled with expanding knowledge in the realm of science? Could we hope, in the long term, for a greater sum of reason and of happiness? Then there were special problems, one of them, whose mystery had long provoked him, being how did conception produce a boy and how did it produce a girl? Would they never manage to scientifically predict gender, or at least explain it? He had dealt with the subject in a very curious treatise, crammed with facts, but concluding basically with the same absolute ignorance in which the most tenacious research had left him. No doubt heredity only excited him the way it did because it remained obscure, vast and unfathomable, like all the still speculative sciences, in which the imagination reigns supreme. Well, a long study he'd done on the hereditary transmission of consumption had just rekindled his wavering faith as a healer doctor, urging him on in the noble and forlorn hope of regenerating humanity.

In short, Doctor Pascal had only one belief: the belief in life. Life was the sole manifestation of the divine. Life was God, the great engine, the soul of the universe. And life had no instrument other than heredity, heredity made the world; which meant that, if you could only understand it, harness it so as to control it, you could make the world however you liked. Because he'd seen sickness and suffering and death up close, a doctor's militant compassion was stirring inside him. Ah, to stop people getting sick, stop suffering, to keep people alive as much as possible! His dream ended in the thought that you could spur on universal happiness, the future city of perfection and bliss, by intervening and ensuring health for all. When everyone was healthy, strong, intelligent, there would be only a superior people, infinitely wise and happy. In India, didn't they make a Brahmin out of a Sudra* in seven generations, thereby experimentally raising the last of the outcasts to the most sublime human type? And, as in his study of consumption, where he had come to the conclusion that the disease was not hereditary, but that any child of a consumptive was a breeding ground where consumption could develop with rare ease, so now he thought only of enriching this breeding ground depleted by heredity so as to give it the strength to resist the parasites or, rather, the deadly ferments which, well before the theory of microbes was put forward, he suspected were present in the organism. Giving strength—the whole problem lay there; and giving strength also meant giving willpower, enlarging the brain by boosting the other organs.

It was around this time that the doctor read an old fifteenth-century medical book, and he was very struck by a form of medicine described there as 'the doctrine of signatures'. To cure a diseased organ, all you had to do was take the same healthy organ from a sheep or an ox, boil it up, and get the patient to drink the broth. The theory was that you could restore like by like, and with diseases of the liver especially, the old book said, cures were too numerous to count. The doctor's imagination was busily applying itself to this. Why not try it? Since he hoped to regenerate enfeebled heirs who lacked nerve substance, all he had to do was provide them with this nerve substance in a normal and healthy state. Only, the method using broth seemed puerile to him, so he came up with the idea of grinding up some sheep's brains with a mortar and pestle, steeping this paste in distilled water, then decanting and filtering the liquid thus obtained. He then experimented on his patients using this solution mixed with Malaga wine, without obtaining any appreciable result. Then suddenly one day, just as he was starting to feel discouraged, he had a brainwave when he was giving a lady suffering from inflammation of the liver an injection of morphine, with the small hypodermic syringe Pravaz* invented. What if he were to try hypodermic injections of his solution? And straightaway, the moment he got home, he experimented on himself, gave himself a shot in the backside, and then repeated the procedure morning and night. The first doses, of only a gram, had no effect. But when he doubled and then tripled the dose, he was thrilled to find when he got up one morning that his legs were as strong as they had been when he was twenty. He gradually increased the dose to five grams and consequently breathed more deeply and worked with a lucidity and an ease that he hadn't felt in years. He was flooded by a great sense of well-being, amazing *joie de vivre*. From then on, after he'd managed to get a syringe manufactured in Paris that could hold five grams, he was surprised by the happy results he obtained with his patients, setting them back on their feet in a matter of days, as though they had a new lease of life—vibrant, active life. His method was still fairly empirical, still primitive, and he sensed all sorts of dangers in it and was particularly afraid of causing embolisms if the solution was not absolutely pure. He later suspected that his convalescents' energy stemmed partly from the fever he produced in them. But he was merely a pioneer; the method would be improved over time. Didn't he already have a miracle here that could make paralysed syphilitics walk, revive consumptives, even give madmen a few hours of lucidity? And at this chance find anticipating the alchemy of the twentieth century, an immense hope opened up before him; he believed he'd discovered a universal panacea, the elixir of life destined to combat human debility, which was the sole real cause of all ills; a veritable scientific Fountain of Youth, which, by giving strength, health, and will, would create an altogether new and superior humanity.

That particular morning in his bedroom—a north-facing room somewhat dark from being so close to the plane trees and furnished simply with an iron bed, a mahogany secretaire, and a large worktable with a mortar and a microscope on it—he was putting the finishing touches to a vial of his home-made brew, taking infinite care as he did so. After pounding some nerve substance from a sheep in distilled water with the pestle, he had had to decant and filter. And he had obtained at last a small bottle of a cloudy, opaline liquid, iridescent with bluish reflections, which he gazed at for a long time in the light as if he held in his hand the regenerating and redeeming blood of the world.

But a few gentle knocks on the door and an urgent voice dragged him out of his reverie.

'What's happening? It's a quarter past twelve, Monsieur, don't you want lunch?'

Downstairs, lunch was indeed waiting in the big cool dining room.

The shutters had been kept closed, only one of them being opened a crack just now. It was a cheery room with pearl-grey wainscot panels, highlighted by blue beading. The table, sideboard, and chairs looked as though they must once have completed the suite of Empire furniture that filled the bedrooms, and against the light background, the old mahogany wood stood out powerfully in its intense red. A polished copper ceiling light, always gleaming, shone like a sun; while on the four walls bloomed four huge bouquets in pastel, of wallflowers, carnations, hyacinths, and roses.

Radiant, Doctor Pascal stepped inside.

'Oh, dear! I got carried away, I just wanted to finish up. Look here, this is completely new and extremely pure, this time, pure enough to work miracles!'

He held up the vial, which he'd brought downstairs with him in his enthusiasm. But then he noticed Clotilde standing there stiff and mute with a grave expression on her face. Bitter resentment at being kept waiting had brought back all her hostility, and having longed to throw her arms round his neck all morning, she remained motionless now, looking chilly and distant.

'Right!' he went on, losing none of his cheerfulness. 'We're still sulking. Now, that's not nice. So, you don't admire this sorcerer's solution of mine that can wake the dead?'

He sat down at the table and, sitting down opposite him, the young woman was forced to reply.

'You know very well, Maître, that I admire everything about you. I'd just like others to admire you, too. And there *is* the death of poor old Boutin...'

'Oh!' he cried without letting her finish. 'The man was an epileptic who succumbed in the middle of a seizure!... Well! Since you're in a bad mood, let's not talk about that any more: you'll upset me and that will spoil my day.'

There were hard-boiled eggs, cutlets, and custard. A silence stretched out, during which, despite her sulks, Clotilde ate heartily, having a healthy appetite which she was not coy enough to hide. He finally spoke, chuckling:

'The thing that reassures me is that you've got such a cast-iron stomach. Martine, give Mademoiselle some bread, why don't you.'

As usual, Martine served them and watched them eat with her quiet familiarity. She would often even chat with them.

'Monsieur,' she said when she'd cut the bread, 'the butcher brought his bill round, should it be paid?'

He looked up and gazed at her in surprise.

'Why are you asking me? Don't you usually pay without consulting me?'

It was in actual fact Martine who held the purse strings. The sums the doctor had invested with Monsieur Grandguillot, the notary in Plassans, produced a nice round sum of six thousand francs in interest. Every quarter, the fifteen hundred francs were put in the servant's hands and she disposed of them in the best interests of the household, buying and paying for everything with the strictest economy, for she was a miser, something they were always ribbing her about. Clotilde was not much of a spender and did not have her own allowance. As for the doctor, he took his pocket money and what he needed for his experiments out of the three or four thousand francs a year he still made and which he shoved to the back of a drawer in the secretaire. He now had quite a hoard, in gold coins and banknotes, though he never knew the exact amount.

'To be sure, I pay, Monsieur,' the servant resumed, 'but only when I'm the one who's gone and got the goods. But this time the bill's so high because of all those brains the butcher's been supplying you with.'

The doctor promptly cut her off.

'Now then! Don't tell me you're going to take sides against me, too? Ah, no! That'd be too much! Yesterday you really upset me, the pair of you, and I was angry. But this has to stop, I don't want this house to become a living hell. Two women against me, and the only ones who even like me a little! You know, I'd rather clear out right now!'

He wasn't annoyed, he was laughing, although his trembling voice gave away the disquiet he felt in his heart. And he added with his cheery air of bonhomie:

'If you're worried about making ends meet this month, my girl, tell the butcher to send my bill separately. And never fear, no one's asking you to dig into your own stash, your sous can lie idle.'

This was an allusion to Martine's small personal fortune. In thirty years, at four hundred francs a year in wages, she had made twelve thousand francs, from which she had taken only what was strictly necessary for her upkeep; and fattened up, almost trebled with the interest, the total value of her savings was now around thirty thousand francs. On an impulse, she had decided not to invest her money with Monsieur Grandguillot, but to put it aside. It was somewhere else, in solid annuities.

'Money that lies idle is honest money,' she said gravely. 'But Monsieur is right, I'll tell the butcher to send a separate bill, since all these brains are for Monsieur's cookery, not mine.'

This explanation made Clotilde smile, amused as she usually was by jokes about Martine's avarice, and the lunch ended on a cheerier note. The doctor wanted to have his coffee out under the plane trees, saying he needed fresh air after being shut away all morning. So the coffee was served on the stone table by the fountain. And how good it was there, in the shade, in the cool murmur of the water, while, all around, the pinewood, the threshing floor, the entire estate lay scorching in the early afternoon sun!

Pascal had smugly brought along the vial of nerve substance and was looking at it as it sat on the table.

'So, Mademoiselle,' he went on with an air of gruff jocularity, 'you don't believe in my elixir of resurrection, yet you believe in miracles!'

'Maître,' Clotilde replied, 'I believe we don't know everything.'

He flapped his hand impatiently.

'But we have to know everything. Listen to me then, you stubborn little thing: not one single departure from the invariable laws that govern the universe has ever been scientifically observed. To this day, human intelligence is the only factor that has played a part. I defy you to find any real will, any kind of intention, outside life as we know it... That's the whole point: there is no will in the world other than the force that drives everything to live, to live a life that's ever more evolved and elevated.'

He had risen to his feet and opened his arms wide, lifted up by such faith that the young woman just stared, amazed to see him looking so young in spite of his white hair.

'Would you like me to tell you my own personal Creed,* since you accuse me of not wanting anything to do with yours? I believe that the future of humanity lies in the progress of reason through science. I believe that the pursuit of truth through science is the divine ideal that man ought to set himself. I believe that all is illusion and vanity outside the treasure trove of truths slowly acquired and which will never again be lost. I believe that the sum of these truths, which are always growing in number, will end up giving man incalculable power—and serenity, if not happiness... Yes, I believe in the ultimate triumph of life.'

He opened his arms even wider to encompass the vast horizon, as if calling as witness the blazing countryside, where the sap of all living things boiled.

'But the perpetual miracle, my child, is life... So open your eyes and look!'

She shook her head.

'I open them obviously, but I don't see everything. You're the one who's stubborn, Maître, not wanting to admit that there is an unknown world out there, a world you will never enter. Oh, I know you're too intelligent not to be aware of it! You just don't want to take it into account; you cast the unknown aside because it would get in the way of your research. You can tell me all you like to set aside the mystery, to start with the known so as to conquer the unknown. I can't do that, myself! The mystery immediately claims me and troubles me.'

He heard her out, smiling, glad to see her becoming animated, and he stroked her blonde curls.

'Yes, I know, you're like the rest, you can't live without illusions and lies... But, well, never mind, we understand each other, even so. Take care of yourself, that's the best part of wisdom and happiness.'

He then changed the subject:

'Well, anyway, you can still come with me and help me on my miracle rounds. It's Thursday, my visiting day. When the heat's died down a bit, we'll set out together.'

She refused at first so as to appear not to yield, but ended up agreeing, seeing the pain she'd caused him. She almost always went with him. They stayed sitting for a long while under the plane trees, until the doctor went upstairs to change. When he came down again, looking spruce in his close-fitting frock coat, with a wide-brimmed silk hat clapped on his head, he talked of harnessing Bonhomme, the horse who, for a quarter of a century, had been taking him on his house calls. But the poor old nag was going blind, and in gratitude for his services and out of affection for his dear self, they hardly ever disturbed him now. That afternoon, he was quite sleepy, his eyes vacant, his legs crippled with rheumatism. So the doctor and the young woman went into the stable to see him and planted a big kiss on either

side of his nostrils, telling him to rest on a nice bale of straw that the
maid brought in. And they decided they'd go on foot.

Clotilde, keeping on her white dress with the red spots, had simply tied a big straw hat, covered in lilac, over her hair, and she looked
charming with her great big eyes and her peaches-and-cream complexion, in the shadow of the vast brim. When she stepped out like
this, on Pascal's arm—she slim and willowy and so young, he radiant, his face illuminated by the whiteness of his beard, and still
vigorous enough to lift her up and over running streams—people
would smile as they passed, would turn and gaze after them, they
were so handsome and happy. That particular day, as they came out
of the Chemin des Fenouillères, at the entrance to Plassans, a group
of old biddies suddenly stopped talking. You would have sworn he
was one of those old kings you see in pictures, one of those powerful
but gentle kings who never grow old, a hand on the shoulder of
a girl as lovely as the day whose dazzling and dutiful youthfulness
buoys them.

They were just turning into the Cours Sauvaire on their way to the
Rue de la Banne when a tall dark-haired young man of about thirty
stopped them.

'Ah, Maître, you've forgotten me! I'm still waiting for your notes,
on consumption.'

It was Doctor Ramond, who'd moved to Plassans two years before
and was building up a sizeable practice. With a magnificent head and
at the peak of his sunny virility, he was adored by women, but thank-
fully he was also extremely intelligent and extremely wise.

'Well, well! Ramond, hello! But not at all, dear friend, I haven't
forgotten you. It's this young miss here. I gave her the notes to copy
yesterday but she hasn't got round to it yet.'

The two young people shook hands, apparently good friends.

'Hello, Mademoiselle Clotilde.'

'Hello, Monsieur Ramond.'

When Clotilde had had a bout of typhoid fever, luckily mild, the
year before, Doctor Pascal had panicked, so much so that he lost confidence in himself and had insisted his young colleague help him and
reassure him. That was how a familiarity, a sort of camaraderie, had
sprung up between the three of them.

'You'll have your notes tomorrow morning, I promise you,' she
went on, laughing.

But Ramond lingered, walking with them to the end of the Rue de la Banne, the start of the old quarter where they were headed. And in the way he lent towards Clotilde, smiling, there was a whole discreet, slowly growing love, impatiently awaiting its hour for the most reasonable of denouements. Apart from that, he listened deferentially to Doctor Pascal, whose works he admired greatly.

'Ah, yes! I just so happen, dear friend, to be going to see Guiraude—you know, the woman whose husband, the tanner, died of consumption five years ago. She's still got two children living: a girl, Sophie, who's about to turn sixteen—luckily I was able to pack her off to the countryside, not far from here, to one of her aunts, four years before her father died; and a boy, Valentin, who's just turned twenty-one—the mother wanted to keep him at home with her, out of a clinging affection, in spite of the appalling consequences I threatened her with. Well, see if I wasn't right to claim that consumption isn't hereditary, but that consumptive parents merely pass on a degenerate breeding ground, in which the disease develops at the slightest contagion. Today, Valentin, who lived in daily contact with his father, is consumptive, whereas Sophie, who grew up in the sunlight, enjoys superb health.'

He gloated, and added, laughing:

'That doesn't mean I won't manage to save Valentin. He's visibly springing back to life again, and even putting on weight since I've been giving him injections. Ah, Ramond! You'll come round to them, my injections, you'll come round to them!'

The young doctor shook hands with both of them.

'But I'm not saying I won't. You know very well I'm always on your side.'

When they were alone again, they stepped up the pace and immediately delved into the Rue Canquoin, one of the darkest and narrowest streets in the old quarter. Blistering as the sun was, the light that reigned there was as dim and cool as in a cellar. It was here, on the ground floor, that Madame Guiraude lived with her son Valentin. She it was who opened the door, thin, exhausted-looking, herself struck with a slow putrefaction of the blood. From morning till night, she crushed almonds with the end of a sheep bone on a big paving stone she held between her knees; and this labour was their only means of living, the son having had to cease all work. Madame Guiraude smiled, though, that particular day, to see the doctor, for Valentin had just eaten a chop, with gusto, in a veritable act of debauchery he hadn't allowed himself for months. Puny, with sparse hair and beard, and prominent cheekbones that were strangely rosy in an otherwise waxen complexion, he had also jumped to his feet to show that he was full of beans. Clotilde was moved to see the way they welcomed Pascal, as if he were the saviour, the long-awaited messiah. These poor people clutched his hands, would have kissed his feet, looked at him with eyes gleaming with gratitude. He could clearly do anything, he was clearly the Almighty, to be able to bring the dead back to life like this! He himself gave an encouraging laugh in the face of a cure that looked so promising. No doubt the patient wasn't cured, perhaps he'd just had a bit of a boost, for he sensed Valentin was more excited and feverish than anything else. But was gaining a few days nothing? He gave him another injection while Clotilde, standing at the window, turned her back; and when they were leaving, she saw him put twenty francs on the table. It often happened that he paid the sick instead of being paid by them.

They made three other visits in the old quarter and then went to see a lady in the new town. When they were back out in the street again, he said:

'You know, if you're up to it, before we call in at Lafouasse's, we might go all the way to La Séguiranne to see Sophie at her aunt's. I'd really like that.'

It was barely two miles away and would be a delightful walk in such glorious weather. So she cheerfully agreed, no longer sulking, and snuggled up to him, happy to be on his arm. It was five o'clock and the slanting sun filled the countryside with a great golden gauze. But as soon as they left Plassans, they had to cut across a swathe of the vast plain, parched and bare, on the right of the Viorne. The recently built canal, which was meant to provide irrigation water that would transform a region dying of thirst, was still not irrigating this patch; and reddish earth and yellowish earth stretched out to infinity in the mournful and shattering glare of the sun, planted only with spindly almond trees and stunted olives, continually pruned and cut back, their branches twisted and gnarled in postures of pain and revolt. In the distance, on the bald slopes, all that could be seen were the pale splotches of bastides,* striped black by the obligatory cypresses. Yet the immense treeless expanse, with its broad desolate folds of land in harsh, sharp hues, preserved lovely classical curves of a severe grandeur.

And on the road lay dust eight inches thick, like snow–dust the slight-est puff of wind whipped up into wide whirling plumes that coated the figs and brambles on both verges with white powder.

Clotilde, who was enjoying herself like a child at the sound of all this dust crackling under her tiny feet, tried to shelter Pascal under her parasol.

'You've got the sun in your eyes. Keep to the left.'

But he soon grabbed the parasol and held it himself.

'You're not holding it properly, and anyway, it's tiring for you. Besides, we're here.'

In the burnt plain, you could already make out a small oasis of greenery, a whole enormous clump of trees. This was La Séguiranne, the property where Sophie had grown up, in the home of her aunt Dieudonné, the sharecropper's* wife. Wherever there was the tiniest spring, the tiniest stream, this blazing land broke out in powerful vegetation, and dense shade then spread along the deliciously deep and fresh byways. Plane trees, chestnuts, and young elms grew vigor-ously. They turned into an avenue of magnificent green oaks.

As they were approaching the farm, a girl making hay in a meadow dropped her fork and came running. It was Sophie, who had recog-nized the doctor and the young lady, as she called Clotilde. She adored them, but could only stand there embarrassed, gawping at them, unable to give voice to the fine feelings with which her heart overflowed. She resembled her brother Valentin; she was short like him, her cheekbones prominent like his, her hair also fair; but out in the country, far from the contagion of the paternal environment, she seemed to have taken on flesh, to stand straight-backed on her strong legs, with her cheeks filled out, her hair thick. And she had really beautiful eyes that shone with health and gratitude. Aunt Dieudonné, who had also been making hay, came over in her turn, shouting out from afar, joking in the rough Provençal way.

'Ah! Monsieur Pascal, we don't need you here! No one's sick!'

The doctor, who'd only come to see this lovely show of health, answered in the same vein:

'I should think not. All the same, here's a girl who ought to be very grateful to us, you and me!'

'That is the plain unvarnished truth, when it comes to you! And she knows it, Monsieur Pascal, she tells me every day that, without you, she'd be like her poor brother Valentin right now.'

'Nonsense! We'll save him, too. He's much better, Valentin. I've just seen him.'

Sophie clasped the doctor's hands, big tears appeared in her eyes. She could only stammer:

'Oh, Monsieur Pascal!'

How they loved him! And Clotilde felt her own tenderness for him grow, fed by all these scattered affections. They lingered for a while, chatting, in the invigorating shade of the green oaks. Then they strolled back towards Plassans, having one more visit to make.

This was to a dingy pothouse, at the confluence of two roads, white with the usual swirling dust. They had just set up a steam mill across the way, using the old buildings of Le Paradou,* a property dating from the previous century. And Lafouasse, the publican, was still doing a bit of trade, thanks to the mill workers and the peasants who brought in their wheat. On Sundays he also had as customers the few residents of the neighbouring hamlet of Les Artaud. But bad luck had struck him and for the past three years he'd been dragging about, complaining of pains the doctor finally recognized as the onset of ataxia;* yet the man stubbornly refused to take on a servant, and went on serving his regulars regardless, hanging onto the furniture as he did so. But now, put back firmly on his feet after ten or more injections, he was already telling anyone who'd listen that he was cured.

He was at his doorstep that very moment, standing tall and looking strong, his face fiery with excitement under his flaming red hair.

'I was waiting for you, Monsieur Pascal. You know, yesterday, I was able to bottle two casks of wine, and without getting tired!'

Clotilde stayed outside, sitting on a stone bench, while Pascal went in to give Lafouasse his injection. She could hear their voices, and the latter, who was extremely delicate despite his well-developed muscles, was complaining that the injection hurt; but that, well, a bit of pain was a small price to pay for good health. Then he got cross, forced the doctor to agree to a glass of something. The young lady would not offend him by refusing a glass of cordial. He carried a table outside, and they absolutely had to have a drink with him.

'To your good health, Monsieur Pascal, and the good health of all the poor buggers you've brought back from the dead!'

Clotilde thought with an inward smile of the gossip Martine had mentioned, of this old father Boutin they accused the doctor of having killed. So he didn't kill all his patients, then, his medication worked real miracles? And her faith in her master came flooding back in the warmth of the love that again stirred her heart. By the time they left, she had gone back to him completely, he could pick her up, carry her off, and dispose of her however he liked.

But a few minutes earlier, sitting on the stone bench, she had been trying to remember a vague story as she gazed at the steam mill. Wasn't it there, in those buildings blackened with coal and today white with flour, that a crime of passion had once been committed? And the story came back to her, with details Martine had provided and allusions the doctor himself had made—a whole tragic love affair that his cousin, the Abbé Serge Mouret, then curé at Les Artaud, had had with an exquisite girl, wild and passionate, who'd lived at Le Paradou.

They were walking back along the road again, and Clotilde stopped, pointing to the vast mournful expanse of stubble-fields, flattened crops, and fields still lying fallow.

'Maître, wasn't there a big garden there once? Didn't you tell me that story?'

Pascal, still full of the wonderful day, gave a shudder and a smile of immensely sad tenderness.

'Yes, Le Paradou, a huge garden, woods, meadows, orchards, flower beds, and fountains, and streams that flowed into the Viorne. A garden abandoned for a hundred years, Sleeping Beauty's garden, overrun once more by nature. As you can see, they've chopped down the woods, broken up the ground, levelled it, and divided it into lots to sell at auction. The springs themselves have dried up, there's nothing there now but this poisoned swamp. Ah! When I pass by here, it breaks my heart!'

She ventured a further question:

'Wasn't it at Le Paradou that my cousin Serge and your great friend Albine fell in love?'

But he'd forgotten she was there, and went on, his eyes far away, lost in the past.

'Albine, my God! I can see her now, sunstruck in the garden, smelling of perfume like a great living bouquet, her head thrown back, her breast heaving with laughter, happy with her flowers, the wild flowers she'd woven into her blonde hair, and tied around her neck and on her bodice, and around her thin bare golden arms. And when she'd committed suicide, suffocating to death amid her flowers, I can see her again, dead, white as a ghost, hands clasped, smiling in her sleep, lying on her bed of hyacinths and tuberoses... She died of love, and how they loved one another, Albine and Serge, in that big Garden of Eden, in the bosom of nature, their accomplice! What a surge of life, sweeping away all the sham ties! What a triumph of life!'

Clotilde was troubled by the ardour of these mumbled words, and gazed searchingly at him. She had never allowed herself to bring up another story she'd heard—about the secret love he'd harboured for a lady, the love of his life, who was dead now, too. They reckoned he'd looked after her without even daring to kiss her fingertips. Up to this point, up to now when he was close to sixty, study and timidity had kept him away from women. But you sensed that he was made for passion, his heart all young and overflowing, despite the white hair.

'And the woman who died, the one they still mourn...'

She checked herself, her voice trembling, her cheeks flushed, without knowing why.

'Serge didn't love her, then, if he let her die?'

Pascal seemed to snap out of his reverie, and he shivered to find her beside him, so young, with such beautiful eyes, burning and bright in the shade of the wide-brimmed hat. Something had just happened, the same current had just shot through them both. They didn't take each other's arm now but walked along side by side.

'Oh, darling! It would all be so wonderful if men didn't spoil everything! Albine is dead, and Serge is now the curé at Saint-Eutrope, where he lives with his sister Désirée, a decent creature, that one, who has the luck to be a halfwit. He's a holy man, I've never said otherwise. You can be a killer and still serve God.'

And he went on, bluntly describing the ugliness of existence, and the foul and execrable nature of humanity, without once dropping his beaming smile. He loved life, and pointed out the sheer, endless persistence of life, unflappably optimistic, despite all the evil, all the heartache it could hold. No matter how awful it might seem, life was necessarily great and good, because people put such tenacious will into living it, the purpose being, no doubt, this same will itself and the great work it unwittingly performed. Of course, he was a scientist, a man of unclouded vision; he didn't believe in an idyllic humanity living in a land of milk and honey—quite the opposite, he saw the vices and defects, and had been exposing them, probing them and cataloguing them for thirty years; but his passion for life, his admiration for the forces of life, were enough to throw him into a state of constant joy, from which seemed to flow naturally his love of others, a brotherly compassion, a fellow feeling, that you could sense beneath the unflinching rigour of the anatomist and the affected impersonality of his studies.

'Oh, well!' he concluded, turning back one last time to the vast and mournful fields. 'Le Paradou is no more, they've ravaged it, defiled it, destroyed it. But who cares! Vines will be planted, wheat will grow, a whole host of new crops; and people will go on falling in love, at grape-gatherings and harvests, long into the future... Life is eternal, all it ever does is begin again and grow.'

He took her arm once more and they walked home, pressed close together, good friends, as the light slowly died away in the sky, in a tranquil lake of violets and roses. And seeing them go past together, the powerful but gentle old king leaning on the shoulder of a charming and dutiful child, buoyed by her youth, the women of the faubourg, sitting at their doors, followed their progress with tender smiles.

At La Souleiade, Martine was watching out for them. From afar, she motioned to them to hurry up. Well! Whatever next! Weren't they going to eat that evening? When they were at close range, she said:

'Ah! You'll have to wait a while, now. I didn't dare put on my leg of lamb.'

They stayed outdoors, enchanted, in the dying light. The pine grove, which was plunged in shadow, gave off the balsamous scent of resin; and from the still-burning threshing floor, where a last rosy reflection was disappearing, a chilliness arose. It was like breathing, a sigh of relief, rest and repose for the entire estate, the emaciated almond trees, the twisted olives, under the great fading sky of unblemished serenity; while, behind the house, the cluster of plane trees was no more now than a mass of gloom, black and impenetrable, where you could hear the fountain singing its eternal crystalline song.

'Look!' the doctor said. 'Monsieur Bellombre's already had his dinner and now he's getting an airing.'

He pointed to a bench next door on which sat a tall, gaunt old man of seventy, with a long face scored with lines, and big staring eyes, very sprucely bundled into a frock coat and cravat.

'That's a wise man,' murmured Clotilde. 'He's happy.'

Pascal cried out in protest.

'That man! I certainly hope not!'

He didn't hate anyone, and only Monsieur Bellombre, this former teacher of the seventh grade, now retired and living in his little house with no one for company but a gardener, deaf and dumb and older than he was, had the knack of exasperating him.

'That man was afraid of life, hear me? Afraid of life! Yes! A hard and stingy egotist! If he banished women from his life, that was only because he was terrified he'd have to pay for ladies' ankle boots. And he's only ever had to deal with other people's children, but they made him suffer: so now he hates all children, they're just fodder for punishment. Afraid of life, afraid of encumbrances and duties, of nuisances and calamities! Afraid of life! What that means is being so terrified of life's sorrows, you reject its joys! Ah, you see, such cowardice infuriates me, it's something I can't forgive. We've got to live, live completely, live life to the full, all of it. Give me suffering and nothing but suffering any day, rather than this renunciation, this being dead to what is alive and human in us!'

Monsieur Bellombre had stood up and was ambling along a path in his garden, taking easy little steps. Clotilde, who was still quietly watching him, finally broke her silence:

'There's joy in renunciation, though. Renouncing the world, not living, saving yourself for the mystery of revealed truth—hasn't that been the essence of the great happiness of the saints?'

'If they haven't lived,' cried Pascal, 'they can't be saints.'

But he could feel her rebelling and about to slip away from him again. In all concern with the beyond, deep down, there is fear and hatred of life. So he reverted to his lovely laugh, so tender and so conciliatory.

'No! That's enough for today; let's not argue any more, let's love each other dearly. And, hear that! Martine's calling us for dinner, let's go and eat.'

3

OVER the next month the uneasiness only grew worse and Clotilde was especially pained to see that Pascal now locked his drawers. He no longer had the quiet confidence in her of days gone by, and she was hurt by this, so much so that if she'd found the cupboard open again, she would have hurled the files into the fire as her grandmother Félicité was urging her to do. They started bickering again, and often didn't speak to each other for at least a couple of days.

One morning, following one such bout of sulking that had been going on since the day before, Martine said, as she served breakfast:

'Just now as I was crossing the Place de la Sous-Préfecture, I saw a stranger going into Madame Félicité's and I thought I recognized him. Yes, if it turns out to be your brother, Mademoiselle, I wouldn't be at all surprised.'

Suddenly, Pascal and Clotilde were on talking terms again.

'Your brother! Was your grandmother expecting him?'

'No, I don't think so. Well, she's been expecting him for over six months. I know she wrote to him again a week ago.'

They questioned Martine.

'Heavens, Monsieur! I can't say. I mean it's four years since I saw Monsieur Maxime, when he spent a couple of hours with us on his way to Italy; he might well have changed a lot. But I did think I recognized him from behind, all the same.'

The conversation continued; Clotilde seemed happy at this event that had finally broken the oppressive silence, and Pascal concluded:

'Good! If it is him, he'll come and see us.'

It was in fact Maxime. He had yielded, after months of saying no, to the pressing entreaties of old Madame Rougon, who still had an open wound to close on this side of the family. The situation went back a long way, and it got worse every day.

When he was seventeen, which was already fifteen years ago, Maxime had had a child with a servant he'd seduced; it was just a silly affair on the part of a precocious boy, and Saccard, his father, and his stepmother, Renée, who was simply vexed by the unworthy choice, had been happy to laugh it off. That was the trouble: the servant, Justine Mégot, was from a nearby village; she was a blonde girl, also seventeen, and sweet and docile; and she'd been packed off to Plassans, with an allowance of twelve hundred francs a year to bring up little Charles. Three years later, she had married a harness-maker from the faubourg there, Anselme Thomas, a hard-working, sensible boy, lured by the allowance. Moreover she'd become a model of good behaviour and had fattened up, apparently cured of the cough that had once raised concerns about a regrettable heredity, due to a long line of alcoholic ancestors. And two more children, born of her marriage, a boy now aged ten and a little girl of seven, both plump and rosy, were doing wonderfully well, so much so that she would have been the happiest and most respected of women if it hadn't been for the trouble Charles caused her at home. Despite the allowance, Thomas detested the boy, the son of another man, and pushed him around— something his mother suffered in silence, as a submissive and uncomplaining wife. And so, although she adored him, she would gladly have handed him back to his father's family.

Charles, at fifteen, scarcely looked twelve, and was stalled at the stumbling mental age of a child of five. Bearing an extraordinary resemblance to his great-great-grandmother, Aunt Dide, the madwoman of Les Tulettes, he had a supple and delicate grace, like one of those bloodless little kings that spell the end of their line, crowned with long pale hair, light as silk. His big clear eyes were vacant and his disturbing beauty had the shadow of death hanging over it. With no brain and no heart, he was nothing but a vicious little dog, who rubbed himself against people to fondle himself. His great-grandmother Félicité, won over by this beauty in which she affected to recognize her blood, had first put him in boarding school, and paid the fees; but he got himself thrown out after six months, accused of unmentionable vices. Three times she had kept at it and moved him to different schools, only to wind up each time with the same shameful expulsion. So, as he would not, absolutely could not, learn anything, and as he defiled everything, they had had to hang onto him and he was passed around between them, within the family. Moved to pity, Doctor Pascal had hoped to cure him, and had only given up on that impossible task after he'd had him at home for nearly a year and become anxious about the contact with Clotilde. And now, when Charles was not at his mother's, where he almost never stayed any more, he could be found at Félicité's or with some other relative, daintily turned out, up to his neck in toys, living like the effeminate little dauphin of an ancient fallen race.

Old Madame Rougon, however, was pained by this bastard, with his royal blond locks, and her plan was to remove him from the rumour mill of Plassans by getting Maxime to take him back to Paris and keep him there. That would be one more vile story about the family erased. But Maxime had long turned a deaf ear, haunted as he was by the constant fear of ruining his existence. After the war, made wealthy by the death of his wife, he had come home to steadily fritter away his fortune in his mansion in the Avenue du Bois-de-Boulogne, having acquired from his precocious debauchery a salutary fear of pleasure, and being above all determined to shun emotions and responsibilities, so as to hold out as long as possible. Sharp pains in his feet, which he believed to be rheumatism, had been tormenting him for some little time; he saw himself already crippled, confined to an armchair; and his father's sudden return to France, Saccard's active new role, had put the finishing touch to his terror. He knew the old squanderer of millions only too well, and trembled to find him bustling around him, playing the old codger, with his friendly mocking laugh. He'd surely get eaten alive if he remained at the man's mercy another day, riveted to the spot by these pains that were spreading to his legs. And he was suddenly so frightened of being on his own that he'd finally yielded to the idea of seeing his son again. If the boy looked sweet, intelligent, and healthy, why not take him home with him? It would give him a companion, an heir who would guard him against his father's machinations. In his selfishness he'd gradually come to see himself loved, pampered, protected; and yet, he may well not have risked such a journey again if his doctor had not sent him to take the waters in Saint-Gervais. From there it was just a short detour to old Madame Rougon's place and he had dropped in without warning that morning, firmly resolved to take the train back that very evening after having quizzed her and seen the boy.

At around two o'clock, Pascal and Clotilde were still sitting by the fountain, under the plane trees, where Martine had served them coffee, when Félicité turned up with Maxime.

'Darling, I've got a surprise for you! Your brother!'

Startled, the young woman rose to her feet before this stranger, wasted and a sickly yellow, whom she barely recognized. Since they'd parted, in 1854, she had only seen him twice, the first time in Paris, the second in Plassans. But she still had a clear picture of him as

elegant and alive. His face had hollowed, his hair had thinned and was
sprinkled with strands of grey. Yet, looking at him, with his fine pretty
head, she eventually saw the familiar grace, disturbingly girlish even
in his premature senility.

'*You're* looking well!' he said simply, embracing his sister.

'But,' she replied, 'for that, you have to live in the sun. Oh, I'm so
happy to see you!'

Pascal, with the eye of a doctor, had probed his nephew to the core.
He embraced him in turn.

'Hello, my boy... She's right, you know, you can be well only in the
sun, like the trees!'

In a flash, Félicité had darted into the house. She came back,
shouting:

'Charles isn't here, then?'

'No,' said Clotilde. 'We saw him yesterday. Uncle Macquart brought
him over, but he's supposed to spend a few days at Les Tulettes.'

Félicité was in despair. She had only come running in the certainty
of finding the boy at Pascal's. Now what? The doctor, in his usual
calm manner, suggested writing to his uncle, who could bring the boy
back the very next morning. But when he realized Maxime was absolutely determined to leave by the nine o'clock train, without staying
the night, he had another idea. He would send someone to look for
a landau at the hire place, so all four of them could go and see Charles
at Uncle Macquart's. It would actually be a delightful drive. It wasn't
even ten miles from Plassans to Les Tulettes: with an hour each way,
they'd still have nearly two hours to spend there if they wanted to be
back by seven. Martine would get dinner and Maxime would have all
the time in the world to eat and catch his train.

But Félicité was agitated, visibly unhappy about this visit to
Macquart.

'Oh, no you don't, if you think I'm going down there, with a storm
coming... It'd be a lot simpler to send someone to collect Charles and
bring him back here.'

Pascal shook his head. You couldn't always bring Charles back
when you wanted to. The boy had no sense and, at times, he'd gallop
away on the slightest whim, like an untamed animal. Old Madame
Rougon, opposed and furious at having no ready reply, ended up
giving in, forced as she was to trust to luck.

'All right! Have it your way! God, what a nuisance!'

Martine ran to get a landau, and before it had struck three the two horses were trotting along the road to Nice, descending the slope that went all the way down to the bridge over the Viorne. They then turned left and skirted around the wooded banks of the river for just under one and a half miles. After that the road went through the gorges of the Seille, a narrow defile between two gigantic walls of rock, baked and turned to gold by the harsh rays of the sun. Pine trees had grown up in the cracks; feathery treetops, scarcely any bigger from below than tufts of grass, fringed the crest and hung over the chasm. It was chaos, a battered landscape, a hall in hell, with its tumultuous twists and turns, its spills of blood-red earth sliding down from every gash, its desolate loneliness disturbed only by the flight of eagles.

Félicité did not open her mouth once but sat there with her brain ticking away, apparently weighed down by her thoughts. It was in fact extremely sultry, with the sun burning behind a veil of great livid clouds. Pascal was almost the only one to speak, moved by his passionate love for this brutal expanse of nature, a love he tried to get his nephew to share. But no matter how he exclaimed, pointed out to him the stubborn determination of the olives and figs and brambles in growing out of the rocks, or the life of those rocks themselves, of this colossal and powerful carcass of the world, from which a sigh could be heard rising, Maxime remained unmoved, gripped by a vague anguish before these blocks of wild majesty whose massiveness overwhelmed him. He preferred to bring his eyes back to his sister, seated opposite. She slowly captivated him, she looked so healthy and happy, with her pretty round head and her straight, perfectly untroubled brow. At times their eyes met and she gave an affectionate smile, and he felt reassured.

But the wildness of the gorge softened, the two walls of rock sank down, and they rode between quiet hillsides, with gentle slopes dotted with thyme and lavender. It was still the wilderness, though, and there were bare patches, greenish or purplish, where the slightest breeze tossed around an acrid scent. Then all of a sudden, after one last turn, they descended into the little valley of Les Tulettes, which was freshened by springs. At the bottom meadows stretched away, divided by tall trees. The village was halfway down, among the olive trees, and Macquart's bastide, a bit removed, sat on the left facing full south. The landau had to take the path that led to the lunatic asylum, whose white walls they could see facing them.

Félicité's silence had darkened, as she didn't like putting Uncle Macquart on show. Yet another one the family would be well shot of when he went! For the greater glory of them all, he should have been lying in the ground a long time ago. But he dug his heels in and carried on, eighty-three years old, an old lush, saturated with drink, seemingly pickled in alcohol. In Plassans he had a terrible reputation as a no-hoper and a crook, and the old men told in hushed voices the shocking story of the bodies that lay between him and the Rougons, an act of betrayal in the troubled days of December 1851, an ambush in which he'd left his comrades, lying with their guts ripped open, on the blood-streamed pavement.* Later, when he'd come back to France, he'd turned down the good job he'd been promised, preferring this little domain at Les Tulettes which Félicité had bought for him. And he'd been living there off the fat of the land ever since, his only remaining ambition being to extend the place, on the lookout as he was once more for good deals, having again found a way to get hold of a long-coveted field as a reward for making himself useful to his sister-in-law when she'd needed to win Plassans back from the Legitimists: another appalling story told in a whisper, of a madman surreptitiously let out of the asylum, crashing through the night, pursuing his revenge, setting fire to his own house, in which four people were burnt alive.* But happily all that was ancient history, Macquart had settled down and was no longer the alarming thug who had made the whole family quake. He showed himself to be extremely polite now, cunningly diplomatic, having retained only the jeering laugh that seemed to mock the rest of the world.

'Uncle's in,' said Pascal, as they drew near.

The bastide was one of those single-storey Provençal constructions with faded roof tiles, its four walls gaudily washed in yellow. In front of the house there was a narrow terrace shaded by ancient mulberry trees, trained downwards to form an arbour, their thick branches writhing and twisting like vines. This was where their uncle smoked his pipe in the summer. Hearing the sound of the carriage, he'd come and planted himself at the edge of the terrace, straightening up to his full and considerable height, dressed neatly in blue serge, with the inevitable fur cap he wore all year round clapped on his head.

When he saw who the visitors were, he sniggered and yelled:

'Well, if it isn't the hoi polloi! Of course, you'll kindly come in and have a drink?'

But Maxime's presence intrigued him. Who was this? What was he doing here, this one? They introduced him, but he immediately cut short the explanations they were reeling off in an effort to help him find his way through the complicated tangle of kinship.

'Charles's father, I know, I know! My nephew Saccard's son, of course! The one who made a good match, and whose wife died...'

He stared hard at Maxime and looked extremely happy to see him already wrinkled at thirty-two, his hair and beard sprinkled with grey.

'Yes, well!' he added. 'We're all getting old... Myself, I don't have much to complain about yet, I'm holding up.'

And he gloated, standing steady on his pins, his face looking boiled and singed, the fiery red of a furnace. For a long time now ordinary brandy had been like pure water to him; only ninety-per-cent pure alcohol still tickled his hardened gullet; and he drank such large shots that he was full of it, his flesh awash, soaked in it like a sponge. The alcohol poured out of his skin in sweat. And at the slightest breath, when he spoke, an alcoholic vapour wafted from his mouth.

'Oh, yes! You're holding up all right, Uncle!' said Pascal, amazed. 'And you've done nothing to help; you have every reason to laugh at us. You know, there's only one thing I'm afraid of, and that's that one day, when you light your pipe, you'll light yourself by the same token, like a bowl of punch.'

Macquart, flattered, chortled loudly.

'Very funny, very funny, junior! A glass of cognac's better than your dirty drugs. You will all have a glass with me, eh? So it can definitely be said your uncle does you all proud. I don't give a damn about backbiters, myself. I've got wheat, I've got olive trees, I've got almond trees, and vines, and land—as much as any burgher. In summer, I smoke my pipe in the shade of my mulberry trees; in winter, I go and smoke it over there, by the wall, in the sun. Eh? Nothing to be ashamed of in an uncle like that! Clotilde, I've got cordial, if you like. And you, Félicité, my dear, I know you prefer anisette. There's a bit of everything, I tell you, there's a bit of everything here!'

He gestured expansively, as if to encompass the well-being he now possessed as an old rogue turned recluse; while Félicité, whom he'd begun to frighten for a moment now, with the listing of his riches, didn't take her eyes off him, ready to step in and cut him off.

'Thank you, Macquart, we won't have anything, we're in a hurry. So where's Charles?'

'Charles, right, fine! In a moment! I know, Papa's come to see his boy. But that won't stop us having a drink.'

When they absolutely refused, he took offence and said with his malevolent smile:

'Charles is not here, he's at the madhouse with the old woman.'

Then he steered Maxime to the end of the terrace and showed him the great white buildings whose internal gardens looked like prison yards.

'There, Nephew, you see those three trees in front of us. Well, above the one on the left there's a fountain, in a courtyard. Follow the ground floor, the fifth window to the right is Aunt Dide's. And that's where the young one is. Yes, I took him there a short while ago.'

This was something the hospital board tolerated. In the twenty-one years that she'd been in the asylum, the old woman had not given her keeper a single qualm. Very quiet, very gentle, immobile in her chair, she spent her days staring straight ahead; and, as the boy liked it there, as she herself seemed to take an interest in him, they turned a blind eye to this infraction of the rules and left him there sometimes for two or three hours at a time, busily cutting out pictures.

But this new disappointment brought Félicité's foul mood to a head. She became angry when Macquart suggested they go as a group, all five of them, to pick up the boy.

'What an idea! You go on your own and come back quickly. We haven't got time to sit around.'

Her barely suppressed rage seemed to amuse her brother, and, from then on, sensing how much she disliked the idea, he insisted, with his sneer.

'But, children! We can see our old mother, the mother of us all, at the same time. Say what you like, we all come from her, you know, and it wouldn't be very polite not to go and say hello, since my great-nephew, who's come from so far away, mightn't have seen her again yet... Myself, I've never disowned her! Not on your life! She's mad, no doubt about it; but it's not every day you see old mothers over a hundred years old—it's worth the trouble to be a bit nice to her.'

There was a silence. A little chill ran through them. It was Clotilde, silent till now, who spoke up first, in a voice full of feeling:

'You're right, Uncle, we'll all go.'

Even Félicité had to agree. They hopped back in the landau, Macquart taking a seat next to the driver. A queasiness had drained

Maxime's tired face of colour; and during the short trip, he questioned Pascal about Charles with an air of paternal interest that masked growing anxiety. The doctor, inhibited by his mother's imperious glances, softened the truth. Well, no! The boy didn't enjoy robust good health—that was actually the reason they gladly left him for weeks on end at their uncle's place in the country; but he was not suffering from any known disease. Pascal did not add that he had, for a time, dreamed of giving him a bit of a brain and muscles by treating him with injections of nerve tissue; but he'd always run up against the same accidental complication, as the tiniest jabs brought on haemorrhages which he'd have to stop every time using pressure bandages: there was a slackening of the tissues due to degeneracy, an oozing of blood that pearled on the skin, and above all there would be nosebleeds, so sudden and so abundant that they didn't dare leave the boy on his own for fear all the blood in his veins would flow out. The doctor ended by saying that, if his intelligence was slow, he had hopes it would develop in an environment that provided more stimulating cerebral activity.

They arrived at the asylum. Macquart, who had been listening, got down from his seat, saying:

'He's a very sweet boy, very sweet. And then, he's so beautiful, an angel!'

Maxime, still more wan, and shivering in spite of the suffocating heat, asked no further questions. He gazed at the vast buildings of the asylum, the wings of the different quarters, separated by gardens, one for men and one for women, ones for subdued lunatics and ones for raving lunatics. A marked cleanliness permeated the place, a mournful loneliness, penetrated by footfalls and the sound of keys. Old Macquart knew all the keepers. Besides, the doors were always open to Doctor Pascal, who'd been authorized to treat some of the internees. They went along a corridor and turned into a courtyard: here it was, one of the ground-floor rooms, a room covered in bright wallpaper and furnished simply with a bed, a wardrobe, a table, an armchair and two chairs. The keeper, who was supposed never to leave her charge, had just slipped out, and the only people there, sitting on either side of the table, were the madwoman, rigid in her armchair, and the boy, on a chair, absorbed in cutting out pictures.

'Go in, go in!' Macquart repeated. 'Oh, there's no danger, she's very sweet!'

Their forebear, Adélaïde Fouque, whom her grandchildren, the whole teeming brood, called by the endearing nickname of Aunt Dide, didn't even turn her head at the noise. From adolescence, hysterical disorders had unbalanced her mind. Violently intense, passionate in love, wracked by fits, she had thus reached the grand old age of eighty-three when appalling grief, a terrible shock to her faculties, had sent her mad. Since that day, twenty-one years ago, she'd experienced complete loss of intelligence, a sudden enfeeblement that ruled out any form of recovery. Today, at a hundred and four, she was still living on like a woman the world had forgotten, a quiet madwoman with an ossified brain, in whom insanity could remain stalled indefinitely without leading to death. Yet old age had caught up with her and had gradually atrophied her muscles. Her flesh seemed to be eaten away by time, she was nothing now but skin and bones, so that she had to be carried from her bed to her armchair. And, although a skeleton who'd yellowed and dried up on the spot, like a century-old tree of which nothing remains but the bark, she sat fully upright against the back of her chair, with only her eyes still alive in her long, thin face. She was staring fixedly at Charles.

Clotilde, quaking a little, went up to her.

'Aunt Dide, we wanted to come and see you... Don't you know who I am? I'm your granddaughter who sometimes comes and gives you a kiss.'

But the madwoman didn't seem to have heard. Her eyes never left the boy, who had just finished cutting out a picture with his scissors, a purple king with a gold cloak.

'Come now, Mother,' Macquart said in turn, 'don't play the fool. You might at least give us a look. Here's a gentleman, one of your grandsons, who's made a special trip, all the way from Paris.'

At that voice, Aunt Dide finally turned her head. She slowly ran her clear vacant eyes over them, one by one, then brought them back to Charles and fell back to contemplating him. No one said another word.

'Since the terrible shock she received,' Pascal finally explained in a low voice, 'this is how she is: all intelligence, all memory seem to have been suppressed. Mostly she keeps quiet, but sometimes she stammers out a whole stream of words that are hard to make sense of. She laughs and cries for no reason, she's a thing that nothing can affect. And yet, I wouldn't dare claim that the darkness is absolute, that memories aren't stored away deep down. Ah, the poor old woman! How I pity her if the light hasn't yet been fully extinguished! What can she have been thinking about, for twenty-one years, if she does remember?'

With a wave of the hand, he brushed away this frightening past with which he was all too familiar. He saw her young again, a tall creature, thin and pale, with frightened eyes, no sooner married than made a widow, by Rougon, that lump of a gardener she'd wanted as a husband; but then throwing herself before her mourning was up into the arms of the smuggler Macquart, whom she'd loved with the love of a she-wolf and whom she didn't even bother to marry. She'd lived in this state of tumult and mayhem for fifteen years, with one legitimate child and two bastards, disappearing for weeks on end only to come back bruised, her arms black and blue. Then Macquart was shot dead, mown down like a dog by a gendarme; and at this first shock she had fossilized, her eyes, sparkling as springwater in her wan face, already the only thing still alive about her; and she'd withdrawn from the world into the bowels of the hovel her lover had left her, living the life of a nun there for forty years, punctuated by appalling fits of hysteria. But the next shock polished her off, drove her insane, and Pascal recalled the atrocious scene, for he had been there: a poor child his grandmother had taken in, her grandson Silvère, victim of the family's hatreds and murderous fights, had had his skull shattered by another gendarme firing a pistol shot, during the suppression of the insurrectionary movement of 1851. She was still spattered with blood.

Félicité, however, had gone over to Charles, who was so absorbed in his pictures that all these people did not disturb him.

'My darling boy, this gentleman is your father. Give him a kiss.'

Everyone then turned their attention to Charles. He was very daintily turned out, in a black velvet jacket and pants with gold braiding. As white as a lily, he really did look like the son of one of the kings he was cutting out, with his big pale eyes and streaming blond hair. But what stood out above all, at that moment, was his resemblance to Aunt Dide, a resemblance that had skipped three generations, leaping from that dried-up centenarian's face, from those worn-out features, to this delicate child's face, it too already looking wiped out, incredibly old, and run down by the erosion of the bloodline. Sitting opposite each other, the idiot child, with his moribund beauty, was like the end of the line of his forebear, the woman who'd been forgotten.

Maxime bent down to plant a kiss on the boy's forehead, but his heart was cold, the boy's very beauty frightened him, and his uneasiness only grew in this room filled with madness, where a whole history of human misery blew from far back in time.

'What a beautiful boy you are, my pet! Don't you love me, just a little?'

Charles looked at him, didn't understand, and went back to his pictures.

But they all remained stunned. Without the closed expression on her face altering in any way, Aunt Dide was crying, floods of tears were rolling from her living eyes and down her dead cheeks. Still not taking her eyes off the boy, she cried slowly without end.

At that, Pascal felt an extraordinary emotion run through him. He took Clotilde's arm and squeezed it hard, although she couldn't understand why. Before his very eyes, the whole line—both the legitimate branch and the illegitimate branch—that had grown from this trunk, already damaged by neurosis, rose up and was on parade. The five generations were there, together, the Rougons and the Macquarts, with Adélaïde Fouque at the root, then his old crook of an uncle, then himself, then Clotilde and Maxime, and lastly, Charles. Félicité filled the place of her dead husband. There was no break, the chain of hereditary succession rolled out in all its logic and implacability, unbroken. And what an age was conjured up, inside that tragic padded cell, where this misery from far back in time blew, and so terrifyingly that despite the shattering heat, every one of them shivered!

'What is it, Maître?' Clotilde whispered, trembling.

'No, nothing!' murmured the doctor. 'I'll tell you later.'

Macquart, who alone continued to sneer, scolded the old woman. The very idea, greeting people with tears, when they'd put themselves out to come and visit you! It wasn't exactly polite. After that, he went back to Maxime and Charles.

'Well, Nephew, there you see him, your boy. He's a picture, isn't he, a credit to you, all the same?'

Félicité hastened to intervene, most unhappy at the turn things were taking and in a hurry now just to get away.

'He certainly is a lovely child and not as backward as people think. Just look how clever he is with his hands. You'll see, when you've sharpened him up in Paris, eh? In ways we couldn't do in Plassans.'

'No doubt, no doubt,' muttered Maxime. 'I'm not saying no, I'll think about it.'

He stood there embarrassed, then added:

'You know, I only came to have a look at him. I can't take him with me now, since I've got to spend a month in Saint-Gervais. But as soon as I get back to Paris, I'll think about it and write to you.'

And, pulling out his watch:

'Jesus! Half past five. You know I don't want to miss the nine o'clock train for all the world.'

'Yes, yes, let's go,' said Félicité. 'There's nothing more for us to do here.'

Macquart vainly endeavoured to delay them with all sorts of stories. He talked about the days when Aunt Dide used to chatter away, and claimed that one morning he'd found her belting out a romantic ballad from her youth. Anyway, he didn't need the carriage, he'd take the boy back on foot, since they were leaving the boy with him.

'Give your papa a kiss, lad, because we know very well when we see each other, but we never know when we'll see each other again!'

With the same startled but indifferent motion, Charles lifted his head and Maxime, disconcerted, planted another kiss on his forehead.

'Behave yourself and look smart, dear boy... And love me just a little.'

'Come, come, we don't have time to waste,' repeated Félicité.

But the keeper came back into the room just then. She was a big sturdy girl, especially assigned to attend to the madwoman. She got her up, put her to bed, got her to eat, and cleaned her up, like a child. And she immediately fell to chatting with Doctor Pascal, who put questions to her. One of the doctor's most cherished dreams was to treat and heal the mad using his method of hypodermic injections. Since, in their case, it was the brain that was in jeopardy, why wouldn't injections of nerve substance give them a bit of resistance, a bit of will, by repairing the lesions in that organ? And so, for a time, he'd thought of experimenting with the medication on the old woman; then he'd had scruples, a sort of holy terror, to say nothing of the fact that insanity, at that age, meant total, irreparable ruin. He'd chosen another subject instead, a hatter named Sarteur, who had been in the asylum for a year by then, having come of his own accord and begged them to lock him up to stop him committing a crime. In his fits, Sarteur was driven by such a need to kill that he would have thrown himself on any hapless passers-by. Small and very dark, with a receding forehead and a profile like the beak of a bird, with a big nose and a very small chin, his left cheek was noticeably bigger than the right.

And the doctor was getting miraculous results with this compulsive man who had had no more attacks for a month. In fact, when asked just now, the keeper replied that Sarteur had calmed down and was going from strength to strength.

'You hear that, Clotilde?' cried Pascal, thrilled. 'I don't have time to see him this evening, we'll come back tomorrow. That's my visiting day. Ah! If only I dared, if only she were still young...'

His eyes went back to Aunt Dide. But Clotilde, who smiled at his enthusiasm, said softly:

'No, Maître, you can't make life anew. Come on now. We're lagging behind.'

It was true, the others had already left the room. Macquart was standing on the doorstep, watching Félicité and Maxime as they walked away, with his usual scoffing air. And Aunt Dide, the forgotten woman, alarmingly thin, remained sitting there, dead still, her eyes once again fixed on Charles, with his exhausted white face framed by his kingly head of hair.

The ride back was extremely uncomfortable. In the heat coming up from the ground, the landau rolled along heavily. Across the stormy sky, dusk was spreading in a smouldering fire the colour of copper. A few vague words were exchanged at first; then, as soon as they entered the gorges of the Seille, all conversation fell away under the disturbing menace of the gigantic rocks, whose walls seemed to be closing in. Wasn't this the back of beyond? Weren't they about to hurtle down some yawning abyss into the netherworld? An eagle flew past and sent up a great cry.

Willows had appeared again and they were trundling along the banks of the Viorne when Félicité, without any prelude, spoke up as if she were continuing a conversation well under way:

'You don't have to worry about his mother—she won't object. She's fond of Charles, but she's a very sensible woman and she can see very well that it's in the child's interests that you should take him. And I have to confess, the poor boy's none too happy at her place, because of course the husband prefers his own son and daughter... Well, you ought to know everything.'

And she went on, no doubt trying to force Maxime's hand and get a formal promise out of him. She talked all the way to Plassans. Then, all of a sudden, as the landau rattled over the cobblestones of the faubourg, she cried out.

'But, look! There she is, the boy's mother. That big blonde in the doorway, there.'

This was the doorway to a harness-maker's shop, where harnesses and halters hung. Justine was taking the air, sitting on a chair, and knitting a stocking, while the little girl and boy played on the ground at her feet. Behind them you could see into the shadowy interior of the shop, where Thomas, a big dark man, was busily sewing a saddle back together.

Maxime had craned his neck out the window, without emotion, simply curious. He was genuinely surprised at this robust woman of thirty-two, who looked so steady and so respectable, with nothing left about her of the wild young thing with whom he'd lost his innocence when they had both just turned seventeen. But perhaps he felt a slight pang at finding her so pretty and serene and plumply full-figured, when he was sick and already incredibly old.

'I'd never have recognized her,' he said.

The landau, which was still rolling on, turned into the Rue de Rome, and Justine, that vision of the past, so different now, disappeared, sinking into the gathering dusk, along with Thomas, the children, and the shop.

At La Souleiade the table was set. Martine had prepared an eel from the Viorne, as well as sautéd rabbit and roast beef. Seven o'clock sounded, they had plenty of time to dine tranquilly.

'Don't torment yourself,' Doctor Pascal said again to his nephew. 'We'll go with you to the railway, it's only ten minutes away. Once you've left your trunk, you only have to get your ticket and hop on the train.'

But when he ran into Clotilde in the hall, where she was hanging her hat and parasol, he said to her in a whisper:

'You know your brother worries me.'

'Why is that?'

'I had a good look at him and I don't like the way he walks. I've never been wrong about that. That boy is threatened with ataxia.'

She went quite pale and repeated, 'Ataxia!'

A cruel picture raised its head, that of a neighbour, a man still young, whom she'd watched for ten years being dragged around by a domestic servant in a little cart. Wasn't it the worst of diseases, the blow of the axe that severed a living being from life?

'But', she murmured, 'he only complains of rheumatism.'

Pascal shrugged his shoulders and, placing a finger to his lips, stepped into the dining room, where Félicité and Maxime were already seated.

The dinner was extremely friendly. The sudden anxiety that had sprung up in Clotilde's heart made her affectionate towards her brother, who was seated beside her. She gladly took care of him, forcing him to take the best bits. She even called Martine back twice, as she was passing the dishes too quickly. And Maxime was more and more captivated by this sister of his, who was so kind, so brimming with health, so sensible, whose charm enveloped him like a caress. She captivated him so completely that a plan gradually formed in his mind, at first vague, then more specific. Since his son, young Charles, had scared him so much with his moribund beauty and his regal air of sickly imbecility, why not take his sister Clotilde home with him? The idea of having a woman about the house certainly terrified him, for he feared them all, having enjoyed them too young; but this one seemed genuinely maternal. On top of that, having an honest woman at home would make a change and be very good. His father, at least, would no longer dare send him girls, as he suspected him of doing, in order to polish him off and grab his money forthwith. Terror and hatred of his father decided him.

'You're not thinking of marrying, then?' he asked her, wanting to test the waters.

The young woman started to laugh.

'Oh, there's no hurry!'

Then, as though making a witty joke, her eyes on Pascal, who'd looked up, she added:

'Who can tell?... I may never marry.'

But Félicité protested. When she'd seen how attached to the doctor the girl was, she'd often hoped for a marriage that would take her away from him and leave him cut off, in a deserted household, in which she herself would become all-powerful, completely in charge. And so she called on her son as a witness: was it not true that a woman ought to marry, that it was unnatural to remain a spinster? Gravely, he nodded, without taking his eyes off Clotilde.

'Oh, yes, one should marry. She's too sensible not to, she'll get married...'

'But why!' Maxime cut in. 'Does she have any real reason to? Only if she wants to be unhappy, maybe—there are so many bad marriages!'

He made up his mind:

'You know what you should do? Well, you should come to Paris and live with me. I've thought about it, and it alarms me a bit to take charge of a child in my state of health. Aren't I a child myself, a sickly thing who needs looking after? You could care for me, you'd be there if I end up losing the use of my limbs.'

His voice had broken in self-pity. He saw himself crippled, he saw her at his bedside, a sister of charity; and, if she agreed to remain a spinster, he'd gladly leave her his fortune, just so his father didn't get it. His terror of being on his own, the need he might well soon have of a sick nurse, made him convincingly touching.

'It would be very good of you, and you'd never have cause to regret it.'

But Martine, who was serving the roast, had stopped dead in shock; and the proposal caused the same surprise all around the table. Félicité was the first to nod approval, feeling the girl's departure would further her plans. She looked at Clotilde, who was still speechless and apparently stunned, while Doctor Pascal went very pale and waited.

'Oh, Brother, Brother!' stammered the young woman, not at first being able to think of anything else to say.

So the grandmother stepped in.

'Is that all you can say? But it's a very good idea, what your brother's proposing. If he's afraid of taking Charles now, you can always go; and you can send for the boy later. Come, now, this all works out perfectly. Your brother's appealing to your heart. Pascal, doesn't she owe him a decent answer?'

With an effort, the doctor regained his composure. But the icy chill that had frozen him was palpable to all. He spoke slowly.

'I say again that Clotilde is extremely sensible and that, if she ought to agree, she will agree.'

Thrown into confusion by this, the young woman rebelled.

'So, Maître, you want to send me away? Of course, I thank Maxime. But to leave everything, my God! Leave all that love me, all that I've loved till now!'

She made a distraught gesture, taking in people and things, embracing all of La Souleiade as a whole.

'But,' Pascal went on, looking straight into her eyes, 'what if Maxime needed you, though?'

Her eyes welled up, and she sat for an instant trembling, for she alone had understood. The cruel vision rose before her once more:

Maxime, crippled, dragged around in a little cart by a domestic servant like the neighbour she used to run into. But her passion protested against her compassion. Did she really have a duty to a brother who, for fifteen years, had remained a stranger to her? Didn't her duty lie where her heart was?

'Listen, Maxime,' she said at last, 'let me think about it, I too need time to reflect. I'll see... Rest assured I'm very grateful to you. And if one day you really did need me, well, no doubt I'd make up my mind then.'

They couldn't get her to commit to more than that. Félicité, feverishly worked up as always, exhausted herself trying; while the doctor now pretended to think she'd given her word. Martine brought in a custard pudding without even attempting to hide her joy. Fancy taking Mademoiselle away! The very idea! So that Monsieur could die of sadness, finding himself all on his own! The incident had also slowed down the last course of the meal. They were still on dessert when half past eight chimed. After that Maxime grew anxious, tapped his foot, and was keen to go.

At the station, where they had all gone with him, he gave his sister one last kiss.

'Don't forget.'

'Never fear,' declared Félicité, 'we're here to remind her of her promise.'

The doctor smiled, and all three waved their handkerchiefs as soon as the train was in motion.

That particular day, after they'd seen the old lady to her door, Doctor Pascal and Clotilde strolled home slowly to La Souleiade and had a wonderful evening there. The uneasiness of the previous few weeks, the unspoken antagonism that had divided them, seemed to have gone. Never had they experienced such sweet peace at feeling themselves so united, inseparable. It was like a return to health after a bout of illness, there was a stirring of hope and *joie de vivre*. They sat for a long while out in the warm night, under the plane trees, listening to the fine crystal voice of the fountain. They didn't even talk but just deeply delighted in the happiness of being together.

4

ONE week later the household had sunk back into the same uneasiness. Pascal and Clotilde once again snubbed each other for whole afternoons, and there were constant mood swings. Martine herself was always cranky. The household of three was becoming a hell.

Then suddenly everything got even worse. A Capuchin friar of great godliness, of the kind that often pass through the towns of the South of France, had come to Plassans to make a retreat. The pulpit of Saint-Saturnin resounded with his shouting. He was a sort of preacher with a cause, an excitable popular orator, whose overblown speech was riddled with imagery. He preached the emptiness of modern science with extraordinary mystical elan, denying the reality of this world, and unlocking the unknown, the mystery of the beyond. All the devout women of the town were overcome.

The very first evening, Clotilde, accompanied by Martine, had been at the sermon, and Pascal could see the feverish excitement she brought back with her. Over the following days her interest became more acute and she came home later, after staying on and spending an hour in prayer in the dark recess of some chapel. She never left the church now, would come home shattered, with the shining eyes of a seer; and the Capuchin's fiery words haunted her. Anger and contempt for everyone and everything seemed to have been visited upon her.

Pascal was concerned and wanted to have it out with Martine. He came down early one morning as she was sweeping the dining room.

'You know I leave you free, you and Clotilde, to go to church if that's what you want to do. I don't intend to weigh on anyone's conscience. But I don't want you making her sick.'

The servant replied, without stopping her sweeping:

'The sick may well be those who think they're not.'

She'd said it with such conviction that he began to smile.

'Yes, I'm the feeble-minded one whose conversion you pray for, while the rest of you enjoy good health and absolute wisdom. Martine, if you two continue to torment me and to torment yourselves, I'll get angry.'

He spoke in a voice so desperate and gruff that the servant stopped in her tracks and looked him in the eye. An infinite tenderness, an

immense desolation passed across her face, the face of a worn-out old
maid, cloistered in his service. Tears filled her eyes and she ran off,
stuttering:

'Ah, Monsieur, you don't love us!'

At that Pascal was disarmed, overwhelmed by a growing sadness.
He felt even more intensely sorry that he'd always been so tolerant,
that he hadn't taken charge uncompromisingly of Clotilde's education and upbringing with all his authority as her overall guardian and
teacher. In his belief that trees grew straight when they weren't ham-
pered, he'd allowed her to grow up as she liked, having simply taught
her to read and write. It had been without a preconceived plan, but
just in the normal course of their life that she had ended up more or
less reading everything and had become passionately interested in the
natural sciences, helping him do his research, correct his proofs,
copy and classify his manuscripts. How he now regretted his disinterestedness! What strong direction he could have given that bright
mind, so keen to learn, instead of letting her stray and lose herself in
this need for the beyond peddled by her grandmother Félicité and the
good Martine! Where he always stuck to the facts, never went beyond
verifiable phenomena, and succeeded in so limiting himself through
his discipline as a scientist, he had seen her endlessly preoccupied
with the unknown, with mystery. It was an obsession with her, an
instinctive curiosity that went as far as torture when it wasn't satisfied. There was a need there that nothing could satisfy, the irresistible
pull of the unattainable, the unknowable. Already when she was little,
and particularly later on in adolescence, she would go straight to the
how and the why and demand to know the ultimate causes. If he
showed her a flower, she would ask why this flower would produce
a seed, and why that seed would germinate. Then it was the mystery
of conception, of the sexes, of birth and death, and unknown forces,
and God, and everything in-between. In just a few questions, she
would drive him every time into the corner of his inevitable ignorance; and when he no longer knew what to say in answer, when
he'd shaken her off with a comical gesture of fury, she would let out
a lovely laugh of triumph, and lose herself again in her dreams, in
the limitless vision of all that we do not know and all that we might
believe. Often she stunned him with her explanations. Her mind,
reared on science, set out from known facts, but with such gusto
that she shot straight up into the firmament of myth. All sorts of

go-betweens floated past, angels, saints, airy supernatural beings, changing matter, giving it life; or else it would be just the one force, the moving spirit of the world, working to dissolve things and beings in one final kiss of love, over fifty centuries. She had done her sums, she'd say.

But never had Pascal seen her so agitated as now. During the week that she'd been following the Capuchin's retreat at the cathedral, she spent every day impatiently waiting for the evening's sermon; and then she'd take herself off there in the over-excited self-communing state of a girl going off to her first amorous tryst. The next day, everything about her would speak of her detachment from external life, from her customary existence, as if the visible world, the necessary actions of every moment, were but a snare and a folly. And so she had more or less abandoned her usual pursuits, yielding to a sort of invincible indolence, in which she'd sit there for hours, with her hands in her lap, her eyes vacant and far away, lost in a distant dream. She had always been so active, such an early riser, but now she got up late, scarcely appeared except for lunch; and it can't have been on her grooming that she spent those long hours, for she was losing her feminine concern for her appearance, barely combing her hair now and dressing sloppily in a frock buttoned up the wrong way—though even this didn't stop her looking adorable thanks to her triumphant youthfulness. The morning walks through La Souleiade she had so loved, racing down the terraces planted with olives and almonds, the visits to the pine grove, sweet with the scent of resin, the long breaks on the burning threshing floor, where she sunbathed—these she did no more. She preferred to stay locked up in her room with the shutters closed, and she couldn't even be heard moving around in there. In the workroom of an afternoon, she was all languishing sloth, doing nothing but drag herself from chair to chair, weary and annoyed with all that had till then interested her.

Pascal was forced to do without her assistance. A note he'd given her to make a clean copy of sat there on her desk for three days. She no longer filed anything, and would not even have stooped to pick a manuscript off the floor. Most tellingly, she had abandoned the pastels, the extremely exact drawings of flowers that were to serve as colour plates in a work of his on artificial fertilization. Some great big mallows, of a new and striking shade of red, had wilted in their vase before she'd finished copying them. And yet for a whole afternoon she was passionately engaged in another mad drawing of dream flowers, this one an extraordinary efflorescence blossoming in wondrous sunlight, a whole burst of golden rays in the form of clusters of flowers along a stem, amidst huge crimson corollas, like open hearts, from which rose pistils that were flares of stars, billions of worlds whirling through the sky like a Milky Way.

'Ah, my poor girl!' the doctor said to her that day. 'Fancy wasting your time on such inventions! I'm still waiting for the copy of these mallows you've let die! You'll make yourself sick, you know. There is no health, no possible beauty even, outside reality.'

Often she wouldn't reply these days, immuring herself in fierce conviction and not wanting to argue. But he had just touched her to the quick of her beliefs.

'There is no reality,' she declared outright.

Amused by such philosophical shoulder-squaring in this overgrown child, he began to laugh.

'Yes, I know. Our senses are fallible, yet we only know the world through our senses, so it may well be that the world does not exist. Well, then, let's usher in madness; let's accept that the most preposterous pipe dreams are possible, let's set ourselves up for nightmare, in a world beyond laws and facts... Can't you see that there are no rules any more, if you do away with nature? That the only point in living is to believe in life, to love life and apply all the powers of our intelligence in getting to know it better?'

She gesticulated in a way that signalled both heedlessness and bravado at once and the conversation came to an end. Now she slashed at the pastel with big strokes of blue crayon, bringing out the glowing blaze against a limpid summer night.

But two days later, after a fresh discussion, things deteriorated further. That evening, Pascal had left the table and gone back upstairs to work in the workroom while she stayed outside, sitting on the terrace. Hours went by and he was surprised and anxious when midnight struck and he still hadn't heard her go up to her room. She had to go through the workroom to get there and he was absolutely certain she hadn't done so while his back was turned. When he went downstairs he saw that Martine was sleeping. But the hall door wasn't locked, so Clotilde had obviously lost sight of the time outside. That happened to her sometimes on hot nights, but she'd never stayed up this late before.

The doctor's anxiety grew when, on the terrace, he saw that the chair she'd have been sitting in so long was empty. He'd hoped to find her asleep in it. If she was no longer there, why hadn't she come back in? Where could she have got to at such an hour? The night was beautiful, a September night, still scorching, with an immense sky, its dark velvety infinity studded with stars; and, deep in this moonless sky, the stars shone so big and bright that they lit the earth. First, he lent over the terrace balustrade, scanned the slopes and the drystone steps that went all the way down to the railway; but nothing stirred, and all he could see were the still, round heads of the stunted olive trees. Then it suddenly occurred to him that she was probably under the plane trees, by the fountain, enjoying the perpetual chilliness of the tinkling water. He ran there, plunging into darkness so dense that even though he knew every tree trunk, he had to walk with his arms out in front of him to avoid bumping into something. Then he beat and groped his way through the shadows of the pine grove without meeting anyone. He ended up calling out, in a muffled voice:

'Clotilde! Clotilde!'

The darkness remained deep and silent. He raised his voice higher.

'Clotilde! Clotilde!'

Not a soul, not a breath. The very echoes of his voice seemed heavy with sleep, his cries were drowned in the infinitely soft lake of blue shadows. And he cried out at the top of his lungs and turned back under the plane trees, went back to the pine grove, panicking, going over the entire estate. Suddenly, he found himself on the threshing floor.

At this hour, the roofless rotunda of the threshing floor, vast and cobbled, slept too. Over the long years since grain had last been hulled there, grass had pushed up between the stones, only to be burnt to gold immediately by the sun and beaten down as though mown, so that it looked like a high-pile carpet. Between the tufts of this luxurious vegetation, the round pebbles never cooled off, and they steamed as soon as twilight fell, releasing into the night the heat stored from so many oppressive hours of daylight.

Bare, deserted, the threshing floor filled out, bigger and rounder, in the shimmering air, beneath the silent stillness of the sky, and Pascal was running across it towards the orchard when he almost fell on a body he hadn't seen, stretched out at full length. He gave a cry of alarm.

'What, you're here?'

Clotilde didn't even bother to answer. She was lying on her back with her hands locked together under her head, looking up at the sky; and in her pale face you could see only her big eyes gleaming.

'To think I've been calling you for a quarter of an hour, I was so worried! Didn't you hear me shouting?'

She finally opened her mouth.

'Yes.'

'Well, then, this is stupid! Why didn't you say anything?'

But she lapsed into her usual silence again and refused to explain, her forehead stubbornly set, her eyes on the heavens.

'Come on, get to bed, you wicked child! You can tell me all about it tomorrow.'

Still she didn't budge; he begged her to go in a dozen times, but she didn't make the slightest move. He ended up sitting down next to her himself, on the close-cropped grass, and he could feel the warmth of the cobbles under him.

'Well, you can't sleep out here. Tell me at least what you're doing here.'

'Looking.'

At that, her big still eyes, wide open and staring, seemed to soar higher, among the stars. She was one with the pure infinity of the summer sky, high among the heavenly bodies.

'Ah, Maître!' she said slowly and evenly, without a pause. 'How small and mean it is, all that you know, besides what is surely up there. Yes, if I didn't say anything, it's because I was thinking about you and I felt so sad… You mustn't think I'm wicked.'

Such a thrill of tenderness had crept into her voice that he was deeply moved. He stretched out on his back beside her. Their elbows touched. They talked.

'I do fear, darling, that your sorrows are irrational. You think of me and you feel sad. But why?'

'Oh! For reasons I'd find hard to explain. I'm not a scientist. But you've taught me a lot, and I've learned even more myself, living with you. Besides, these are things that I feel… I'll try and tell you, though, since we're here, so completely alone, and it's so lovely!'

Her full heart was overflowing, after hours of reflection in the intimate peace of the beautiful night. He didn't speak for fear of throwing her.

'When I was little and listened to you talk about science, it seemed to me that you were talking about God, you were so fired up by hope and faith. Nothing seemed impossible to you any more. With science, we were going to fathom the secret of the world and make the dream of perfect human happiness come true. According to you, we were moving ahead in giant leaps. Each day brought its discovery, its certainty. Another ten years, another fifty years, another hundred years perhaps, and the heavens would be opened, we'd stare truth in the face. Well, the years go by and nothing opens and the truth is in retreat.'

'You're too impatient,' he answered, simply. 'If it takes ten centuries, we'll just have to wait.'

'It's true, I can't wait. I need to know, I need to be happy right away. And to know everything at once, and be happy completely and for good! You see! That's what's so painful, not being able to attain complete knowledge in a single bound, not being able to settle down and rest in total bliss, free of scruples and doubts. Is this living, advancing into the darkness at such a slow pace, not being able to enjoy an hour's serenity without worrying where the next blow is coming from? No! Give me all knowledge and all happiness in a day! Science promised them to us and if it can't deliver them to us, then it has failed.'

At that he, too, began to get excited.

'But that's crazy, little girl, what you're saying there! Science isn't revelation. It moves along at its human pace, its very effort is its glory. And then again, it's just not true—science never promised happiness.'

She cut in sharply.

'What do you mean, not true! Open those books of yours upstairs. You know very well I've read them. They're overflowing with promises! To read them, you'd think we were marching towards conquest of the earth and sky. They demolish everything and vow to replace everything—by sheer reason, soundly and wisely. No doubt it's childish of me, but when someone has promised me something, I want them to give it to me. My imagination goes to work, the thing has to be truly beautiful for me to be pleased with it. It would've been easier not to promise me anything! And now, at this point in time, when my longing is so aroused and so painful, it's wrong of you to tell me that no one promised me anything.'

He waved his hand in protest again, in the great still night.

'Anyway,' she continued, 'science has wiped the slate clean, the earth is bare, the sky is empty, and what do you want me to do with myself, even if you find science not guilty of the hopes I've formed? I can't live without certainty and happiness. What solid ground will I build my house on, since the old world has been demolished and no one's in much of a hurry to build the new one? The whole ancient city has come tumbling down in this disaster caused by examining and analysing; and all that's left of it is a panicked population thrashing about in the ruins, not knowing what stone to lay their head on, camping out in the storm, demanding a solid and permanent refuge where they can make a fresh start... So you shouldn't be surprised if we're discouraged or impatient. We can't wait any longer. Science is too slow and has gone bankrupt,* so we prefer to fall back—yes!— on bygone beliefs which, for centuries, were enough to make the world happy.'

'Ah, but that's just it!' he cried. 'We are indeed at the turn of the century, weary and unnerved at the alarming mass of knowledge raked up in our time. But it's this eternal need for falsehood, the eternal need for illusion that wears humanity down and takes us back to the lulling spell of the unknown. Since we'll never know everything, what's the good of knowing anything more? From the moment that acquired truth fails to provide immediate and certain happiness, why not be satisfied with ignorance, that dark narrow bed on which humanity has heavily slept away its early infancy? Yes! This is the desperate backlash of mystery, it's a reaction to a hundred years of experimental inquiry. And it could hardly be otherwise; we have to expect desertions when we can't satisfy every need at once. But it's nothing more than a pause, the forward march will continue, out of our sight, up there in boundless space.'

For a second they were silent, as they lay there motionless, their eyes lost among the billions of worlds shining in the dark sky. A shooting star flashed across the constellation of Cassiopeia in an arrow of light. And the illuminated universe, above, slowly turned on its axis, in sacred splendour, while the tenebrous earth around them gave off only a faint exhalation, like the sweet warm breath of a sleeping woman.

'Tell me,' he asked in his good-natured tone, 'is it this Capuchin of yours who's set your head in a whirl tonight?'

She answered candidly:

'Yes, he preaches things to the congregation that really upset me. He speaks against everything you've ever taught me, and it's as if the science I owe to you had turned to poison and were killing me... My God! What am I to do?'

'My poor child! It's terrible to eat yourself up like this! And yet, my mind's still easy on your account because you're well balanced; you've got a good solid little round noggin, as I've often told you. You'll calm down. But what havoc there must be in people's brains if someone as sane as you is muddled! Don't you have faith, then?'

She held her tongue and sighed, while he added:

'Of course, from the simple viewpoint of happiness, faith is a reliable walking stick, it makes walking easy and smooth, when we have the luck to have it.'

'Oh, I don't know any more!' she said. 'There are days when I believe, and there are others when I side with you and your books. You're the one who's upset me, it's because of you that I'm in turmoil. And the whole problem may well lie there—in my revolt against you—the one I love. No, don't say a thing! Don't tell me I'll calm down. Right now that would only make me angrier. You deny the supernatural. Mystery, for you, is merely the unexplained, is it not? You even concede that we'll never know everything; so, the sole interest in living is unending conquest of the unknown, the eternal effort to know more. Ah! I know too much already to believe, you've already more than persuaded me, and there are times when it seems to me that I'm going to die of it.'

He took her hand, lying on the warm grass, and squeezed it hard.

'But it's life that frightens you, little girl! And how right you are to say that the only happiness lies in unremitting effort! From this day forward, resting in blissful ignorance is just not possible. We can't hope for a break of any kind, or for any kind of peace in wilful blindness. We have to keep going, to move on regardless, in step with life, which always moves on. All the things that people propose, all these steps backwards into the past, this return to dead religions, religions patched up temporarily, adjusted to fit new needs—all that is a trap. So get to know life, love life, live it the way it ought to be lived: there is no other wisdom.'

With an angry jerk she freed her hand and her voice when she spoke expressed a simmering disgust.

'Life is vile, how do you expect me to live it, and yet be happy and at peace? Your science shines a terrible light on the world, your analysis pokes into all our human wounds just to expose the horror. You say everything, and you speak crudely, you leave us with nothing but nausea at living beings and things, without any possible consolation.'

He cut her off with a cry of fervent conviction.

'Say everything, yes! So as to know everything and cure everything!'

She was roused to fury at that and sat upright.

'If only equality and justice existed in this nature of yours. But you say so yourself, life is for the fittest, the weak inevitably perish—because they're weak. No two beings are equal, whether in health, or beauty, or intelligence: it's all left to chance encounters, to random selection. And the whole thing comes crashing down once great and sacred justice ceases to exist!'

'It's true,' he said in an undertone, as though talking to himself, 'there's no such thing as equality. A society based on equality could not survive. Down through the ages, people thought they could remedy evil with charity. But the world broke down; and today, what they're proposing is justice. Is nature just? I think of it more as logical. Logic may well be a higher, natural form of justice that goes straight to the sum total of the common task, to the ultimate great labour.'

'Well, then, don't you see?' she cried. 'The justice that crushes the individual for the good of the race, that destroys the weakened species so the winning species can fatten up... No! That's criminal! All it gives us is obscenity and murder. He was right, tonight, at church: the earth has gone bad, and all science does is expose the rot. It's up above that we need to seek refuge, all of us. Oh, Maître! I'm begging you, let me save myself, let me save *you*!'

She burst into tears and the noise of her sobbing rose, wild and heart-racking, in the pure unsullied night. He tried in vain to soothe her, but she only spoke over him.

'Look, Maître, you know how much I love you, you mean everything to me. It's because of you that I'm so tormented, I can hardly breathe with the pain when I think that we don't agree, that we'd be separated forever if we both died tomorrow. Why won't you believe?'

He tried to reason once more.

'Come now, darling, you're being silly.'

But she was on her knees now, and she grabbed his hands and clung to him with a feverish grip. And she begged him more loudly, in such an outcry of despair that the dark countryside, far and wide, sighed.

'Listen, he said in church... that we must change our life and do penance, all our past mistakes must be consumed by fire. Yes! Your books, your files, your manuscripts... Make this sacrifice, Maître, please, I'm imploring you on my knees. You'll see what a wonderful life we'll lead together then.'

At last, he rebelled.

'No! This is too much, stop!'

'Yes! If you know anything about me, Maître, you'll do what I want. I can't tell you how unhappy I am, even loving you as I do. Something's missing in our affection. Till now it's been empty and fruitless and I have an irresistible need to fill it—oh!—with all that's divine and eternal. What could we be missing if not God? Kneel with me, pray with me!'

He pulled away, angry now himself.

'Stop it, you're raving. I left you free, leave me free.'

'Maître, Maître! It's our happiness I want! I'll take you away, far away. We'll live in seclusion in God.'

'Stop it!... That, never!'

They sat for a while afterwards, face to face, mute and menacing. All around them La Souleiade spread its nocturnal silence, with the light shadows of its olive trees and the gloom of its pines and plane trees, where the saddened voice of the spring sang on; and above their heads it seemed the vast star-studded sky shivered and turned pale, although dawn was still a long way off.

Clotilde lifted her arms as though to point out the boundlessness of the shivering sky. But in an irascible move Pascal grabbed her hand again and forced it to the ground. And not another word was spoken. They were beside themselves, violent and hostile. This was a fierce falling-out.

Suddenly she pulled her hand back and leapt aside, like a proud untameable animal, rearing; then she ran off through the night, towards the house. The clackety-clack of her boots could be heard on the pebbles of the threshing floor, before the sound grew muffled over the sandy soil of a garden path. Already mortified, he called her back urgently. But she wasn't listening, didn't answer, kept running. Gripped by fear, heart heavy, he bolted after her and rounded the stand of plane trees just in time to see her storming into the hall. He rushed in at her heels, raced up the stairs, and hurled himself at her bedroom door just as she was violently shooting home the bolts on the lock. And there he stopped and calmed down, with great effort, resisting the urge to cry out, to call her again, to kick in the door just to see her, to convince her, to keep her all to himself. For a while, he just stood there motionless before the silence of the room, from which not even the sound of breathing emerged. No doubt she was lying face down across the bed, stifling her cries and sobs with a pillow. He finally decided to go downstairs again and shut the hall door, then he went back up softly to listen and see if he could hear her moaning; and day was breaking by the time he went to bed, in despair, choking with tears.

From then on it was all-out merciless warfare. Pascal felt watched, tracked, threatened. He was no longer at home in his own house, no longer had a home: the enemy was always there, forcing him to be afraid of everything, to lock everything away. One after the other, two vials of the nerve substance he'd been manufacturing were picked up off the floor in pieces; and he had to barricade himself in his room, where he could be heard muffling the sound of his pestle, without even showing himself at mealtimes. He no longer took Clotilde along on visiting days, because she discouraged his patients with her attitude of aggressive incredulity. But whenever he went out, the only thing he was in a hurry to do was to swiftly go home, for he was terrified of finding his locks forced and his drawers ransacked, on his return. He no longer got the young woman to file or copy out his notes, since several of them had gone, as though carried away by the wind. He no longer even dared get her to correct his proofs, having noticed that she had cut a whole passage from an article because the idea expressed in it offended her Catholic faith. And so she remained idle, prowling through the rooms, having all the time in the world to watch for an opportunity that would deliver her the key to the big cupboard. That must have been her dream, the plan she mulled over during her long silences, eyes glinting, hands restless: to get the key, open up, take everything, destroy everything, in an auto-da-fé that would be pleasing to God. The few pages of a manuscript he'd left on the corner of the table while he went to wash his hands and put on his frock coat disappeared, leaving only a pinch of ash at the back of the fireplace. One evening as he was coming home in the gloaming, having lingered by a sick man's side, a mad terror had taken hold of him as soon as he reached the faubourg when he saw thick black smoke rising up in swirling clouds, befouling the pale sky. Wasn't it La

Souleiade going up in flames, lock, stock and barrel, lit by the bonfire of his papers? He raced home and only recovered when he saw, in a neighbouring field, a fire of roots slowly giving off smoke.

What absolute torture it is, the torment of the scientist who feels himself threatened like this, in his intellect and in his works! The discoveries he has made, the manuscripts he counts on leaving to posterity: these are his pride and joy, these are living beings, his own blood, offspring; and destroying them, burning them, means burning his own flesh. In this perpetual ambush of his thought, Pascal was tortured above all by the idea that the enemy, who was within, inside his very heart, was someone he could not drive out, and that he loved her regardless. He was left disarmed, utterly defenceless, not wanting to take action and having no other recourse than to keep his eyes open vigilantly at all times. The enemy was closing in from every direction. He felt he could hear the little thieving hands slipping into his pockets, and he had no peace any more even with the doors locked, fearing he'd be robbed through the cracks.

'You miserable child,' he yelled one day, 'you're the only thing I love in the world yet you're the one killing me! You love me, too, though; you're only doing all of this because you love me, and it's abominable. It'd be better if we had done with it straightaway and threw ourselves in the water with stones round our necks!'

She didn't reply, her honest eyes alone spoke, ardently, saying that she would like nothing better than to die then and there, if it were with him.

'So, if I died tonight, suddenly, what would happen tomorrow? You'd empty out the cupboard, you'd empty out the drawers, you'd make a big pile of all my works and you'd burn them? You would, wouldn't you? Don't you know that would amount to real murder, as if you'd killed someone? And what abominable cowardice, killing thought!'

'No,' she said in a muted voice, 'killing evil, stopping it from spreading and springing up again!'

All their attempts at explanation only made them angry again. And there were some terrible exchanges. One night when old Madame Rougon stumbled into one such altercation, she stayed behind with Pascal after Clotilde had run up to her room. A silence prevailed. Despite the air of anguish she'd put on, there was a glint of joy deep in her twinkling eyes.

'But your poor home is sheer hell!' she finally cried.

The doctor waved his hand to avoid answering. He had always felt his mother was behind the young woman, whipping up her religious beliefs, using this stirring of revolt to sow trouble in his home. He had no illusions, he knew perfectly well that the two women had seen each other that day and that it was to that encounter, to a whole skilful process of poisoning, that he owed the shocking scene that was still making him shake. No doubt his mother had come to assess the damage and see if they weren't now getting close to the end.

'It can't go on like this,' she continued. 'Why don't you part ways, since you no longer get along? You ought to pack her off to her brother Maxime's. He wrote to me again the other day, asking for her.'

He straightened up, drained of colour but forceful.

'Part in anger? Ah, no! No! I'd never get over the remorse, the wound would never heal. If she does leave one day, I'd like us to be able to love each other from afar. But why would she leave? Neither of us is complaining.'

Félicité realized she'd been a bit too quick off the mark.

'Well, if you like fighting, that's nobody's business but your own. Only, allow me to tell you, my poor boy, that in this case I'm rather on Clotilde's side. You force me to admit I saw her a short while ago. Yes! It's better that you know, even though I promised to keep quiet. Well, she isn't happy, she does complain, and quite a lot. As you can imagine, I pulled her up, I told her she had to show complete obedience... That doesn't stop me from having trouble understanding you these days, or from thinking you're doing everything you can to make yourself unhappy.'

She sat down, and forced him to sit, in a corner of the room where she seemed delighted to have him alone, at her mercy. Several times already she had used similar tactics to force him to explain himself, but he had always eluded her. Even though she'd been torturing him for years and there was nothing he didn't know about her, he remained a deferential son and had vowed to himself never to abandon this resolutely respectful stance. And so as soon as she broached certain subjects, he took refuge in absolute silence.

'Come now,' she continued, 'I can understand you not wanting to give in to Clotilde; but to me? If I begged you to sacrifice those abominable files, there, in that cupboard, for me! Let's suppose for a second that you suddenly died and that those papers fell into the hands of outsiders: we'd all be dishonoured. That's not what you want, is it? So, what is your aim? Why do you persist in playing such a dangerous game? Promise me you'll burn them.'

He held his tongue, but was finally compelled to respond:

'Mother, I've already pleaded with you, let's not talk about it. I can't help you.'

'But honestly!' she cried. 'Give me one good reason. Anyone would think our family meant no more to you than that passing herd of cattle over there. You're part of it, however. Oh! I know you do everything you can, not to be. I'm sometimes amazed myself, I wonder where on earth you can have come from. But I still think it's shameful on your part to lay yourself open like this, disgracing us all, without stopping to think of the grief you're causing me, your own mother. It's a wicked business, that's all there is to it.'

He was shocked and yielded for a moment to the need to defend himself, despite his vow of silence.

'You're heartless and you're wrong. I've always believed in the necessity, in the absolute efficacy of the truth. It's true I reveal all about the others and about myself; but that's because I firmly believe that in revealing all, I'm doing the only possible good. To start with, those files aren't meant for the public, they're just personal notes, which it would be painful to me to part with. And then, I know full well that those aren't the only things you'd burn: all my other works would be thrown on the fire, too, wouldn't they? And I won't have it, do you hear! Never, while I'm alive, will a single line of writing here be destroyed.'

But he already regretted having said so much, for he saw it only made her draw closer, press him, force him to have it out in the cruellest way.

'Well, go on, speak up, tell me just what it is you hold against us. Yes, me for example, what do you hold against me? Surely not having struggled so hard to bring you all up. Ah! Our fortune was a long time in the making! If we enjoy a bit of prosperity today, we've certainly earned it. Since you saw it all and you put it all down in those pathetic papers of yours, you can attest to the fact that the family did more favours for others than anyone ever did for us. Twice, without us, Plassans would have found itself in a fine pickle. So it's only natural if all we got for our pains is ingratitude and envy—so much so that even today the whole town would still be thrilled with any scandal that would cover us in mud. You can't want that, and I'm sure you'll do justice to the dignity of my bearing since the fall of the Empire and the calamities from which France will surely never rise again.'

'Leave France out of it, Mother!' he said, breaking his silence again, so deftly had she touched what she knew were his sore points. 'France is tough, and I think it's well on the way to astounding the world with the speed of its recovery. Of course, there are plenty of rotten elements. I haven't hidden them, I may well have put them too much on show. But you don't understand me very well at all if you think I believe in the ultimate downfall of everything, because I point out sores and lesions. I believe in life, which is constantly eliminating harmful bodies and making new flesh to fill wounds, and always moving forward no matter what towards health and constant renewal, amid impurities and death.'

He was aware that he was getting carried away, and he made an angry gesture and said nothing more. His mother had decided to weep, a few tiny tears, brief and painful, that dried instantly. And she returned to the fears that had thrown a gloom over her old age, she too implored him to make his peace with God, at least out of consideration for his family. Didn't she set an example of courage? The whole of Plassans, the Saint-Marc quarter, the old quarter and the new town—didn't they all pay homage to the noble way she resigned herself to fate? She asked only for a show of support, she required all her children to make an effort similar to her own. And so, she cited the example of Eugène, that great man, who had fallen from such a height, and who really only wanted now to be a simple deputy, defending till his last breath the vanished regime from whence he'd derived his glory. She was also full of praise for Aristide, who never despaired, who had won another excellent position under the new regime, despite the unjust catastrophe that had buried him for a time among the ruins of the Union universelle.* Would he, Pascal, remain apart, would he do nothing to see she died in peace, in the joy of the final triumph of the Rougons? He who was so intelligent, so affectionate, so good! Come now, it was just not possible! He would go to Mass the following Sunday and he would burn those sordid papers, the mere thought of which made her sick. She begged, ordered, threatened. But he didn't react again, he was composed once more, invincible in his pose of great deference. He didn't want a debate, he knew her too well to hope to convince her or to dare discuss the past with her.

'So!' she cried when she sensed he was unshakeable. 'You're not one of ours, I've always said so. You bring disgrace on us.'

He bowed his head.

'Mother, you'll think about it and you'll forgive me.'

That day, Félicité was beside herself when she left, and as she ran into Martine at the front door, by the plane trees, she unburdened herself, not knowing that Pascal, who had just gone into his bedroom, where the windows were open, could hear every word. She gave vent to her resentment, swore she'd get her hands on the papers somehow and destroy them, since he wasn't willing to sacrifice them himself. But what struck a chill into the doctor's soul was the restrained way in which Martine quietened his mother down. She was obviously in on the plot, she kept saying they had to wait, not rush anything, that she and Mademoiselle had vowed to get the better of Monsieur by not leaving him an hour's peace. It was a promise, they would reconcile him to the good Lord, because it was just not possible that a saintly man like Monsieur could be without religion. And the two women dropped their voices gradually to a whisper, a hushed murmur of gossiping and scheming, in which he only caught the odd word, orders given, measures taken, an assault on his personal independence. When his mother finally left, he saw her, with her light step and her girlishly slim figure, walking away looking extremely pleased.

Pascal then had a moment of hopelessness, of absolute despair. He asked himself what good it was to struggle, since all the people he was attached to were allied against him. That Martine, who would have thrown herself into the fire at a simple word from him, was betraying him like this, for his own good! And Clotilde was in league with the servant, plotting in corners, getting her to help her lay traps! Now he really was alone; the only people around him were traitors and they were poisoning the very air he breathed. Those two at least loved him, and he might have wound up mollifying them; but from the moment he knew his mother was behind them, egging them on, he knew why they were so relentless, and he gave up all hope of winning them back. In his timidity as a man who had lived for scholarship, cut off from women despite his passionate nature, the idea that there were three of them who wanted to control him, to bend him to their will, crushed him. He was always conscious that one or other of them was at his back; when he shut himself away in his room, he sensed them on the other side of the wall; and they haunted him, left him with the constant fear that he'd be robbed of any thought, if he were to let it be seen at the back of his skull even before he'd formulated it.

This was far and away the time in his life when Pascal was the most unhappy. The perpetual state of defensiveness in which he was forced to live broke him; and it sometimes felt to him as though the ground under his home was giving way beneath him. He now felt acute regret that he'd never married and that he didn't have any children. Had he himself been frightened of life? Wasn't he being punished for his self-ishness? This yearning for a child overwhelmed him at times and lately his eyes would be wet with tears whenever he ran into bright-eyed little girls out in the street who smiled at him. True, there was Clotilde. But that was another sort of affection, marred now by turbu-lence, and not a calm, infinitely sweet affection, like the affection for a child with which he'd have liked to rock his aching heart to sleep. On top of that, what he wanted most of all, now that he felt he was coming to the end of his life, was continuation, a child who would have carried it on. The more he suffered, the more he felt he'd have found consolation in passing on that suffering, with his faith in life. He believed himself to be exempt from the physiological defects of his family; but even the thought that heredity sometimes skipped a generation and that, in any son of his, the disorders of his forebears could reappear, did not deter him. Despite the rotten old rootstock, despite the long line of execrable kin, he still yearned for this unknown son, some days, as you hope for an unexpected gain, for rare hap-piness, the stroke of luck that brings solace and riches to last a life-time. In the shock to his other attachments, his heart bled because it was too late.

On a sultry night at the end of September, Pascal could not sleep. He opened one of the windows in his room. The sky was black, there had to be a storm passing in the distance, as a continual rumble of thunder could be heard. He could only just make out the sombre mass of the plane trees, their mournful green highlighted now and then, against the gloom, by flashes of lightning. And his soul was full of anguish as he relived the past few awful days, with their fresh feuds, agonizing betrayals and suspicions, torturing him ever more intensely. All of a sudden, a sharp recollection made him start. In his fear of being plundered, he had adopted the policy of carrying the key to the cupboard on him at all times. But that particular afternoon, suffering from the heat, he had taken off his jacket and he remembered seeing Clotilde hang it on a hook in the workroom. A sudden bolt of terror shot through him: if she'd felt the key in the bottom of his pocket, she would have taken it. He rushed over and fumbled through the jacket, which he'd simply flung over a chair. The key was gone. At this very moment, he was being burgled; he was sure of it. The clock struck two. He didn't bother getting dressed again but stayed in a simple pair of pants, with his feet bare inside his slippers, and his chest bare under his unbuttoned nightshirt; and he banged open the door and leapt into the room, candle in hand.

'Ah!' he cried. 'I knew it! Thief! Murderer!'

And it was true. Clotilde was there, undressed like him, her feet bare in her canvas mules, her legs bare, her arms bare, her shoulders bare, her body only scantily covered by a short petticoat and her chemise. As a precaution she had not brought a candle but had merely pulled back the shutters on one of the windows; and the uninterrupted lightning of the storm that was passing out in front, heading south in the dark sky, was enough for her, bathing things in a livid phosphorescence. The old cupboard, with its broad sides, was wide open. Already, she had emptied the top shelf, taking the files down by the armful and throwing them on the long table in the middle of the room where they lay piled up pell-mell. And for fear of not having time to burn them, she was feverishly putting them in bundles, having decided to hide them and then send them on later to her grandmother, when the sudden light of the candle, illuminating her from head to foot, froze her where she stood, looking surprised and ready to fight.

'You're stealing from me and you're murdering me!' Pascal said again furiously.

She was still holding one of the files in her bare arms. He tried to take it off her. But she hugged it to her as hard as she could, mulish in her work of destruction, without a hint of embarrassment or remorse, a combatant who has right on her side. He then threw himself at her, blinded, frantic; and they fought. He grappled with her in her nakedness, and he handled her so roughly that he hurt her.

'Kill me, then!' she stammered. 'Kill me, or I'll rip everything up!'

But he held her, bound to him, in a grip so fierce she could hardly breathe.

'When a child steals, she gets punished!'

A few drops of blood had appeared along her round shoulder, near her armpit, where a bruise was starting to appear under the delicate silky skin. And for a moment he felt her so out of breath and panting, so divinely virginal, with her fine willowy figure, her slender tapering legs, her supple arms, her slim body and tiny hard breasts, that he released her. With one last effort, he wrested the file from her.

'And now you can help me put them back up there, damn it! Come here, start by sorting them on the table. Do as I say, you hear!'

'Yes, Maître!'

She went to him and she helped him, broken in, broken by that manly grip which felt as though it had penetrated her flesh. The candle, which was burning with a high flame in the sultry night, illuminated them; and the distant rumble of thunder did not let up. The window, open on the storm, looked to be ablaze.

5

FOR a moment, Pascal stood looking at the files, piled up in what seemed to be an enormous heap, thrown together randomly as they were over the long table that took up the middle of the workroom. In the jumble, several of the blue cardboard folders had fallen open and the documents were spilling out—letters, newspaper clippings, official stamped documents, handwritten notes.

Already, to reclassify the bundles, he was busy looking for the names written on the folders in capital letters, when, with a determined gesture, he snapped out of the sombre reflections into which he had lapsed. And he turned to Clotilde, who stood there waiting stiffly, mute and white as a ghost:

'Look, I've never allowed you to read these papers, and I know you've respected my wishes. Yes, I had scruples. It's not that you're ignorant, like other girls, since I've let you learn all there is to know about men and women, and that's certainly only bad for people of bad character. But what was the good of plunging you too early into the terrible truth about human beings? So I've spared you the history of our family, which is the history of all families, of humanity as a whole: a lot of bad and a lot of good...'

He broke off, appeared to strengthen in his resolve, composed again now and full of unbounded energy.

'You're twenty-five, it's time you knew. And then again, our life together just can't go on: you're living and making me live in a nightmare, flying off into fantasy-land the way you do. I'd prefer reality to be laid out before us, no matter how abysmal it may be. Maybe the jolt will make you the woman you're meant to be. We're going to reclassify these files together, and then go through them and read them, and it's going to be a terrible lesson in life!'

As she still didn't move, he added:

'We need to see clearly, light the other two candles there.'

A great need for clarity assailed him and he would have liked the blinding light of the sun; he didn't think even the three candles shed enough light, so he went to his room to get the two double-armed candelabras in there. Seven candles were now blazing away. Neither of them, in their disarray, he with his chest exposed, she with her left shoulder stained with blood and her arms and throat bare, even saw the other. It was past two now but neither of them was remotely aware of the time: they were about to spend the night immersed in this passionate quest for knowledge, without the need for sleep, beyond time and space. The storm, which was still raging along the horizon visible through the open window, roared louder than ever.

Never before had Clotilde seen Pascal's eyes burn with such feverish excitement. He had been overexerting himself for several weeks, and his mental anguish had made him brusque at times, in spite of his conciliatory good nature. But it seemed that an infinite tenderness, all quivering with humane compassion, was welling inside him, now that he was about to delve into the painful truths of existence; and something very protective and immensely noble, from deep within, rose to the fore so that he could exonerate, in front of this girl, the appalling avalanche of facts. He was ready for it now; he would tell all, since one must tell all to cure all. Wasn't the story of these people, who were so close to them, the ultimate proof of inescapable evolution? Such was life and it had to be lived. No doubt she would emerge from it toughened, full of tolerance and courage.

'They're turning you against me,' he went on, 'they're making you do appalling things, and what I want to do is give you back your moral integrity. When you know, you can decide for yourself and act. Come closer, read with me.'

She did as he said. Yet the files, which her grandmother talked about with such fury, frightened her a bit; while a certain curiosity was aroused and was growing inside her. Besides, in spite of being so quashed by the virile authority that had just gripped and broken her, she was holding back. So couldn't she at least hear him out, and read with him? Didn't she reserve the right to resist him or to commit herself after that? She waited.

'Let's have a look, would you like to?'

'Yes, Maître, I would!'

First he showed her the Rougon-Macquart Family Tree. He didn't normally lock it up in the cupboard, but kept it in the desk in his room, from where he'd taken it while he was collecting the candelabras. For over twenty years he'd been keeping it up to date, recording the births, deaths, and marriages, and other important family matters, setting out each case in brief notes according to his theory of heredity. It was a large sheet of paper, yellowed with age, its folds cut by wear, on which rose a symbolic tree drawn in bold outline, its branches spreading and subdividing into five rows of big broad leaves. Each leaf bore a name and contained, in tiny handwriting, a biography, a hereditary case.

A scholar's joy had taken hold of the doctor at the sight of this artefact twenty years in the making, in which the laws of heredity, as defined by him, were applied so clearly and so completely.

'Look, then, little girl! You know most of it, you've copied out enough of my manuscripts to follow... Isn't it beautiful, such a discrete set of data, a document so definitive and so complete there isn't a single gap? You'd think it was a laboratory experiment, a problem posed and solved on the blackboard... You see, down at the bottom, there's the trunk, the common stock, Aunt Dide. Then the three branches emerge, the legitimate branch, Pierre Rougon, and the two illegitimate ones, Ursule Macquart and Antoine Macquart. Then more branches rise, and ramify: on one side, there are Maxime, Clotilde and Victor, Saccard's three children, and Angélique, the daughter of Sidonie Rougon; on the other side, Pauline, Lisa Macquart's daughter, and Claude, Jacques, Étienne and Anna, the four children of Gervaise, Lisa's sister. There's Jean, their brother, at the end there. And note that, here, in the middle, what I call the knot, the legitimate shoot and the illegitimate shoot join together in Marthe Rougon and her cousin François Mouret, to give rise to three new ramifications, Octave, Serge and Désirée Mouret; while further along, descended from Ursule and the hatter Mouret, there's Silvère, whose tragic death you know about, and Hélène and her daughter Jeanne. Lastly, right up here at the top, are the latest offshoots, the son of your brother Maxime, our poor Charles, and two other dead infants, Jacques-Louis, the son of Claude Lantier, and Louiset, the son of Anna Coupeau. In all, five generations, a human tree that already, in five springs, five springtides of humanity, has grown new stock, thanks to the flowing sap of never-ending life!'

He was becoming animated now and started pointing out cases, his finger moving over the old yellow paper as if it were an anatomical drawing.

'I repeat, it's all here... See the way preference works, in direct inheritance: the favouring of the mother, Silvère, Lisa, Désirée, Jacques, Louiset, yourself; or of the father, Sidonie, François, Gervaise, Octave, Jacques-Louis. Then there are the three cases of mixing: through the direct joining of parts, Ursule, Aristide, Anna, Victor; through random distribution, Maxime, Serge, Étienne; and through blending, Antoine, Eugène, Claude. I've even had to specify a fourth, and most remarkable, case: exactly even blending, Pierre and Pauline. And variations establish themselves, the favouring of the mother for example often goes with physical resemblance to the father, or the opposite occurs; similarly, with mixing, one factor or another is favoured physically and morally, depending on circumstances...* Then there's indirect inheritance, involving the collaterals: I've only got one well-established example of this: the striking physical resemblance of Octave Mouret to his uncle Eugène Rougon. I've also only got one example of influence inheritance: Anna, the daughter of Gervaise and Coupeau, bore an incredible resemblance to her mother's first lover, Lantier, especially when she was a child, as if he'd impregnated* the mother once and for all time. But where I've got abundant examples is for reversion inheritance: the three clearest cases are Marthe, Jeanne and Charles all resembling Aunt Dide, with the resemblance thus skipping one, two, or three generations. That experience is surely exceptional, because I don't much believe in atavism; it seems to me that the new elements contributed by the partners, the accidents and infinite variation in the mix must very rapidly erase specific traits, in such a way as to take the individual back to the general type... And there remains innateness, Hélène, Jean, Angélique. That's the combination, the chemical mix whereby the physical and moral traits of the parents merge, without a trace of either of them apparently finding its way into the new being.'

There was a momentary silence. Clotilde had listened with profound attention, trying to understand. He stood there now, engrossed, his eyes still on the Tree, needing to assess his work objectively, and he went on slowly, as if talking to himself:

'Yes, it's as scientific as possible. But I've only put in the members of the immediate family. I should have given equal parts to the spouses, the fathers and mothers coming in from outside whose blood is mixed in with ours and has thereby altered it. I actually did draw a strictly mathematical tree, with the fathers and mothers being passed on to the progeny evenly, by halves, from generation to generation, so that, in Charles, for instance, Aunt Dide's part is just a twelfth—but that was absurd, since the physical resemblance there is total. So I decided it was enough just to indicate the elements coming in from outside, noting the marriages and the new factor these always introduce... Ah, these sciences that are still in their infancy, these sciences where hypotheses merely babble and stumble about and the imagination still holds sway! They're the realm of poets as much as of men of science! Poets lead the way as pioneers, in the vanguard, and they often discover virgin lands, point the way to solutions that are just out of sight. There's a latitude there that's all theirs, a gap between acquired, definitive truth and the unknown quantity from which tomorrow's truth will be hacked out... What a tremendous fresco there is to paint, what a colossal human comedy and tragedy to write, on heredity, which is the very Genesis of families, and societies, and of the world!'

His eyes became unseeing as he lost himself, pursuing his thought. But then with a sudden jerk he returned to the files, throwing the Tree aside:

'We'll come back to that a bit later. For you to understand here and now, events must be restaged and you must see them in action, all these protagonists, labelled here with simple notes summing them up. I'll call out the files, you'll pass them to me one by one—and I'll show you, I'll tell you what each one contains, before I put it back up there on the shelf. I won't follow alphabetical order, but the order of the facts themselves. I've long wanted to devise such a system of classification. So, now, look for the names on the folders. Aunt Dide first.'

At that moment, an edge of the storm lighting up the skyline clipped La Souleiade at a slant and burst over the house in an absolute deluge of rain. But they didn't even shut the window. They didn't hear the claps of thunder or the constant drumroll of the torrent beating down on the roof. Clotilde passed him the file bearing the name of Aunt Dide in capital letters, and he took out papers of all sorts, old notes he'd made, and he began to read.

'Give me Pierre Rougon... Give me Ursule Macquart... Give me Antoine Macquart...'

Silent, she continued to do as she was told, her heart heavy with anguish at all she was hearing. And the files paraded past, released their documents, and returned to pile up again in the cupboard.

They started at the beginning, with Adélaïde Fouque, the tall unhinged girl, the original nerve injury, giving birth to the legitimate branch, Pierre Rougon, and to the two illegitimate branches, Ursule and Antoine Macquart, that whole gory bourgeois tragedy, framed by

the *coup d'état* of December 1851, with the Rougons, Pierre and
Félicité, salvaging order in Plassans, and spattering their just-forming
fortune with Silvère's blood, while Adélaïde, grown old, the miserable
Aunt Dide, was locked up in Les Tulettes like a ghostly symbol of
atonement and hope against hope.* After that the pack hounds of
appetite were unleashed, a supreme appetite for power in Eugène
Rougon, the great man, the eagle-like genius of the family, full of
disdain, above vulgar interests, loving power for its own sake, conquering Paris in old boots alongside the rogue adventurers of the
approaching empire, moving from presidency of the Conseil d'État
to a ministerial portfolio. He was a man made by his gang, a whole
greedy bunch of patrons who supported him yet preyed upon him;
defeated briefly by a woman, the lovely Clorinde, whom he'd desired
madly, but so genuinely strong, burning with such a strong need
to be on top, that he regained power thanks to a betrayal of his
whole life, as he marched onwards to his triumphal enthronement as
vice-emperor.*

In Aristide Saccard, appetite threw itself into sordid pleasures,
money, women, and wild excess—a devouring hunger that put him
out on the street, the instant the hounds went in for the kill and the
hot quarry was carved up, in the squall of unbridled speculation gusting through the town, boring holes in it everywhere you turned and
rebuilding it. Outrageous fortunes were built up in six months,
squandered and built up again, in a gold binge that gradually made
the man himself so intoxicated it got the better of him, causing him,
when the body of his wife Angèle was not yet cold, to sell his name in
a bid to get his hands on the first essential hundred thousand francs,
by marrying Renée; then leading him later, during a financial crisis, to
tolerate incest, to turn a blind eye to the love affair between his second
wife and his son Maxime, in the flashy magnificence of Paris making
merry.* And it was Saccard again, a few years after that, who cranked
up the enormous moneymaking machine of the Banque universelle,
Saccard never vanquished, Saccard bigger than ever, elevated to the
wheeling and dealing of a great financier, understanding the fierce
and civilizing role of money, giving, winning and losing battles at the
Bourse like Napoleon at Austerlitz or Waterloo, and burying under an
avalanche of disaster a whole universe of paltry little people, before
dropping his natural son Victor into the shadowy netherworld of
crime. Victor then disappeared, fleeing through the dismal nights,

while Saccard himself, under the unmoved protection of unjust nature, was loved by the adorable Madame Caroline, no doubt as a reward for his deplorable life.*

A great spotless lily had grown in the compost there, when Sidonie Rougon, her brother Saccard's obliging go-between, procuress of a hundred sleazy transactions, coupled with a stranger and begat the pure and holy Angélique, the little embroiderer with the nimble fingers who wove from the gold of chasubles a dream of her prince charming, taking wing and soaring so far off among her companions the saints, so little made for harsh reality that she obtained the grace to die of love, the day of her wedding, at Félicien de Hautecœur's first kiss, as the bells pealed, sounding the glory of her royal nuptials.* The knot joining the two branches, the legitimate and the illegitimate, was tied at that point and Marthe Rougon married her cousin François Mouret. But that peaceful pairing slowly unravelled, ending in the worst of catastrophes, with a sweet sad woman caught up, used, and ground down in the vast war machine mounted to conquer a town, and her three children were almost torn from her, and she left her very heart in the rough clutches of the Abbé Faujas, and the Rougons saved Plassans for the second time, while she lay dying by the light of the fire in which her husband, mad with pent-up rage and a lust for revenge, burned along with the priest.*

Of the three children, Octave Mouret was the daring conqueror, a clear-headed man, resolved to ask women for the throne of Paris, who fell into the clutches of a crassly decadent bourgeoisie and had a terrible sentimental education there, going from the capricious rejection of one woman to the craven abandonment of another, and sampling the disadvantages of adultery right down to the slimy dregs. But he remained happily active, industrious and pugnacious, and gradually extricated himself, rising again regardless from the dirty basement of this rotten world, which you could hear cracking apart.* Octave Mouret victorious revolutionized high-end commerce, killed off the unambitious little shops of the old-style trade, planted in the middle of a feverish Paris the colossal palace of temptation, sparkling with cut-glass chandeliers and overflowing with velvet, silk and lace, made a king's fortune exploiting women and lived in smiling scorn of them, till the day an avenger in the shape of a young girl, the very simple and sensible Denise, tamed him, and held him captive at her feet distraught with pain, until she finally did him the favour—and she so poor—of marrying him, at the height of the success of his Louvre, under the teeming golden hail of the takings.*

There remained the other two children, Serge Mouret and Désirée Mouret—she innocent and healthy like a happy young pup, he refined and mystical, stumbling by accident into the priesthood after a nervous episode of the kind his line of the family were prone to, before reliving the story of Adam and Eve, this time in the legendary Paradou. Here he was born again just to love Albine, to have her and to lose her, in the bosom of great complicit nature, before being recaptured by the Church, and going on to fight the eternal war on life, battling for the death of his sexuality, throwing on Albine's dead body the handful of dirt of the officiating priest at the very time when Désirée, the loving friend of animals, was going wild with joy in the midst of the warm fecundity of her farmyard.*

Further along, a glimpse into a sweet but tragic life opened up: Hélène Mouret lived peacefully with her young daughter Jeanne, on the heights of Passy, overlooking Paris, that boundless and bottomless human sea in full view of which the painful history unfolded. Hélène's sudden passion for a passing stranger, a doctor, called in by chance one night to her daughter's bedside, Jeanne's morbid jealousy, the instinctive jealousy of a born lover competing for her mother's love and already so ravaged by jaundiced passion that she died of the sin—a terrible price for her mother to pay for one hour of desire in an otherwise virtuous life, with the poor dear dead girl lying up there all alone under the cypresses in the silent cemetery, before Paris everlasting.*

With Lisa Macquart began the illegitimate branch, fresh and sturdy in this woman who flaunted the prosperity of a full stomach, when she stood in a bright apron on the doorstep of her charcuterie and smiled upon Les Halles, where the hunger of a nation rumbled, in the time-honoured battle of the Fat and the Thin, with the thin Florent, her brother-in-law, hated and hunted down by the fat fish-wives, the fat shopwomen. The fat charcutière herself, unfailingly honest but unforgiving, had had the man arrested as a Republican illegally returning from exile, convinced as she was that she was thereby working towards the good digestion of all decent folk.*

From such a mother sprang the sanest and most humane of girls, Pauline Quenu: the poised, level-headed one, the virgin, who knew all there was to know about life and accepted it, so passionate in her love of others that, in spite of the rebellion sparked by her fertile puberty, she gave away her fiancé Lazare to a friend, then rescued the child of the dissolved couple and became his true mother, always sacrificed, ruined, but triumphant and gay, in her little patch of monotonous wilderness, facing the wide open sea, amidst a whole host of sick people who howled their pain and didn't want to die.*

Then Gervaise Macquart turned up with her four children, lame, pretty, hard-working Gervaise, whose lover, Lantier, threw her out on the street in the slums, where she ran into the zinc-worker Coupeau, a good and sober workingman whom she married. She was so happy at first, with three women working for her in her laundry, but then she went under with her husband and sank into the inevitable decadence of the milieu, he slowly overcome by alcohol, so possessed by it that he went stark raving mad and died, she herself perverted, turning into a lazy slob, finally polished off by the return of Lantier and the quiet ignominy of a *ménage à trois*, forever after a pitiable victim of complicit destitution, which ended up killing her one evening, her stomach empty.*

Gervaise's eldest son, Claude, had the mournful genius of a great mentally unbalanced painter, suffering from the crazy impotence of feeling he had a masterpiece in him, but that his unruly fingers would never let him get it out; a giant wrestler forever battered and fulminating, a martyr crucified by his art, adoring women, but sacrificing his wife Christine, so loving and for a time so loved, to the woman not yet created, whom he could see in divine detail but whom his brush could not raise up on canvas in all her naked perfection. This devouring passion for bringing forth, this insatiable need to create, caused such appalling distress when it couldn't be satisfied that he wound up hanging himself.*

Jacques, for his part, contributed crime, the hereditary defect that turned into an instinctive craving for blood, the fresh young blood running from the slashed-open chest of a woman, the first comer, any woman passing by on the footpath, an abominable sickness he fought but that caught up with him again in the course of his love affair with the submissive and sensual Séverine. She herself was thrown into a state of constant terror by this tragic history of murder, and he stabbed her one night in a fit of rage at the sight of her white bosom. This savage human beast then charged off among the speeding trains, while the engine he mounted roared away, but his beloved engine ground him to a pulp one day before going out of control and hurtling, driverless, towards untold disasters in the distance.*

Étienne, in his turn, driven out, lost, surfaced in the black coal country one freezing March night, and went down into the voracious pit. He loved the sad Catherine, who was stolen from him by a brute, and he shared the miners' dismal life of poverty and sordid promiscuity till the day when hunger, fanning revolt, drove across the barren plain a bellowing multitude of starving poor who wanted bread and marched on in the crumbling ruins and the burning wreckage, under threat of fire from the troop whose rifles went off on their own, a terrible convulsion heralding the end of a world; for the avenging blood of the Maheus rose up later, with Alzire dying of starvation, Maheu killed by a bullet, Zacharie killed by a coal gas explosion, while Catherine lay in the ground, and only La Maheude survived, mourning her dead and going back down the mine to earn her thirty sous, while Étienne, the miners' defeated leader, haunted by the prospect of future political action, took himself off one mild April morning lured by the first muffled sounds of a thrusting new world, whose germination would soon blast open the earth.*

Nana subsequently became the revenge—Nana, this girl who sprang up on the social dungheap of the slums, the golden fly who took wing and soared above the putrefaction below, whom people tolerated but hid, carrying in her fluttering wings the ferment of destruction, rising up and corrupting the aristocracy, poisoning men just by landing on them, in the depths of palaces through whose windows she flew, toiling unwittingly at ruin and death, with the stoical Vandeuvres setting himself on fire; the melancholy Foucarmont roaming the China seas; the disaster of Steiner's being reduced to living like an honest man; the smug imbecility of La Faloise; and the tragic collapse of the Muffats; and Georges's white corpse, watched over by Philippe who'd only got out of prison the day before. The stinking air of the epoch was so contagious that Nana herself decayed and died of black smallpox which she'd caught on her son Louiset's deathbed, while under her windows, Paris went by, drunk, struck by war fever and racing headlong towards the collapse of everything.*

Lastly there was Jean Macquart, the workman and soldier who went back to being a peasant, grappling with the hard earth that makes you pay for every grain of wheat with a drop of sweat, above all wrestling with country people whom bitter desire and the slow and arduous conquest of the soil consume with a burning need to possess that is always being stoked, the Fouans in old age surrendering their fields as if they were surrendering a chunk of their flesh, the Buteaus in their frenzy going as far as parricide to hasten inheritance of a little patch of lucern, stubborn Françoise dying from the stroke of a scythe, without talking, not wanting even a clod of dirt to leave the family— this whole tragedy of simple and instinctive people, not fully freed from the original primitive savagery, the whole human stain over the noble earth, which alone remains immortal, this earth that is the mother from which we come and to which we return, she whom we love to the point of committing crimes, who continually makes life anew for her unknown ends, even out of the misery and abomination of human beings.*

It was Jean again who, having become a widower and having enlisted at the first rumours of war, contributed the inexhaustible reserve, the fount of eternal youth that the earth holds, Jean the humblest and steadiest soldier in the ultimate débâcle, driven along in the awful and fatal storm which, sweeping through the Empire from the border at Sedan, threatened to blow his homeland away; always wise, circumspect, unwavering in his hope, loving with brotherly affection his comrade Maurice, the deranged son of the bourgeoisie, with the holocaust destined to be expiation, Jean crying tears of blood when inexorable fate chose him of all people to hack off that damaged limb, then, at the end of it all, after the never-ending defeats, the atrocious civil war, the provinces lost, the billions to pay, starting again, returning to the land that was waiting for him, to the great and arduous task of making all France anew.*

Pascal paused. Clotilde had handed him all the files, one by one, and he had run through them all, abstracted and reclassified them, and put them all back on the top shelf in the cupboard. He was out of breath, exhausted by such a prolonged sprint through this living humanity; while she, not making a sound, not moving, giddy and reeling from this overflowing river of life, was still waiting, incapable of thought or judgement. The storm continued to beat down on the black countryside with its endless drumroll of teeming rain. Lightning had just struck a nearby tree with an awful cracking noise. The candles flared in fright in the wind from the wide-open window.

'Ah!' he said, gesturing once more at the files. 'There's a world, a society, a whole civilization in there, the whole of life is there, in all its manifestations, good and bad, hammered out in the forge fire that sweeps all along. Yes, our family could, today, provide a broad enough sample for science, which hopes one day to mathematically define the laws governing irregularities of the nerves and blood that show up in a bloodline, following an initial organic lesion. These irregularities determine—in each individual in that bloodline according to their different environments, feelings, desires, and passions—all the natural and instinctive human manifestations, whose results go by the names of virtues and vices. And it's also a historical document; it tells the story of the Second Empire, from the *coup d'état* to Sedan, for our family rose from the people, then spread throughout the whole of contemporary society, invaded all walks of life, propelled by outbreaks of unbridled appetite, by the essentially modern impulse, this crack of the whip that drives the lower classes to seek pleasure, as they move upwards across the social body...* The beginnings, as I told you: they started out from Plassans; and here we are in Plassans again, back where we started.'

He broke off once more, his speech slowed by reverie.

'What a mass of horror I've stirred up, all these experiences, some sweet, some terrible, all these joys, all these sorrows, flung by the shovel load onto this colossal heap of facts and deeds! There is pure history, the Empire built on blood, first reckless and harshly authoritarian, conquering rebellious towns, then slowly unravelling into chaos, collapsing into blood, into such a sea of blood that the whole nation nearly drowned in it... There are social studies here, of small tradespeople and big business, prostitution, crime, the land, money, the bourgeoisie, the people—the kind that go bad in the cesspit of the slums, the kind that rebel in the great industrial hubs, that whole burgeoning growth stemming from almighty socialism, its womb swollen from bearing the new age. There are simple human studies, intimate pages, love stories, the struggle of hearts and minds against unjust nature, the crushing of those who cry out at tasks too hard for them, the cry of goodness sacrificing itself, victorious in pain. There is fantasy, flights of fancy beyond reality, vast gardens blossoming all year round, cathedrals with fine spires exquisitely wrought, tales of the supernatural dropping down from paradise, ideal affections soaring back up to heaven in a kiss... There's something of everything there, the best and the worst, the vulgar and the sublime, flowers, muck, tears, laughter, the river of life itself endlessly carrying humanity along!'

He picked up the Family Tree, which was still lying on the table, and spread it out, running his finger over it again, now listing the members of the family who were still living. Eugène Rougon, fallen monarch, was in the Chamber, witness and imperturbable defender of the old world swept away in the downfall. Aristide Saccard, having sloughed off his old skin, had fallen on his feet again as a Republican, the editor of a leading newspaper, already making fresh new millions; while his son Maxime squandered his revenue, in his little mansion on the Avenue du Bois-de-Boulogne, proper and prudent now, and threatened with a terrible disease; and his other son Victor had not reappeared, must still be prowling around somewhere in the shadows of crime, since he wasn't in the hulks, let loose by the world into the future, into the dark unknown of the scaffold. Sidonie Rougon, who disappeared from view for a long while, tired of sleazy jobs, was now of nun-like austerity and had just withdrawn into the darkness of some religious house, as treasurer of the Œuvre du Sacrement, set up to assist in marrying off child-mothers. Octave Mouret, proprietor of the big department store The Ladies' Paradise, whose colossal fortune just kept on growing, had had, towards the end of winter, a second child with his wife Denise Baudu, whom he adored, although he was starting to play up a bit again. The Abbé Mouret, curé at Saint-Eutrope, at the bottom of a boggy gorge, had cloistered himself away there with his sister Désirée, in great humbleness, refusing all advancement from his bishop, and awaiting death like a holy man who rejected treatment, even though he was suffering from the onset of consumption. Hélène Mouret lived very happily, away from everything, idolized by her new husband, Monsieur Rambaud, in the little property they owned not far from Marseilles, by the sea; but she had no children from her second marriage. Pauline Quenu was still in Bonneville, at the other end of France, facing the vast ocean, alone now with little Paul since the death of Uncle Chanteau, resolved never to marry but to devote herself entirely to the son of her cousin Lazare, who'd become a widower and gone to America to make his fortune. Étienne Lantier, back in Paris after the Montsou strike, later became implicated in the insurrection of the Commune, whose ideas he had upheld with a vengeance; he had been sentenced to death, then pardoned and deported, so that he now found himself in Noumea; it was even said that he'd married there without further ado and had a child, but no one actually knew whether it was a girl or a boy. Lastly, Jean Macquart, discharged after the week of bloodshed, had come back to settle down near Plassans, at Valqueyras, where he'd had the luck to marry a robust girl, Mélanie Vial, the only daughter of a well-heeled peasant whose land he was turning to good account; and his wife, who'd fallen pregnant on their wedding night, had given birth to a boy in May and was two months' pregnant again, in one of those cases of teeming fertility that leave mothers no time to breastfeed their babies.

'Of course, yes,' he went on in a hushed voice, 'the bloodlines degenerate. There is real exhaustion there, rapid decline, as if our people, in their rage for pleasure, in the gluttonous satisfaction of their appetites, burned too fast. Louiset* died in the cradle; Jacques-Louis,* a halfwit, was carried off by a nervous disease; Victor* reverted to a feral state, running off into who knows what mysterious depths of darkness; our poor Charles, so beautiful and so frail: these are the last boughs of the Tree, the last pale shoots in which the powerful sap of the big branches doesn't seem able to rise. The worm was in the trunk, now it's in the fruit and is devouring it. But we should never despair, families are the everlasting future. They go back, beyond the common ancestor, through the unfathomable strata of the different lines who have lived, right back to the very first being; and they will go on growing without end, they will spread and ramify endlessly, to the end of time. Look at our Tree: it only covers five generations, it doesn't even amount to a blade of grass in the human forest, colossal and dark, whose peoples are the great age-old oaks. But just think of its immense roots holding all the soil together, think of the incessant unfurling of its upper leaves that then mingle with the other leaves, and of the sea of treetops, endlessly churning in the eternal fertilizing breath of life... Well, hope lies there, in the daily reconstitution of the line through the new blood that comes in from outside. Every marriage supplies different elements, good or bad, the effect of which is, after all, to prevent progressive, mathematically calculable degeneracy. Flaws are corrected, defects eliminated, an inevitable equilibrium is restored after a few generations, and it's the average man who always ends up emerging, indistinct humanity, doggedly persisting in its mysterious labour, marching onwards to its unknown goal.'

He paused and took a deep breath.

'Ah! Our family—what will become of it? What being will it finally end in?'

Then he kept going, not counting any more on the survivors he'd named, having classified those particular individuals and knowing what they were capable of, but full of passionate curiosity about the children who were still in their infancy. He'd written to a colleague in Noumea for precise information about Étienne's wife and the child she was supposed to have given birth to; but he had received nothing back and feared that, on that side, the tree would remain incomplete. He was better informed about the two children of Octave Mouret, with whom he remained in correspondence: the little girl was still alarmingly puny, while the little boy, who took after his mother, was becoming magnificent. His strongest hope, in any case, lay in Jean's children, of which the firstborn, a big boy, seemed to be bringing renewal, the young sap of bloodlines that go off and get their hands dirty in the soil and are reinvigorated by it. He went to Valqueyras occasionally and came back happy from that oasis of fertility, from the quiet sensible father, always at his plough, and from the simple cheerful mother, with her broad hips, capable of bearing a whole teeming horde. Who knew where the healthy branch would come into the world? Maybe the wise and mighty one they'd been waiting for would spring up there. The worst of it, for the beauty of his Tree, was that these little boys and girls were still so young he couldn't classify them yet. And his voice mellowed as he spoke of this hope for the future, these blond heads, with all the unavowed regret and yearning of his celibacy.

Pascal went on looking at the Tree spread out in front of him, then cried:

'But just look how complete it is, how decisive! Go on, look! I tell you again that every possible case of heredity is in there. To finalize my theory all I had to do was base it on this set of facts. Well, what's so wonderful is that you can put your finger on how individuals springing from the same stock can appear radically different, while being merely logical modifications of common ancestors. The trunk explains the branches, which explain the leaves. With your father, Saccard, as with your uncle, Eugène Rougon, so opposite in their temperaments and their ways of life, the same shoot has created the dissolute appetites of the one, and the overweening ambition of the other. Angélique, that pure lily, comes from the seedy Sidonie, in the surge of rapture that makes women mystics or passionate lovers, depending on the environment. Mouret's three children are swept along by an identical impetus, which makes the intelligent Octave a millionaire rag-trader, the believer Serge a poor country curé, the imbecile Désirée a beautiful and happy girl. But the example is even more striking with Gervaise's children: neurosis is passed on and Nana sells herself, Étienne rebels, Jacques kills, Claude is a genius; whereas Pauline, their first cousin on one side, is the triumph of decency, the kind of woman who fights and sacrifices herself... It's heredity, life itself that hatches imbeciles, madmen, criminals, and great men. Some cells abort, others take their place, and you get a rogue or a complete lunatic in the place of a man of genius or an ordinary, decent man. And humanity rolls on, carrying the lot along with it!'

Then his thinking took a new turn and he added:

'And what about animal life, the animal who suffers and loves, who's like a rough draft of man: this whole kindred animal world that lives off our life!... Yes, I'd have liked to put the animals on the Ark, to give them their place in our family, show how they're always part of us, completing our existence. I've known cats whose presence made for the mysterious charm of the household, dogs who were adored, whose death was mourned and left their owners inconsolable with grief. I've known goats, cows, donkeys who mattered greatly and whose personality played such a paramount role that their story really should be written... And, well! Our own Bonhomme, that poor old horse of ours who has served us for a quarter of a century—don't you think he's mixed some of his blood in with ours and is now one of the family? We've changed him just as he has acted a little on us, so that we end up being made in the same image; and that's so true that when I see him now, half-blind, with his eyes cloudy and his legs crippled with rheumatism, I kiss him on both cheeks like some poor old relative who's fallen into my care... Ah, animals! All that creeps along, all that whines below man—what a place for immense fellow feeling we'd have to make for them in any history of life!'

It was a final cry, into which Pascal poured the extreme elation of his love for all beings. He had gradually worked himself up and finally come to the confession of his faith in the never-ending and victorious labour of living nature. And Clotilde, who hadn't spoken a word till then, quite washed out from the calamity of so many facts falling on top of her, finally opened her mouth to ask:

'Well, Maître, and what about me in all that?'

She had placed one of her thin fingers on the leaf of the Tree where she saw her name written down. He had passed over that leaf. But she insisted.

'Yes, me, what am I, then? Why didn't you read me my file?'

For a second he remained speechless, as though surprised at the question.

'Why? No reason. It's true, I've got nothing to hide from you. You see what's written there: "Clotilde, born in 1847. Favouring of the mother.* Reversion inheritance, with moral and physical predomin-ance of her maternal grandfather..." Nothing could be clearer. Your mother won out in you; you have her keen appetite, and you also have a lot of her stylishness, her indolence at times, her submissiveness. Yes, you're very feminine like her, without really realizing. I mean you love to be loved. On top of that, your mother was a great reader of novels, a dreamer who loved to stay in bed for whole days at a stretch, musing over a book; she was mad on nursery stories, had her cards read and went to fortune tellers; and I've always felt you got your preoccupation with the mysteries of life, your anxiety about the unknown, from her... But what really makes you who you are, by giv-ing you a dual nature, is the influence of your grandfather, Commander Sicardot. I knew him, he was no genius but at least he had a lot of integrity and energy. Without him, quite frankly, I don't think you'd amount to much, since the other influences aren't exactly good. He's given you the best part of your personality, the courage to fight, high-mindedness and frankness.'

She had listened closely to him and nodded slightly to say that that was exactly right, that she wasn't hurt, despite the little stab of pain that made her lips tremble at these new details about her family, about her mother.

'Well,' she said, 'and what about you, Maître?'

This time he didn't hesitate:

'Oh, me! What's the good of talking about me? I'm not part of the family! You can see what's written there: "Pascal, born in 1813. Innateness. Combination, in which the physical and moral character-istics of the parents blend, without a trace of either apparently recur-ring in the new being..." My mother's told me often enough that I don't belong, that she didn't know where I could have come from!'

This came as a cry of relief, coming from him, a kind of burst of involuntary joy.

'You see, the people never get it wrong. Have you ever heard anyone in this town call me Pascal Rougon? No! People have always said
Doctor Pascal, full stop. That's because I'm the odd one out. And it
may not be very nice of me, but I'm delighted, because there are some
legacies that really are too heavy to bear. However much I may love
them all, my heart still beats with glee when I feel myself to be alien,
different, that I have absolutely nothing in common with them. Not
to belong, not to be one of them, my God! It's a breath of fresh air, it's
what gives me the courage to put them all down there on paper, to lay
them bare in these files, and still find the courage to go on living!'

He finally stopped talking and there was a silence. The rain had
stopped, the storm was moving away, only thunderclaps could now be
heard, more and more distant; while, from the fields, still dark but
cool and fresh, a delectable smell of wet earth rose through the open
window. In the stilled air, the candles burned away with a tall tranquil
flame.

'Ah!' Clotilde said simply, with a sweeping gesture of despair.
'What to be?'

One night she had cried out in anguish, on the threshing floor, that
life was vile, how could one live it and yet be happy and at peace?
Science shone a terrible light on the world, its analysis poked into all
human wounds just to expose the horror. And now it had just spoken
more crudely still, sharpening the disgust she already felt for beings
and things by throwing her own family, completely naked, onto the
slab of the dissecting room. The muddy river had rolled before her
for nearly three hours and it brought the worst of revelations, the
sudden terrible truth about those closest to her, dear beings, the
people she was supposed to love: her father exalted through financial
crimes, her incestuous brother, her unscrupulous grandmother, covered
in the blood of the just, the others almost all depraved, drunks, prof-
ligates, murderers, the monstrous efflorescence of the human tree.
The shock was so violent that she couldn't find her feet, stunned and
hurt as she was to learn about the whole of life this way, in one blow.
Yet the lesson was somehow made inoffensive, in its very violence, by
something grand and good, a breath of profound humanity that had
swept it along from start to finish. Nothing bad had happened to her,
she felt as if she'd been whipped by a raw sea breeze, the kind of
storm wind that fills your lungs and invigorates them with good clean
bracing air. He had told all, speaking freely even about his own

mother, while keeping up his deferential attitude towards her in the manner of a scientist who does not judge the facts. To tell all in order to know all, to cure all—wasn't that the cry he'd uttered that beautiful summer's night? And although she remained shaken, blinded by the too-bright light, she understood him finally, thanks to the very exorbitance of what he'd just revealed to her, and she admitted to herself that what he was attempting here was an immense work. In spite of everything, it was a cry of sanity, of hope in the future. He spoke as a benefactor who, since heredity made the world, wanted to set down its laws to make use of it, and to make a new and happy world afresh.

Then again, wasn't there more than mud in this overflowing river whose floodgates he'd opened? So much gold had flowed by, mixed in with the grasses and flowers of the riverbanks! Hundreds of creatures went on flying past her still, and she remained haunted by faces of great charm and goodness, the fine profiles of young girls and serenely beautiful women. All passion lay bleeding there, whole hearts opened up in outbursts of love. They were numberless, the Jeannes, Angéliques, Paulines, Marthes, Gervaises, Hélènes. From those and from the other women, even the not-so-good, and even from the terrible men, the worst of the pack, rose a kindred humanity. And it was precisely that breath of air she had felt pass, that current of broad sympathy he had just injected into his rigorous science lesson. He didn't seem to be moved, he'd maintained the dispassionate attitude of the lecturer; but in his heart of hearts, what wounded kindness there was, what frantic devotion, what a gift of his whole being to the happiness of others! His entire *œuvre*, constructed with such mathematical precision, was suffused with this painful sense of kinship, right down to its cruellest ironies. Hadn't he spoken to her about animals as if he were the older brother of all poor living creatures who suffer? Suffering enraged him, but the anger he felt was part and parcel of aiming so high, and he had only become brutal in his hatred of the artificial and the fleeting, dreaming as he did of working not for the polite society of a moment, but for the whole of humanity at all the solemn hours of its history. It may even have been this revolt against the prevailing vulgarity that had made him throw himself into theories and their application, and the challenge of being bold. And the *œuvre* remained humane, overflowing with the immeasurable sob of beings and things.

Besides, wasn't that life? There is no absolute evil. No man is ever bad in everyone's eyes, he is always a source of delight to someone; which means that when you stop looking from a single point of view, you end up realizing that every being has a purpose. Those who believe in a God should tell themselves that, if their God doesn't strike evildoers down, it's because he sees the progress of his work as a whole and cannot stoop to the particular. The labour that ends begins again, the living as a totality remain admirable for their courage and industry; and the love of life overcomes all. This gigantic labour of mankind, this obstinate persistence in living, is their excuse, redemption. So, from on high, all you could see was this continual struggle, and a lot of good too, despite everything, even if there was a lot of bad. You reached a point where you made allowances for everybody, you forgave, you felt only infinite compassion and intense charity. This was where the safe harbour surely lay, awaiting those who have lost faith in dogmas, who would like to know why they are alive, in the midst of the apparent injustice of the world. You have to live for the effort of living, to leave a stone that will one day go to shape some far-off and mysterious edifice; and the only peace possible, on this earth, lies in the joy of having made such an effort.

Another hour had passed, the whole night had slipped by in this terrible lesson in life, without either Pascal or Clotilde being aware of where they were, or of time flying. Worn out from work for some weeks, and already ravaged by his life of suspicion and grief, Pascal gave a nervous start as though suddenly waking up.

'Well, now you know everything, so does your heart feel strong, galvanized by reality, full of forgiveness and hope? Are you with me?'

But, startled herself by the alarming moral shock she'd received, she shuddered and was unable to collect her thoughts. Inside her the old beliefs had been so soundly trounced and such a brave new world was dawning, that she didn't dare consult herself and judge. She felt she'd been seized and swept up into the almighty power of truth. She bowed to it but was not convinced.

'Maître', she stammered, 'Maître...'

They stood there for a moment, face to face, looking at each other. Day was breaking, a dawn of delicious purity, far away in the great clear sky, washed by the storm. Not a cloud now stained the pale azure, tinged with pink. The whole chirruping awakening of the wet countryside came in through the window, while the candles, which were burning down, paled in the growing light.

'Tell me, do you still want to destroy everything, burn everything, here? Are you with me, with me completely?'

At that moment, he thought she was going to throw her arms around his neck and sob. A sudden burst of emotion seemed to propel her. But then they saw each other in their semi-nakedness. She hadn't caught sight of herself till then, but now became aware that she had nothing on but a petticoat, that her arms were bare, her bare shoulders scarcely covered by stray locks of her loose hair; and looking down, she saw, there on her shoulder, near her left armpit, the few drops of blood and the bruise he'd given her in struggling to subdue her in a brutal hold. And deep down she felt extraordinary turmoil, the certainty that she was going to be vanquished, as if, through that hold, he really had become her master, in all things and for all time. The sensation spread and she was overwhelmed, helplessly swept away beyond her will, gripped by the irresistible need to abandon herself.

She promptly straightened up, trying to think. She had wrapped her bare arms around her bare chest. All the blood in her veins had rushed to the surface of her skin in a dark flush of shame. And she turned to flee, darting off with all her exquisitely light grace.

'Maître, please, leave me alone... I'll see...'

With the swiftness of a panicked virgin, she took refuge, as she had done once before, in her room. He heard her slam the door and lock it. He stood there, alone, and, suddenly overcome by immense discouragement and sadness, wondered if he'd been right to tell all, if the truth would germinate in this dear adored creature, and grow there one day into a crop of happiness.

6

THE days went by. October started out gloriously, the warm passion of summer generously ripening into a fiery autumn, without a cloud in the sky. Then the weather turned, terrible winds blew, and a final storm cut channels into the slopes. And inside the bleak household at La Souleiade, the approach of winter seemed to bring with it infinite gloom.

This was a new kind of hell. There were no more stinging arguments between Pascal and Clotilde. Doors were no longer slammed, loud shouting no longer forced Martine to mount the stairs at all hours. Now, they barely spoke to each other, and not a word had been uttered about the scene of that night. He, through some unexplained scruple, an odd bashfulness he himself was not aware of, didn't feel like resuming the conversation and demanding the answer he longed for—a pledge of faith in him and of her respectful submission. She, after the great moral shock that had transformed her to the core, was still thinking, hesitating, struggling, putting off a decision so as not to give in, still instinctively rebelling. And the misunderstanding only grew worse, within the great desolate silence of the miserable house where there was no happiness any more.

It was, for Pascal, one of those times when he suffered appallingly, without a word of complaint. The apparent peace did nothing to reassure him—quite the opposite. He had lapsed into deep mistrust, fancying that they were still lying in wait and that, even though they seemed to be leaving him alone, it was only to gather in the shadows and hatch the vilest plots. His anxiety in fact intensified, and every day he expected some disaster—for his papers to be swallowed up at the bottom of an abyss that would suddenly open up, or for all of La Souleiade to be razed to the ground, carried off, smashed to smithereens. The assault on his thinking, on his moral and intellectual life, in being thus masked, became even more unnerving, intolerable, to the point where he went to bed every night with a fever. Often, he would give a start and swivel round, feeling he was about to catch the enemy in some treacherous act behind his back; but there would be no one there, nothing but the thumping of his own heart in the dark. At other times, gripped by a suspicion, he would remain on the lookout for hours, hidden behind his shutters, or else lurking in ambush at the end of a corridor; but not a soul ever stirred, all he would hear was the violent throbbing of his temples. He was left wrung out by it all, never went to bed any more without inspecting every room, no longer slept, waking up at the slightest sound, panting, ready to defend himself.

And the thing that intensified Pascal's suffering was the nagging, overpowering thought that this injury was being inflicted on him by the one creature in the world he loved, the adored Clotilde, whom he'd been watching grow ever more beautiful and enchanting for twenty years, whose life till then had blossomed like a full fragrant bloom, sweetening his own. Clotilde, for the love of God! She who filled his heart with a feeling of utter love he'd never examined! She who had become his joy, his courage, his hope, a whole new burst of youth in which he felt himself come alive again! When she went by, with her delicate neck, so round, so fresh, he felt rejuvenated, awash with health and gladness, as if at the return of spring. His whole existence till then explained how he'd been possessed like this, taken over and filled by this child, who had already stolen his heart when she was still only little, and then, as she grew, had gradually taken up all the room there. Since he had moved for good to Plassans, he had been leading the life of a monk, cloistered among his books, well away from women. He had only been known to feel passion for one woman, the one who'd died, the one whose fingertips he'd never even kissed. True, he went off to Marseilles now and then and stayed the night; but those were sudden escapades, always with the first woman to happen along, and soon over. He hadn't really lived, he had a whole reservoir of virility bottled up inside him and now, with the threat of encroaching old age, the sap was roaring as it rose. And he'd have become passionately attached to an animal, a stray dog picked up in the street who'd licked his hands; but it happened to be Clotilde he loved, the little girl who was suddenly a desirable woman, and possessed him now and tortured him by turning into his foe.

Pascal, so carefree, so kind, swiftly became unbearably bad-tempered and harsh. He flared up at the slightest word, bullied the startled Martine, who looked up at him with the apologetic eyes of a beaten animal. From morning till night, he paraded his distress through the despairing house, his face so thunderous no one dared say a word to him. He never took Clotilde out with him now, went out alone on his house calls. And it was alone that he came home one afternoon, badly shaken by an accident, with a man's death on his conscience as a risk-taking medical innovator. He'd gone to give Lafouasse, the publican, his injection, the man's ataxia having suddenly advanced so far that the doctor felt he was doomed. Yet he persisted in battling on regardless and kept up the man's treatment; but as luck would have it, that particular day the syringe had sucked up, from the bottom of the vial, a speck of dirt that had eluded the filter. To make matters worse, he'd managed to puncture a vein and a drop of blood had actually appeared. He'd immediately become alarmed, seeing the publican swiftly lose colour, choke, and break out into big beads of cold sweat. When death struck like a thunderbolt, the man's lips turning blue, his face black, he finally understood. It was an embolism, and he could only blame the deficiency of his preparations, the fact that his whole method was still so primitive. No doubt Lafouasse had been doomed, he might only have lived another six months at most and that, in appalling pain; but the brutality of what had happened was no less inescapable, this dreadful death. And what desperate regret, what a jolt to his faith, what rage against useless and murderous science Pascal had felt! He'd returned home livid and only reappeared the next day after staying shut up in his room for sixteen hours, flung across his bed fully clothed, scarcely breathing.

The afternoon of that particular day, Clotilde, who sat sewing next to him in the workroom, ventured to break the heavy silence. She looked up and watched him flicking through a book, searching for information he was unable to find.

'Maître, are you sick? Why don't you say so? I'll look after you.'

He kept his nose in his book, and muttered in a hollow voice:

'Sick? What's it to you? I don't need anyone.'

Wanting to placate him, she went on:

'If something's worrying you, and you're able to tell me, it might help. Yesterday you came home so dejected! You mustn't let yourself be disheartened like that. I spent the night worrying. I got up three times and stood outside your door, listening, tormented by the idea that you were in pain.'

As gently as she had spoken, it was as if he'd been lashed by a whip. In his morbidly weakened state, a sudden surge of rage made him thrust the book away and shoot to his feet, quivering.

'So, you spy on me now, I can't even retire to my room without people coming and gluing their ears to the walls... Yes, they even listen to the beating of my heart, they're waiting for me to die so they can ransack everything, burn everything here.'

And his voice rose, and all the unjust suffering he felt came out in accusations and threats.

'I forbid you to trouble yourself about me... Have you got anything else to say to me? Have you thought about it, can you put your hand in mine, faithfully, and tell me we agree?'

But she didn't speak again, she just went on staring at him with her big clear eyes, still openly wanting not to give in; while he, further infuriated by this stance, lost all restraint.

Waving her away, he stammered out:

'Go away! Go on! I don't want you anywhere near me! I don't want enemies anywhere near me! I don't want anyone near me, driving me mad!'

She rose, white as a ghost, and walked out of the room, perfectly erect, without looking back, taking her needlework with her.

In the month that followed, Pascal tried to take refuge in work, toiling away desperately around the clock. He would stick at it now for whole days on end, alone in the workroom, and he even spent the nights going back over old documents, recasting all his works on heredity. It was as if he'd been seized by a violent need to convince himself of the legitimacy of his hopes, a need to force science to provide him with the certainty that humanity could be created anew, made healthy at last and altogether superior. He no longer went out, abandoned his patients, lived in his papers, without fresh air, without exercise. And after a month of such overexertion, which wrecked him without alleviating his domestic woes, he fell into such a state of nervous exhaustion that illness, which had been brewing for a while, broke out with alarming force.

Now, when he got up in the morning, Pascal felt annihilated with fatigue, heavier and wearier than when he'd gone to bed the night before. His whole being was under constant strain, his legs felt limp after five minutes walking, his body felt shattered at the slightest effort, he was unable to make a move without it ending in a pang of acute pain. At times, the ground beneath his feet would suddenly seem to wobble. Constant buzzing in his ears made him giddy, dizzy spells made him shut his eyes as if to protect himself from a hail of sparks. He suddenly hated wine, hardly ate a thing any more, had trouble with his digestion. Then, in the middle of the apathy that came with this growing sluggishness, he'd suddenly burst into fits of rage, frenzies of pointless activity. His equilibrium was thrown and, made irritable by feebleness, he would swing to violent extremes of mood for no apparent reason. At the slightest emotion, tears would fill his eyes. He ended up locking himself away in such convulsions of despair that he would heave with sobs for hours, without any immediate cause for sorrow, simply overwhelmed by the immense sadness of the world.

But his sickness got distinctly worse after one of his trips to Marseilles, one of those bachelor's escapades he sometimes went on. Perhaps he'd hoped a bout of debauchery would be a potent distraction, would bring relief. He stayed only two days and came back looking battered, morally and physically depleted, with the haunted face of a man who has lost his virility. This was an unmentionable humiliation, a fear which desperately concerted efforts had changed to a certainty, and which only added to his lack of confidence as a lover. He had never thought all that was important. Now, he was possessed by it, convulsed, overcome with misery, so much so that he contemplated suicide. It was no use telling himself it was probably only temporary, that some morbid cause had to be at the bottom of it: the feeling that he was impotent depressed him no less; and he was like a pubescent boy, in front of women, deprived of coherent speech by desire.

Around the first week in December, Pascal had sudden unbearable attacks of neuralgia. The bones of his skull creaked, making him feel his head would split open at any moment. Informed of this, old Madame Rougon decided one day to go and see how her son was. But she slipped into the kitchen, hoping to talk to Martine first. Looking scared and disconsolate, Martine told her that Monsieur was going mad, to be sure; and she described his peculiar ways, the never-ending stamping about in his room, the way he locked all the drawers, and patrolled the house from top to bottom till two in the morning. It brought tears to her eyes, and she ended up venturing the opinion that a devil may well have entered Monsieur's body, and that they'd do well to alert the curé at Saint-Saturnin.

'Such a good man,' she kept saying, 'you'd gladly be drawn and quartered for him! What a sorry thing it is, not being able to get him to church, when that would cure him at once, without fail!'

But Clotilde, who had heard her grandmother Félicité's voice, came in. She too wandered through the empty rooms, and lived most of the time in the abandoned salon on the ground floor. She didn't speak, though, but merely listened with that reflective, expectant air of hers.

'Ah, it's you, puss. Hello!… Martine's been telling me a devil's got into Pascal's body. That's my view too—only, this particular devil is called pride. He thinks he knows everything, he's the emperor and the pope rolled into one, and naturally, when people don't fall into line, it infuriates him.'

She shrugged her shoulders, full of boundless contempt.

'I'd laugh, myself, if it wasn't so sad… That boy knows nothing whatever—that's just it: he hasn't lived, he's stayed cooped up with his nose in his books like a fool. Put him in a smart drawing room and he's as innocent as a newborn babe. As for women, he doesn't know the first thing about them…'

Forgetting who she was talking to, this girl and the spinster servant, she lowered her voice, confidentially:

'Well, you see! You pay for that too, being too well behaved. No wife, no mistress, nothing. That's what's ended up curdling his brain.'

Clotilde didn't stir. Her eyelids alone moved, slowly closing over her big thoughtful eyes; but then she raised them again and kept up her act as a poor creature cut off from the world, unable to say a word about what was happening inside her.

'He's up there, isn't he?' Félicité went on. 'I came to see him, as this has to stop, it's too silly for words!'

On that note, she went upstairs, while Martine went back to her pots and pans and Clotilde wandered through the empty house again.

Upstairs, in the workroom, Pascal sat apparently stupefied, his nose in a book wide open in front of him. He could no longer read, the words swam past him, vanished, made no sense. But he went on desperately trying, it killed him to see that he was losing even his ability to work, which until now had been so powerful. His mother wasted no time, and chided him immediately, tore the book from him and flung it on a table, shouting that, when you were sick, you looked after yourself. He stood up with an angry jerk, ready to drive her out, just as he had driven out Clotilde. But instead he made one last effort of will and reverted to his usual deference.

'Mother, you know very well I've never wanted to argue with you… Leave me alone, please.'

She stood her ground, taking him to task over his continual mistrust. He was the one putting himself into a fever, always imagining enemies were surrounding him with traps, watching him so as to burgle him. Would any man of sound mind imagine people persecuting him like that? And, while she was at it, she accused him of getting a little too carried away with his discovery, his famous elixir that cured all ills. It was no good thinking you were God. All the more so as disappointments were only the crueller; and she made an allusion to Lafouasse, the man he'd killed: naturally, she realized that that couldn't have been pleasant for him, for it was indeed enough to make anyone take to their bed.

Pascal, who was still managing to control himself, kept his eyes on the ground and merely replied:

'Mother, please, leave me alone.'

'Oh, no! I won't leave you alone,' she shouted with her usual vehemence, fierce in spite of her great age. 'That's exactly why I've come—to give you a bit of a shove, and pull you out of this fever that's eating you alive... No, things can't go on like this, I won't sit by and let us become the laughing stock of the whole village again, with the way you're carrying on... I want you to get yourself better.'

He shrugged his shoulders and said in an undertone, as if talking to himself, making a troubling observation:

'I'm not sick.'

But, at that, Félicité started up, beside herself.

'What, not sick! What do you mean, not sick! Only a doctor could fail to look at himself like this. Good God! My poor boy, all those who come near you are struck by it: you're going mad with pride and fear!'

This time Pascal swiftly raised his head and looked her straight in the eye, while she carried on:

'That's what I wanted to tell you, since no one else would. I'm right, aren't I? You're old enough to know what you ought to do... A person fights back, you think of other things, you don't let yourself be overcome by some obsession, especially when you're from a family like ours... You know what they're like. Watch out, and get yourself better.'

He had gone pale but went on staring at her, as though probing into her to find out what there was of her in him. And he merely said in reply:

'You're right, Mother. Thank you.'

When he was alone again, he fell back into the chair at his table and tried to resume reading his book. But he was no more able than before to focus his attention and understand the words, the letters blurred before his eyes. The remarks his mother had made buzzed in his ears, and an anguish that had been mounting inside him for some time, grew, settled, and now haunted him with a sense of immediate, clearly defined, danger. Two months earlier he'd boasted so triumphantly of not being part of the family, but was he now about to get the most appalling refutation of this? Would he have the pain of seeing the family defect spring up again in his own marrow? Would he spend his life in terror at feeling himself to be in the clutches of the hereditary monster? His mother had said it: he was going mad with pride and fear. The presumptuous notion, the fanatical certainty he'd had of eliminating suffering, giving men willpower, making humanity anew, healthy and nobler—this was surely just the onset of delusions of grandeur. And, in his fear of being ambushed, in his compulsion to watch out for the enemies he sensed bent on destroying him, he easily recognized the symptoms of persecution mania. All the abnormalities in the bloodline ended up in the same terrible case: rapid-onset madness, then general paralysis, and death.

From that day forward, Pascal was possessed. The state of nervous exhaustion to which overwork and grief had reduced him, left him utterly defenceless, at the mercy of this haunting fear of madness and death. All the morbid sensations he had been experiencing, the immense fatigue on waking, the buzzing, the dizziness, right down to his attacks of indigestion and sudden crying fits, stacked up, one on top of the other, as so many certain proofs of the imminent breakdown with which he believed he was threatened. When it came to himself, he completely lost his fine and subtle powers of diagnosis as an observant doctor; and although he continued to reason, it was only to muddle everything and pervert everything, under the mental and physical depression in which he dragged himself around. He was no longer master of his own actions, was close to being mad, persuading himself, hour by hour, that he would go mad.

He spent whole days over that pale December burying himself deeper in his illness. Every morning he tried to escape the haunting dread, but he would come back no matter what and shut himself up in the workroom and take up the tangled thread of the day before. The lengthy study he'd done of heredity, his massive research work, all his labours, wound up poisoning him, providing him with endlessly renewed causes for anxiety. To the ever-present question he put himself about his specific hereditary case, the files were there, providing answers that covered all the possible combinations. Those combinations appeared so numerous now that he lost his bearings in them. If he'd got it wrong, if he couldn't set himself apart as a remarkable case of innateness, should he put himself in the category of reversion inheritance, skipping one, two, or even three generations? Was his case more simply a manifestation of latent inheritance, something that would supply fresh proof in support of his theory of germ plasma? Or should it be seen merely as evidence of the particularity of successive resemblances, with the sudden appearance of an unknown ancestor, at the close of his life? From the moment these questions began gnawing at him, he had no rest, but threw himself into tracking down the original source of his case, combing through his notes, rereading his books. And he analysed himself, monitored his every sensation so as to draw data on which he could assess himself. The days when his mind was lazier, when he believed he was experiencing peculiar problems with his vision, he inclined towards a predominance of the original nervous lesion; while, if he thought he was being attacked in the legs, his feet feeling leaden and sore, he imagined he was suffering from the indirect influence of some ancestor who'd come into the family from outside. Everything was mixed up, and he reached a point where he no longer recognized himself, amidst the imaginary troubles assaulting his distressed organism. And every night, the conclusion was the same, the same death knell tolled inside his skull: heredity, terrifying heredity, fear of going mad.

One day early in January, Clotilde unintentionally witnessed a scene that broke her heart. She was sitting by a window in the workroom, reading, hidden by the high back of her armchair, when she saw Pascal come in, after he'd been out of sight, cloistered in his room, since the day before. With both hands he was holding up to his eyes an unfolded sheet of yellowed paper she recognized as the Family Tree. He was so absorbed, his eyes so fixed, that she could have shown herself without his noticing her. He spread the Tree on the table and continued staring at it, with his terrified questioning look, gradually defeated and pleading, his cheeks wet with tears. Why, in God's name wouldn't the Tree answer him! Why wouldn't it tell him which ancestor he took after, so that he could write down his case, on his own leaf, alongside the others? If he was destined to go mad, why couldn't the Tree tell him so, clearly? That would have calmed him down, since he believed he was suffering only from uncertainty. Tears blurred his vision, but he went on looking, overpowered by this need to know that was finally causing his reason to fail. Clotilde had to hide when she saw him go to the cupboard and swing both doors open. He grabbed a fistful of files, flung them on the table, and flicked through them furiously. It was the scene of the terrible night of the storm starting all over again, the nightmare gallop, the parade of all these phantoms, conjured up, looming up from out of the mass of old papers. As they passed, he threw at each one of them a question, a fervent prayer, demanding to know the origin of his sickness, hoping for a word, a murmur that would give him some certainty. At first he let out only an indistinct stammer; then words formed, scraps of sentences.

'Is it you?... Is it you?... Is it you?... Oh, old mother, the mother of us all, are you the one destined to pass your madness on to me?... Is it you, the alcoholic uncle, the old rogue of an uncle, whose inveterate drunkenness I'll be paying for?... Is it you, the ataxic nephew, or you, the mystic nephew, or you, the idiot niece, who brings me the truth by showing me one of the forms of the lesion I'm suffering from?... Or is it you, the second cousin who hanged himself, or you, the second cousin who committed murder, or you, the second cousin who died of rottenness,* all these tragic ends heralding my own, my moral decline inside a padded cell, the appalling decomposition of my body?'

And the gallop continued, they all reared up and raced past at the speed of a gale. The files came to life, fleshed out, jostled each other, in a stampede of suffering humanity.

'Ah! Who'll tell me, who'll tell me, who'll tell me?... Is it this one who died mad? This one who was carried off by consumption? This one who suffocated from paralysis? This one who was killed very young by malnutrition?...* Who's got the poison I'm going to die from? What is it—hysteria, alcoholism, tuberculosis, scrofula? And what's it going to turn me into—an epileptic, an ataxic, or a lunatic?... A lunatic! Who said a lunatic? They *all* say it, a lunatic, a lunatic, a lunatic!'

Pascal was choking on sobs. Feeling faint, he dropped his head among the files and cried non-stop, his body heaving. And gripped by a sort of religious terror and feeling the fatality that governs bloodlines, Clotilde quietly walked away, holding her breath; for she knew only too well that he would have been horribly ashamed if he'd sensed she was there.

A long period of soul-destroying bleakness followed. January was very cold. But the sky remained wonderfully cloudless, the sun shone unfailingly every day in the unblemished blue; and, at La Souleiade, the windows of the workroom, facing south, turned it into a green-house, keeping the temperature there delectably mild. They didn't even light the fire, the sun never left the room, laying a gauze of pale gold in which flies, spared by the winter, slowly flew around. There was no sound in there apart from the quivering of their wings. It was sleepily still and warm, like a patch of spring that had been sealed off and preserved inside the old house.

It was there one morning that Pascal in his turn overheard some-thing, the tail end of a conversation, that made his suffering much worse. He hardly ever left his room before lunch these days, and so it was Clotilde who received Doctor Ramond, ushering him into the workroom, where they'd begun chatting quietly, huddled together in the bright sunlight.

This was the third time in a week that Ramond had come round. Personal circumstances, above all the need to firmly consolidate his position as a Plassans doctor, compelled him not to put off marrying any longer; and he wanted a decisive answer from Clotilde. Twice before already, other people had been in the way, preventing him from speaking. As he only wanted to hear the answer from her, he had resolved to clear things up with her directly in a frank and open con-versation. Their camaraderie, and shared level-headedness and integr-ity, encouraged him to take this approach. And he was winding up, smiling and gazing into her eyes.

'I assure you, Clotilde, this is the best course for us to take... You know I've loved you for a long time. I feel deep affection and esteem for you. But if that's not enough, there's also the fact that we'll get on perfectly and be very happy together, I'm certain of it.'

She had not cast her eyes down, but returned his candid gaze with a friendly smile. He really was very handsome, in the absolute prime of youth.

'Why', she asked, 'don't you marry Mademoiselle Lévêque, the solicitor's daughter? She's prettier and richer than I am, and I know she'd be so happy... My dear friend, I fear you're making a silly mis-take choosing me.'

He remained unruffled, seemingly convinced of the rightness of his decision.

'But I don't love Mademoiselle Lévêque, I love you. Besides, I've thought everything through and I can only tell you again that I know exactly what I'm doing. Say yes, you yourself couldn't make a better choice.'

At that she became solemn, and a shadow flitted across her face, the shadow of the thoughts, of the inward, almost unconscious battles that had kept her silent for many long days.

'Well then, my friend, since it's quite serious, allow me not to give you an answer today, let me have another few weeks. Maître is really very sick, and I'm troubled, too; and you wouldn't want to get me on an impulse... I assure you I'm also very fond of you. But it would be wrong to make a decision right now, there's too much misery at home... So, we're agreed, no? I won't keep you waiting long.'

To change the subject, she added:

'Yes, Maître worries me. I wanted to see you, wanted to tell you—you especially... The other day, I caught him crying his eyes out, and it's clear to me that he's haunted by fear of going mad... The day before yesterday, when you were talking to him, I could see you were studying him. Tell me honestly, what do you think of his condition? Is he in danger?'

Doctor Ramond let out a cry of protest. 'No, no! He's overdone it and come a cropper, that's all!... How can a man of his calibre, who's spent so much time looking into nervous diseases, be so off the mark? It really is dispiriting if the clearest and most vigorous minds can shut down like this!... In his case, that brainwave of his, the hypodermic injections, would be just the thing. Why doesn't he inject himself?'

But the young woman gestured in despair and said that Pascal didn't listen to her any more, that she couldn't even speak to him now, so he added:

'Well then, I'll talk to him.'

It was at that moment that Pascal emerged from his room, drawn by the sound of voices. But seeing them both so close together, so animated, so young and so beautiful, in the sunlight, as though cloaked in sunlight, he stopped dead at the door. His eyes widened and his pale face fell.

Ramond had taken Clotilde's hand, wanting to keep her a bit longer.

'That's a promise, isn't it? I'd like the wedding to take place this summer... You know how much I love you, and I'll be waiting for your answer.'

'Of course,' she replied. 'Before another month goes by, everything will be settled.'

Pascal was so dazed he reeled. So now this lad, a friend, a student, had infiltrated his house to rob him of what was his! He should have anticipated this development, but the sudden news of a possible wedding surprised him, crushed him as though it were some unforeseen catastrophe, in which his life would finally come crashing down in ruins. This creature he had moulded, whom he thought of as his, was about to take herself off without regret, she was about to leave him to die all alone, in his own little hole! Only the day before, she had caused him such pain he'd wondered if he wouldn't part company with her, pack her off to her brother, who was still clamouring for her. For a moment, he'd even decided to go ahead with this separation, so they could both have some peace. But now to suddenly find her there with this man, to hear her promising an answer, to think that she was about to marry, that she'd soon leave him—this was a terrible stab to the heart.

He strode in heavily and the two young people turned round, slightly embarrassed.

'Well, hello Maître! We were just talking about you,' Ramond said brightly at last. 'Yes, we were conspiring, I have to confess... Look, why don't you administer to yourself? You don't have anything serious, you'd be back on your feet in a fortnight.'

Pascal, who had dropped onto a chair, kept his eyes on them. He had the strength to get himself under control, and no trace of the injury he had received showed on his face. He would surely die of it, yet no one in the world would suspect what particular malady had carried him off. It was a relief for him, though, to be able to take offence and vehemently refuse to swallow as much as a glass of herbal tea.

'Administer to myself! What's the point?... Isn't the jig up for this old carcass of mine?'

Ramond insisted, smiling with his usual quiet composure.

'You'll bury the lot of us. This is just an irregularity, and you know very well you have the cure... Inject yourself...'

He was unable to continue, and that was the final straw. Pascal flew into a rage, asked if they wanted him to kill himself the way he'd killed

Lafouasse. His injections! Now there was an invention he had every reason to be proud of! He disowned medicine, vowed he'd never touch another sick person again. When you were no longer good for anything, you curled up your toes, and that was better for all concerned. It was, moreover, what he intended to do, and as quickly as possible.

'Rubbish!' Ramond concluded, deciding to take his leave for fear of inflaming him further. 'I leave you in Clotilde's hands, so my mind's completely at ease... Clotilde will take care of things.'

But that morning Pascal had received the ultimate blow. He took to his bed as soon as the light faded and stayed there till the following night, without once opening his door. Clotilde became anxious after a while, and banged violently on the door with her fist: not a breath, not a murmur in reply. Martine herself came up and begged Monsieur, through the keyhole, to at least tell her if he needed anything. A deathly silence reigned, it felt as if the room were empty. Then, on the morning of the second day, as Clotilde tried the handle on the off-chance, the door yielded; perhaps it had been unlocked for hours. She was able to freely enter this room in which she had never set foot. It was a big room, made cold by its north-facing aspect, but all she could see was a small, curtainless iron bed, a shower bath in a corner, a long blackwood table, a few chairs, and on the table, and on rows of shelves running along the walls, a whole alchemy set, mortars, burners, apparatuses, cases of surgical instruments. Pascal was up and dressed and sitting on the edge of the bed, which he'd worn himself out making, unassisted.

'Won't you let me look after you, then?' she asked, moved and fearful, not daring to go too far in.

He waved his hand in defeat.

'Oh, you can come in! I won't hit you, I don't have the strength.'

From that day forward, he could tolerate her being near him, and he allowed her to attend to him. But he was awkwardly capricious, all the same, and didn't want her coming in whenever he was in bed, gripped by a kind of morbid bashfulness; and he would make her send Martine instead. He rarely stayed in bed, anyway, but would drag himself from chair to chair, powerless to do any kind of work. His illness got even worse, and he finally reached the point of utter despair, ravaged by migraines and stomach aches, without the strength, as he expressed it, to put one foot in front of the other, convinced every morning anew that he'd be sleeping that night at Les Tulettes, stark raving mad. He was wasting away and his face always looked sorrowful, and tragically beautiful, framed by his flowing white hair, which he continued to comb out of one last remaining shred of vanity. And although he agreed to let them look after him, he rudely rejected all remedies, having lost his faith in medicine.

He was now Clotilde's sole concern. She weaned herself off all else; first she started going to Low Mass, rather than High, then she stopped going to church altogether. In her eager longing for some kind of certainty and happiness, it seemed as if she was starting to be satisfied with this job that took up every minute of her time, centred on a beloved being, whom she would have liked to see cheerful and kind again. It meant giving all of herself, a certain self-neglect, a need to build her happiness on someone else's happiness; and doing so unconsciously, motivated only by her womanly heart, as she went through this crisis that was changing her profoundly without her caring to examine it. She still kept silent about the conflict that had divided them, it hadn't occurred to her yet to throw her arms around his neck and proclaim that she was his, that he could live again, since she was giving him her all. In her mind, she was just an affectionate daughter, watching over him the way any other relative would have done. And it was all very pure, very chaste, all thoughtful attentions, perpetual kindnesses, such an invasion of her life that the days now flew past, free of torment about the hereafter, filled only with the desire to heal him.

Where she faced a real battle, though, was in trying to get him to inject himself. He would flare up, disown his discovery, call himself an imbecile. And she would shout back. She was the one, these days, who had faith in science, and got indignant to see him doubt his genius. For a long while, he resisted; then, sapped of energy, yielding to the power she now assumed over him, he simply tried to spare himself the affectionate fight she would pick with him every morning. Right from the first injections, he experienced great relief, even if he refused to admit it. His head began to clear, his strength gradually returned. And so she triumphed, feeling a surge of pride in him, extolling his method, appalled that he didn't admire himself as an example of the miracles he could perform. He smiled, and began to see his case clearly. What Ramond had said was true, it must have been simple nervous exhaustion. Maybe he would pull through after all.

'Well! You're what's curing me, little girl,' he would say, without wanting to admit his hopes. 'Remedies, you see, only work if the right person administers them.'

The convalescence dragged on, lasting the whole month of February. The weather remained clear and cold, but not a day went by without the sun warming up the workroom with its stream of pale rays. And yet there were relapses, bouts of black melancholy, times when the invalid plunged back into his terror-stricken state; while his carer, in great distress, had to go and sit at the other end of the room so as not to inflame him further. Once again he despaired of ever recovering. He became bitter, and aggressively sarcastic.

It was on one of these bad days that, having gone to the window, Pascal spotted his neighbour, Monsieur Bellombre, the retired teacher, circling his trees checking to see if they had lots of budding fruit. The sight of the old man, so proper and so upright, perfectly serene in his selfishness, apparently never a prey to illness, suddenly threw him into a fit.

'Ah!' he growled. 'There's a man who'll never push himself too hard, who'll never risk his hide giving himself grief!'

And off he went from there, launching into an ironic encomium on selfishness. Being all alone in the world, having no friend, no wife, no child of one's own—what bliss! That hard-hearted miser who, for forty years, only had to box the ears of other people's children, who had retreated into solitude, without so much as a dog, but only a deaf-and-dumb gardener, older than he was himself—did he not represent the greatest possible sum of happiness on this earth? Not a single responsibility, not a single duty, not a single worry other than that of his precious health! He was a wise man, all right, he'd live to a hundred.

'Ah! Being afraid of life—honestly, there is no greater cowardice… To think I sometimes regret not having a child of my own about the place! Do we have any right to bring miserable creatures into the world? We need to kill off bad heredity, kill off life… The only decent man, fancy, turns out to be that old coward!'

Monsieur Bellombre continued peacefully circling his pear trees, in the March sun. He took care not to move too briskly, but conserved his vigorous old age. As he encountered a pebble on the path, he poked it aside with the end of his cane, then walked on at a leisurely pace.

'Just look at him! Isn't he well preserved, isn't he handsome, doesn't he unite all the blessings of Heaven in his dear self! I don't know anyone happier.'

Clotilde, who had kept quiet, was pained by Pascal's sarcasm, which she sensed was fraught with sadness. She usually defended Monsieur Bellombre and now felt a cry of protest mounting. Tears sprang to her eyes and she simply replied, in a hushed voice:

'Yes, but he isn't loved.'

That put an abrupt end to the distressing scene. As though he'd received a shock, Pascal turned round and looked at her. Unexpected compassion filled his eyes with tears, too, and he walked away so as not to cry.

Several more days passed, marked by this alternation of good and bad moments. Pascal's strength was returning, but only very slowly, and he was driven to despair by not being able to get back to work again without breaking out in copious sweat. If he'd persisted he would surely have fainted. And as long as he wasn't working he felt indeed that the convalescence would drag out. Yet he once again took an interest in his customary research pursuits, and he reread the last pages he'd written; but with this reawakening of the scholar in him, his old worries returned. At one stage he sank into such a slump that the entire house virtually disintegrated: people could have robbed him, taken everything, destroyed everything, and he wouldn't even have been aware of the disaster. Now, he'd gone back to being on the lookout, and he would pat his pocket to assure himself that the key to the cupboard was still there.

But one morning, when he'd slept in and only emerged from his room at around eleven o'clock, he caught sight of Clotilde in the workroom, quietly absorbed in doing an extremely accurate pastel drawing of a flowering almond branch. She looked up, smiling; and, picking up a key lying next to her, on her desk, tried to give it to him.

'Here, Maître!'

Astonished, not knowing what to make of it, he examined the thing she held out to him.

'What's this?'

'It's the key to the cupboard which must have fallen out of your pocket yesterday. I found it here this morning.'

At that, Pascal took the key, feeling extraordinarily moved. He looked at it, he looked at Clotilde. So, it was over? She wouldn't torment him any more, she wouldn't be furiously determined to steal everything, burn everything, any more? Seeing her also deeply moved, he felt his heart fill with boundless joy.

He grabbed her and hugged her.

'Ah, little girl, what if we managed not to be too unhappy!'

Then he went to his desk and opened a drawer and threw the key in, just as he used to do before.

From that moment, he recovered his strength and his convalescence progressed more swiftly. Relapses were still possible as he remained badly shaken. But he was able to write again, and the days weren't quite as oppressive. The sun also perked up, and it was already so warm in the workroom that they sometimes had to half close the shutters. He refused to see visitors, barely tolerated Martine, and had them tell his mother he was sleeping whenever she came to ask after him, as she did every now and then. And he was only happy in this delightful solitude, nursed by the rebel, yesterday's enemy, today's dutiful disciple. Long silences lay between them without making them feel uncomfortable. They reflected, and they dreamed, in an atmosphere of immense peacefulness.

One day, though, Pascal seemed very solemn. He was now convinced that his illness was purely accidental and that the issue of heredity had played no role in it. But that didn't fill him with any less humility.

'My God!' he murmured. 'How insignificant we are! I thought I was so strong, I was so proud of my sanity! And yet a bit of grief and a bit of fatigue nearly drove me mad!'

He fell silent, musing further, and his eyes lit up as he managed to get himself under control. Then, in a moment of wisdom and courage, he made up his mind.

'If I'm feeling better, I'm happy for you most of all.'

Clotilde didn't understand and looked up.

'Why's that?'

'Because of your wedding, of course... Now we'll be able to fix a date.'

She was stunned.

'Ah, that's right, my wedding!'

'Why don't we settle right now on the second week in June?'

'Yes, the second week in June; that would be good.'

They said no more; she brought her gaze back to her needlework, while he sat there motionless, his eyes far away, his face solemn.

7

THAT day, when she reached La Souleiade, old Madame Rougon spotted Martine in the vegetable garden planting leeks; and, making the most of the opportunity, she headed straight for the servant to have a chat and drag information out of her before stepping into the house.

Time was slipping by, and she was most aggrieved at what she called Clotilde's desertion. She strongly sensed that she would never again get to the files through her. The child was going astray, she'd been reconciled to Pascal since she'd been looking after him, and she was becoming so corrupted that her grandmother had not seen her at church again. So she'd gone back to her original idea, which was to get the girl out of the way, then defeat her son when he was on his own, weakened by isolation. Since she hadn't managed to persuade the girl to go and join her brother, she was now madly plumping for the marriage, and she would have liked to throw her at Doctor Ramond the very next day, unhappy as she was at the continual delays. She'd come running, this particular afternoon, driven by a feverish need to hasten things along.

'Hello, Martine… How is everyone here?'

The servant, who was on her knees with her hands full of dirt, raised her pale face, which she was protecting from the sun with the aid of a handkerchief tied over her coif.

'Well, the same as usual, Madame, middling.'

And they chatted away. Félicité treated her like a confidante, a devoted old maid who was now one of the family, someone you could say anything to. She began by questioning her, wanted to know if Doctor Ramond had been over that morning. He had, but as far as Martine knew, they'd only talked about this and that. At this news, Félicité despaired, for she herself had seen the young doctor the day before and he had confided in her, told her how dejected he was not to have a definite answer, in a hurry now to at least get Clotilde's word. It could not go on like this, the girl would have to be forced to commit herself.

'He's too nice,' she cried. 'I told him so, too. I knew very well that yet again this morning, he wouldn't dare demand a straight answer…

But I'm going to make it my business. We'll soon see if I don't force that girl to come to a decision.'

Composing herself, she added:

'My son's back on his feet now, he doesn't need her.'

Martine, who had resumed planting her leeks, bent double at the waist, swiftly straightened up.

'Ah! That's for sure!'

And her face, worn out by thirty years of domestic service, lit up with a rekindled flame. This was because a wound had been bleeding inside her ever since her master had been almost completely unable to bear her near him. The whole time he was ill, he had kept her away, accepting her services less and less, and finally shutting his bedroom door to her. She was dimly aware of what was going on and was tortured by an instinctive jealousy, in her worship of this master who'd owned her, heart and soul, for so many long years.

'No, of course we don't need Mademoiselle! I'm quite enough for Monsieur.'

Then, although normally so discreet, she went on to talk about her work in the garden, said she found the time to do the vegetables so they didn't have to pay for a day-labourer. The house was big, all right; but if you weren't frightened of work, you could get through it. Then again, when Mademoiselle left them, that'd be one less person to wait on, after all. And her eyes glimmered unconsciously at the thought of the profound solitude, the blessed peace in which they'd live, after the girl was gone.

She dropped her voice.

'It'll upset me because Monsieur will of course be so upset. I'd never have believed I'd wish for people to part ways like that... Only, Madame, I think like you do that it has to happen, because I'm very much afraid Mademoiselle will end up going bad here and that'll mean one more soul lost to the good Lord... Ah! It's sad, my heart's so heavy sometimes, it's bursting!'

'They're up there, the two of them, aren't they?' said Félicité. 'I'll go up and have a word, and I'll see to it personally that they put an end to this business once and for all.'

When she came down again an hour later, she found Martine still crawling around on her knees in the soft dirt, finishing her planting. Upstairs, as soon as she had got started and told them how she'd spoken to Doctor Ramond and he'd seemed impatient to know his

fate, she saw that Pascal agreed with her: he was solemn and he nodded as if to say he found Ramond's impatience only natural. Clotilde
herself had stopped laughing and seemed to be listening deferentially.
But she expressed some surprise. Why was she being rushed? Maître
had set the wedding for the second week in June, so she had two whole
months ahead of her. She would speak to Ramond about it very soon.
Marriage was so serious that she could surely be left to give it some
thought and commit herself only at the last minute. What's more,
she said these things in her virtuous manner, like someone determined to make a decision. And Félicité had had to be satisfied with
the evident desire the two of them felt that things should take the
most reasonable turn.

'To tell you the truth, I think it's done,' she concluded. 'He doesn't
seem to be putting any obstacles in the way, and she only seems to
want to act without haste, like any girl who intends to make up her
mind completely before committing herself for life... I'll give her
another week to think about it.'

Martine, squatting on her heels, stared at the ground, her face the
picture of gloom.

'Yes,' she muttered in an undertone, 'Mademoiselle's been doing
a lot of thinking of late... I bump into her all over the place. You talk
to her, she doesn't answer. It's like when people are coming down with
an illness and their eyes go all funny... Something's up, she's not herself any more, not herself...'

And at that she grabbed the dibble again and stuck in a leek, keen
to get on with her work; while old Madame Rougon, feeling somewhat easier, went off, certain, she said, that the marriage would take
place.

Pascal did, indeed, seem to accept Clotilde's marriage as if it were
decided on, inevitable. He hadn't spoken to her about it again; the rare
allusions they made to it between themselves, in their never-ending
conversations, left them serene; and it was simply as if the two months
they still had to live together would go on forever, an eternity whose
end they would never see. She, especially, would look at him with
a smile, and put off all vexations and decisions till later, with a sweetly
dismissive wave of the hand that indicated she trusted to life in all its
goodness. He, cured, getting stronger by the day, only grew sad the
moment he returned to the solitude of his room, at night, when she
had gone to bed. He would feel cold, a sharp chill would come over

him to think that a time was coming when he'd always be alone. Was it the onset of old age that made him shiver like this? Far off in the distance, it looked to him like a land of darkness, in which he could already feel all his energies dissolving. And he then regretted not having a wife, not having a child, and yearning would fill him with rebellion, and wring his heart with unbearable agony.

Ah, if only he'd lived! Some nights he even cursed science, which he accused of having robbed him of the best years of his life. He had let himself be devoured by work, and it had eaten up his brain, eaten up his heart, eaten up his muscles. And the only thing all that lonely passion had given birth to was books, ink-blackened paper that the wind would no doubt blow away, books whose cold pages froze his hands whenever he opened them. No warm woman's breast to press against his own, no soft child's hair to kiss! He had lived alone in his icy single bed, the bed of a self-absorbed scholar, and he'd die in it, alone. But was he really to die that way? Would he never taste the happiness enjoyed by ordinary street-porters, ordinary carters whose whips cracked below his windows? He grew panicky at the idea that he needed to hurry, for time would soon run out. All his untapped youth, all his repressed pent-up desires came surging back then through his veins, in a tumultuous flood. He vowed to love again, to come alive again and so drain to the last drop the passions he had never drunk, taste them all, before he was an old man. He would knock on doors, he would stop passers-by, he would roam through town and country. But then, the next day, when he'd had a good wash and got out of his room, all this feverish restlessness would subside, the torrid tableaux would fade away, and he went back to being his timid self. Then, the following night, fear of loneliness would throw him back into the same insomnia, his blood would burn again, and he would feel the same despair, the same rebellion, the same craving not to die without having known the love of a woman.

During those raging nights, his eyes wide open in the dark, he dreamed the same dream over and over. A girl, a traveller, was going past on the road, a girl of twenty, wonderfully beautiful; and she came in and knelt before him, with an air of submissive adoration, and he married her. She was one of those love pilgrims, like the ones you find in the old stories, who have followed a star to come and restore health and strength to a very powerful old king, covered in glory. He was the old king, and she adored him, working the miracle, she being only twenty, of giving him some of her youthfulness. He emerged triumphant from her arms, having recovered his courage and faith in life. In a fifteenth-century Bible he owned, illustrated with primitive wood engravings, one image in particular inspired him, and that was of old King David returning to his room, his hand on the bare shoulder of Abishag, the young Shunammite. He read the text on the opposite page: 'King David was old, and could get no heat, even though they covered him in clothes. So his servants said to him: "We will seek a young virgin for our lord the king, so that she may stand before the king, and cherish him, and lie in his bosom, and warm our lord the king." And so they sought in all the lands of Israel for a fair damsel and they found Abishag, a Shunammite, and brought her to the king. And the damsel was very fair and cherished the king, and ministered to him...'* The old king's chill—wasn't it the same chill that froze him now, as soon as he got into bed alone, beneath the grim ceiling of his room? And the girl traveller, the love pilgrim his dream brought him, wasn't she the devotional and docile Abishag, the passionate subject who gives herself completely to her master, for his sole good? He saw her there always, a slave happy to be annihilated in him, responsive to his every desire, of such stunning beauty that she was enough to furnish him with everlasting joy, of such sweetness that he felt himself immersed in scented oil just being near her. Then, as he sometimes leafed through the antique Bible, other engravings filed past and his imagination would lose itself in this vanished world of patriarchs and kings. What faith in the longevity of man, in his creative force, in his almighty power over womankind, with these extraordinary stories of hundred-year-old men still getting their wives pregnant, taking their servants to their beds, entertaining young widows and virgins who happened to be passing by! There was the centenarian Abraham, father of Ishmael and Isaac, husband of his own sister Sarah, obeyed master of his handmaid Hagar.* There was the enchanting idyll of Ruth and Boaz, the young widow turning up in the Bethlehem countryside during the barley harvest, and coming to lie down, one balmy night, at the feet of the master, who understands the right she is claiming, and marries her as her kinsman through marriage, according to the law.* There was the whole unbridled thrust of a strong and tenacious people, whose toil was destined to conquer the world, these men whose virility was never sated, these women who were always fertile, this stubborn, teeming race continuing on through all kinds of crimes, adulteries, acts of incest, amorous adventures beyond the realm of age or reason. His own dream, gazing on these primitive old engravings, ended up taking on a certain reality. Abishag came into his dismal room and lit it up and filled it with perfume, opened her bare arms, her bare body, all her divine nakedness, to make him the gift of her magnificent youth.*

Ah, youth! He was ravenous for it! In the twilight of his life, this passionate longing for youth was his revolt against the old age that loomed, a desperate desire to turn back time and start again. And mingled with this need he felt to start again, there was more, for him, than just a yearning for those first tastes of happiness, the inestimable value of days long gone, over which memory casts its spell; there was also an absolute determination to enjoy his health and his strength this time round, not to miss out on any of the joy of loving. Ah, youth! How he would have sunk his teeth into it, how he would have lived it over again, voraciously eating it all and drinking it all up, before he got old. He was overcome with anguish when he pictured himself again at twenty, slim-hipped, with the healthy vigour of a young oak, dazzling white teeth and thick black hair. With what brio he would have celebrated them, these gifts he'd once scorned, if by some miracle they were given back to him! And youth in a woman, any girl passing by, aroused him, stirred him deeply. Quite often this went beyond the individual to embrace the very idea of youth, the pure smell and the glow emanating from it, bright eyes, wholesome lips, rosy cheeks, and above all a delicate neck, silky and round, shaded by straggling curls at the nape; and, to him, youth always appeared fine and tall, exquisitely slender in its easy nakedness. His eyes would follow the apparition, his heart would be swamped with boundless desire. Youth alone was good and desirable, it was the flower of the world, the only beauty, the only joy, the only real good, along with health, that nature could bestow on a human being. Ah, to start again, to be young again, to have in your arms, all to yourself, all of young womanhood!

Now that the fine April weather had covered the fruit trees in flowers, Pascal and Clotilde resumed their morning walks around La Souleiade. These were his first sorties as a convalescent, and she would steer him to the already scorching threshing floor, taking him down the paths of the pine grove and bringing him back close to the terrace, which was sliced up by bars of shadow from the two centenarian cypresses that provided the only shade. The sun was turning the old flagstones white there and the vast horizon rolled away beneath the sparkling sky.

One morning, when Clotilde had been running around, she came back all excited and shaking with laughter, so giddy that she went up to the workroom without taking off her garden hat or the light piece of lace she'd tied around her neck.

'Ah!' she said. 'I'm hot!... And how silly of me not to get rid of these downstairs! I'll take them back down in a minute.'

When she'd first stepped inside, she had flung the lace on an arm-chair. And she tugged at the ribbons on the big straw hat, in a hurry to untie them.

'Ah, wouldn't you know it! Now I've gone and tightened the knot. I'll never get this off, you have to come to my rescue.'

Pascal was also excited by the lovely walk and felt cheered to see her so beautiful and so happy. He came over, had to stand facing her, very close.

'Wait, put your chin up... Oh, you keep moving, how do you expect me to see what I'm doing?'

She laughed all the louder and he saw the way the laughter swelled her breast with a wave of sound. His fingers got tangled under her chin, at that delicious part of the neck, and he accidentally touched the warm silk of her skin there. She was wearing a very low-cut dress with a scooped neck, and he breathed all of her in through the open-ing, a living bouquet of womanhood rising up, the pure smell of her youth, warmed up in the hot sun. All of a sudden, he was dazed and felt as if he was going to faint.

'Stop! I can't do anything if you won't keep still!'

A rush of blood made his temples throb, his fingers strayed, while she leant back further, unwittingly offering the temptation of her virginity. She was the apparition of magnificent youth in person, with bright eyes, wholesome lips, rosy cheeks, and above all a delicate neck, silky and round, shaded by straggling curls at the nape. And he was conscious of how fine she was, how willowy, with her small bosom, blossoming so exquisitely!

'There, it's done!' she cried.

Without knowing how, he had untied the ribbons. The walls were spinning, he could still see her, bareheaded now, with her luminous face, shaking her golden curls out as she laughed. And he was afraid he'd take her in his arms again, kiss her madly, in all the places she was showing some of her naked flesh. So he dashed away, carrying the hat, which he still had in his hand, and stammering:

'I'll go and hang it in the hall... Wait for me, I need to speak to Martine.'

Downstairs he took refuge in the abandoned salon and locked himself in securely, fearing she might get worried and come down looking for him. He was aghast and haggard, as though he'd just committed a crime. He spoke out loud, shuddering at the first cry that shot out of his mouth: 'I've always loved her, desired her to distraction!' Yes, ever since she had become a woman, he had adored her. And suddenly he saw clearly, he saw the woman she'd become, when, from the sexless imp, this gorgeous creature made for love had emerged, with her long shapely legs, her strong slender body, her round breasts, her round neck, her round supple arms. The nape of her neck and her shoulders were a pure milky-white, like lustrous white silk, infinitely soft. And it was monstrous, but it was absolutely true, he was hungry for all that, ravenously hungry for that youthfulness, for that perfect flower of flesh that smelled so good.

Then, having dropped onto a rickety chair, his face buried in both hands as if he no longer wanted to see the light of day, Pascal burst out sobbing. Oh, God! What was to become of him? A little girl his brother had left in his care, whom he had brought up like a good father should, and who had now turned into this temptress of twenty-five, womanhood in her overwhelming almighty power! He felt as defenceless and weak as a child—more so.

And over and above the physical desire, he still loved her with an immense tenderness, smitten as he was with her moral and intellectual distinction, her emotional integrity, her subtle mind, so fearless and so sharp. Even the discord between them, all that anxiety over the mysteries of religion she was tormented by, had ended up making her precious to him, as a being different from him, in whom he had rediscovered something of the world's infinity. He liked it when she rebelled and stood up to him. She was both student and companion; he saw her as he had moulded her, with her big heart, her passionate honesty, her unfailing good sense. And she was just as necessary and attentive to him as ever, he couldn't imagine being able to breathe the air in a place where she would no longer be, he needed her breathing, the swirl of her skirts around him, her thoughts and her affection by which he felt enveloped, her glances, her smile, her whole everyday womanly life, which she had given to him, which she could not be so cruel as to take away. The thought that she was going to go was like the sky falling on his head, the end of everything, the final darkness. She alone existed in all the world, she was the only noble and good woman, the only intelligent and wise woman, the only beautiful woman, so beautiful it was a miracle. Why, then, since he adored her and he was her master, didn't he go back upstairs and take her in his arms again and kiss her like the idol she was? They were both perfectly free, she knew everything there was to know about the facts of life, she was old enough to be a woman. It would be bliss.

Pascal had stopped crying and now rose to his feet, ready to head for the door. But all of a sudden he dropped back onto the chair, overcome by fresh sobs. No! It was vile, it was impossible! Suddenly the white hair on his skull felt like frost; and he hated himself for being so old—fifty-nine!—when she was only twenty-five. Once more he shivered in terror, knowing for certain that she possessed him, that he would be powerless against the daily temptation. And he saw her getting him to untie the ribbons on her hat, calling him, forcing him to lean over her from behind to correct some detail in her work; and he saw himself blinded, bewitched, mauling her neck, mauling the nape of her neck, by the mouthful. Or else, and this was even worse, in the evening, when they would both delay sending for the lamp, languishing as complicit night slowly fell, and then tumbling helplessly to their downfall, reaching the point of no return in each other's arms. He was swept by a burst of violent anger at a development that was not only likely but inevitable, if he could not find the courage to let her go. It would be the worst of crimes on his part, an abuse of trust, a sordid seduction. He felt so revolted that he rose bravely this time, and found the strength to go back up to the workroom, fully resolved to fight.

Upstairs Clotilde had quietly gone back to doing a drawing. She didn't even turn her head, but contented herself with saying:

'You took your time! I was beginning to think Martine was ten sous out in her accounts.'

This routine joke about the servant's avarice made him laugh. And he, too, quietly went and sat at his table. They didn't speak again till lunchtime. A great sweetness flooded him, calmed him, now that he was near her. He risked a look at her, and was moved by her fine profile, her air of seriousness, as if she were a little girl acting grown up and concentrating hard. Had he simply had a nightmare downstairs? Was it going to be as easy as this for him to control himself, after all?

'Ah!' he cried, when Martine called them. 'I'm famished! You see if I don't get my muscles back!'

She gaily came and took his arm.

'That's the spirit, Maître! A person needs to be happy and strong!'

But that night, in his room, the agony started all over again. At the idea of losing her, he had to stuff his face in the pillow to stifle his cries. The pictures in his head became clearer, he saw her in the arms of another man, giving to another man the gift of her virginal body, and he was tortured by excruciating jealousy. He would never manage to be heroic enough to consent to such a sacrifice. All sorts of contradictory plans collided in his poor overheated brain: to put her off the marriage and keep her close to him, without her ever suspecting his passion; to go away with her, travel from town to town, keep both their brains busy with endless study, and that way preserve their master–student companionship; or even, as a last resort, to pack her off to her brother so she could be his sick nurse, lose her rather than hand her over to a husband. And at every one of these solutions, he felt his heart break and cry out in anguish, in his urgent need to possess her, body and soul. He was no longer content with her mere presence, he wanted her to himself, for himself, in himself, such as she rose up, radiant, against the darkness of his room, in her perfect nakedness, arrayed only in her loosely flowing hair. His arms embraced empty space and he leapt out of bed, tottering like a man intoxicated; and it was only in the great black calm of the workroom, his bare feet on the parquet floor, that he woke from this sudden madness. Where had he been going, for God's sake? To knock on the door of this sleeping child? Perhaps burst it open with a shove of the shoulder? The pure soft breathing he thought he could hear, in the deep silence, hit him in the face, knocked him backwards, like a sacred blast. And he went back to his room and threw himself down on his bed in a fit of shame and horrible despair.

When he got up the next day, shattered by insomnia, Pascal was resolved. He had his usual daily shower and felt bolstered, saner. The decision he'd come to was to force Clotilde to give her word. Once she had formally agreed to marry Ramond, it seemed to him that this irrevocable solution would bring him relief, would rule out any insane hopes he might have. It would mean one more barrier, an insurmountable one, between him and her. He would, from that moment, be armed against his desire, and if he went on suffering, suffering was all it would be, without this hideous dread of turning into a man without morals, of getting up one night to take her ahead of the other man.

When he explained to Clotilde that morning that she couldn't dither any longer, that she owed it to the fine young man who'd been waiting so long to give him a decisive answer, she seemed at first amazed. She looked him square in the face, straight in the eye; and he found the strength not to be disconcerted, but simply pressed the point with a vaguely disappointed air as though saddened to have to say these things to her. Finally, she gave a faint smile and turned her head away.

'So, Maître, you want me to leave you?'

He did not answer directly.

'My darling, I'm telling you it's getting ridiculous. Ramond would have every right to take offence.'

She went and tidied up some papers on her desk. Then, after another pause, she said:

'That's funny, now you're siding with Grandmother and Martine. They've been at me to get it over with... I thought I still had a few more days. But really, if all three of you are going to gang up on me...'

She didn't finish and he didn't push her to make herself clearer, either.

'So,' he asked, 'when would you like me to tell Ramond to come round?'

'But he can come round whenever he likes, I've never minded him visiting... Don't worry, I'll let him know we're expecting him, one of these afternoons.'

Two days later the scene was repeated. Clotilde had done nothing and, this time, Pascal was vehement. He was in too much pain, he had panic attacks the moment she was no longer there to calm him down with her sunny openness. And he demanded, in harsh terms, that she behave like a responsible girl and not toy any longer with a man who was honourable and who loved her.

'For heaven's sake! Since it's got to be done, let's get it over with! I warn you, I'm going to send word to Ramond to be here tomorrow, at three.'

She had listened, eyes on the ground, mute. Neither of them seemed to want to broach the question of whether the marriage had actually been decided on; but they acted as though a decision had been made previously, and was absolutely definite. When he saw her lift her head again, he trembled, for he had a sudden inkling: he sensed she was on the point of saying she had examined her heart and decided to decline the marriage proposal. What would happen to him then, what would he do, God! Already he was flooded with boundless joy and a mad fear. But she was watching him, with that discreet and tender smile that never left her lips these days, and she answered with apparent meekness:

'As you like, Maître. Send him word to be here tomorrow, at three.'

Pascal had such an appalling night that he got up late, pretending his migraines had come back. He only felt some relief under the freezing cold water of the shower. Then, at around ten, he went out, saying he was going himself to Ramond's. But the excursion had a different purpose: he knew that, at a second-hand clothes dealer in Plassans, there was a bodice all in old Alençon lace, a marvel just lying there, waiting for a lover's crazily generous impulse; and the idea had come to him, in all the torments of the night, to make a present of it to Clotilde, who could embellish her wedding dress with it. This bitter idea of decking her out himself, of making her really beautiful and dressing her all in white for her to bestow her body, soothed his heart, worn out from sacrifice. She knew the bodice, she'd admired it with him one day, wonderstruck, only wanting it so she could drape it over the shoulders of the Virgin at Saint-Saturnin, an antique Virgin carved in wood and worshipped by the congregation. The second-hand clothes dealer handed it to him in a small cardboard box which he could conceal and which he hid at the back of his secretaire as soon as he got home.

At three o'clock, when Doctor Ramond appeared, he found Pascal and Clotilde in the workroom, where they'd been waiting for him, excited and unnaturally cheery, though they'd avoided mentioning his visit again among themselves. Now there was laughter, a big, loud welcome of exaggerated cordiality.

'I see you're completely well again, Maître!' the young man said. 'You've never looked sturdier.'

Pascal shook his head.

'Oh, sturdier, maybe! Only my heart's no longer in it.'

This involuntary admission spurred a movement from Clotilde, who was watching them as if, through the very force of circumstance, she couldn't help but compare them. There was Ramond, the handsome doctor, adored by women, with his smiling face and magnificent head, and his black beard and powerfully luxuriant black hair, all the lustre of his youthful virility. And there was Pascal who, with his white hair and his white beard, that still thick snowy fleece, had conserved the tragic beauty he'd acquired over the six months of torture he had just been through. His sorrowful face had aged slightly, only his big eyes were the same, and they were the eyes of a child, brown eyes, lively and limpid. At that moment, though, every one of his features expressed such sweetness, such heightened goodness, that Clotilde ended up fixing her gaze on him, with profound tenderness. There was a silence, a little shiver that ran through everyone's heart.

'Well then, children,' Pascal began again heroically, 'I believe you have things to say to each other... I have to attend to something downstairs, but I'll be up again shortly.'

And off he went, beaming at them.

As soon as they were alone, Clotilde, utterly frank as always, went to Ramond with both hands outstretched. She took his hands in hers and held them while she spoke.

'Listen, my friend, I'm going to cause you a lot of pain... But you mustn't be too angry with me, as I swear I love you deeply as a friend.'

He understood immediately and went very pale.

'Clotilde, please, don't give me an answer now, take your time, if you'd like to think about it further.'

'There's no point, my friend, my mind's made up.'

She looked at him with her beautiful honest eyes, not letting go of his hands, so that he could clearly feel that she was both coolly collected and loving. He was the one who went on, quietly:

'So, you're saying no?'

'I'm saying no, and I assure you it hurts me to do so. Don't ask me any questions, you'll know everything later.'

He had taken a seat, broken by the emotion he was keeping in check, a stable and self-possessed man whose equilibrium was not supposed to be thrown by even the greatest emotional blow. Never had any sorrow overwhelmed him like this. He sat there speechless as she, standing, continued:

'And above all, my friend, don't think I've been flirting with you... If I let you hope, if I kept you waiting for my answer, it's because

I truly didn't know my own heart… You can't imagine what a crisis I've gone through, an absolute tempest in complete darkness, and I'm only just finding my way again at last.'

Finally he spoke.

'Since you don't want me to, I won't ask any questions… Anyway, there's only one question for you to answer. Don't you love me, Clotilde?'

She didn't hesitate, but said gravely, with a heartfelt sympathy that softened the frankness of her answer:

'It's true, I don't love you, I only feel the truest affection for you.'

He rose to his feet and waved away the kind words she was still searching for.

'It's over, we won't speak about it ever again. I wanted you to be happy. Don't worry about me. Right this moment, I feel like a man whose house has just fallen on his head. But I'll just have to get out from under it.'

His pale face was suddenly flushed, he was choking and he went to the window and then came back, his feet heavy, trying to regain his self-command. He gulped in air. In the painful silence, they could hear Pascal noisily coming back up the stairs to announce his return.

'Please,' Clotilde murmured quickly, 'let's not say anything to Maître just yet. He doesn't know what I've decided, I want to break it to him myself, gently, since he was so keen on this marriage.'

Pascal stopped in the doorway. He was staggering, out of breath, as if he'd taken the stairs too fast. But he still had the strength to smile at them.

'Well then, children, are you agreed?'

'Why, yes, of course,' Ramond replied, shaking just as hard as he was.

'So, it's all settled?'

'Completely,' Clotilde piped up in turn, suddenly feeling faint.

At that, Pascal stepped inside and, leaning on the furniture, made his way to his worktable, where he flopped into his armchair.

'Ah! Ah! As you can see, I'm still none too steady on my pins. It's this old carcass of a body… Never mind! I'm very happy, very happy, my children, your happiness will fix me up again.'

But then, when Ramond had taken himself off after a few minutes of conversation, Pascal's turmoil seemed to return on finding himself alone again with Clotilde.

'It's all over, well and truly over, you swear?'

'Absolutely over.'

After that he didn't say another word, just nodded, as though repeating that he was delighted, that it was perfect, that they could all now live in peace. He closed his eyes and pretended to be falling asleep. But his heart was beating hard enough to burst and his determinedly closed eyelids held back tears.

That evening, at around six, Clotilde went downstairs to give Martine an order and Pascal took advantage of the opportunity to put the little box containing the lace bodice on her bed. She came back up and wished him the usual good night; and he had been back in his room for a good twenty minutes and was already in his shirtsleeves, when there was a loud burst of glee at his door. A small fist knocked, a young voice cried out, laughing all the while:

'Come, come and see!'

He couldn't resist opening his door at this youthful appeal, infected by such contagious joy.

'Oh! Come and see, come and see what a little birdie has dropped on my bed!'

And she marched him to her room without his being able to object. She had lit the two candles there, and the whole welcoming old room, with its wall hangings of such a delicate faded pink, looked as if it had been converted into a chapel; and on the bed, like an altar cloth, offered up to the worship of the faithful, she had laid out the bodice in old Alençon lace.

'No, you can't imagine!... Just think, I didn't even see the box at first. I did my little chores that I do every night, I got undressed, and it wasn't till I went to hop into bed that I spotted your present... Ah! What a shock, my heart missed a beat! I knew I'd never be able to wait till tomorrow morning, so I slipped a petticoat back on and came running to get you!'

Only then did he notice that she was half naked, like the night of the storm when he'd caught her in the act of stealing his files. And she looked divine, with the willowy fineness of her virginal body, and her shapely legs and her supple arms, and her slender chest with its small hard breasts.

She had taken his hands and was holding them in her own small hands, captivating hands made for caressing.

'You're so kind! Thank you so much! Such a marvel, such a beautiful present, and for a nobody like me!... And you remembered, you remembered I'd admired it, this old work of art, I told you the Virgin

of Saint-Saturnin alone was worthy of wearing it on her shoulders...
I'm so happy, oh, so happy! For it's true—I love nice things, I love
nice things so much, you know, that I sometimes wish I had quite mad
things to wear, frocks woven out of sunbeams, veils as fine as air, made
of the blue of the sky... How beautiful I'll be! How very beautiful!'

Radiant in her excited gratitude, she pressed herself against him,
keeping her eyes on the bodice, and forcing him to marvel with her.
Then her curiosity was suddenly pricked.

'But tell me, why have you given me this gorgeous present?'

Ever since she'd come running to get him, with such a loud burst
of glee, Pascal had been floating on a cloud. He was moved to tears by
such loving gratitude, and he stood there, without the terror he'd
dreaded, soothed, on the contrary, thrilled, as if some great miraculous happiness were drawing near. This room, which he never entered,
had the peacefulness of sacred places that satisfy our unslaked thirst
for the impossible.

His face, however, expressed some surprise, and he replied:

'This present, my darling, is for your wedding dress, of course.'

She, now, stood there for a second stunned, seeming not to com-
prehend. Then, smiling the strange soft smile she'd been wearing for
the past few days, she brightened up again.

'Ah, yes, that's right, my wedding!'

She became serious once more and asked:

'So, you're getting rid of me, it was so you wouldn't have me around
any more that you were so keen for me to get married... You still feel
I'm your enemy, is that it?'

He felt the torment return and looked away, wanting to be heroic.

'My enemy, yes, well, you are, aren't you? We've both put each
other through so much pain, these past few months! It's better that
we part... Besides, I don't know what you think, you never gave me
the answer I was waiting for.'

In vain she tried to catch his eye. She began talking about that terrible night when they'd gone through the files together. It was true, the
shock to her whole being had been so violent, she still hadn't told him
if she was with him or against him. He was right to demand an answer.

She took his hands again and forced him to look at her.

'And it's because I'm your enemy that you're sending me away?...
Listen to me! I am not your enemy, I am your servant, your creation, and
your possession. Do you hear? I am with you and for you, for you alone!'

He shone, boundless joy sparkled in his eyes.

'I'll put it on, this lace bodice, oh yes! It will be worn on my wedding night, because I want to be beautiful, very beautiful—for you... Don't tell me you still don't know! You are my master, it's you I love...'

With a frantic gesture he tried to close her mouth, but to no avail. She finished with a cry.

'And it's you I want!'

'No, no! be quiet! you're driving me insane!... You're engaged to another man, you've given him your word, luckily all this madness is impossible.'

'The other man—I compared him to you and I chose you... I sent him away, he's gone and he won't be back... There are only the two of us, it's you I love, and you love me, I know that perfectly well, and I'm giving myself to you...'

A shiver shot through him, but he was already no longer fighting, swept up as he was into the eternal desire—to hold and breathe in through her all the delicacy and scent of a woman in her prime.

'Take me, then, since I'm giving myself to you!'

It was not a fall from grace, life in all its glory bore them aloft, and they became one in rapturous elation. The spacious complicit bedroom, with its old-fashioned furniture, seemed suddenly full of light. And they had no more fear or pain, or scruples: they were free, she gave herself knowing what she was doing and wanting to do it, and he accepted the supreme gift of her body as if it were a priceless blessing that he had won through the strength of his love. The place, the time, the difference in their ages all vanished. All that remained was immortal nature, the passion that possesses and creates, the happiness that insists on being. She, enthralled and delicious, gave out only a soft cry as she lost her virginity; and he, in a sob of ravishment, embraced her fully, thanking her, without her knowing what he meant, for having made a man of him again.

Pascal and Clotilde went on lying in each other's arms, drowning in a wave of ecstasy, exquisitely joyous and triumphant. The night air was soft, the silence had a tender calmness. Hours and hours went by in this bliss of savouring their joy. At once she had murmured in his ear, in a caressing voice, slowly and over and over:

'Maître, oh! Maître! Maître...'

And that one word, the word she used to use, in days gone by, now took on a profound significance, widened and drew itself out, as if it expressed the whole gift of her being. She said it over and over again with grateful ardour, a woman who now understood and yielded. Wasn't this mystical theology defeated, reality accepted, life honoured, with love at last experienced and satisfied?

'Maître, Maître, this has been coming for so long, I must tell you and confess my sins... It's true I used to go to church so as to be happy. The sad thing was that I couldn't believe: I wanted so much—too much—to understand, and their dogmas insulted my intelligence, their paradise felt to me like a childish invention... And yet, I didn't think the world stopped at sensation, I believed there was a whole unknown world that we should acknowledge—and that, Maître, I still believe. It's the notion of a hidden world, which even the happiness I've finally found, in your arms, will not erase... But this need for happiness, this need to be happy right away, to have some kind of certainty—how I suffered because of it! If I went to church, it was because something was missing and I was looking for it. My anguish was caused by this irresistible desire to satisfy my longing... You remember what you used to call my eternal need for illusion and lies. One night, out on the threshing floor, under a great starry sky—you remember? I loathed your science, I was incensed at the ruins it leaves scattered around, I averted my eyes from the hideous wounds it lays bare. And I wanted to take you away, Maître, to somewhere secluded, where both of us were unknown, somewhere far away from the world, where we could live in God... Ah! What torture, to be thirsty, and to flounder, and not be gratified!'

Gently, without a word, he kissed her on both eyelids.

'Then, Maître, you remember after that', she continued in her airy voice, as light as a breath, 'there was the great moral shock, the night of the storm, when you gave me that terrible lesson in life, as you went through your files in front of me. You'd already told me: "Know life, love it, live it the way it ought to be lived." But what a vast and horrifying river, driving everything along towards a human sea that it keeps on swelling endlessly for the sake of the unknown future!... So you see, Maître, the secret labour, inside me, started with that. It's there, in my heart and in my flesh, that the bitter force of reality was born. At first it was as if I'd been annihilated, the blow was so violent. I couldn't find my way again, I kept quiet because I had nothing definite to say. After that, little by little, the change occurred, even if I made a few final attempts to resist, so as not to admit defeat... But the truth was growing inside me a little more every day. I knew very well that you were my master, that there was no happiness apart from you, apart from your science and your goodness. You were life itself, tolerant and generous, telling all, accepting all, just for the love of health and effort, believing in the work of the world, making this labour that we all carry out with passion the very meaning of life, by inciting us to live, to love, to make new life, again and again, despite our abominations and our sorrows... Oh, living, living is the great task, it's the world's work carried on, and doubtless consummated in a night!'

Silent, he smiled and kissed her on the mouth.

'And, Maître, if I've always loved you, from earliest childhood, it was, I do believe, that terrible night that you branded me and made me yours... You remember you held me so violently I couldn't breathe. I was left with a bruise and drops of blood on my shoulder. I was half naked and it felt as if your body had entered mine. We wrestled, but you were stronger, and it left me with the need for a protector. At first I thought I'd been humiliated; then I saw that it was just an infinitely sweet act of submission... The whole time, I felt you inside me. Your every gesture, even at a distance, thrilled me, for it felt as if your hand had brushed my skin. I would have liked you to take me in your arms again and crush me till I melted in you, forever. And I was aroused, I sensed you felt the same desire, that the violence that had made me yours had made you mine, that you were struggling not to grab me as I went past, and hold on to me... Already, when you were sick and I was looking after you, I felt somewhat satisfied. That's when I knew. I stopped going to church, and I started being happy around you, you became certainty... Remember, I cried out to you on the threshing floor that there was something missing in our affection. It was empty, and I needed to fill it. What could we be lacking, if it wasn't God, the reason the world exists? And it was in fact a kind of divinity, complete possession, the act of love and of life.'

She began babbling after that and he laughed at their victory; and they made love again. The whole night was a beatitude, in that happy room, fragrant with the scent of youth and passion. When first light appeared, they flung the windows wide open to let in the spring. The fertilizing April sun rose in an immense sky of unblemished purity, and the earth, heaving with the quivering of sprouting seeds, gaily sang out their nuptials.

8

THEN came happy possession, the happy idyll. Clotilde was the new lease of life that had come to Pascal late, in his old age. She brought him sunshine and flowers, filling her lover's skirts full of them; and she gave him this youthfulness after thirty years of hard work on his part, when he was weary already, and fading, from having descended into the abysmal realm of human affliction. He came back to life under her big bright eyes, in the pure air of her breath. It meant renewed faith in life, in health, in strength, in new beginnings.

That first morning, after their wedding night, Clotilde was the first to leave the bedroom, though only around ten o'clock. In the middle of the workroom, she at once noticed Martine, planted squarely on her legs, looking alarmed. The night before, when he followed the young woman, the doctor had left his bedroom door open; and the servant, entering freely, had just noticed that the bed hadn't even been slept in. Then she'd had the shock of hearing the sound of voices coming from the other bedroom. She was so stunned, she looked quite comical.

And Clotilde, jubilant, radiant with happiness, bursting with an extravagant joy that swept all before it, threw herself at her and cried:

'Martine, I'm not going!... Maître and I, we got married.'

The old servant reeled under the blow. A wrench, terrible pain drained all colour from her poor face, worn out as it was from her nun-like self-denial, and framed by her white coif. She didn't utter a word, but spun on her heels, went downstairs and collapsed in her kitchen, her elbows on her chopping block, where she sobbed behind clasped hands.

Clotilde, anxious, disconsolate, followed her. And she tried to understand and console her.

'Come now, don't be silly! What's got into you?... Maître and I will love you just the same, we'll always keep you on... Just because we're married doesn't mean you'll be worse off. Just the opposite, the house will be gay now, from morning till night.'

But Martine only sobbed harder, wildly.

'At least answer me. Tell me why you're upset, why you're crying... Aren't you pleased to know Maître's so happy, so incredibly happy!... I'll go and call him, Maître, and he'll make you say something.'

At that threat, the old servant all of a sudden shot to her feet and rushed to her room, which was off the kitchen; and she slammed the door shut furiously and locked herself in. The young woman called, knocked, wore herself out, in vain.

Pascal ended up coming down at the noise.

'What on earth...?'

'It's that mule of a Martine! Imagine, she started sobbing when she heard of our happiness. And she's barricaded herself in, she won't budge.'

She did not budge, in fact. Pascal called and knocked in his turn. He railed, he relented. One after the other, they tried again. There was no answer, nothing came from the little room but a deathly silence. And they pictured it, that little room, maniacally clean, with its walnut chest of drawers and its monastic bed, hung with white curtains. No doubt the servant had thrown herself on that bed, in which she had slept alone all her adult life, so she could bite into her bolster and stifle her sobs.

'Oh well, too bad!' Clotilde finally said, in the selfishness of her joy. 'Let her sulk!'

Then, grabbing hold of Pascal with her cool hands, and lifting up to him her charming face, which still burned with an ardent desire to give herself to him and be his, she said:

'Do you know what, Maître, I'll be your servant today.'

He kissed her on her eyelids, overcome with gratitude; and she immediately began busying herself with lunch, throwing the kitchen into turmoil. She draped herself in a huge white apron and looked enchanting, her sleeves rolled up, showing her delicate arms, as though to take on some enormous task. As it happened there were cutlets already sitting there and she cooked them very nicely. She added scrambled eggs and even did the fried potatoes to perfection. And it was an exquisite lunch, interrupted twenty times by Clotilde in her zealous haste to run and get bread, water, a forgotten fork. If he'd let her, she'd have gone down on her knees to serve him. Ah, if only they were alone, if only there were just the two of them, in this big tender-hearted house, and they could feel far away from the rest of the world, and have the freedom to laugh and love one another in peace!

The whole afternoon they lingered over the housework, swept, made the bed. He had wanted to help her. It was a game, and they had fun like gleeful children frolicking. But still, every now and then, they would return to Martine's door and knock. Come now, this was madness, surely she wasn't going to let herself starve to death! Had anyone ever seen such a pig-headed woman, when no one had done anything or said anything to her! But the knocking always reverberated in the mournful emptiness of the bedroom. Night fell and this time they had to see to dinner, which they ate from the same plate, huddled together. Before going to bed they made one last effort, threatened to break the door down, but when they glued their ears to the wood, they didn't pick up so much as a shiver. And the next day, on waking, they were seized with serious concern when they went downstairs and saw that nothing had been moved and that the door remained tightly shut. It had been twenty-four hours since the servant had given any sign of life.

But although they had only been gone an instant, when they went back to the kitchen Clotilde and Pascal were amazed to see Martine seated at her table, picking the best leaves from a bunch of sorrel, for their lunch. She had taken back her place as servant without a sound.

'What on earth was wrong with you?' Clotilde cried out. 'Are you going to say something, now?'

She lifted her sad face, ravaged by tears. A great calm had come over it, however, and all that could be seen there now was forlorn old age in all its resignation. She looked at the young woman with an air of boundless reproach; then she bowed her head again without a word.

'So, are you angry with us?'

Faced with her mournful silence, Pascal intervened.

'Are you angry with us, my good Martine?'

At that, the old servant looked at him with her adoration of old, as if she loved him enough to put up with everything and stay on, regardless. She spoke at last.

'No, I'm not angry with anyone... Master is free. All is well, as long as he's happy.'

The new life became established from that moment. Twenty-five-year-old Clotilde, who had remained childlike so long, blossomed into a flower of love, exquisite and full. Since her heart had come to beat with love, the intelligent tomboy she had been, with her round head and short curly hair, gave way to an adorable woman, a fully fledged woman who loves to be loved. Her great charm, in spite of the science

she'd picked up randomly from her reading, was her virginal innocence, as though her unconscious wait for love had caused her to hold
back the gift of her being, her annihilation in the man she would one
day love. Of course, she had given herself as much out of gratitude
and admiration as out of tenderness, happy as she was to make him
happy, feeling joy at being no more than a small child in his arms,
a thing of his that he worshipped, a precious possession, that he
kissed on bended knee, in a fanatical private religion. The devout girl
of the past lived on in this docile self-surrender into the hands of an
old and all-powerful master from whom she derived her consolation
and her strength; and, beyond sensation, she once more experienced
the sacred thrill of the believer she remained. But more than anything,
this amorous creature, so womanly, so prone to swoon, offered the
delicious example of a woman who was robust and genial, one who
tore into her food with gusto, and brought with her some of the spir-
itedness of her grandfather the soldier, filling the house with the supple flurry of her limbs, the fresh bloom of her skin, the slender grace
of her waist, of her neck, of her whole young body, so divinely fresh.

And Pascal had himself become handsome again, through love, his
the serene beauty of a man who had remained vigorous despite his
white hair. The sorrowful countenance of the months of grief and
suffering he'd just endured was gone; his kind face had resurfaced,
with his big lively eyes, still so boyish, and his fine features beaming
with goodness; while his white hair and beard grew thicker, in a leo-
nine abundance whose snowy flow made him look younger still. He
had for so long lived the solitary life of a tirelessly hard-working man,
without vices, without debauchery, that he swiftly recovered his virility, which he'd kept in abeyance and which now resurged, rushing to
find satisfaction at last. He came back to life with a vengeance, a young
man's fire exploding in gestures, shouts, and a continual need to let
off steam and live. Everything became new and fabulous again to him,
the tiniest patch of the vast view filled him with wonder, a simple
flower threw him into ecstasy at its perfume, a word of everyday tenderness, weakened by use, moved him to tears, as if it were a completely fresh invention of the heart that millions of lips had not staled.
Clotilde's 'I love you' was an endless caress, the superhuman thrill
of which nobody else in the world could know. And along with health,
along with beauty, gaiety also returned to him, that tranquil gaiety
he once owed to his love of life and which was now lit up with the

sunshine of his passion, with all the reasons he had to find life better than ever.

Together, the two of them—youth in flower, mature strength, both so wholesome, so gay, so happy—made a radiant couple. For a good long month they shut themselves away and didn't once stir from La Souleiade. At first, the bedroom alone was enough for them, this room hung with an old and touching printed calico the colour of dawn, with its Empire furniture, its huge stiff chaise longue, and its tall monumental cheval-glass. They couldn't look without delight at the ornamental clock on the mantelpiece, an ormolu clock on which smiling Love gazed at sleeping Time. Wasn't that an allusion? They sometimes joked about it. A whole affectionate complicity came to them this way from the smallest objects, from these incredibly sweet old things, in this room where others had loved before them, where she herself, now, reintroduced her springtime freshness. One evening, she swore she'd seen, in the cheval-glass, a very pretty lady who was taking her clothes off and was certainly not her; then, once more in the grip of her need for fantasy, she dreamed out loud that she would appear like that, a hundred years later, to a woman in love in the next century, one happy night. He, enthralled, adored this room, in which he recognized all of her, even in the air he breathed there; and he lived in it, he no longer inhabited his own dark, icy room, which he'd rush out of as if out of a cave, with a shiver, the rare times he needed to go in. After that, the room where they also both liked to be was the vast workroom, where everything reminded them of their old habits and their past affection. They would stay there all day, though scarcely doing a scrap of work. The big carved oak cupboard stood there slumbering, doors closed, like the bookcases. On the tables, papers and books sat in piles, undisturbed. Like young newly-weds, they were taken up completely with their passion, beyond the realm of their old occupations, beyond the reach of everyday life. The hours seemed all too short, as they savoured the enchantment of being nestled together, often in the same big old armchair, happy with the peacefulness induced by the high ceiling, with this domain that was so entirely theirs, devoid of luxury and order, cluttered with familiar things and brightened up, from morning to night, by the lovely rekindling warmth of the April sun. Whenever he was seized with remorse and talked about working, she would bind her supple arms around his and keep him all to herself, laughing, not wanting him to get sick again from too much work. And, downstairs, they also liked the dining room, so cheery with its light-coloured wainscot panels, highlighted in blue, its old mahogany furniture, its big pastels of flowers, and copper ceiling light, always gleaming. They would wolf down their food there and only ran away, after each meal, to go back upstairs to their treasured solitude.

Then, when the house felt too small, they had the garden, the whole of La Souleiade. Spring advanced with the sun and as April waned, it brought out the roses. And what joy it was, this estate, so completely walled in, where nothing from the outside world could trouble them! There would be long hours of idling on the terrace oblivious to all care, facing the immense vista laying out the shady course of the Viorne and the slopes of Saint-Marthe, from the rocky ridges of the Seille to the powdery remotenesses of the valley of Plassans. Their only shade there came from the two centenarian cypresses, standing at each end like two enormous green altar candles, that could be seen from seven miles away. Sometimes they'd go down the slope for the sheer pleasure of coming back up the giant steps, clambering over the little drystone walls that held up the soil, checking to see whether the stunted olive trees and the spindly almonds were growing. More often they went for delicious walks in the pine grove under the fine needles, all drenched with sun and giving off a potent scent of resin; they'd do endless circuits around the enclosure wall, behind which could only be heard, now and then, the loud noise of a cart on the narrow Chemin des Fenouillères; or they paused and caught their breath, enraptured, on the ancient threshing floor, from where you could see all of the sky and where they liked to stretch out, tenderly remembering their tears of the time when their love, as yet unacknowledged even to themselves, erupted in squabbling beneath the stars. But their favourite retreat, the one into which they always ended up disappearing, was the quincunx of plane trees, the dense shade they cast, now a tender green, looking like lace. Underneath, enormous boxtrees that once formed the borders of the vanished French garden made a sort of labyrinth, of which they could never find the end. And the trickling water of the fountain, the eternal pure crystal vibration, seemed to them to sing in their hearts. They would sit there by the mossy basin, letting the twilight descend, gradually plunged into darkness beneath the trees, their hands joined, their lips meeting, while the water that could no longer be seen endlessly drew out its flutey note.

Right up to the middle of May, Pascal and Clotilde shut themselves away like this, without even stepping beyond the gate of their retreat. But one morning, as she was lingering in bed, Pascal vanished and came back an hour later; and finding her still in bed, gorgeously dishevelled, her arms bare, her shoulders bare, he clipped two brilliants on her ears, having just run and bought them after remembering that that day was her birthday. She adored jewellery, and was surprised and delighted, and didn't want to get up again she found herself so beautiful, undressed like this, with these stars at either side of her cheeks. From then on, no week passed without his ducking out once or twice of a morning to bring back some present. Any excuse was good enough for him, a feast day, a whim, simple joy. He took advantage of days when she felt like lazing around, arranged things so he was back home before she got up, and would deck her out himself, in bed. Rings were followed by bracelets, a necklace, a slender tiara. He would take out the other jewellery every time and make a game of putting every piece on her at once, while they laughed away. She was like an idol, sitting up in bed with her back against the pillow, covered in gold, with a gold band in her hair, gold on her bare arms, gold over her bare breasts, completely naked and divine, streaming with gold and precious stones. Her feminine vanity was delightfully gratified, and she let herself be loved on bended knee, sensing strongly that this was merely an exalted form of love. Yet she was beginning to scold a bit, to make sensible disapproving noises, for they were becoming absurd, finally, these presents, which she then had to cram together at the back of a drawer, without ever actually using them since she never went anywhere. They were completely forgotten after the moment of satisfaction and gratitude they procured in their novelty. But he wouldn't listen to her, carried away as he was by this veritable mania for giving, and unable to resist the urge to buy a thing as soon as the idea of giving it to her sprang to mind. It was the largesse of a big heart, a compelling desire to prove to her that he was always thinking of her, pride in making her the most gorgeous, the happiest and most desirable of women, as well as an even more profound love of giving, that drove him to divest himself, not to withhold an iota of his money, his flesh, his life. And then again, how good it was when he felt he'd given her real pleasure, when he saw her throw her arms around his neck, quite flushed, with big smacking kisses for thanks! After the jewels came frocks, frippery, toiletries. The room was becoming cluttered, the drawers were full to overflowing.

One morning, she got annoyed. He had produced a new ring.

'But I've told you, I never even put them on! And, look, if I did put them on, I'd have rings all the way to my fingertips!... Do be reasonable.'

He stood there abashed.

'So I didn't make you happy?'

She had to take him in her arms and swear to him, with tears in her eyes, that she was blissfully happy. He was so good to her, he did absolutely everything he could for her! But, as he had ventured, that particular morning, to talk about refurbishing the room, hanging fabric on the walls, laying a carpet, she implored him once again.

'Oh, no, no! For pity's sake!... Don't you touch my old room, everything in it brings back happy memories; it's where I grew up, where we first made love. I'd feel as though we were no longer at home.'

As for the household, Martine's stubborn silence condemned these excessive and needless outlays. She had adopted a less familiar attitude as if, in the new situation, she'd stepped back from her role as friendly housekeeper to her old rank of servant. Towards Clotilde, especially, she changed, treating her as a young lady, mistress of the house, not so much loved as obeyed. Whenever she went into the bedroom, whenever she served them in bed together, her face would wear its air of submissive resignation, worshipping her master always as she did, indifferent as she was to the rest. Two or three times, however, in the morning, her face appeared ravaged, her eyes swollen with tears, and she would avoid answering questions directly, saying it was nothing, that she'd caught a chill. And she never mentioned the presents filling the drawers, she seemed not even to see them, would wipe the drawers and tidy them up without a word of admiration or blame. But every fibre of her being was outraged by this mania for giving, which was evidently beyond her comprehension. She protested in her own way by overdoing her thrift, reducing the household expenditure, and running such a tight ship that she found a way of paring back the most trifling petty expenses. In this way she cut the milk down by a third, and only put out sweets now on Sundays. Pascal and Clotilde didn't dare complain but laughed behind her back at this extreme avarice, and started in again with the jokes that had kept

them amused for ten years, telling each other that, whenever she but-
tered the vegetables, she'd toss them in the colander so as to rescue
the butter that came through.

But, that particular quarter, she was keen to go through the
accounts. As a rule, she went herself to see the notary, Maître
Grandguillot, every three months, to collect the fifteen hundred
francs' interest, which she would then spend as she saw fit, recording
the expenses in a book. The doctor had stopped checking it years
ago, but now she brought it in and insisted he cast an eye over it.
He refrained, declared everything in order.

'It's just that, Monsieur,' she said, 'I've been able to put some
money aside, this time. Yes, three hundred francs... here.'

He looked at her, stunned. Normally she only just managed to
make ends meet. By what miracle of meanness had she been able to
save such a sum? He ended up laughing.

'Ah, my poor Martine! So that's why we've been having all those
potatoes! You're the best little saver there is, but you really could spoil
us a bit more.'

This discreet reproach cut her so deeply that she finally allowed
herself to allude to what was going on.

'Heavens, Monsieur! When we're throwing so much money out the
window, on one side, we'd do well to be cautious on the other.'

He understood but didn't get angry; on the contrary, he was
amused by the lesson.

'Ah, ha! So it's my accounts you're going over with a fine-tooth
comb! But you know, Martine, I, too, have savings lying idle.'

He was talking about the money his patients still gave him sometimes and which he threw into a drawer in his secretaire. For over
sixteen years, he'd been putting away nearly four thousand francs a year,
every year, and this would have ended up making a real little hoard,
gold and notes combined, if he hadn't been taking out, from day to
day, without counting, fairly large sums for his experiments and his
passing fancies. All the money for the presents came from that drawer
and, these days, he was opening it all the time. Besides, he thought of
it as inexhaustible; he was so used to taking what he needed out of it,
that it never occurred to him to worry that it might one day run out.

'Surely a person can enjoy his savings,' he went on chirpily. 'Since
you're the one who goes to the notary, Martine, you know very well
I've got my annuities set aside.'

To this she said, in the flat voice of misers haunted by the night-mare of some always looming disaster:

'And what if they all disappeared?'

Pascal gazed at her, thunderstruck, but contented himself with a vague expansive gesture in reply, since the possibility of some calamity had never even entered his mind. He thought avarice was driving her batty, and he laughed about it that night with Clotilde.

In Plassans, the presents were also cause for endless gossip. What was happening at La Souleiade, this very particular and very ardent flare-up of love, had become news, had spread, had cleared fences, no one knew exactly how, through that communicative force that fuels the curiosity of small towns, always on the alert. The servant, certainly, was not talking; but her manner perhaps sufficed, and word travelled even so; people had no doubt been keeping an eye on the amorous couple, over the walls. And then the present-buying had started, confirming everything, making everything worse. When the doctor combed the streets, early in the morning, went into jewellers', drapers', milliners', eyes would be riveted on the windows, his smallest purchases would be noted, and the whole town would know, the same evening, that he'd given yet another hooded silk stole, blouses trimmed with lace, a bracelet studded with sapphires. It was turning into a scandal, this uncle who had seduced his niece, who was squandering money on her as if he were a young man, who was decking her out as if she were some holy Virgin. The most extraordinary stories were starting to circulate, and people pointed La Souleiade out to each other as they went past.

But it was old Madame Rougon especially who went into a paroxysm of indignation. She had stopped going to her son's house on learning that Clotilde's marriage to Doctor Ramond was off. They had tricked her, they weren't fitting in with any of her designs. Then, after a good long month without contact, during which she hadn't been able to make head or tail of the pitying looks, the discreet expressions of sympathy and vague smiles that accompanied her everywhere she went, she had suddenly found out all about it, and it hit her like a blow to the head with a club. And to think that, when Pascal was sick, during that whole business when he'd behaved like a surly cur, she had ranted and raged, in her pride and fear, so as not to become the laughing stock of the town yet again! It was worse this time, the height of scandal, a brazen love affair the locals were gloating over!

Once again, the legend of the Rougons was in peril, her hapless son was evidently incapable of doing anything but destroy the family glory, so hard won. And so, in the heat of her fury, she who had made herself the custodian of that glory, determined to purge the legend by any means, clapped her hat on her head and ran to La Souleiade, with all the girlish briskness of her eighty years. It was ten o'clock in the morning.

Pascal, who was delighted at the complete break with his mother, was luckily not in, having been out and about for an hour or so in quest of an old silver buckle he thought could be used on a belt. And so Félicité stumbled on Clotilde, just as she was finishing getting dressed but still in a camisole, arms bare, hair loose, and as fresh and bright as a rose.

The first clash was brutal. The old lady poured out her feelings, waxed indignant, spoke angrily about religion and morals. At last, she wound up.

'Answer me, why have you done this dreadful thing, thumbing your nose at God and men?'

Smiling, and perfectly respectful with it, the young woman heard her out.

'But because we wanted to, Grandmother. We're free, aren't we? We don't have a duty to anyone.'

'No duty! What about me! And the family! Now they'll drag us through the mud again, if you think I enjoy that!'

All of a sudden her rage subsided. She looked at the girl and found her adorable. In her heart of hearts, what had happened didn't much surprise her, she couldn't actually care less, she just wanted it to end in a dignified manner so as to shut up the gossips. And wanting to be conciliatory, she exclaimed:

'Well then, get married! Why don't you get married?'

Clotilde stood there for a moment, surprised. Neither she nor the doctor had thought of marriage. She began to smile again.

'Will it make us any happier, Grandmother?'

'It's not about you, as I said it's about me, about all your relations... How, my dear child, can you joke about these sacred things? Have you lost all shame?'

But the young woman, without reacting, sweet as ever, made a broad sweep of her arm, as if to say she could not be ashamed of her sin. My God! When life entailed so much depravity and weakness, what harm had they done by indulging in the great happiness of being all to each other, under the dazzling sky? Apart from that, she didn't try to argue.

'No doubt we'll get married, since you'd like us to, Grandmother. He'll do whatever I want... But later, there's no rush.'

And she kept up her cheery equanimity. Since they lived away from society, why worry about society?

Old Madame Rougon had to take herself off, making do with this vague promise. From that moment on, about town she affected to have cut all ties with La Souleaide, that den of iniquity and shame. She didn't set foot there again and nobly bore the grief of this new affliction. But she didn't just lay down her arms, she remained on the lookout, ready to take advantage of the slightest opportunity to recover her position, with that tenacity that had always brought her victory.

It was then that Pascal and Clotilde stopped cloistering themselves away. It wasn't that they wanted to provoke people, they had no desire to respond to the nasty rumours by parading their happiness. It simply occurred as a natural extension of their joy. Their love had slowly needed more room, needed to stretch out, first beyond the bedroom, then beyond the house, and now beyond the garden and into the township, into the vast surrounds. It filled everything, it gave them the world. So the doctor quietly resumed his visits, taking the young woman along, and they would go off together through the walkways, through the streets, she on his arm, in a light-coloured dress, with a sprig of flowers in her hair, he buttoned up in his frock coat, with his broad-brimmed hat on his head. He was all white; she was all blonde. They sallied forth, heads high, straight-backed and smiling, so radiantly happy that they seemed to be walking in a golden nimbus. At first, there was a huge commotion, the shopkeepers came and stood at their doors, women leant out of windows, passers-by stopped to follow them with their eyes. People whispered, they laughed, they pointed them out to each other. It looked likely that this outbreak of hostile curiosity would even end up spreading to the street urchins and make them throw stones. But they were so beautiful, he stately and triumphant, she so young, so biddable and proud, that everyone soon felt an invincible urge to make allowances. People could not help but envy and love them, in what became an enchanted epidemic of tenderness. They cast a spell that turned hearts round. The new town, with its bourgeois population of officials and nouveaux riches, was the last to be won over. The Saint-Marc quarter, for all its rigorous conservatism, at once showed itself welcoming, discreetly tolerant, as they walked along the deserted footpaths, tufted with grass, past the silent and closed old mansions, from which emanated the lingering scent of lost loves. But it was above all the old quarter that swiftly made them welcome, this district where the common people, instinctively moved, felt the charm of legend, the deep-rooted myth of the couple, with the beautiful young woman lending support to her regal, rejuvenated master. They adored the doctor there for his goodness, and his companion quickly became popular, greeted by signs of admiration and praise the moment she appeared. The couple themselves, though, even if they seemed unaware of the initial hostility, now clearly sensed the forgiveness and melting affection that surrounded them; and this made them even more beautiful, and their happiness shone over the entire town.

One afternoon as Pascal and Clotilde turned into the Rue de la Banne, they saw Doctor Ramond on the other side of the street. Only the day before, in fact, they'd learned he'd decided to marry Mademoiselle Lévêque, the solicitor's daughter. That was definitely the most reasonable course of action, since in his position he really couldn't afford to wait any longer and the young woman, who was very pretty and very rich, loved him. He himself would certainly come to love her in time. So Clotilde was more than happy to give him a smile by way of congratulating him as a true friend, and Pascal greeted him with an affectionate wave. For a moment, Ramond was a little taken aback at running into them and stood there embarrassed, not knowing what to do. He made a move to cross the street. But a sense of tact must have restrained him, perhaps he felt it would be insensitive to break in on their dream, to invade the intimate isolation that they maintained even when being jostled in the street. And he restricted himself to a friendly salute, and a smile with which he forgave their happiness. It was, for all three of them, a very sweet moment.

Around this time, Clotilde kept herself entertained for several days with a large pastel, in which she evoked the tender scene between old King David and Abishag, the young Shunammite. And it was a sublime evocation, one of those soaring compositions into which her other self, the visionary, poured her taste for the mystical world. Against a background of scattered flowers, flowers shooting out like a shower of stars, of a barbarous luxuriance, the old king appeared face on, his hand resting on Abishag's bare shoulder; and the girl, very white-skinned, was naked to the waist. He was dressed sumptuously in a completely straight robe, heavy with precious stones, and wore the royal headband on his snowy hair. But she was even more sumptuous, with nothing but the lily-like silkiness of her skin, her slim-waisted willowy figure, her small round breasts, and her supple and exquisitely graceful arms. He held sway, a powerful and loved master leaning on this subject chosen from among all others, and she so proud to have been chosen, so delighted to give her king the restorative blood of her youth. Her whole translucent and triumphant nakedness expressed the serenity of her submission, the easy, absolute gift she made of her person, before the assembled multitude, in the broad light of day. And he was very grand and she was very pure, and there emanated from them something like a star-like radiance.

Up until the very last minute, Clotilde had left the faces of the two characters indistinct, in a sort of blur. Pascal joked about it, moved as he looked over her shoulder, guessing what she intended to do. And so it was, she filled in the faces with a few strokes of crayon: Old King David was him, and she was Abishag, the Shunammite. But they were enveloped in a dreamlike splendour; it was them deified, with long locks, all white for one, all blonde for the other, that covered them in an imperial mantle, their features exaggerated by ecstasy and heightened by the blissful happiness of angels, gazing and smiling with everlasting love.

'Oh, darling!' he cried. 'You've made us too beautiful, you've gone off into wonderland again—yes!—you remember, like in the days when I used to scold you for putting all those fantastic flowers from some other world up there.'

And he pointed to the walls, along which bloomed the weird and wonderful parterre of earlier pastels, that unreal flora that had sprouted in the middle of paradise.

But she gleefully protested.

'Too beautiful? We can't be too beautiful! I assure you, it's the way I feel us to be, the way I see us—it's the way we are... Here! look, and see if it isn't simple reality.'

She had taken the old fifteenth-century Bible, which was lying next to her, and she showed him the primitive wood engraving.

'You can see for yourself, it's exactly the same.'

He began to laugh, softly, before this serene but extraordinary assertion.

'Oh, you laugh! You can't see beyond details in the drawing. But it's the spirit you have to enter into... And look at the other engravings, see how it's the same thing again and again! I'll do Abraham and Hagar, I'll do Ruth and Boaz, I'll do them all, all the prophets, the shepherds and kings to whom the humble girls, relatives and servants, gave their youth. They're all beautiful and happy, you can see for yourself.'

At that they stopped laughing as they leant over the antique Bible while she turned the pages with her slender fingers. He stood behind her, his white beard mingling with her girlish blonde hair. He smelled all of her, breathed in all of her. He had put his lips to the delicate nape of her neck, and he kissed her burgeoning youth while the primitive wood engravings went on filing past, that whole biblical world conjured up from these yellowing pages, this unbridled thrust of a strong and tenacious people whose toil was destined to conquer the world, these men whose virility was never sated, these women who were always fertile, this stubborn, teeming race continuing on through all kinds of crimes, acts of incest, amorous adventures beyond the realm of age or reason. And he was filled with emotion, with boundless gratitude, because his very own dream was coming true, his love pilgrim, his Abishag, had just entered his waning life, making it green again and sweetly fragrant.

Then, without ceasing to breathe all of her in, he softly murmured a question in her ear:

'Oh, your youth, your youth! I'm hungry for it; it nourishes me! But you're so young... aren't you hungry for it yourself, for youth, now you've had me, when I'm so old, as old as the world?'

She gave a start of astonishment, and turned her head and looked at him.

'You, old?... Never! You're young, younger than I am!'

And she laughed, flashing her dazzlingly white teeth, so that he couldn't help laughing with her. But he insisted, trembling a little:

'You didn't answer me... Don't you feel hungry for youth, too, being so young yourself?'

She now pushed out her lips and kissed him, murmuring softly in her turn:

'There's only one thing I'm hungry and thirsty for: to be loved, to be loved regardless of everything, more than anything, the way you love me.'

The day Martine spotted the pastel, tacked to the wall, she contemplated it for a second in silence, then she made the sign of the cross, without it being clear whether she'd seen God or the Devil pass by. A few days before Easter, she'd asked Clotilde to go with her to church, and when the latter said no, she had discarded for a second the mute deference she adhered to these days. Of all the new things in the house that amazed her, the one she remained devastated by was her young mistress's sudden irreligion. And so she allowed herself to revert to her old tone of remonstration and scold the girl as she had done when she was little and wouldn't say her prayers. Did she no longer fear the Lord? Did she no longer quake at the thought of going to hell and burning there for all eternity?

Clotilde could not suppress a smile.

'Oh! You know, hell has never worried me much... But you're wrong in thinking I no longer have religion. If I've stopped going to church it's because I worship elsewhere, that's all.'

Martine, mouth agape, looked at her without catching on. That was it, Mademoiselle was well and truly lost. Never again did she ask her to go with her to Saint-Saturnin. But her own worship intensified further and ended by turning into a mania. You never ran into her now, outside working hours, carrying the eternal stocking she knitted even while walking. As soon as she had a spare minute, she would run to church and stay there, deep in never-ending prayers. One day when old Madame Rougon, always on the lookout, found her behind a pillar an hour after she'd first seen her there, Martine began to blush, making excuses like a servant caught doing nothing.

'I was praying for Monsieur.'

Meanwhile, Pascal and Clotilde were expanding their domain further, extending their walks every day, pushing on now beyond the town and into the wide open countryside. And one afternoon when they'd set off for La Séguiranne, they felt deeply stirred as they skirted the dismal cleared ground where once the enchanted gardens of Le Paradou had lain. The vision of Albine rose up, and Pascal once more saw her blossoming like spring. He would never have believed, in the past, when he'd already considered himself so old, going in there to smile at that little girl, that she'd have been dead for years by now when life had made him the gift of a similar spring, sweetening his decline. Clotilde, having felt the vision pass between them, lifted up her face to him in a renewed need for tenderness. She was Albine, the eternal woman in love. He kissed her on the lips, and without their exchanging a word, a great thrill ran through the flat ground, sewn with wheat and oats, where Le Paradou had once billowed with a profusion of beautiful greenery.

Now, Pascal and Clotilde walked across the parched, bare plain in the crackling dust of the roadways. They loved this brutal expanse of nature, these fields planted with spindly almond trees and stunted olives, these stretches of bald slopes, where the pale splotches of bastides grew whiter, accentuated by the black stripes of hundred-year-old cypresses. They were like ancient landscapes, like those classical landscapes you see in the paintings of the old schools, with their harsh hues and their majestic, nicely balanced lines. All the fierce suns of the past, which seemed to have baked this countryside, flowed into their veins; and they were made more alive and more beautiful, under the ever-blue sky, from which streamed down the bright flame of perpetual passion. Protected somewhat by her umbrella, Clotilde glowed, as happy basking in the light as a plant that thrived in full sun; while he, flourishing again, felt the burning sap of the soil rising in his limbs, in a surge of virile joy.

This walk to La Séguiranne was an idea of the doctor's, as he'd learned, through Aunt Dieudonné, that Sophie was about to be married to a local miller lad; and he wanted to see if they were well, if they were happy in that neck of the woods. A delicious coolness refreshed them at once as they stepped into the lofty avenue of holm oaks. On both sides, the springs that fed this great canopy flowed endlessly. And as it happened, when they got to the sharecroppers' house, they actually stumbled on the lovers, Sophie and her miller, locked in a passionate kiss by the well; for the aunt had just left for the wash house down below, behind the willows of the Viorne. Extremely embarrassed, the couple just stood there going red. But the doctor and his companion laughed benignly, and the reassured lovers told them the wedding was set for Midsummer's Day, that that was indeed a long way off, but would finally come round all the same. Sophie had grown even more beautiful and healthy, saved from the hereditary disease, and thrusting up robustly like one of the trees, feet in the wet grass of the springs, bare head in the hot sun. Ah, this boundless blazing sky—what life it breathed into beings and things! There was only one thing still causing her pain, and tears appeared at the corners of her eyes when she talked about her brother Valentin, who might not see out the week. She had had news the day before, he was finished. And the doctor had to lie a bit to console her, for he himself was expecting the inevitable end any moment. When they left La Séguiranne, Clotilde and he, they walked back to Plassans at a slower pace, moved by the happiness of such healthy love, shot through with the faint chill of death.

In the old quarter, a woman Pascal was treating told him Valentin had just died. Two neighbours had had to go and get Guiraude, who had been clinging desperately to the body of her son, howling, half crazed. He stepped inside, leaving Clotilde at the door. Finally, they took the path back to La Souleiade in silence. Ever since he'd resumed his visits, he seemed only to do them out of a sense of professional duty, no longer extolling the miracles of his medication. This death, what's more, Valentin's death—well, he was amazed it had taken so long, was convinced he'd prolonged the patient's life by a year. Despite the extraordinary results he got, he knew full well that death would remain inevitable, invincible. Yet, the way he'd kept it at bay for months ought to have pleased him, staunched the regret, still bleeding inside him, at having inadvertently killed Lafouasse a few months before his time. But that didn't look to be the case, and a solemn frown creased his brow as they returned home together alone. But there he had a fresh emotional jolt, when he saw, sitting outside under the plane trees where Martine had seated him, a man he instantly recognized as Sarteur, the hatter, the inmate of Les Tulettes he'd gone to inject for such a long time; and the fascinating experiment seemed to have succeeded, the injections of nerve substance had produced willpower, since the madman was here, released from the asylum that very morning, swearing he no longer had fits, that he was completely cured of the sudden homicidal rage that would have made him throw himself on a passer-by and strangle him. The doctor looked at him as he sat there, small, very dark, his forehead receding, his face beaky like a bird's, with one cheek noticeably bigger than the other, now perfectly sane and gentle, brimming with a gratitude that made him kiss his saviour's hands. Pascal ended up being moved, and sent the man away fondly, advising him to take up his old working life again, as that was the best physical and moral hygiene.

Then he composed himself and sat at the table, talking merrily of other things.

Clotilde watched him, amazed, and even a little affronted.

'What's wrong, Maître, aren't you just a bit pleased with yourself?' He joked.

'Oh, with myself, never!... And with medicine, you know, it depends on the day!'

It was that night, in bed, that they had their first row. They'd blown out the candle and were lying in the pitch-black darkness of the room in each other's arms, she so slender, so fine, pressed against him, as he folded her fully in his embrace, her head on his heart. But she lost her temper with him for not having any pride left, she went back over her grievances of the day, rebuking him for not glorying in Sarteur's cure, and even in Valentin's death, so long delayed. She was the one, now, who was passionate about his reputation. She reminded him of his cures: hadn't he healed himself? Could he deny the effectiveness of his method? A tremor shook her as she evoked the great dream he'd once had: of fighting debility, the single cause of sickness, of healing suffering humanity, making it healthy and altogether superior, spurring on happiness, the future city of perfection and bliss, by intervening, ensuring health for all! And he held the elixir of life, the universal panacea that unlocked this tremendous hope!

Pascal said nothing, his lips on Clotilde's bare shoulder. Then he murmured:

'It's true, I healed myself, I've healed others, and I *do* still believe my injections are effective in many cases... I'm not disowning medicine; my remorse over a painful accident, like what happened to Lafouasse, doesn't make me unjust... Besides, work has been my passion, it's work that has consumed me till now, it was by wanting to prove to myself that it was possible to revitalize decrepit humanity and make it vigorous at last and intelligent, that I nearly died, not so long ago... Yes, a dream, a beautiful dream!'

With both her supple arms she hugged him in her turn, merging with him, at one with his body.

'No! A reality, the reality of your genius, Maître!'

At that, as they lay intertwined, he lowered his voice further, so that his words were no more than a confession, barely more than a faint exhalation.

'Listen, I'm going to tell you something I'd never tell anyone else in the world, something I don't even say out loud to myself... Correcting nature, intervening, altering it and thwarting its ends—is that a commendable task? Healing, delaying a person's death for his personal pleasure, prolonging that pleasure most likely to the detriment of the species—isn't that undoing what nature wants to do? And dreaming of a healthier, stronger humanity, modelled on our notion of health and strength—have we really got the right? What are we doing there, what are we meddling in when we interfere in this labour of life, whose means and ends are unknown to us? Maybe everything is all right as it is. Maybe we risk killing love, genius, life itself... Listen, I confess this to you alone, I've been gripped by doubt, I tremble at the thought of this twentieth-century alchemy of mine, I've come to believe that it's nobler and healthier to let evolution take its course.'

He broke off, adding so softly she could hardly hear him:

'You know, these days, I inject them with water. You yourself have remarked that you don't hear me pounding away any more; and I told you I had some solution in reserve... The water relieves them, there is doubtless some kind of simple mechanical effect, there. Ah! Relieving, preventing suffering—that, of course, is something I still want! It may well be my ultimate weakness, but I can't stand seeing anyone suffer, suffering drives me mad, it's a monstrous and pointless cruelty of nature... The only reason I still treat people at all now is to prevent suffering.'

'Well, then, Maître,' she said, 'if you no longer want to heal, you mustn't tell all any more, since the only thing that justified the appalling necessity of exposing wounds was the hope of closing them up.'

'No, no! We have to know, to know no matter what, and not hide anything, and reveal everything about people and things!... Ignorance is never bliss, only certainty makes for a peaceful life. When we know more, surely we'll accept everything... Don't you see that wanting to heal all, to regenerate all, is a misguided ambition that stems from our egotism; it's a revolt against life, which we declare bad because we judge it from the standpoint of our own interests! I feel strongly that I'm more serene, that my mind is more open and uplifted, since I've come to respect evolution. It's my passion for life that has triumphed, to the point where I no longer quibble with it over its ends, to the point where I trust in it totally, lose myself in it, without wanting to make it anew according to my conception of good and bad. Life alone is sovereign, life alone knows what it's doing and where it's going, I can only endeavour to get to know it so as to live it the way it asks to be lived... And, you see, I've only understood life since you became mine. While I didn't have you, I was looking for the truth elsewhere, I was floundering in this obsession with saving the world. You came along, and now life is complete, the world is saved every hour of the day by love, by the immense and never-ending work of all that lives and reproduces, throughout space... Life! Faultless life, almighty life, everlasting life!'

That act of faith alone now quivered on his lips, a sigh spelling his abandonment to higher forces. She herself no longer argued, but abandoned herself too.

'Maître, I want only what you want—nothing else; take me and make me yours, so I die and am reborn, in you!'

They made love. Then there was more whispering, plans made for an idyllic life, a quiet, active existence in the country. It was this simple prescription of an invigorating environment that all the doctor's experience came down to, in the end. He hated towns. You could only thrive and be happy out in the vast plains, under the hot sun, provided you renounced money, ambition, even the arrogant excesses of intellectual efforts. Did nothing but live and love, till your patch of land, and have beautiful children.

'Ah!' he went on softly. 'If only we had a child, a child of our own, one day...'

He could not go on, overwhelmed with emotion at the idea of becoming a father so late in life. He usually avoided talking about it, would turn his head away, his eyes moist with tears, whenever they were out and about and some little girl or boy smiled at them.

She said, then, simply and with quiet certainty:

'He'll come!'

For her, it was the natural and indispensable consequence of the act of love. In every one of her kisses there was the thought of a child; to her, every love affair that did not have a child as its aim seemed pointless and sordid.

This was actually one of the things that had made her lose interest in novels. She was not, as her mother had been, a great reader; the flight of her imagination was enough for her and she very quickly got bored with made-up stories. But more than anything, she was always amazed and outraged to see that, in romance novels, no one ever worried about children. They were never even anticipated, and when, by chance, one came along in the middle of an affair of the heart, it was a catastrophe, a stunning surprise, and a considerable embarrassment. Never did the lovers, when they abandoned themselves in each other's arms, seem to realize that they were engaging in a life-giving act and that a baby might result. And yet her studies in natural history had shown her that the fruit was nature's sole concern. It was the only thing that mattered, it was the only goal, every precaution was taken to ensure that the seed was not wasted and that the parent plant bore fruit. Yet man, on the contrary, in civilizing, in refining love, had discarded the very idea of the fruit. The sexual organs of the protagonists, in elegant novels, were nothing more than passion machines. The characters adored each other, took each other, dropped each other, endured a thousand deaths, kissed each other, killed each other, unleashed a storm of social ills—all for pleasure, outside the laws of nature, without their even appearing to remember that in making love you made babies. It was immoral and moronic.

She brightened up and repeated herself, speaking into his neck, with the alluring insolence of a woman in love and a little flustered.

'He'll come... We're doing all the right things, so what makes you think he won't?'

He didn't answer straightaway. She felt him shiver in her arms as a wave of regret and doubt swept over him. Then he murmured sadly:

'No! It's too late... Think, darling, of my age!'

'But you're young!' she cried once more, in a fit of passion, warming him up and covering him with kisses.

The next minute they were laughing about it. And they fell asleep in this embrace, he on his back, hugging her to him with his left arm, she wrapping his whole body round with all four of her supple outstretched limbs, her head on his chest, her blonde hair spread out and mingling with his white beard. The Shunammite slumbered, her cheek on the heart of her king. And amidst the silence, in the big pitch-black room, so tender-hearted towards their lovemaking, all that now existed was the soft sound of their breathing.

9

ALL through the town and all through the surrounding countryside, Doctor Pascal continued his doctor's house calls. And almost always Clotilde was on his arm, going with him into the homes of the poor.

But as he'd admitted to her in a whisper, one night, these visits were hardly anything more now than tours of duty designed to bring relief and consolation. If, in the past, he'd already ended up practising only with reluctance, that was because he'd become aware of just how meaningless therapeutics* was. Medical empiricism depressed him. Once medicine stopped being an experimental science and became an art, he despaired of the infinite complications in disease and cure that could arise, depending on the individual patient. Treatments changed with hypotheses: how many people must have been killed in the past by methods now abandoned! The doctor's flair became all-important, the healer was nothing more than a luckily gifted soothsayer, feeling his way and pulling off cures haphazardly as his genius dictated. And this explained why, after practising for a dozen or so years, Pascal had more or less abandoned his patients to throw himself into pure research. Then, when his major works on heredity had for a moment revived his hopes in intervening, in using his hypodermic injections to heal, he had once again become passionate about medicine, until the day when his faith in life, which had driven him to assist its action by restoring the vital forces, had grown further and given him the greater certainty that life took care of itself, was the sole maker of health and strength. And he only kept up his visits, smiling placidly all the while, to patients who clamoured loudly for him and found themselves miraculously relieved, even when he only injected them with clear water.

Clotilde now occasionally allowed herself to joke about it. She remained, in her heart of hearts, a devotee of the mystery of revealed truth; and she gleefully claimed that, if he performed miracles like this, it was because he had the power in him to do so, like a true beneficent God! But he would then gaily turn the curative virtue of their joint visits back on her, claiming he never cured anyone any more when she wasn't there, that she was the one who brought a whiff of the other world, the essential unknown force. Accordingly, the rich people, the bourgeois, whose homes she did not venture into, continued to moan and groan, with no possible relief. This affectionate contest amused them, and they set out every time as if on the path of new discoveries, and would exchange knowing looks whenever they were with patients in their homes. Ah, that harlot, suffering! It disgusted them, it was the sole thing they still went off to fight, and how happy they were when they thought they'd beaten it! They felt themselves divinely rewarded whenever they saw the cold sweats dry up, the screaming mouths stilled, the dying faces come back to life. It was their love, obviously, that they were taking around and that soothed this little corner of suffering humanity.

'Dying's nothing, it's in the nature of things,' Pascal often said. 'But suffering—what for? It's vile and stupid.'

One afternoon, the doctor went with Clotilde to see a patient in the little village of Sainte-Marthe; and, as they were going by rail, to spare Bonhomme, they had an encounter at the station. The train they were waiting for was coming from Les Tulettes, Sainte-Marthe being the first stop in the opposite direction, heading to Marseilles. As soon as the train pulled in, they ran and were just opening a door when they saw old Madame Rougon step down from the carriage which they'd thought was empty. She was no longer speaking to them, and she hopped down lightly, despite her age, and went off looking stiff and very dignified.

'It's the first of July,' Clotilde said when the train moved off. 'Grandmother's coming back from her monthly visit to Aunt Dide at Les Tulettes... Did you see the look she gave me?'

Pascal was basically happy at this falling-out with his mother, which freed him from the constant anxiety of her presence.

'Oh well!' he said simply. 'When people don't get on it's best not to keep company.'

But the young woman remained fretful and pensive. In a small voice she said:

'I thought she looked different, her face paler... And, did you notice? She's usually so proper, but she only had one glove on, a green one, on her right hand... I don't know why, but she gave me quite a shock.'

He was disturbed too, at that, and made a vague gesture. His mother would surely end up getting old, like everyone else. She still got too agitated, too worked up. He described how she was planning to leave her fortune to the town of Plassans so they'd build an old people's home that would bear the Rougon name. They were both smiling when he cried:

'Oh, but of course! We're off to Les Tulettes ourselves tomorrow, to see our patients. And you know I promised to take Charles to Uncle Macquart's.'

Félicité was indeed coming back that day from Les Tulettes, where she regularly went on the first of every month, to see how Aunt Dide was. For years she had taken a passionate interest in the mad woman's health, amazed to find her still going strong, furious at her stubborn persistence in living on beyond the usual allotted years, in what was a veritable miracle of longevity. What a relief it would be, that fine day when she could at last bury this inconvenient witness to the past, this ghost of hope against hope and atonement, who conjured up the family's—still vivid—abominations! Yet, when so many others had gone, she, demented and preserving only a spark of life in her eyes, seemed to have been overlooked. That particular day, she had again found her in her armchair, dried-up and straight-backed, immutable. As the keeper said, there was no reason now why she should ever die. She was a hundred and five.

When she left the asylum, Félicité was outraged. She thought of Uncle Macquart. Yet another one who cramped her style, thwarting her by clinging on with exasperating determination! Although he was only eighty-four, a mere three years older than she was, he seemed ridiculously old to her, exceeding the allowed limits. A man who played holy hell, who'd been dead drunk every night for sixty years, too! Good people, sober people, were departing this world; he was flourishing, blossoming, bursting with health and joviality. Once, after he'd come and settled at Les Tulettes, she'd given him presents of wine, liqueur, brandy, in the unavowed hope of ridding the family of a crafty devil who really was dirt, from whom they could expect only unpleasantness and shame. But she'd quickly realized that all that alcohol only seemed to have the opposite effect, keeping him nice and sprightly, his face sunny, a glint of mockery in his eye; and she had cut off the supply of presents, since the would-be poison was simply fattening him up. She was still terribly bitter about it and could have killed him, if she'd dared, every time she saw him again, ever steadier on his tosspot's feet, laughing in her face, knowing full well she was waiting for him to die, and gloating over the fact that he wasn't giving her the pleasure of burying him, and along with him, the old dirty family linen, the blood and mire of the two conquests of Plassans.

'You see, Félicité,' he would often say, with that appalling sneer of his, 'I'm here to protect our old mother, and the day we decide to die, the two of us, it'll be out of kindness to you! Yes! Just to save you the trouble of running to see us, like this, out of the goodness of your heart, every month.'

Normally, these days, she spared herself the disappointment of getting off at her brother's house, and would merely ask about him at the asylum. But this time, as she'd just learned there that he was on an extraordinary bender and hadn't sobered up in a fortnight, probably so drunk that he no longer left the house, she was assailed by curiosity and decided to see for herself what sort of state he'd got himself into. So on her way back to the station she took a detour via his bastide.

It was a glorious day, a hot, radiant summer's day. To left and right of the narrow path she was forced to take, she looked at the fields he'd made sure he was given in the past, all this rich earth, the price of his discretion and good behaviour. In the bright sunshine, the house, with its pink roof tiles and its walls gaudily washed in yellow, looked quite pleasingly cheery to her. Under the ancient mulberry trees on the terrace, she savoured the delicious freshness and enjoyed the wonderful view. What a worthy and modest retreat, what a perfect little patch of happiness for an old man, who would end, amid this peace, a long life filled with goodness and duty!

But she didn't see him, she didn't hear him. The silence was profound. The only sound was the bees, buzzing around tall mallow plants. And on the terrace, there was only a little yellow dog, a *loubet* as they're called in Provence, stretched out full length on the bare earth, in the shade. He knew the visitor and raised his head, growling, on the verge of barking; then he laid back down and didn't stir again.

Suddenly, in the solitude, in the joyous sunshine, she felt a strange little shiver run down her spine and she called out:

'Macquart! Macquart!'

Under the mulberry trees, the door of the bastide stood wide open. But she didn't dare go inside; the empty house, yawning like this, alarmed her. She called again:

'Macquart! Macquart!'

Not a sound, not a breath of air. The heavy silence fell again, only the bees buzzed, louder, around the tall mallows.

Shame at her fear finally overcame Félicité and she bravely stepped inside. On the left, in the hall, the door to the kitchen, where her brother usually sat, was shut. She pushed it open but couldn't make anything out at first, as he must have closed the shutters to shield himself from the heat. Her first reaction was just to feel her throat tighten at the violent stench of alcohol that filled the room: it seemed as if every piece of furniture was reeking of the stench, the whole house was permeated with it. But when her eyes adjusted to the semi-darkness, she finally spotted her brother. He was sitting by the table, on which stood a glass and a bottle of ninety-per-cent pure alcohol, completely empty. Hunched in his chair, he was sleeping soundly, dead drunk. The sight brought back her anger and scorn.

'Come now, Macquart, it's ridiculous and disgraceful to get into such a state!... Wake up, now, this is shameful!'

His sleep was so deep, you couldn't even hear him breathing. She raised her voice, loudly clapped her hands, to no avail.

'Macquart! Macquart! Macquart!... Oh! Urrgh!... You're disgusting, my dear man!'

And she gave up on him, made herself at home, walked around freely, turned things upside down. On her way along the dusty road from the asylum, a burning thirst had taken hold of her. Her gloves were hindering her so she took them off, and lay them on a corner of the table. Then she had the luck to stumble across the jug, so she washed a glass and filled it to the brim, and was about to drain it when an extraordinary spectacle shook her up so much she put the glass down next to her gloves, without drinking a drop.

She could see more and more clearly in the room, lit up as it was by thin streaks of sunlight coming in through the cracks in the old disjointed shutters. She distinctly saw her brother, still neatly dressed in blue serge, and wearing the inevitable fur cap that he wore all year round. He'd put on weight over the past five or six years and was a real lump of lard, spilling over in rolls of fat. And she'd just noticed that he must have fallen asleep while smoking, for his pipe, a short black pipe, had fallen on to his knees. Suddenly, she froze, stunned: the smouldering tobacco had spread, his trousers had caught fire, and through the hole in the material, already as big as a hundred-sou piece, you could see his bare thigh, red flesh, with a small blue flame coming from it.

At first Félicité thought it was his linen, drawers or an undershirt, that was burning. But there was no room for doubt, she could definitely see bare flesh, and the little blue flame was escaping from it, volatile, flickering, like a flame wandering over the surface of a bowl of lit alcohol. It was still scarcely any higher than the flame of a night light, so silently gentle, so unstable, that the slightest flutter of air shifted it. But it was growing and spreading rapidly, and the flesh was splitting, and the fat was starting to melt.

An involuntary cry shot from Félicité's throat.

'Macquart! Macquart!'

Still he didn't budge. He had to be completely unconscious, drunkenness had obviously thrown him into a sort of coma, an absolute paralysis of feeling; for he was alive, you could see his chest rising on a slow and even breath.

'Macquart! Macquart!'

Now the fat was oozing from the cracks in his skin, stoking the flame that was licking at his stomach. And Félicité realized her brother was taking fire, right there, like a sponge soaked in brandy. He himself had been saturated with the stuff for years, and the strongest, the most flammable, at that. He would blaze away in a little while, without a doubt, from head to toe.

So she stopped trying to rouse him, since he was sleeping so soundly. For a good long minute she was bold enough to gaze on, alarmed, then gradually resolved. Her hands, though, had begun to shake with a little tremor she could not control. She was choking, she grabbed the glass of water again with both hands and drank it in one go. And she was just tiptoeing out of the room when she remembered her gloves. She went back, and thought she picked them both up off the table, as she anxiously fumbled about. At last she slipped out, shutting the door again carefully, gently, as if she were afraid of disturbing someone.

When she found herself back on the terrace, in the bright sun, in the pure air, facing the immense horizon lapped by sky, she let out a sigh of relief. The countryside was deserted, no one surely had seen her enter or leave. The only thing still there was the yellow *loubet*, sprawled out, and he didn't even deign to lift his head. And so off she went, trotting along at her usual fast pace, her girlish figure swaying slightly. A hundred paces down the track, although she fought it, an irresistible force made her turn around and take one last look at the house, sitting there so serene and so cheery, halfway up the hill, at the end of a beautiful day. Only in the train, when she went to put on her gloves, did she see that one of them was missing. But she was sure it had fallen on the railway platform as she was stepping up into the carriage. She thought she was perfectly calm, but she went on sitting there with one hand gloved, the other bare, something that, for her, could only be the result of powerful inner turmoil.

The next day Pascal and Clotilde took the three o'clock train to Les Tulettes. Charles's mother, the harness-maker, had brought the boy over, since they seemed so keen to take him to see Pascal's old uncle, with whom he was supposed to spend the whole week. Fresh wrangling had thrown the household into disarray: the husband positively refused to put up any longer with this child of another man's, this prince's son, so sluggish and slow. As it was Grandmother Rougon who clothed him, he was in fact that day all dressed again in gold-braided black velvet, like a little lord, a page of a bygone era, on his way to court. And during the fifteen minutes the trip took, in a compartment they had to themselves, Clotilde amused herself taking off his bonnet to buff up his wonderful blond hair, those royal locks, which fell in curls to his shoulders. But she was wearing a ring, and having run her hand over his neck, she was startled to see that her caress had left a bloody mark. You couldn't touch the boy without beads of red dew pearling on his skin: it was a slackening of the tissues so aggravated by degeneracy that the slightest bruising brought on a haemorrhage. The doctor immediately became concerned, asked him if he still had nosebleeds as often as he used to. But Charles scarcely knew what to answer, said no at first, then remembered, and said he'd bled a lot the other day. He did indeed seem weaker, was reverting to childhood as he grew older, his intelligence never having sparked into life and now growing dimmer. This big boy of fifteen didn't look as old as ten, he was so beautiful, so like a little girl with his complexion as pale as a flower that had sprung up in the shade. Moved to pity, her heart heavy, Clotilde, who had kept him on her knees, sat him back on the seat when she realized he was trying to slip his hand through the opening in her bodice, driven by the precocious and instinctive urge of a small depraved animal.

At Les Tulettes, Pascal decided they would take the boy to his uncle's first. And they clambered up the fairly steep slope of the path. From a distance, the little house looked as cheery as it had the day before in the bright sunlight, with its pink roof tiles, its yellow walls, and its green mulberry trees, thrusting out their twisted branches and covering the terrace with a thick roof of leaves. A delicious peace flooded this patch of secluded stillness, this retreat fit for a sage, where all you could hear was the buzzing of bees around the tall mallows.

'Ah, that old rascal of an uncle,' Pascal murmured, smiling, 'I envy him!'

But he was surprised not to see him already standing at the end of the terrace. And, as Charles had started galloping off, dragging Clotilde, to go and see the rabbits, the doctor continued climbing up on his own, and was amazed, at the top, to find no one there. The shutters were closed, the front door was wide open. The only one there was the yellow *loubet*, on the doorstep, his four legs stiff, his hair standing on end, howling in a soft and constant wail. When he saw the visitor coming, and no doubt recognizing him, he fell silent for a second, went to stand further away, then started again softly wailing.

Pascal was filled with fear and could not hold back the anxious call that rose to his lips.

'Macquart! Macquart!'

No one answered, the house kept up a deathly silence, sitting there with its only door wide open, forming a black hole. The dog went on howling.

He grew impatient, and shouted louder:

'Macquart! Macquart!'

Nothing stirred, the bees buzzed, the immense serenity of the sky enveloped this patch of solitude. And so he made up his mind. His uncle may well be sleeping. But as soon as he pushed open the door on the left, to the kitchen, an appalling stench escaped, an unbearable stench of flesh and bones that have fallen onto a brazier. Inside the room he could hardly breathe, choked as he was by a sort of thick vapour, a stagnant, nauseating cloud. The thin streaks of light filtering through the cracks didn't allow him to see much. But when he rushed to the fireplace, he abandoned his initial idea of a fire, because there had been no fire, all the furniture around him looked to be intact. And so, not knowing what was going on and feeling he was about to pass out in the poisoned air, he ran and wrenched open the shutters. Light streamed in.

At that point, what the doctor could see filled him with astonishment. Every object was in its place; the glass and the empty bottle of proof spirit were on the table; only the chair where his uncle must have been sitting bore traces of fire, the front legs blackened, the straw seat half burnt. What had happened to his uncle? Where could he have got to? In front of the chair, on the tiled floor marked by a pool of fat, there was only a small heap of ash, and lying next to it, Macquart's pipe, a black pipe that hadn't even smashed in falling. All of his uncle was there, in this handful of fine ash, and he was also in the reddish-brown cloud that was going out the open window, and in the layer of soot that had covered the entire kitchen, a horrible wool-grease of vaporized flesh, enveloping everything, oily and foul to the touch.

It was the finest case of spontaneous combustion a medical man ever observed. The doctor had of course read of some surprising ones, in various scientific treatises, among others one involving a shoemaker's wife, a sozzlepot of a woman who'd fallen asleep on her foot warmer and of whom they'd found only a foot and a hand. He himself, until now, had been sceptical, and had not accepted, like the ancients, that a body soaked in alcohol gave out an unknown gas capable of spontaneously igniting and devouring flesh and bones. But he could no longer deny it; it explained everything, re-establishing the facts: the drunken coma, absolute unconsciousness, the pipe falling on to the clothes which then caught fire, the flesh saturated with drink burning and splitting, the melting fat, part of which ran down to the floor, the other part of which set off the combustion, and everything in the end—muscles, organs, bones—being consumed as the entire body went up in the blaze. All of his uncle was there, with his blue serge clothes and the fur hat he wore all year round. Clearly, as soon as he began to burn like a bonfire, he must have tumbled forward, which explained why the chair was barely blackened; and nothing of him remained, not a bone, not a tooth, not a nail, nothing but this little heap of grey dust that the draught from the doorway threatened to sweep away.

Clotilde had come in, meanwhile, although young Charles remained outside, captivated by the constant howling of the dog.

'Oh, my God! What a smell!' she said. 'What is it?'

And when Pascal explained the extraordinary catastrophe she shuddered. She had already picked up the bottle to examine it, but put it back down in horror, feeling it to be wet and sticky with their uncle's flesh. You couldn't touch anything, the tiniest things seemed to be coated with this yellowish grease that stuck to your hands.

A shiver of horrified disgust ran through her and she wept, stammering:

'What a sad death! What an awful death!'

Pascal had recovered from his initial shock and almost smiled.

'Awful, why?... He was eighty-four, and he didn't suffer... I think it's magnificent, a death like that for this old crook of an uncle, who never—God! we can say it, now!—led a particularly moral life... You remember his file. He had some truly terrible and sordid things on his conscience, but that didn't stop him from settling down later on, and growing old surrounded by all the good things in life, like a good old joker, rewarded for the great virtues he never had. And here he is dying in state, like the prince of drunks, flaring up all on his own, and being consumed in a funeral pyre lit by his own body!'

Marvelling, the doctor set the scene with his usual sweeping gesture.

'You see?... To be so drunk you don't even know you're alight, to flare up like a midsummer bonfire, go up in smoke, right down to the last bone!... Eh? You see Uncle, taking off into outer space, first spreading to the four corners of this room, dissolving into thin air and floating, coating all the things that used to belong to him, then disappearing in a cloud of dust out that window, when I opened it, and soaring up into the open air, filling the sky... It's a wonderful death! Vanishing, leaving nothing of yourself behind, just a little heap of ash and a pipe, next to it!'

And he picked up the pipe, to have, he added, a relic of his uncle, while Clotilde, who felt she'd detected a hint of bitter mockery in his outburst of lyrical admiration, once again, with a shiver, expressed her nausea and dismay.

But she had just spotted something, under the table, some remains perhaps.

'Look there, that scrap!'

He bent down and was surprised to pick up a woman's glove, a green glove.

'What!' she cried. 'That's Grandmother's glove, you remember, the glove she was missing last night.'

They looked at each other, and the same explanation occurred to them both at once: Félicité had certainly been there, the day before; and a sudden conviction formed in the doctor's mind, the certainty that his mother had seen his uncle catch fire, and that she hadn't put him out. For him this was based on several clues—the way the room had already completely cooled down again by the time they arrived, the number of hours he calculated were needed for combustion. He could clearly see that the same thought was dawning in the terrified eyes of his companion. But since it seemed impossible ever to know the truth, he pictured the simplest story out loud.

'No doubt your grandmother stepped in to say hello to Uncle when she was coming back from the asylum, before he started drinking.'

'Let's get out of here now!' cried Clotilde. 'I'm suffocating, I can't stay here another second!'

Pascal wanted to go and register the death, anyway. He walked out behind her, locked the house up, and put the key in his pocket. And outside, they once again heard the *loubet*, the little yellow dog, who hadn't stopped howling. He had taken refuge between Charles's legs and the boy, amused, was pushing him with his foot and listening to him whine, baffled.

The doctor went straight to Monsieur Maurin, the notary in Les Tulettes, who happened to be the mayor of the municipality as well. A widower for ten years or so, living with his daughter, also widowed and childless, he had maintained good neighbourly relations with old Macquart, and had sometimes looked after young Charles at home for whole days at a stretch, his daughter having taken an interest in the boy, who was so beautiful and so much to be pitied. Monsieur Maurin was alarmed, he wanted to go back with the doctor to establish undeniably that it was an accident, and promised to draw up a valid death certificate. As for a religious ceremony, a funeral, that seemed rather problematic. When Pascal went back into the kitchen, with the notary, the wind came in through the door and sent the ashes flying, and when they forced themselves piously to collect some, all they really managed to do was rake up the scrapings from the floor, a lot of age-old filth in which very little of his uncle could possibly remain. So, bury what? It would be better to forget about it. They forgot about it. Besides, their uncle hadn't exactly been a practising Catholic, and so the family was content to have Masses said later for the repose of his soul.

The notary, however, immediately declared that there was a will, lodged with him at his office. He summoned the doctor without delay for the day after the next, with the aim of officially communicating its contents to him, as he felt able to tell him his uncle had chosen him as his executor. And being a decent man, the notary wound up offering to look after Charles till then, clearly realizing that the young lad, bullied so badly at his mother's, was becoming a nuisance, with all that was going on. Charles seemed thrilled and he stayed behind at Les Tulettes.

It was not till very late, by the seven o'clock train, that Clotilde and Pascal were able to return to Plassans, after the doctor had finally visited the two patients he was supposed to see. But two days later, when they returned together for the appointment with Monsieur Maurin, they had the unpleasant surprise of finding old Madame Rougon installed at the notary's. She had naturally heard of Macquart's death and come running, fidgeting with impatience and erupting into effusive grief. The reading of the will was, however, perfectly straightforward, without incident: Macquart had earmarked all he could squeeze out of his small fortune to have himself raised a superb tomb, in marble, with two monumental angels, wings folded and weeping. It was his own idea, based on a memory he had of a similar tomb he'd seen abroad, in Germany perhaps, when he was a soldier. And he tasked his nephew Pascal with seeing to the execution of the monument, because, he added, Pascal was the only one in the family with any taste.

While the will was being read, Clotilde sat outside in the notary's garden, on a bench in the shade of a very old chestnut tree. When Pascal and Félicité reappeared, there was an extremely awkward moment, since they hadn't spoken to each other again for months. Yet the old lady feigned perfect ease, not making any allusion to the new situation, but giving them to understand that they could meet and put on a united front before the world without having to clear things up or be reconciled to do so. But she made the mistake of overplaying the great sorrow the death of Macquart caused her. Pascal, who knew that she was secretly leaping for joy, that she was absolutely thrilled at the thought that the family wound, this abomination of an uncle, was about to heal over at last, yielded to a growing impatience, a mutinous rage that was welling inside him. He couldn't help but fasten his eyes on his mother's gloves, which were black.

Precisely at that moment, she was lamenting, in a syrupy voice:

'And it wasn't exactly wise, at his age, to persist in living alone, like a wolf! If only he'd had a servant in the house!'

The doctor then spoke, without being clearly aware of what he was doing, propelled by such an irresistible need that he was quite alarmed to hear himself say:

'But what about you, Mother, since you were there, why didn't you put him out?'

Old Madame Rougon went shockingly white. How did her son know? She looked at him for a moment, agape, while Clotilde went just as pale at the now blatant certainty of the crime. It was a confession, this terrified silence that had fallen between mother, son, and granddaughter, the simmering silence in which families bury their domestic tragedies. The two women could think of nothing to say. The doctor, in despair at having spoken when he was usually so careful to avoid vexatious and pointless arguments, was madly trying to take back what he'd said, when a new catastrophe rescued them from this terrible embarrassment.

Félicité had decided to take Charles back, not wanting to abuse the kind hospitality of Monsieur Maurin; and the latter, having packed the boy off after lunch to the asylum to spend an hour with Aunt Dide, had just sent his servant there with the order to bring the boy back immediately. And it was at that very moment, while they were waiting for him in the garden, that the servant reappeared, sweating, out of breath and agitated, and shouting from afar:

'Oh God! God! Come quickly... Monsieur Charles is covered in blood...'

They took off, terrified, all three, for the asylum.

That particular day, Aunt Dide was having one of her good days, and was nice and calm, nice and sweet, sitting up straight in the chair in which she had spent so many long hours, for twenty-two years, staring into space. She looked to have lost even more weight, any remaining muscle had disappeared, and her arms and legs were now just bones, covered in the parchment of her skin; and her keeper, the sturdy blonde girl, had to carry her, get her to eat, and dispose of her as if she were a thing that you move around and put back. The ancestress, that forgotten woman, tall, gnarled, frightening, remained motionless, with only her eyes alive, those clear eyes as sparkling as spring water, in her thin dried-up face. But that morning a sudden flood of tears had streamed down her cheeks, and she had started jabbering incoherently, which seemed to prove that even in the midst of her senile exhaustion and the irreparable torpor of insanity, the slow hardening of the brain was not yet complete: memories remained stored, glimmers of intelligence were possible. After that she had recovered her stony face, indifferent to others and to events, sometimes laughing at some mishap, at a fall, most often seeing and hearing nothing, in her endless contemplation of emptiness.

When Charles was brought in, the keeper set him up straightaway at the little table, facing his great-great-grandmother. She kept a bundle of pictures for him, of soldiers, captains, and kings, dressed in purple and gold, and she gave them to him, along with her pair of scissors.

'There, play quietly with these and be a good boy. You see how nice Grandmother is today. You must be nice too.'

The boy looked up at the madwoman, and they both gazed at each other. At that moment, their extraordinary resemblance was as clear as day. Their eyes especially, their empty, limpid eyes, seemed to lose themselves in each other's eyes, identical. Then, there was the physiognomy, with the worn-out features of the centenarian leapfrogging three generations to reappear in this delicate boy's face, already seemingly worn out too, incredibly old and run down by the erosion of the bloodline. They didn't smile at each other, but examined each other in depth, with an air of solemn imbecility.

'Ah, well!' continued the keeper, who had got into the habit of talking to herself so as to enjoy herself with her madwoman. 'They certainly can't disown each other. Whoever made one made the other. The spitting image... Come on, then, laugh a bit, have fun, since you like being together so much.'

But any prolonged attention tired Charles and he was the first to break off, looking down, apparently interested in his pictures; while Aunt Dide, who had an amazing ability to hold her gaze, continued staring at him indefinitely, without once batting an eyelid.

For a while the keeper bustled about the little room, full of sunshine and all brightened up by its vivid wallpaper with blue flowers. She made the bed now that it had been aired and put the linen away on the shelves in the cupboard. Usually, she took advantage of the boy's presence to take some time off. She wasn't supposed to leave her charge even for a second; but when he was there, she'd ended up taking the risk of entrusting her to him.

'Listen carefully,' she said, 'I have to go out now, but if she stirs, if she needs me, you ring the bell, you call me at once, won't you?... You understand, you're a big boy now, you know how to call someone.'

He looked up again and nodded to show he'd understood and that he'd call. And when he found himself alone with Aunt Dide, he went back to his pictures, quietly. This went on for fifteen minutes in the profound silence of the asylum, where only muffled prison sounds could be heard, a furtive footfall, the jingling of a bunch of keys, then, at times, loud shouting, swiftly silenced. But on this scorching hot day, the boy must have been fatigued and sleep soon caught up with him; his head, white as a lily, seemed to droop under the too-heavy helmet of his kingly hair: he let it fall gently among the pictures and fell asleep, one cheek pressed against the gold and purple kings. The lashes of his closed eyelids cast a shadow, and life beat feebly in the little blue veins of his delicate skin. He was angelically beautiful, with the indefinable corruption of a whole line spread over his soft face. And Aunt Dide gazed at him with her empty gaze, in which there was neither pleasure nor pain, the gaze of eternity turned on the world.

Yet after a few minutes, a spark of interest seemed to ignite in her clear eyes. An event had just occurred, a red drop was dangling at the edge of the boy's left nostril and getting bigger. This drop fell, then another one formed and followed it. It was blood, a bloody dew that was pearling without any bruising, without any contusion this time, but coming out all on its own and disappearing, through the erosion of degeneracy. The drops turned into a thin trickle that ran over the gold in the pictures. These were soon drowned in a little pool that made its way towards a corner of the table; then the drops started forming again, crashed down one by one, heavy, dense, onto the tiled floor of the room. And the boy slept on, with his divinely calm air of a cherub, without his even being aware that his life was slipping away; and the madwoman went on gazing at him, apparently more and more interested, but not alarmed, more amused, her eye held by all this as by the blowflies she often watched whizzing around for hours.

A few more minutes went by and the red trickle grew bigger, the drops followed each other more rapidly, making a light plash, monotonous and persistent, as they fell. Charles stirred at one point, opened his eyes, saw he was covered in blood. But he wasn't frightened, he was used to this bloody spring that came out of him at the slightest knock. He let out a moan of boredom. Instinct, though, must have alerted him, as he then became scared, whined louder, and stammered out a confused cry for help.

'Maman! Maman!'

Already he must have been too weak, for an invincible drowsiness took hold of him again and he let his head drop back down. His eyes closed again, and he appeared to fall back to sleep as if he wanted to carry on his moaning in a dream, the soft wail growing more and more reedy and forlorn.

'Maman! Maman!'

The pictures were flooded, his gold-braided black velvet jacket and pants were becoming soiled with long streaks; and the red trickle, persistent, had begun to flow again from his left nostril, without let-up, running through the bright red pool on the table and crashing to the floor, where a puddle was finally forming. A loud cry from the madwoman, a terrified call would have been enough. But she didn't cry, she didn't call; she sat motionless, with the staring eyes of a forebear watching fate play out, as though she'd dried out there on the spot, gnarled, her limbs and her tongue tied by her one hundred years, her brain ossified by insanity, incapable of willing or acting. And yet the sight of the red trickle was beginning to rouse her with emotion. A tremor flitted across her lifeless face, heat was rising to her cheeks. Finally one last moan reanimated her completely.

'Maman! Maman!'

At that, inside Aunt Dide, a dreadful struggle visibly took place. She brought her skeletal hands to her temples as if she felt her skull exploding. Her mouth opened quite wide, but no sound came out: the frightening tumult mounting inside her was paralysing her tongue. She tried to force herself to get up, to run; but she had no muscles left and she remained rooted to the spot. Her whole poor body was shaking with the superhuman effort she was making to cry for help, without being able to break out of her prison of senility and madness. Her face convulsed, her memory wide awake, she was forced to see everything.

And it was a slow and very gentle death, the spectacle lasting a good few minutes more. Charles lay there, silent now, as though fast asleep again, and went on losing blood from his veins, which were emptying out endlessly with only the faintest sound. His lily whiteness intensified, becoming the pallor of death. His lips were losing their colour, turning a pale pink; then they went white. And just before expiring, he opened his big eyes and fixed them on his great-great-grandmother, who was able to watch the last glimmer of life flare in them. The rest of his waxen face was already lifeless, while his eyes were still alive.

They still had a certain limpidity, a brightness. Suddenly, they emptied and went out. It was the end, this death of the eyes; and Charles died without a shudder, exhausted like a spring whose water has completely drained away. Life no longer beat in the veins of his delicate skin, there was nothing now but the shadow of his eyelashes over his white face. But he remained exquisitely beautiful, with his head lying in the blood, in the middle of his streaming royal blond hair, like one of those bloodless little dauphins who weren't able to carry the abysmal legacy of their line and who fall asleep from old age and imbecility as soon as they reach fifteen.

The boy had just exhaled his last short breath when Doctor Pascal entered, followed by Félicité and Clotilde. And as soon as he saw the amount of blood that had flooded the tiled floor, Pascal cried out:

'Oh, God! It's what I feared. The poor little thing! No one was here, it's over!'

But all three stood there terrified at the extraordinary spectacle unfolding before them. Aunt Dide, who looked taller, had almost succeeded in lifting herself up; and her eyes, fixed on the little dead boy, so white and so peaceful, on the red blood spilled, the pool of blood that was now clotting, were lit up with a thought, after a long sleep of twenty-two years. The terminal lesion of insanity, that night of the brain nothing could repair, was not complete enough, no doubt, for a dim, stored memory not to be suddenly rekindled under the terrible blow that had struck her. And once more the forgotten woman lived, emerged from her nothingness, sound and devastated, like a spectre of horror and pain.

For a moment she went on panting. Then with a shiver she managed to stammer a single word only:

'Gendarme! Gendarme!'*

Pascal, and Félicité, and Clotilde, understood. They looked at each other involuntarily and shuddered. That word brought back the whole violent life of the old mother, the mother of them all—the furious passion of her youth, the long suffering of her mature years. Already two moral shocks had shaken her terribly: the first, at the height of her wild love life, when a gendarme had shot dead, like a dog, her lover, the smuggler Macquart; the second, many years later, when another gendarme had taken his pistol and shattered the skull of her grandson Silvère, the insurgent, victim of the family's hatreds and murderous feuds. Blood had always spattered her. And a third moral shock was now finishing her off, blood was spattering her afresh, this weakened blood of her line which she had just seen flow so slowly and which was all over the floor, while the royal white child, his veins and heart empty, lay still.

Three times, seeing her whole life before her, that life red with passion and with torment and dominated by the image of the law as atonement, she stammered:

'Gendarme! Gendarme! Gendarme!'

And then she collapsed onto her chair. They thought she was dead, struck down.

But at last the keeper came back, made excuses, certain she'd be dismissed. When Doctor Pascal helped her get Aunt Dide back onto her bed, he saw that she was still alive. She was not to die till the following day, at the age of a hundred and five years, three months, and seven days, of cerebral congestion,* brought on by the last shock she had received.

Pascal told his mother, there and then, that this would happen.

'She won't go twenty-four hours, tomorrow she'll be dead... Ah! Uncle, and now this poor child, then her, one after the other, so much misery and grief!'

He cut himself off, only to add in a quieter voice:

'The family's thinning out, the old trees are falling and the young ones are dying on their feet.'

Félicité must have thought this was a fresh allusion. She was sincerely upset by the tragic death of young Charles. But, even so, beyond the pang of grief, an immense sense of relief was shaping itself inside her. The following week, when they'd stopped shedding tears, what peace of mind it would be to tell oneself that the whole abomination of Les Tulettes was no more, that the glory of the family could finally rise up and shine in legend!

Then suddenly she remembered that she hadn't replied, at the notary's, to her son's involuntary accusation, and she spoke about Macquart again, out of bravura.

'You see now, servants are useless. There was one here, and she didn't stop anything; Uncle could have had himself taken care of all he liked, he'd still be in ashes, at present.'

Pascal dipped his head, with his habitual air of deference.

'You're right, Mother.'

Clotilde had fallen to her knees. Her beliefs as a fervent Catholic had revived, in this room filled with blood and madness and death. Her eyes were streaming with tears, her hands were joined together, and she prayed ardently for the dear souls who were no more. Dear God, let their sufferings be well and truly over, let them be forgiven their sins, let them be resurrected only for a new life of eternal bliss! And she interceded with all her fervour, in horror of a hell that, after this miserable life, would perpetuate suffering for all eternity.

From that sad day on, Pascal and Clotilde went about visiting their sick patients with a more compassionate outlook, snuggled together as they walked. Perhaps he had become even more acutely aware of his powerlessness in the face of the inevitability of sickness. The only wise policy was to let nature take its course, eliminate dangerous elements, and work only towards nature's ultimate labour of health and strength. But losing relatives, relatives who suffer and die, leaves the heart with a grudge against sickness, and an irresistible need to fight it and defeat it. And never had the doctor experienced joy as great as when he succeeded, with an injection, in quelling a fit, in seeing the howling patient calm down and fall asleep. She, on their return, worshipped him, and was very proud of him, as if their love were the solace they brought as a last sacrament to the poor world.

10

ONE morning, as she did every quarter, Martine got Pascal to give her a receipt for fifteen hundred francs so she could go and draw what she called 'their funds', at Grandguillot the notary's. The doctor seemed surprised the due date had come round again so soon: never had he been less interested in money matters than he was now, shifting the worry of settling everything onto her. And he was with Clotilde, out under the plane trees, revelling in their unrivalled *joie de vivre*, refreshed deliciously by the eternal song of the spring, when the servant returned, alarmed, in the grip of an extraordinary emotion.

She couldn't speak for a moment, she was so out of breath.

'Oh, God! Oh, God!... Monsieur Grandguillot's gone!'

Pascal didn't follow at first.

'Well, my girl, there's no rush, you can go back another day.'

'No, no, no! He's *gone*, do you hear, gone for good...'

And with that, the floodgates burst, the words gushed, her violent emotion poured out.

'I get to the street, I see from a distance that they're people standing outside the door... A chill comes over me, I sense something bad's happened. And the door's shut, there's not a shutter open, like someone had died in there... They told me at once that he'd bolted, that he didn't leave a sou behind, that families are ruined...'

She put the receipt down on the stone table.

'Here! Here's your note! It's all over, we haven't got a sou left, we'll starve to death!'

She was overcome with tears and sobbed hard with all the distress of her miser's heart, distraught at this loss of a fortune and terrified of the misery that loomed.

Clotilde sat there shocked, speechless, her eyes on Pascal, who seemed more incredulous than anything else, at first. He tried to calm Martine. There, there! She shouldn't be so scared. If she'd only heard about this business from the people in the street, she may well be reporting mere hearsay, wildly exaggerated. Monsieur Grandguillot on the run, Monsieur Grandguillot a thief—it was glaringly obvious that that was monstrous, impossible. A man of such impeccable integrity! A firm loved and respected by all Plassans, for over a century! Money was safer there, they said, than in the Banque de France.

'Think, Martine, a disaster like that wouldn't happen in a flash, nasty rumours would have been circulating, ringing alarm bells well in advance... Good God! All that long-standing probity doesn't founder overnight.'

At this, she gave a wave of despair.

'Well, Monsieur, that's what I'm so upset about because, you see, it makes me a bit responsible... I *have* been hearing stories for weeks... You people, naturally, hear nothing, you don't even know if you're alive...'

Pascal and Clotilde shared a smile, since it was perfectly true that their love lifted them out of this world, taking them so far away, so far above it, that none of the sounds of ordinary life reached them.

'Only, as they were truly filthy, these stories, I didn't want to trouble you with them, I thought people were lying.'

She finished by telling them that, while some accused Monsieur Grandguillot simply of gambling on the Bourse, others reckoned he had women, in Marseilles. In short, orgies, disgusting depravities. And she started sobbing again.

'Oh God! God! What's going to become of us? We really will starve to death!'

Shaken at that, and moved to see Clotilde's eyes also fill with tears, Pascal tried to think back, to clear his mind a little. In bygone days, when he was practising in Plassans, he had deposited a total of one hundred and twenty thousand francs at Monsieur Grandguillot's in several instalments, and the annual interest had already been enough for him to live on for the past sixteen years; and, each time he'd made a deposit, the notary had given him a receipt for the sum deposited. That, no doubt, would allow him to establish his position as a private creditor. Then a dim memory dawned at the back of his mind: without being able to specify the exact date, he remembered that, at the notary's request, and following a discussion in which the notary had explained why he should do so, he had handed the man a power of attorney authorizing him to use all or part of his, Pascal's, money in mortgage investments; and he was even sure that, on that power of attorney, the name of the authorized agent had remained blank. But he didn't know if the document had ever been put to use, as he had never bothered finding out how his funds were invested.

Once again her miser's anguish caused Martine to erupt:

'Ah, Monsieur, you've certainly reaped what you've sowed! Who else goes around throwing their money away like that! *Myself*, you hear, *I* know what I've got in my account every quarter, down to the last centime, and I can tell you, since I've got the figures and the denominations at my fingertips.'

For all her desolation, an unconscious smile had crept over her face. It came from knowing she'd managed to satisfy her stubborn lifelong passion, with her four hundred francs in wages barely dented, saved up and invested over thirty years, and finally amounting, through compound interest, to the enormous sum of twenty thousand francs or more. And this hoard of treasure was intact, sound, set aside in a special account, in a safe place no one knew about. It made her beam with pleasure and stopped her insisting further.

Pascal protested again.

'Well, who says all our money's lost! Monsieur Grandguillot had a personal fortune, and I don't suppose he's carried his house and his estates off with him. We'll see, we'll get to the bottom of this business, I can't come at the idea that he's a common thief... The only nuisance is that we'll have to wait.'

He was saying these things to reassure Clotilde as he could see she was only getting more anxious. She looked at him, she looked around them at La Souleiade, concerned only with his happiness, wanting more than anything to go on living there forever as they had in the past, to go on loving him forever in the depths of this benign seclusion. And he, hoping to calm her, reverted to his carefree insouciance, never having lived for money and not imagining that you could lack it and suffer because of that lack.

'Anyway, I've got money!' he finally cried. 'What's she talking about, Martine, saying we haven't got a sou left and that we'll starve to death!'

And on that note, he gaily rose to his feet and forced them both to follow him.

'Come on, then! I'll show you money! And I'll give Martine some so she can make us a decent dinner tonight.'

Upstairs in his room, before them both, he triumphantly pulled down the front of the secretaire. It was here, at the back of a drawer, that for close to sixteen years he had thrown the banknotes and gold that his last patients brought him of their own accord, without his ever asking them for a thing. Nor had he ever known the exact amount of his little hoard, taking out whatever he liked, for his pocket money, his experiments, his donations to charity, his presents. For a few months now, he'd been making frequent and serious visits to the secretaire. But he was so used to finding the sums he needed there, after years of natural economy, leading a modest life with almost nothing in expenses, that he'd come to think his savings were inexhaustible.

So he laughed easily.

'You'll see! You'll see!'

And he stood there completely astounded when, after rummaging around frantically among a mass of statements and bills, he could only muster the sum of six hundred and fifteen francs—two bank-notes of a hundred francs each, four hundred francs in gold, and fifteen francs in small change. He shook the other papers, felt in the corners of the drawer, protesting.

'But that's just not possible! There's always been money here, there was still heaps of it just days ago!... It must have been all these old bills that had me fooled. I swear that just the other week I saw some, I touched it, a lot of it...'

He was so amusingly sincere, his amazement was so guilelessly unfeigned, that Clotilde couldn't help laughing. Ah, this poor master of hers, what a woeful businessman he was! But when she noticed Martine's sorry look, her absolute despair over this paltry sum of money that now represented their livelihood, the three of them together, she herself was overcome with compassionate distress, and her eyes welled with tears as she murmured:

'My God! It's me you spent it all on. I'm the reason we're ruined, the only reason, if we have nothing left!'

He had actually forgotten the money he'd taken out for the presents. That was where the leak was, obviously. It put his mind to rest to make the connection. And since, in her anguish, she spoke of taking everything back to the shopkeepers, he got angry.

'Take back what I've given you! But you'd be taking a bit of my heart back with it! No! I'd rather starve to death, I want you to be the way I always wanted you!'

Then suddenly feeling confident, seeing a boundless future opening up ahead, he added:

'Anyway, we won't starve tonight, will we, Martine?... With what's there, we'll go far.'

Martine shook her head. She would undertake to go two months with what was there, maybe three, if they were extremely sensible, but no further. In the past, the drawer had always been topped up, a bit of money was always coming in from somewhere; whereas now, the takings were down to nil, ever since Monsieur had abandoned his patients. So they couldn't count on help from outside. And she concluded, saying:

'Give me the two hundred-franc notes. I'll try and make them last a whole month. After that, we'll see... But be very careful, don't touch the other four hundred francs in gold, shut the drawer and don't open it again.'

'Ah, as for that,' cried the doctor, 'you can rest easy! I'd rather cut off my hand.'

All was thus settled. Martine would keep independent control of this, their last remaining resources; and they could rely on her thrift, they were sure she'd pare back every possible centime. As for Clotilde, who had never had her own allowance, she wouldn't even notice the lack. The only one who would suffer was Pascal, from not having his freely available, inexhaustible hoard any more; but he had now formally agreed to let the servant pay for everything.

'So! There you are, then!' he said, relieved, jubilant, as if he'd just done an amazing deal that would ensure their livelihood forever more.

A week went by and nothing seemed to have changed at La Souleiade. In the rapture of their love, neither Pascal nor Clotilde seemed to have any idea any more that misery was looming. But one morning when Clotilde had gone to the market with Martine, the doctor, left behind on his own, received a visit that filled him at first with a sort of terror. It was the second-hand clothes dealer who had sold him that treasure, the old Alençon lace bodice, his very first present. He felt so weak in the face of any potential temptation that he trembled. Before the woman had even opened her mouth, he began putting up a defence: No! No! He couldn't, he wouldn't buy anything; and, hands thrust out, he prevented her from taking anything out of her little leather bag. But she, as oily and affable as they come, just smiled, certain of victory. In an unstoppable, ingratiating voice she began to speak, to tell him a story: Yes! A lady she couldn't name, one of the most distinguished ladies in Plassans, had been struck by misfortune and was now reduced to letting go of a piece of jewellery; then she dwelt on what a wonderful bargain it was, since this piece had cost more than twelve hundred francs, but they were resigned to parting with it for five hundred. Taking her time, she opened her bag, despite the doctor's alarm and growing anxiety, and she pulled out a thin neck chain, mounted, simply, with seven pearls at the front; but the pearls had a roundness, a brilliance, a translucence that were admirable. It was all very refined, very pure, exquisitely fresh. He immediately saw the necklace around Clotilde's delicate neck, as a natural adornment of that silken flesh whose floral taste was always on his lips. Any other piece of jewellery would have needlessly over-embellished it, these pearls would speak only of her youth. And already he had taken it in his trembling fingers, and he felt a fatal reluctance to hand it back. Yet he kept resisting, swore he didn't have five hundred francs, while the dealer droned on, in her even voice, stressing how cheap it was, which was true. After another fifteen minutes, when she felt she had him, she decided, suddenly, to let the necklace go for three hundred francs; and he gave in, his mania for giving was the stronger, his need to give pleasure, to adorn his idol. When he went to get the fifteen gold coins from the drawer, to pay the dealer, he was convinced the business at the notary's would get sorted out and they would soon have lots of money.

Afterwards, as soon as he was alone again, with the necklace in his pocket, Pascal was filled with childlike glee as he prepared his little surprise, waiting for Clotilde's return and overcome with impatience. And when he spotted her, his heart beat ready to burst. She was very hot, the burning August sun was setting the sky on fire. And so she was keen to change her frock, happy with her walk as she was, and she laughed as she told him how Martine had just pulled off a bargain, getting two pigeons for eighteen sous. Choking with emotion, he followed her into her room and, when she'd stripped to her slip, with her arms bare, and her shoulders bare, he pretended to notice something on her neck.

'Wait! What have you got there? Show me.'

He was hiding the necklace in his hand and managed to put it on her, running his fingers over her neck as if he wanted to make sure she had nothing there. But she put up a struggle, with much mirth.

'Stop that! I know there's nothing there… Now then, what are you up to, what have you got that's tickling me?'

He grabbed her in an embrace and marched her over to the long cheval-glass, where she could see herself in full. At her neck, the thin chain was a mere golden thread, and she saw the seven pearls springing up there, like milky stars, softly gleaming against the silk of her skin. It was childish and delicious. She immediately let out a delighted laugh, the cooing of a flamboyant dove preening.

'Oh, Maître, you're so kind!... So you only ever think of me?... You make me so happy!'

And the joy in her eyes, that joy of a woman and a lover, thrilled to be beautiful, to be adored, was his exquisite reward for his folly.

She threw her head back, radiant, and pushed out her lips. He leant down and they kissed.

'Are you pleased?'

'Oh, yes, Maître, pleased as anything!... Pearls are so soft, so pure! And these ones really suit me!'

For a moment more she admired herself in the mirror, innocently proud of the fair bloom of her skin beneath the lustrous pearl-drops. Then, hearing the servant moving around in the next room, and yielding to a need to show herself off, she broke away and ran to her, in her slip, bare-chested.

'Martine! Martine! See what Maître's just given me!... Well, aren't I beautiful!'

But at the sight of the spinster's stern, suddenly ashen face, her joy was spoiled. Perhaps she was aware of the heart-rending jealousy that her dazzling youth produced in that poor creature, worn out in the silent resignation of her domestic service, worshipping at her master's altar. But in any case that was the initial reaction of a fleeting moment, unconscious for the one, scarcely suspected by the other; and what was left was the visible disapproval of the thrifty housekeeper, looking askance at the costly present and condemning it.

Clotilde suddenly felt a slight chill.

'Only', she murmured, 'Maître has been rooting around in his secretaire again... They're very dear, aren't they, pearls?'

Pascal, embarrassed in his turn, protested, explained what a wonderful bargain it had been, and at great length told them all about the second-hand clothes dealer's visit, yapping away, not pausing for breath. Incredibly cheap: you couldn't not buy.

'How much?' the young woman asked, with genuine anxiety.

'Three hundred francs.'

At that, Martine, who had not yet opened her mouth, awful in her silence, could not hold back a cry:

'God Almighty! Enough to live on for six weeks, and we don't have any bread!'

Huge tears spurted from Clotilde's eyes. She would have torn the necklace from her neck if Pascal hadn't stopped her. She spoke of giving it back without further ado, and stuttered, distraught:

'It's true, Martine's right... Maître's mad, and I'm mad too, keeping this for a minute longer, in the situation we're in... It would burn my skin. Please, let me take it back.'

But to that he would never agree. He simply despaired with them both, acknowledged his mistake, declared that he was incorrigible, that they should have taken all the money off him. And he ran to the secretaire, brought over the remaining hundred francs and forced Martine to take them.

'I tell you I don't want any more, not even a sou! I'd only spend it... Here! Martine, you're the only one of us with any sense. You'll make that money last, I know you will, until our affairs are sorted out... And you, darling, keep that, don't hurt my feelings. Give me a kiss and go and get dressed.'

There was no more talk of this calamity. But Clotilde kept the necklace on around her neck, under her dress; and it was charmingly discreet, this little piece of jewellery, so fine, so pretty, hidden from all, that she alone felt on her. Sometimes, in private, she would smile at Pascal and quickly whip the pearls out of her bodice to show him, without a word, and then swiftly put them back again on her warm bosom, deliciously stirred. It was their madness she was reminding him of, with an overwhelming feeling of gratitude, a radiant joy that remained always just as vivid. She never took them off again.

A life of penury, but sweet nevertheless, began from then on. Martine had made a precise inventory of the household's resources, and things were dire. Only the potato supply promised to be substantial. As bad luck would have it, the oil in the earthenware jar was reaching the bottom just as the wine in the cask was running out. La Souleiade, no longer having either vines or olive trees, barely produced more than a few vegetables and a little fruit, pears which weren't yet ripe, and some vine-arbour grapes that would now be their only treat. Lastly, bread and meat needed to be bought daily. So right from day one the servant rationed Pascal and Clotilde, cutting out the sweets of old, the custards, the patisseries, and cutting main dishes down to a subsistence allowance. She had resumed all her old authority and treated them like children, no longer even consulting them now about what they wanted or liked. It was she who set the menus, who knew better than they did what they needed, and she was motherly, too, lavishing infinite care on them, working the miracle of giving them even more satisfaction for their paltry money, and only occasionally bullying them when it was in their interests, as you bully young children who won't eat their soup. And it seemed that this strange motherliness, this final self-immolation, this tranquillity produced by the illusion with which she surrounded their love, gratified her a little too, took her out of the secret despair into which she had sunk. Since she'd been watching over them like this, she had got back her little white face—the face of a nun vowed to celibacy—and her calm eyes the colour of ash. When, after the endless potatoes and the cheap little cutlet lost among the vegetables, she managed, some days, to serve them crêpes without compromising her budget, she exulted, and laughed to see them laughing.

Pascal and Clotilde were happy with everything, but that didn't stop them from poking fun at her when she wasn't there. The old jokes about her avarice started again, they claimed she counted the peppercorns, so many peppercorns per plate, to eke them out further. When there was hardly any oil on the potatoes, when the cutlets were reduced to a mouthful, they would exchange a quick glance, wait for her to leave the room and smother their mirth in their serviettes. They made fun of everything, they laughed at their impoverishment.

At the end of the first month, Pascal finally thought about Martine's wages. Usually, she helped herself to her forty francs from out of the common kitty she controlled.

'My poor girl,' he said to her one night, 'what are you going to do for your wages, since there's no money left?'

She stood there for a second, eyes on the ground, looking dismayed.

'Yes, well, Monsieur! I'll just have to wait.'

But he could see there was something she wasn't saying, that she had come up with some scheme but didn't know how to put her offer to him. And so he encouraged her.

'So, well, providing Monsieur agrees, I'd prefer it if Monsieur signed me a document.'

'What do you mean, a document?'

'Yes, a document where, every month, Monsieur would say he owes me forty francs.'

Pascal immediately drew up the document, and she was very happy with it, and gripped it carefully, as if it were good solid money. It clearly made her feel easier. But for the doctor and his companion, the document was fresh fodder for amazement and humour. What on earth was this extraordinary power money had over some people? Here was this old maid, who served them on her knees, who adored him especially, to the point of having given up her life for him, and who accepted this idiotic guarantee, this scrap of paper, which was worthless if he couldn't pay her!

Besides, so far neither Pascal nor Clotilde showed any great merit in keeping calm in adversity, since they didn't yet feel this adversity. They lived above it, far away, high up, in the happy and bountiful land of their passion. Sitting down to a meal, they took no notice of what they were eating, could make believe they were dining on princely viands, served on silver plates. They weren't aware of the privations growing around them, of the fact that the servant was famished, feeding on their crumbs; and they sailed through the empty house as if it were a palace hung in silk, crammed full of riches. It was certainly the happiest time in their love affair. The bedroom was a world in itself, this bedroom covered in old printed calico the colour of dawn, in which they could never exhaust their limitless passion, the endless happiness of being in each other's arms. Next came the workroom, which held glowing memories of the past, so much so that they lived there in the daytime, as if luxuriously wrapped in the joy of having already lived there so long together. Then, outside, over every nook and cranny of La Souleiade, the sumptuous summer had pitched its blue tent, resplendent with gold. In the morning, along the fragrant paths of the pine grove; at noon, under the dark shade of the plane trees, refreshed by the song of the spring; at night, on the terrace as it cooled or on the still warm threshing floor, bathed in the dim blue light of the first stars, they aired in ecstasy their existence as paupers, whose only ambition was to live together forever, in absolute disdain for all the rest. The earth was theirs, with all its treasures and feasts and dominions, since they had each other.

Towards the end of August, however, things deteriorated further. They sometimes had anxious moments, in the middle of this life free of ties or duties, free of work, which they found so sweet but felt was impracticable, wrong, to live all the time. One night Martine declared she only had fifty francs left, and that they'd have trouble surviving two weeks, even if they stopped drinking wine. On top of that, the news was grave; Grandguillot the notary was definitely insolvent, individual creditors themselves would not get a sou. At first, people had been able to count on the house and two farms that the absconding notary had inevitably left behind; but it was now certain that those properties were held in his wife's name and while he was now in Switzerland, they said, enjoying the beauty of the mountains, the wife occupied one of the farms, which she was busy improving, quite unruffled, far from the tedious vexations of their ruin. Plassans, convulsed, told how the wife put up with the husband's depravities, going so far as to allow him the two mistresses he'd taken with him to the shores of the great lakes. And Pascal, with his usual insouciance, even neglected to go and see the public prosecutor to talk about his case, sufficiently informed by everything he heard, and wondering what the point was of raking up this sordid story, since nothing good or useful could come of it now.

And so at La Souleiade, the future looked menacing. Dire poverty lay just around the corner, a moment away. Clotilde, who was extremely sensible deep down, was the first to be scared. She kept up her sunny ebullience while Pascal was around; but, being more forward-looking than he, in her womanly tenderness she became stricken with real terror as soon as he left her for a moment, wondering what would happen to him, at his age, burdened as he was with such an unwieldy household. For several days, she secretly developed a plan: to work, to earn money, a lot of money, with her pastels. People had gasped in admiration so many times at her singular and peculiarly individual talent that she took Martine into her confidence and charged her, one fine morning, to go and offer several of her fantastical bouquets of flowers to the artists' supplier in the Cours Sauvaire, who was, it was claimed, related to a Paris painter. The express condition was not to show anything in Plassans, to send everything off somewhere far away. But the result was disastrous, the merchant was startled by the strangeness of her imagination, and the unbridled force of her workmanship, and he declared that it would never sell. She despaired at this, fat tears filling her eyes. What use was she? It was distressing and shameful to be good for nothing! And the servant had to console her, to explain to her that not all women were born to work, apparently, that some grew like flowers in gardens, just to smell good, while others were the wheat of the earth and got flattened and provided food.

But Martine was chewing over a different plan, which was to persuade the doctor to take up his practice again. She ended up talking about it to Clotilde who promptly pointed out the drawbacks, the almost physical impossibility of such an endeavour. As it happened, she herself had talked about it again with Pascal only the day before. He too was worried and thought of work as the only chance of salvation. The idea of reopening a consulting room was the first thing that came to him. But for so long he'd been the doctor of the poor! How could he think of getting people to pay him when he hadn't asked for money for so many years? Wasn't it too late, anyway, at his age, to start over again in a career? To say nothing of the absurd stories that circulated about him, the whole fairy tale they'd made up about his being a crackpot genius. He wouldn't win back a single patient, it would be a pointless cruelty to force him to try, as he'd surely emerge from the experiment with his heart bruised and his hands empty. Clotilde was actually doing her level best to talk him out of it; and Martine soon realized these were good reasons and she too proclaimed that they had to stop him from risking such heartache. Besides, as she was talking, a new idea had popped into her head when she remembered an old account book she'd found in a cupboard and in which, in bygone days, she'd recorded the doctor's visits. Many people had never paid, so many that a list of them took up two full pages of the account book. Now they were in trouble, why not ask these people for the amounts they owed? She and Clotilde could well act without telling Monsieur, who had always refused to turn to the law. And this time, Clotilde sided with her. It was quite a conspiracy: she herself noted the money owing and prepared the bills, which the servant then delivered. But Martine did not get a sou anywhere, she was told from door to door that they'd have a look, that they'd call in later at the doctor's. Ten days went by and no one came, and there was only six francs left in the house, just enough to live on for another two or three days.

When Martine returned the following day empty-handed from a fresh approach at a former patient's, she took Clotilde aside and told her she'd just been chatting to Madame Félicité at the corner of the Rue de la Banne. No doubt the woman had been lying in wait for her.

She still hadn't set foot again in La Souleiade. Even the misfortune that had struck her son, this sudden loss of money that had the whole town talking, hadn't brought her any closer to him. But she was biding her time, simmering with excitement; she only kept up her pose as a rigidly conservative mother who couldn't condone certain sins, because she was certain of finally having Pascal at her mercy, counting indeed on his being forced to call on her for help any day now. When he didn't have a sou left and came knocking on her door, she would dictate her terms, make him marry Clotilde or, better still, demand that Clotilde go. But the days passed and she didn't see any sign of him. And that was why she'd stopped Martine, putting on a concerned face, asking for news, seeming to be amazed they hadn't come to her for money, all the while giving Martine to understand that her dignity prevented her from making the first move.

'You ought to talk to Monsieur about it and persuade him,' the servant concluded. 'Why wouldn't he turn to his mother, after all? It'd only be natural.'

Clotilde was horrified.

'Oh, never! I will never do such a thing. Maître would only get angry and he'd be right. I really do think he'd rather starve to death than eat Grandmother's bread.'

So, two days later, at dinner, as Martine was serving them leftover boiled beef, she warned them.

'I have no money left, Monsieur, and tomorrow there'll only be potatoes, without oil or butter... You've been drinking water for three weeks. Now, you'll have to do without meat.'

They were amused, still joked.

'Have you got any salt, dear girl?'

'Why, yes, Monsieur, just a bit.'

'Well, potatoes with salt are very good when you're hungry.'

She went back to her kitchen, and in hushed voices they started scoffing at her extraordinary avarice again. She would never offer to lend them ten francs, even though she had her little hoard hidden away somewhere, in a safe place that no one knew. What's more, they laughed about it without holding it against her, for the idea would no more occur to her than it would to take down the stars and serve them those.

That night, however, as soon as they'd gone to bed, Pascal sensed that Clotilde was restless, tormented by insomnia. So out of habit, as they lay in each other's arms in the warm darkness, he got her to confess and she ventured to tell him how anxious she was for him, for herself, for the whole household. What would become of them with absolutely no resources? For a second, she was on the point of mentioning his mother. But then she lost her nerve, and merely owned up to the steps they'd taken, she and Martine: finding the old account book, drawing up bills and dispatching them, claiming the money all over the place, to no avail. In different circumstances, he would have been really aggrieved and angry at this confession, hurt that they'd acted behind his back, going against everything he'd stood for his whole professional life. He remained silent at first, deeply affected, and that was proof enough of how great his secret anguish was at times, beneath the cheery indifference to misery he liked to feign. But then he forgave Clotilde, hugging her frantically to his chest, and he finally told her she'd done well, that they couldn't go on living like this any longer. They stopped talking but she knew he could not sleep, that, like her, he was trying to think of a way of getting the money for their daily needs. Such was their first unhappy night, a night of shared suffering, when she despaired of the torture he was doing to himself, and when he couldn't bear the idea of knowing she had no bread to eat.

At lunch the next day they ate only fruit. The doctor had remained taciturn all morning, clearly struggling. And it was only at around three o'clock that he made up his mind.

'Come on, we have to stir ourselves,' he said to his companion. 'I don't want you fasting again this evening. Go and get a hat, we're going out together.'

She looked at him, waiting to see.

'Yes, since people owe us money and they wouldn't give it to you, I'll go and see if they refuse to give it to me as well.'

His hands were shaking, the idea of getting paid this way, after so many years, had to be costing him horribly; but he forced himself to smile, and put on a brave face. But she sensed the enormity of his sacrifice from his shaky voice, and felt violently agitated.

'No, Maître! don't go, if it's too painful… Martine could always go back.'

But the servant, who was there, very much agreed with Monsieur.

'Well! And why shouldn't Monsieur go? There's never any shame in claiming what you're owed… Isn't that so? To each his due… I think it's a fine thing, myself, that Monsieur is finally showing he's a man.'

And so, as of yore, in the days when all was bliss, old King David, as Pascal sometimes jokingly called himself, went out on the arm of Abishag. Neither one of them was yet in rags, he still had his frock coat, sprucely buttoned up, while she wore her pretty red-spotted linen dress; but consciousness of their misery doubtless diminished them, made them feel they were no more now than two paupers, taking up little room, quietly slipping past the houses. The sunny streets were almost deserted. A few looks caused them some embarrassment, but they did not step up the pace, their hearts were so heavy.

Pascal wanted to start with a former magistrate whom he'd treated for a kidney infection. He entered the house, after leaving Clotilde on a bench in the Cours Sauvaire. But he was deeply relieved when the magistrate, anticipating his request, told him he only got his pension in October and would pay him then. At the home of an old lady, a septuagenarian, and paralytic, it was a different story: she took exception to the fact that they'd sent her bill by a rather rude domestic servant; so much so that he hastened to offer her his apologies, giving her all the time she liked. Next he climbed three flights of stairs to see a tax-office clerk, whom he found still unwell, and just as poor as he was, so that he didn't even dare put his request. From there, a string of old patients filed past, one after the other, including a haberdasher, the wife of a barrister, an oil merchant, and a baker, a host of well-off people; and they all turned him away, some making excuses, some simply refusing to see him in the first place—one person even pretended not to follow. There remained the Marquise de Valqueyras, the sole representative of a very old family, extremely rich and famously tight-fisted, a widow, with a little girl of ten. He had saved her till last, as she really terrified him. He finally rang the bell at her antique mansion, at the end of the Cours Sauvaire, a monumental construction from the days of Mazarin. And he was there so long that Clotilde, who was strolling under the trees, became worried.

At last when he reappeared after a good half an hour, she joked, relieved.

'What was it? She had no loose change?'

No, of course, at the Marquise's place, too, he had got nothing. The woman had complained that her tenant-farmers had stopped paying her.

'Just fancy,' he went on, to explain why he was gone so long, 'the little girl's sick. I fear she's coming down with typhoid fever... So, she wanted me to have a look at her, and I examined the poor little thing...'

An irresistible smile spread across Clotilde's lips.

'So you let her have a free consultation?'

'Well, what else could I do?'

She took his arm again, deeply moved, and he felt her press it hard to her heart. For a moment they walked haphazardly along. It was over, all that remained for them to do was to go back home, empty-handed. But he refused, and persisted in wanting more for her than the potatoes and water that awaited them. When they'd gone back up the Cours Sauvaire, they turned left into the new town; and it seemed as if bad luck was battening down on them, blowing them adrift.

'Listen,' he said finally, 'I've got an idea... If I went to Ramond, he'd gladly lend us a thousand francs, which we could pay him back when our affairs are sorted out.'

She didn't answer immediately. Ramond, whom she'd rejected, who was now married, set up in a house in the new town, in a fair way to becoming the handsome doctor of the day and making a fortune! Luckily she knew him to be high-minded and big-hearted. If he hadn't come back to see them, that was surely out of discretion. Whenever he ran into them, he would greet them so delightedly, so pleased at their happiness!

'Does that bother you?' Pascal asked guilelessly, since he would certainly have opened his house, his wallet, and his heart to the young doctor.

She rushed to respond.

'No, no! We've never been anything other than open and affectionate with each other. I think I caused him a lot of pain, but he's forgiven me... You're right, we don't have any other friends, so we have to turn to Ramond.'

Bad luck went on hounding them, though. Ramond was away, holding consultations in Marseilles and he wouldn't be back till the following night; and it was the young Madame Ramond, an old friend of Clotilde's, three years her junior, who received them. She seemed a bit embarrassed, though she was very pleasant. But the doctor, naturally, did not make his request, and simply explained his visit by saying he missed Ramond.

Out in the street, once again, Pascal and Clotilde felt alone and lost. Where could they take themselves off to now? What could they try? And they were forced to wander about again, aimlessly.

'Maître, I didn't tell you,' Clotilde murmured, finding sudden courage, 'it seems Martine ran into Grandmother... Yes, Grandmother was worried about us, asked her why we didn't go to her if we were in distress... Oh, and look! There's her door down there...'

They were, in fact, in the Rue de la Banne, and could see the corner of the Place de la Sous-Préfecture. But he had just registered what she was saying and silenced her.

'Never, do you hear!... And don't you go there, either. You're only saying that because you hate seeing me out on the streets like this. I feel sick at heart, too, to think that you're here with me and you're suffering. Only, it's better to suffer than do something we'd always regret... I won't, I can't.'

They left the Rue de la Banne and headed into the old quarter.

'I'd far rather turn to strangers... Maybe we still have some friends, but only among the poor.'

And resigned to asking for charity, David continued on his way on Abishag's arm, the old beggar-king went from door to door, leaning on the shoulder of his amorous subject, whose youth remained his sole support. It was almost six o'clock, the heat was going out of the sun, the narrow streets were filling up; and, in this populous neighbourhood, where they were loved, people greeted them, people smiled at them. A touch of pity mingled with the admiration, for no one was ignorant of their ruin. And yet they seemed to have an even nobler beauty, he all white, she all blonde, thus humbled. You could feel that they were even more united and together, their heads still high, and still proud of their radiant love, but struck by misfortune, he tottering, while she, with her brave heart, held him upright. Workmen in smocks passed them with more money in their pockets than they had. But no one dared offer them the sou that you don't begrudge the hungry. In the Rue Canquoin, they decided to stop at Guiraude's: but she had died in her turn, the week before. Two other attempts failed. After that, all they could do was dream of getting a loan of ten francs somewhere. They'd been pounding the pavements for three hours.

Ah, this Plassans, with the Cours Sauvaire, the Rue de Rome, and the Rue de la Banne carving it up into three districts; this Plassans with its closed windows; this town corroded by sunlight, apparently dead, yet hiding beneath its stillness a busy nightlife of club houses and gambling—they crossed it another three times, walking more slowly now, at the limpid end of a scorching August day! On the Cours, rickety old coaches that took people to the mountain villages were waiting, unharnessed; and, in the dark shade of the plane trees, at the doors of the cafés, customers who could be seen there from seven o'clock in the morning, watched them and smiled. In the new town, too, where the domestics stationed themselves on the doorsteps of the posh houses, they felt less sympathy than in the deserted streets of the Saint-Marc quarter, whose old mansions maintained a friendly silence. They wended their way back to the heart of the old quarter, and went all the way to Saint-Saturnin, the cathedral, whose chapter garden shaded the apse, a place of delightful peace from which they were driven by a pauper who himself begged alms from them. There was a lot of building going on around the railway station, a new suburb was springing up there, and they headed towards it. Then they returned one last time to the Place de la Sous-Préfecture, propelled by a sudden burst of fresh hope, thinking they'd end up running into someone, that money would be offered to them. But still they were attended only by the town's smiling forgiveness, at seeing them so united and so beautiful. The pointy little flint stones from the Viorne that paved the streets hurt their feet. And in the end they had to return to La Souleiade with nothing, the two of them, the old beggar-king and his amenable subject, Abishag, the girl in the flower of her youth bringing the ageing David home, stripped of his possessions and weary from having tramped around the highways and byways in vain.

It was eight o'clock and Martine, who was waiting for them, understood that there would be no cooking for her to do that evening. She claimed she'd eaten; and as she looked ill, Pascal sent her straight to bed.

'We'll manage all right without you,' Clotilde said. 'Since the potatoes are already on, we'll get them ourselves.'

The servant, in a bad mood, yielded, muttering under her breath: when you've eaten everything, what's the point of sitting down to table? But before she shut herself in her room, she said:

'Monsieur, there's no more oats for Bonhomme. I thought he looked funny, and Monsieur should go and see him.'

Seized with anxiety, Pascal and Clotilde raced away to the stable. The old horse was indeed lying on his straw, dozing. For the past six months, they hadn't taken him out because of his legs, crippled with rheumatism; and he had gone completely blind. No one knew why the doctor kept the old horse alive, even Martine had reached the point of saying they should put him down, out of simple pity. But Pascal and Clotilde always protested, horrified, as if people had talked of finishing off an old relative who wasn't moving on fast enough. No! He had served them for over a quarter of a century, and he would die at home with them, of a natural death, like the worthy soul he had always been! And, that night, the doctor did not neglect to examine him closely. He lifted up his hoofs, looked at his gums, listened to his heart.

'No, there's nothing wrong with him,' he said in the end. 'It's old age, that's all... Ah! My poor old friend, no more gadding about the countryside together for us!'

The idea that he was out of oats tortured Clotilde. But Pascal reassured her: a horse that age, who was no longer working, didn't need much! So she grabbed a handful of grass from the heap the servant had left there, and it was a joy for both of them when Bonhomme consented, out of sheer love and affection, to eat the grass from her hand.

'Ha!' she said laughing. 'I see you've still got an appetite, don't you try and tug at our heartstrings... Goodnight! Sleep tight!'

And they left him to doze off again after they had each planted a big kiss on either side of his nostrils, as always.

Night was falling and they suddenly decided not to stay downstairs in the empty house, but instead to lock everything up and carry their dinner upstairs, to the bedroom. She briskly took up the dish of potatoes, along with the salt and a good carafe of unadulterated water, while he took charge of a basket of grapes, the first to be picked from an early ripening vine that grew on a trellis below the terrace. They shut themselves in and set a small table, with the potatoes in the middle between the salt mill and the carafe, and the basket of grapes on a chair beside it. And it was a wonderful feast that reminded them of the exquisite breakfast they'd had, the day after their nuptials, when Martine refused to talk to them. They felt the same rapture at being alone, serving themselves and eating, huddled together, from the same plate.

This night of utter destitution that they had done everything in the world to avoid brought them the most delicious hours of their existence. Since they'd come home and had ensconced themselves in the big friendly bedroom, seemingly a thousand miles from that uncaring town they'd just tramped around, the sadness and fear had vanished, right down to the very memory of that awful afternoon, wasted on futile expeditions. Insouciance had wrested them back from everything outside their love, and they no longer knew if they were poor, if they'd have to seek out a friend the following day so they could dine at night. What was the good of dreading misery and going to so much trouble, since all they needed, to be perfectly happy, was to be together?

Yet he became frightened.

'God! We were so afraid that it would come to this one night! Is it rational for us to be this happy? Who knows what tomorrow holds in store for us?'

But she put her tiny hand over his mouth.

'No! Tomorrow, we'll love each other just as we love each other today... Love me with all your might, the way I love you.'

Never had they eaten with such gusto. She showed her usual appetite, a beautiful girl with a cast-iron stomach, wolfing down the potatoes with much laughter, saying they were wonderful, better than the most fabled viands. And he too recovered the appetite he'd had as a young man of thirty. Large draughts of pure water tasted heavenly to them. After that the grapes, their dessert, sent them into raptures, such fresh clusters, the blood of the earth gilded by the sun. They ate too much and were tipsy on the water and fruit, on gaiety especially. They could not remember ever having had such a feast. Their very first breakfast, with its great profusion of cutlets, and bread and wine, hadn't produced this intoxication, this thrill at being alive, in which the joy of being together was all they needed, changed the earthenware into gold plate, the pitiful pauper's food into celestial fare, such as the gods themselves never taste.

Night had completely drawn in and they hadn't lit a lamp, happy to go straight to bed. But the windows remained wide open on the vast summer sky, and the night breeze blew in, still scorching, charged with a remote scent of lavender. Over the horizon, the moon had just risen, so big and so full that the whole room was bathed in a silvery luminescence and they saw each other, as if in a dreamlike splendour, infinitely dazzling and soft.

And then, arms bare, neck bare, breasts bare, she brought the banquet she'd provided for him to a close, magnificently, making him the royal present of her body. The night before, for the first time, they had felt the chill of anxiety, an instinctive dread at the approach of the hard times looming. But now the rest of the world once more seemed forgotten, it was like one supreme night of beatitude that bountiful nature had decided to grant them, blinding them to all that lay out-side their passion.

She opened her arms and surrendered, gave herself completely.

'Oh, Maître! I wanted to put myself to work for you but I found out I'm a good-for-nothing, incapable of earning even a mouthful of the bread you eat. All I can do is love you, give myself to you, be your moment of pleasure... But it's enough for me to be your pleasure, Maître! If you only knew how glad I am that you find me beautiful, since I can make you a present of that beauty. It's all I've got, and I'm so happy I make you happy.'

He held her in an ecstatic embrace and murmured:

'Oh, yes! You're beautiful! the most beautiful, the most desired woman in the world!... All those poor jewels I've decked you out in, the gold, the precious stones—they're not worth the tiniest patch of your silky skin. A single one of your fingernails, a single strand of your hair, are riches beyond price. I'll kiss your eyelashes, devoutly, one by one.'

'But Maître, listen carefully: what gives me joy is that you're old and I'm young, because the present of my body delights you even more that way. If you were young like me, my body wouldn't give you as much pleasure, and I wouldn't get as much happiness... I'm only proud of my youth and my beauty for your sake, I only glory in them because I can offer them to you.'

He started to shake violently and his eyes welled with tears, feeling her to be so completely his, and so adorable, and so precious.

'You make me the richest, the most powerful of men, you fill me to the brim with all good things, you pour me out the most exquisite sensual pleasure that can fill a man's heart.'

And at that she gave even more of herself, she gave herself right down to the blood in her veins.

'Take me then, Maître, so I disappear in you and dissolve... Take my youth, take it all in one draught, in a single kiss, and drink it down in one gulp, drain it dry so there's nothing left but a drop of honey on your lips. You'll make me so happy, it is I, once more, who'll be grate-ful to you... Take my lips, Maître, since they're untainted, take my breath since it's pure, take my neck since it's sweet to the mouth that kisses it, take my hands, take my feet, take all of my body, since it's

a barely opened bud, a delicate silk, a perfume you get drunk on...
You hear me, Maître! Let me be a living bouquet and breathe me in!
Let me be a delicious ripening fruit and bite into me! Let me be
a never-ending caress and revel in me!... I am your plaything, the
flower that's grown at your feet to please you, the water that runs to
refresh you, the sap that bubbles up to make you feel young again.
And I'm nothing, Maître, if I'm not yours!'

She gave herself, and he took her. At that moment, a reflection of
moonlight illuminated her in her supreme nakedness. She appeared
like the beauty of womankind itself, in its everlasting springtime.
Never had he seen her so young, so white, so divine. And he thanked
her for the present of her body as if she'd given him all the treasures
of the earth. No gift can equal that of a young woman who gives herself, and who gives the flow of life, a child perhaps. They thought
of that child and their happiness was only intensified, in this royal
banquet of youth that she served him and that would have been the
envy of kings.

11

YET the very next night the anxious insomnia returned. Neither Pascal nor Clotilde spoke about their uneasiness; but in the darkness of the saddened room, they lay for hours side by side, pretending to be asleep, both thinking of the worsening situation. Each of them forgot their own distress and feared only for the other. They had had to resort to getting into debt, Martine was now buying their bread and wine and a bit of meat on credit, and she was filled with shame, moreover, being forced to lie and be extremely careful doing so, since everyone was aware of the household's ruin. The idea of mortgaging La Souleiade had of course occurred to the doctor; but that was a last resort, the only thing he had left was the property, which was valued at twenty-thousand-odd francs, although he probably wouldn't even get fifteen thousand if he sold it; but if he did sell it, then real destitution would begin and they'd be dossing down on the cobblestones, with not even a stone of their own on which to lay their heads. So Clotilde begged him to wait, not to do anything irrevocable as long as things were not absolutely desperate.

Three or four days went by. They were going into September, and the weather, unfortunately, was breaking up: there were terrible storms that ravaged the district, and one of La Souleiade's enclosure walls was knocked down and couldn't be put up again, a whole section had collapsed leaving a yawning gap. Already the people at the baker's were becoming uncivil. Then one morning when the old servant had brought back some beef for a *pot-au-feu*, she burst into tears, said the butcher was palming off inferior cuts on her. A few days more and credit would be out of the question. They absolutely had to think of something, find funds somewhere, for the little daily outlays.

One Monday, as another week of torment began, Clotilde wandered about, agitated, all morning. She seemed to be in the throes of some inner struggle and only appeared to come to a decision after lunch, seeing Pascal reject his share of a bit of leftover beef. And very calmly and resolutely, she went out with Martine afterwards, having placed in the servant's basket a small parcel, rags that she wanted to donate to charity, she said.

When she came back a couple of hours later, she was pale. But her big eyes, so pure and so frank, sparkled. She went straight to the doctor, looked him in the face and confessed her sins.

'Forgive me, Maître, for I have just broken your rule, and I know I'm about to cause you a lot of pain.'

He didn't know what she meant and became uneasy.

'So, what have you done?'

Slowly, without taking her eyes off him, she pulled an envelope out of her pocket and took a few banknotes from it. The light suddenly dawned on him and he let out a cry:

'Oh, God! The jewellery, all the presents!'

And although usually so kind and gentle, he was roused to a painful fury. He grabbed both her hands, almost did her violence, crushing the fingers holding the banknotes.

'My God! What have you done, you dreadful girl!... That's my whole heart you've sold! *Our* whole heart went into that jewellery and now you've gone and taken it back with them—for money!... Jewellery that I gave you, mementoes of our most sublime moments, your very own property, yours alone—how can you expect me to take that money back and profit by it? Can it be, did you stop to think of the awful grief it would cause me?'

Gently, she replied:

'What about you, Maître? Do you really think I could leave us in the sorry state we're in, with hardly a crust of bread to eat, when I had those rings here, the necklaces, the earrings, just lying there at the back of a drawer? But my whole being was outraged, I'd have felt myself to be a hoarder, a selfish monster, if I'd kept them any longer. And although it upset me to part with them—oh, yes! I admit it, I was so upset I almost couldn't work up the courage—I'm quite positive I only did what I had to do, as a woman who always does what you ask and who adores you.'

Then, as he hadn't let go of her hands, tears welled in her eyes, and she added in the same gentle voice, with a faint smile:

'Don't squeeze quite so hard, will you, you're actually hurting me.'

At that, he cried too, reeling, thrown into profound emotional turmoil.

'I'm a brute, getting angry like this... You did the right thing, you couldn't do otherwise. Forgive me, it's so hard for me to see you dispossessed... Give me your hands, your poor hands, and I'll make them better.'

He took her hands again delicately and covered them with kisses, finding them precious beyond price, bare and so fine, stripped of rings like this. Relieved and happy now, she told him about her escapade, how she had taken Martine into her confidence and how the two of them had gone to the second-hand dealer, the woman who'd sold him the bodice in old Alençon lace. Finally, after interminable scrutiny and haggling, the woman had given them six thousand francs for the lot. Once again, he suppressed a gesture of despair: six thousand francs! When that jewellery had cost him more than three times that much, twenty thousand francs at least.

'Listen,' he said after a long pause, 'I'll take the money, since it comes from your big heart. But I want us to be very clear that it's yours. I swear to you I'll be even more of a miser than Martine from now on, I'll only give her the few sous strictly necessary for our upkeep, and you'll find whatever's left of the total amount in the secretaire, assuming that I may never actually be able to top it up again completely and give it all back to you.'

He sat down, pulled her onto his knees and hugged her, still trembling with emotion. Then he whispered in her ear:

'So you sold everything, absolutely everything?'

Without a word, she wriggled free a little and fumbled inside her bodice in that pleasing way she had. She smiled, blushing, and at last pulled out the thin chain on which the seven pearls gleamed like milky stars; and it felt as if she were bringing out a bit of her intimate nakedness, that the whole living perfume of her body wafted from this single piece of jewellery, worn against her skin, in the most hidden mystery of her person. She then swiftly put it back, made it disappear.

He, blushing with her, felt a great bolt of joy. And he kissed her with desperate passion.

'Ah! You're the sweetest thing, and I love you so much!'

But that evening, memory of the jewellery sold still sat like a heavy weight on his heart and he could not look at the money, in his secretaire, without feeling pain. The imminence of poverty, the inevitability of poverty, oppressed him; but what made his distress even more agonizing was the thought that he was old, that he was already sixty, because it rendered him useless, incapable of earning a woman a happy life; and he woke up with a jolt to the whole disturbing reality, out of his deceitful dream of everlasting love. In an instant he sank into despond, and he felt quite ancient: this turned him cold, filled him with a kind of remorse, with hopeless anger at himself, as if he were suddenly conscious of having done something terrible in his life.

Soon after this he had an appalling illumination. When he was on his own one morning, he received a letter, postmarked Plassans in fact, and he studied the envelope, surprised that he didn't recognize the handwriting. The letter wasn't signed and after the first few lines, he gestured in irritation, ready to tear the thing up; but instead he sat down, trembling, feeling a sudden compulsion to read it to the end. Besides, the style was perfectly civilized, the long sentences ran on, tactful and considerate, like the sentences of a diplomat whose sole aim is to convince. It was demonstrated to him, with a profusion of sound arguments, that the scandalous situation at La Souleiade had gone on too long. If passion, to a certain extent, explained the initial sinful lapse, a man of his age and in his position was making himself absolutely contemptible by continuing to compound the sad fate of the young kinswoman he had led astray. Everyone knew the hold he had over her, and it was conceded that she prided herself on sacrificing herself for him; but surely it was up to him to see that she couldn't love an old man, that she merely felt pity and gratitude, and that it was high time to release her from this senile love affair, which she would emerge from disgraced, socially demoted, neither wife nor mother? Since he could no longer even leave her any money, it was hoped he would do the decent thing and find the strength to part with her so as to ensure her happiness, if there was still time. And the letter ended with the maxim that bad behaviour always ended up being punished.

From the opening words, Pascal knew that this anonymous letter was from his mother. Old Madame Rougon must have dictated it, he could even hear the modulations in her voice. But having begun reading it in a fit of anger, he ended the reading pale and shivering, seized by the chill that now shot through him at any time of day. The letter was right, and it shone light on his uneasiness, made him see that the remorse he felt was all about being old, being poor, and yet holding on to Clotilde regardless. He got to his feet, planted himself in front of a mirror and stood there for a long while, his eyes gradually clouded by tears, in despair at the lines on his face and at his white beard. The deathly feeling of cold that chilled him to the marrow was the idea that, now, separation would be necessary, unavoidable, inevitable. He drove the idea away, couldn't imagine he'd ever end up accepting it;

but it was bound to return anyway, and he wouldn't be able to live for a minute without being assailed by it, without being torn apart by this battle between his love and his reason, until the terrible night when he would resign himself and give in, having used up all his nerve and tears. In his current cowardly state, he shuddered at the mere thought of one day finding such courage. This was indeed the end, there was no turning back, he had become frightened for Clotilde, she was so young, and all that was left to him was to do his duty and save her from himself.

Haunted by the words, by the turns of phrase in the letter, he first tortured himself trying to persuade himself that she didn't love him, that all she felt for him was pity and gratitude. It would, he believed, have made the break easier if he'd been convinced she was sacrificing herself and that by holding on to her any longer, he was simply satisfying his monstrous selfishness. But it was useless studying her and putting her to various tests—he always found her as loving as ever and as passionate as ever in his arms. He was distraught at this result, which went against the dreaded solution by making her even dearer to him. And so he strove to prove to himself that their separation was necessary, and he went through all the reasons why. The life they'd been leading for the past few months, this life without ties or duties, without work of any kind, was no good. For himself, he felt he was fit only to crawl away and sleep in the ground, somewhere; but, for her, wasn't it a detrimental existence, one from which she'd emerge workshy and spoiled, incapable of resolve? He was corrupting her, was making an idol of her, amid the booing and hooting of scandal. Then, in a sudden flash, he pictured himself dying and leaving her all on her own, out on the street, with nothing, despised. No one took her in, she roamed the streets, forever without a husband or children. No! No! That would be a crime; he could not, for the sake of the few days of happiness remaining to him, leave her—*her* of all people—nothing but this legacy of shame and destitution.

One morning when Clotilde had gone out by herself on some errand in the neighbourhood, she came back shattered, all pale and shivering. And as soon as she was upstairs and they were alone, she almost fainted in Pascal's arms. She stammered a few disjointed words.

'Oh, my God!… God!… Those women…'

He was alarmed and pressed her with questions.

'Come now! tell me! what happened?'

At that, the blood rushed to her face, turning it bright red. She hugged him tightly, hiding her face against his shoulder.

'It's those women... I'd crossed over into the shade and, as I was shutting my parasol, I accidentally knocked over a child... And they all ganged up against me and yelled things. Oh, the things they yelled! Like I'd never have any myself, any children! That children didn't grow in creatures like me!... And other things, God! Things I can't repeat, that I didn't even understand!'

She began sobbing. He was livid, but couldn't think of anything to say, so he kissed her frantically while crying with her. The scene formed a picture in his mind, he saw her set upon, smeared with obscenities. Eventually he mumbled:

'It's my fault, it's because of me that you're going through this... Listen, we'll go away, far away, somewhere where they don't know us, where people will greet you, where you'll be happy.'

But, seeing him crying, she bravely made an effort, straightened up and swallowed her tears.

'Ah! How mean of me to do this to you! And I promised myself so many times I wouldn't say a word! But then, when I got home, I felt so sick at heart that everything just came pouring out... See, it's over, don't be upset... I love you.'

She was smiling, and she took him gently in her arms again and kissed him in her turn, as if he were a desperate man, who had to be lulled out of his suffering.

'I love you, I love you so much, I could get over anything! You're all the world, so what does anything or anyone that isn't you matter? You're so good, you make me so happy!'

But he went on crying and she started to cry again, too, and for a long while all they felt was fathomless sadness, a distress in which their kisses mingled with their tears.

When Pascal was alone again, he judged himself to be a monster. He could not go on wrecking the life of this child he adored. That very evening something happened that at last brought him the opening he'd been looking for till then, in terror at actually finding it. After dinner, Martine took him aside with an air of great secrecy.

'I saw Madame Félicité, Monsieur, and she told me to give you this letter, and I'm supposed to say that she would have brought it to you herself if her good name didn't prevent her from coming here any more... She begs you to send back Monsieur Maxime's letter and let her know what Mademoiselle's answer is.'

It was indeed a letter from Maxime. Félicité, delighted to have received it, was using it as a weapon after waiting in vain for dire straits to deliver her son to her. Since neither Pascal nor Clotilde had come asking her for aid or support, she was yet again changing tack, reverting to her original plan of separating them; and, this time, the opportunity seemed decisive. Maxime's letter was pressing, and he had addressed it to his grandmother so that she would plead his cause with his sister. He now had full-blown ataxia, and already he could no longer walk except on the arm of a servant. But the thing he deplored most was a bad mistake he'd made—a pretty brunette had wormed her way into his home, and he hadn't been able to resist; in fact, he'd left what remained of his health in her arms; and the worst of it was that this man-eater, he now knew for sure, was a secret present from his father. Saccard had sent her to him, like a true gentleman, to ensure that he got his hands on his son's inheritance all the faster. So, after throwing her out, Maxime had barricaded himself in his mansion, showing his father himself the door, but frightened he'd see the man slip back in through a window one morning. He was terrified of being on his own and desperately clamoured for his sister, as he wanted her to be a bulwark against these dastardly schemes, and, well, because she was a sweet upright woman who would take care of him. The letter gave it to be understood that if she treated him well, she would not regret it; and he ended by reminding the young woman of the promise she'd made to him during his trip to Plassans, of joining him if, one day, he really needed her.

Pascal stood frozen to the spot. He read it again, all four pages of it. What was being offered was the separation, on terms acceptable to him, advantageous for Clotilde, so easy and so natural a move that they'd have to agree at once; but despite the effort of his reason, he felt so unsure, so irresolute still, that he had to sit down for a moment, his legs shaky. Yet he wanted to be heroic, and so he pulled himself together and called Clotilde.

'Here! Read this letter your grandmother's passed on to me.'

Clotilde read the letter attentively to the end, without a word, without a movement. Then, perfectly matter-of-factly, she said:

'Well, you'll answer, won't you?... I refuse.'

He had to force himself not to let out a cry of joy. Already, as if a different self had taken the floor, he heard himself say, quite reasonably:

'You refuse, it just isn't possible... We should think about it, though, let's wait till tomorrow before giving an answer, and we can talk it over, if you like?'

But she was stunned at this and became agitated.

'Leave you! Why?! Really, you'd agree to it?... What madness! We love each other, so why on earth would we part, why would I go up there, where no one loves me?! Come now, have you thought about it? It would be too silly for words.'

He avoided going down that track, spoke of promises made, of duty.

'Remember, darling, how upset you were when I warned you Maxime was in danger. Now, here he is cut down by illness, crippled, all alone, calling you to his side!... You can't leave him in that situation. There's a duty there for you to fulfil.'

'A duty!' she cried. 'What duty can I possibly have to a brother who's never bothered for a second with me? My only duty lies where my heart is.'

'But you promised. I promised for you, I said you were sensible... You're not going to make a liar of me.'

'Sensible, you're the one who isn't sensible. It's totally senseless for us to part when we'd both die of sorrow.'

And she cut him off with a sweeping gesture, furiously ruling out all discussion.

'Anyway, what's the good of arguing? Nothing could be simpler, only one word's needed. Do you want to send me away?'

He let out a cry.

'Me, send you away, good God!'

'Well then, if you're not sending me away, I'm staying.'

She was laughing now, and she ran to her desk and wrote two words, in red pencil, across her brother's letter: 'I refuse.' And then she called Martine and absolutely insisted Martine take the letter back in an envelope that instant. He was laughing too, flooded with such happiness that he let her go ahead. The joy of holding on to her swept all before it, even his reason.

But that very night, when she'd fallen asleep, what remorse he felt at having been so weak! Once again he'd simply yielded to his craving for happiness, to the sensual pleasure of finding her there every night, snuggled against his side, so fine and soft in her long chemise, covering him with the fresh scent of her youth. After her, he would never love again; and his whole being cried out at having the woman and love itself wrenched away from him like this. He broke out in a sweat of agony when he pictured her gone and saw himself alone, without her, without all that was warm and softly caressing in the air he breathed, her breath, her subtle mind, her fearless integrity, that dear physical and moral presence, as necessary now to his life as daylight itself. She needed to leave him and he had to find the strength to die of it. Without waking her, all the while holding her asleep on his heart, her chest lifted by a child's shallow breathing, he lay there hating himself for being so spineless, and he sized up the situation with terrible lucidity. It was over: a life commanding respect, and a fortune, were waiting for her up there; he couldn't be such a selfish old man as to keep her any longer in her poverty-stricken state, getting about under a hail of abuse. And so, faltering at feeling her so adorable in his arms, so trusting, a subject who'd given herself to her old king, he vowed to be strong, not to accept the sacrifice of this child, to restore her to happiness, to life, even if it were against her will.

From that moment the struggle of self-denial began. A few days passed and he had so successfully got her to see the harshness of her 'I refuse' on Maxime's letter, that she'd written at some length to her grandmother to justify her refusal. But she still wouldn't leave La Souleiade. As he had descended to extreme frugality so as to make as small a dent as possible in the money from the jewellery, she outdid him and ate her bread dry, chirruping with laughter as she did so. One morning, he even caught her giving Martine tips on thrift. Ten times a day, she would stare at him, throw her arms around him, cover him with kisses, trying to fight the appalling idea of separation, which she now saw glinting constantly in his eyes. Then all of a sudden, she had a new argument to wield. After dinner one night, he was racked with palpitations and nearly passed out. This surprised him as he had never had a problem with his heart, and he simply assumed that his nervous disorder was coming back. Since he'd come to know the great delights of the flesh on a daily basis, he'd been feeling less robust, with the odd sensation that something fragile, deep inside him, had broken. She immediately became worried, anxiously attentive. Ah, well! now surely he'd stop talking about her going? When you loved people and they were sick, you stayed with them and looked after them.

And so the battle was never-ending. It was a continual clash between tenderness and selflessness, the sole goal for each of them being the happiness of the other. But although, for him, the emotion he felt at seeing her so kind and loving only made the necessity of her going all the crueller, he realized that that necessity was becoming more imperative with each passing day. His decision was now categorical. He was merely racking his brains, still tremulous, hesitant, trying to find a way to persuade her. He pictured the scene of tears and despair in his mind: what would he do? What would he say to her? How would they manage, either of them, to embrace one last time and part, never to see each other again? But the days went by and he could think of nothing, and he started calling himself a coward again every night when, the candle blown out, she took him in her cool fresh arms once more, happy and triumphant at defeating him this way.

Often she poked fun, with a hint of tender malice.

'Maître, you're too good, fancy keeping me on.'

But this would annoy him and he would become agitated, and glum.

'No, stop! Don't talk about my goodness! If I were really good, you'd have been up there long ago, living in affluence and enjoying respect, with a whole wonderful tranquil life ahead of you, instead of clinging on here, reviled and poor and without any prospects, being the sad companion of an old lunatic like me!... No! I'm nothing but a coward and a degenerate!'

She would swiftly shut him up. And it was in reality his goodness that was bleeding, the immense goodness that he owed to his love of life, and that he spread over living beings and things in his constant concern for the happiness of all. Didn't being good mean wanting her to be happy, making her happy, at the cost of his own happiness? He needed to have that particular goodness, and he really felt that he would acquire it, and be decisive, be heroic. But like those poor souls bent on suicide, he was waiting for the opportunity, the right moment and the means to attempt it.

One morning he got up at seven, and she was quite surprised to find him already sitting at his table when she went into the workroom. For many a long week he hadn't once opened a book or picked up a pen.

'Well, well! You're working?'

He didn't lift his head, answered as though absorbed:

'Yes, it's the Family Tree, I haven't even updated it.'

For a few minutes she stood behind him, watching him write. He was completing the notes for Aunt Dide, Uncle Macquart, and little Charles, recording their deaths, putting in the dates. Then, as he still didn't budge, apparently having forgotten she was there waiting for the kisses and laughter of other mornings, she walked over to the window and back, for want of something to do.

'So, it's serious, we're working?'

'Of course, you can see I should have entered these deaths already last month. And I've got a heap of jobs waiting for me, over here.'

She stared at him, searching his eyes piercingly as she did lately, as though constantly questioning him.

'Fine! Let's work... If you have any research jobs I can do, any notes for me to copy, give them to me.'

And from that day forward, Pascal pretended to throw himself completely into work again, as if in earnest. It was one of his theories, anyway, that absolute rest had no benefit, that it should never be prescribed, not even to the chronically overworked. A man lives only through the external environment in which he is immersed; and the sensations he takes in from it are transformed in him into movement and thoughts and deeds; which means that, if there is absolute rest, if you continue to take in sensations without giving them back, digested and transformed, this produces congestion, discomfort, an inevitable loss of equilibrium. He himself had always felt that work was the best regulator of his existence. Even on days when he wasn't well, he'd get down to work in the morning and would recover his balance. Never did he feel better than when he was carrying out a task he'd set himself and methodically sketched out in advance, so many pages by the same time every morning; and he compared that task to a balancing pole that kept him on his feet, amid the everyday woes, the falterings and failures. And so he blamed indolence, the idle state he'd been living in for weeks, as being the sole cause of the palpitations that left him gasping for air at times these days. If he wanted to get himself better, he had only to take up his great work again.

For hours, Pascal would elaborate on these theories, explaining them to Clotilde with feverish, exaggerated enthusiasm. He seemed once more to be possessed by the love of science that, until his sudden passion for her, had exclusively consumed his life. He kept telling her he couldn't leave his work unfinished, that he still had so much to do if he wanted to erect a lasting monument! Concern about the files seemed to take hold of him again, and once more he opened the big cupboard twenty times a day, took the files down from the top shelf and continued to add to them. His ideas on heredity were already evolving, and he'd have liked to review everything, revise everything, take the natural and social history of his family as a basis to build a comprehensive synthesis, a summing-up, drawn with a broad brush, of humanity as a whole. Then, alongside that, he revisited his treatment using hypodermic injections, wanting to expand on it: an obscure vision of a new therapeutics, a vague and dimly intuited theory, was taking shape in his mind, based on his conviction and personal experience, regarding the positive and dynamic influence of work.

Now, every time he sat down at his table, he complained.

'Life's too short, I'll never have enough time!'

It was indeed as if he didn't have a moment to lose. And one morning, out of the blue, he looked up and said to his companion, who was making a copy of a manuscript by his side:

'Listen carefully, Clotilde... If I die...'

She protested, alarmed.

'The very idea!'

'If I die, listen carefully... You lock the doors immediately. You keep the files to yourself, don't show them to anybody. And when you've gathered my other manuscripts together, you give them to Ramond... Do you hear! Those are my last wishes.'

But she cut him off, refused to listen.

'Stop it! You're being silly!'

'Clotilde, swear that you'll keep the files and give my other papers to Ramond.'

In the end, she did swear, serious now, her eyes full of tears. He swept her into his arms, also very moved, and covered her with kisses as if his heart had abruptly opened again. Then he collected himself and spoke of his fears. Since he'd been forcing himself to get back to work, they seemed to have taken hold of him again, and he kept watch over the cupboard, claimed to have seen Martine prowling around. Couldn't the old maid's blind devotion be whipped up, couldn't she be driven to some evil act by being persuaded she was saving her master? Suspicion had already caused him so much suffering! But he relapsed, under the threat of his imminent isolation, into his old torment, into this torture endured by the man of science threatened and persecuted by his own people, in his own home, in his very flesh, in the work of his brain.

One evening when he'd reverted to the subject with Clotilde, he let slip:

'You know, when you're no longer here—'

She went completely white, and when she saw that he'd stopped himself with a shudder, she said:

'Oh, Maître! You're still mulling over that outrage? I can see it in your eyes, you're hiding something from me, you're thinking something I no longer share... But if I go and you die, who'll be here to protect your work?'

He felt she was getting used to the idea of going after all, and he found the strength to reply airily:

'Do you really think I'd allow myself to die without seeing you again? I'll write to you, for heaven's sake! You'll be the one who comes and closes my eyes.'

At that, she dropped onto a chair and sobbed.

'My God! Can it be? Can you actually want us to live apart, and soon, when we never leave each other even for a minute, when we live in each other's arms! And yet, if the child had come...'

'Ah! Guilty as charged!' he snapped, cutting her off. 'If the child had come, you would never have gone... Can't you see that I'm too old and that I despise myself! With me, you'd remain childless, you'd have the particular pain of not being a whole woman, a mother! Go, then, since I'm no longer a man!'

In vain she strove to calm him down.

'No, I know very well what you think, we've said it twenty times: if a child isn't the result, the act of love is just a useless obscenity... The other night, you threw down that novel you were reading because the hero and heroine were stunned at having made a baby without even knowing they could, and wanted only to get rid of it... Ah! I've longed for it so much, I'd have loved it so much, your child!'

That day, Pascal seemed to bury himself even deeper in work. He now kept at it for four or five hours at a stretch, whole mornings or afternoons, without looking up once. He exaggerated his zeal, forbade anyone to disturb him, even to address a single word to him. But sometimes, when Clotilde had tiptoed out, needing to give orders below or run some errand, he would furtively check that she was no longer there, then drop his head on the edge of the table, utterly dejected. This was a painful relaxation of the extraordinary effort he had to make, whenever he felt her near him, to stay at his table and not take her in his arms, not hold her there for hours, softly kissing her. Ah, work! How ardently he turned to it as the only refuge in which he could hope to numb himself, to deaden himself completely! But more often than not he couldn't work and had to put on an act, pretend to concentrate, his eyes glued to the page, those sad eyes that would cloud with tears, while his mind agonized, muddled, slippery, always filled with the same picture. Was he now to discover that even work was bankrupt, he who had believed it to be all-important, the sole creator, the regulator of the world? Did he now have to discard that old tool, renounce action, do no more than live, and love beautiful passing strangers? Or was it merely the fault of his senility if he was becoming incapable of writing a page, just as he was incapable of making a child? Fear of impotence had always tormented him. While he sat there with his cheek to the table, sapped of strength, overwhelmed by misery, he dreamed he was thirty years old and that, every night, in Clotilde's arms, he drew the energy he needed for the following day's work. And the tears ran down his white beard; but if he heard her coming back upstairs, he would swiftly sit up and grab his pen again, so that she'd find him just as she'd left him, apparently deep in thought, where there was nothing but distress and emptiness.

It was now the middle of September and two interminable weeks had passed in this state of unease without bringing any solution, when one morning, to her great surprise, Clotilde saw her grandmother Félicité step in. The day before, Pascal had run into his mother in the Rue de la Banne and, impatient to get the sacrifice over with, not finding the strength to make the break himself, he had confided in her, despite his repugnance, and begged her to come over the next day. As it happened, she had just received a second letter from Maxime in which he sounded completely desperate.

First, she explained her presence.

'Yes, it's me, pet, and for me to set foot in here again, as you know, I'd have to have serious reasons indeed... Really, in all honesty, you've lost your head, but I can't stand back and let you ruin your life like this without spelling things out for you one last time.'

She promptly read out Maxime's letter in a tearful little voice. He was stuck in an armchair, apparently stricken with a fast-developing, extremely painful form of ataxia. And so he demanded a definite answer from his sister, still hoping she would come, and agitated at the idea of being reduced to looking for some other sick-nurse. That was what he'd be forced to do, however, if he was abandoned to his sad predicament. And when she finished her reading, Félicité intimated just how regrettable it would be to let Maxime's fortune fall into unknown hands; but, above all, she spoke of duty, of the help owed to a relative, she, too, pretending there had been a formal promise.

'Come now, pet, try to remember. You told him that if ever he needed you, you'd go and join him. I can still hear you... Isn't that right, Son?'

Pascal had been silent from the moment his mother arrived, and now, pale and head bowed, he let her pretend, replying only with a slight nod.

Félicité then summed up all the reasons he himself had given Clotilde: the appalling scandal that now had people resorting to insult, the looming destitution, so oppressive for them both, the impossibility of continuing to live such a worthless life in which he, already getting old, would lose what health he still had, and she, so young, would end up throwing her whole life away. What future could they hope for, now that it had come to poverty? It was stupid and cruel to dig your heels in like this.

Completely straight-backed, her face a mask, Clotilde kept silent, refused even to discuss it. But since her grandmother was pressing her, harassing her, she finally said:

'Once again, I have no duty to my brother whatsoever, my duty lies here. He can do what he likes with his fortune, I don't want any part of it. When we're too poor, Maître will send Martine away and keep me on as servant.'

She finished with a flourish of her hand. Oh, yes! She'd devote herself to her prince, give him her life, sooner beg along the highways and byways, leading him by the hand! Then, when they'd returned home, just as they had done the evening of the day they'd gone door to door, she'd give him the gift of her youth and warm him in her unsullied arms!

Old Madame Rougon nodded, chin thrust out.

'Before being his servant, you'd have done better starting out as his wife. Why didn't the two of you get married? That would have been simpler and more correct.'

She reminded her granddaughter that one day she'd come to insist they get married so as to hush up the growing scandal, and the young woman had seemed surprised, had said that neither she nor the doctor had thought of it, but that, if need be, they'd get married all right, only later, since there was no rush.

'Get married, I'm all for it!' cried Clotilde. 'You're right, Grandmother.'

And she turned to Pascal:

'You've told me a hundred times you'd do whatever I wanted... Marry me, you hear. I'll be your wife and I'll stay. A wife doesn't leave her husband.'

But he replied only with a gesture, as if he feared his voice would betray him and that he would accept, with a cry of gratitude, the eternal bond she was offering him. His gesture could mean hesitation, or rejection. What was the good of this marriage *in extremis*, when everything was falling apart?

'Doubtless', Félicité went on, 'those are fine sentiments. You've arranged it all very nicely in that little head of yours. But marriage won't provide you with an income; and meanwhile, you cost him a lot of money, you're a very heavy burden on him.'

These words had an extraordinary effect on Clotilde, who whipped round to face Pascal, her cheeks flushed, her eyes flooded with tears.

'Maître! Is that true, what Grandmother just said? Have you got to the point where you now resent the money I cost here?'

He had gone even whiter and didn't move a muscle, sitting slumped as though crushed. But in a distant voice, as if talking to himself, he murmured:

'I've got so much work to do! I'd so like to get back to my files, my manuscripts, my notes, and finish my life's work!... If I were on my own, I might be able to get through it all. I'd sell La Souleiade—oh, for a song, it's not worth much! I'd go and set myself up in a little room somewhere, with all my papers. I'd work from morning to night and I'd try not to be too unhappy.'

But he would not look at her, and in her agitation, she was not about to be fobbed off with this painful mumbled excuse. She was growing more terrified by the second, as she now knew that the inevitable was about to be said.

'Look at me, Maître, look me in the face... And please, I'm begging you, be brave, choose between your work and me, since you seem to be saying that you're sending me away so you can get more work done!'

The moment for the heroic lie had come. He lifted his head and looked her in the face, bravely; and with the smile of a dying man who welcomes death, he found his voice of exquisite goodness once more:

'Don't get so excited!... Can't you just do your duty like everyone else? I've got a lot of work to get through, I need to be on my own; and you, darling, should join your brother. Go, then, it's all over.'

There was a terrible silence for a few seconds. She went on staring hard at him in the hope he would relent. Was he really telling the truth, wasn't he sacrificing himself for her future happiness? For a moment, she had the subtle feeling that that was exactly what he was doing, as if a chilling breath, emanating from within him, had warned her.

'So you're sending me away for good? You won't let me come back soon?'

He remained brave and seemed to answer with another smile that you didn't go off only to spin on your heels and come straight back; and everything blurred, her perception dimmed, and she actually managed to believe that he'd chosen work, genuinely, as a man of science for whom work prevails over any woman. She had gone very pale again, waited a bit longer in the excruciating silence; then, slowly, with her air of loving and absolute submission, she said:

'All right, Maître, I'll leave whenever you like and I won't come back till the day you call me back.'

This was the severing blow. There was no turning back. Moving fast, Félicité, surprised at not having needed to say more, tried to get them to set the departure date. She congratulated herself on her tenacity, believed she'd outflanked them. It was Friday, and it was agreed Clotilde would leave on the Sunday. A telegram was even sent to Maxime.

Already the mistral had been blowing for three days. But that night it redoubled in violence, and Martine announced that it would last at least another three days, according to popular opinion. The winds of late September are terrible throughout the valley of the Viorne. And she went up to all the rooms to make sure the shutters were tightly shut. When the mistral blew, it came from over the rooftops of Plassans and hit La Souleiade at a slant, on the little plateau on which it was built. And it was rage, a furious merciless whirlwind that lashed the house and shook it from cellar to attic, day and night, without a single pause. Tiles flew off, window locks were torn away, while inside, the wind rushed through the cracks in a wild roaring lament, and the doors, left open even for a second, slammed shut with the great reverberating boom of a canon. It was as if they had to withstand a whole siege, amid the tumult and anguish.

The next day, it was in this mournful house rattled by the gale that Pascal tried to busy himself, alongside Clotilde, with the preparations for her departure. Old Madame Rougon was not to return till the Sunday, when it came time to say goodbye. When Martine learned of the imminent separation, she stood there in shock, speechless, her eyes lighting up briefly with a flash of fire; and as they'd sent her out of the room, saying they'd manage to deal with the trunks without her, she went back to her kitchen and threw herself into her routine jobs there, looking as though she knew nothing about the catastrophe that was about to shatter their life together. But at the slightest summons from Pascal, she came running, so swift, so nimble, her face so luminous, bathed in the sunshine of her keenness to serve him, that she seemed to have become a girl again. He himself never left Clotilde for a minute, helping her pack, wanting to satisfy himself that she really was taking everything she'd need. Two big trunks sat open in the middle of the room, which was a mess, with parcels and clothes trailing everywhere; and all the furniture, all the drawers, were ransacked again and again. And this toil, this overwhelming concern not to forget anything, helped a little to dull the aching pain both of them felt in the pit of their stomachs. They were distracting themselves for a moment: he was extremely solicitous, making sure there was no wasted space, using the hat compartment for small bits and pieces, slipping boxes between the chemises and the handkerchiefs; while she, taking down her dresses, folded them on the bed, waiting to put them in last, in the top rack. Then when, a little weary, they straightened up and found themselves face to face, they smiled at each other at first, then held back sudden tears, reminded of the irremediable unhappiness which wracked them again, body and soul. But they remained firm, even if their hearts were bleeding. Oh, God! So it was true they had already stopped being together? And that's when they heard the wind, the terrible wind, which threatened to rip the house apart.

How many times, over that last day, did they go to the window, drawn by the storm, hoping it would sweep the world away! While the

mistral is gusting, the sun doesn't stop shining, the sky remains
a steady blue; but it's a leaden blue, turbid with dust; and the yellow
sun grows pale in the shimmering light. They watched the immense
white plumes of dust swirling up from the roads in the distance, the
bent, wildly waving trees, which all looked as if they were fleeing
in the same direction, at the same breakneck speed, the entire countryside parched and exhausted under the violence of this relentlessly
even breath, bowling along endlessly with its rumbling thunder.
Branches broke off and vanished, roofs were lifted off and carted so
far they were never found again. Why couldn't the mistral take them,
together, and hurl them down there, in that unknown land, where
people are happy? The trunks were nearly done when he tried to open
a shutter again after the wind had just slammed it shut; but the wind
rushed in so hard through the half-open window, she had to run to his
aid. They put all their combined weight against it and finally managed to shoot the bolt home. Inside the room the last of Clotilde's
things had been blown around helter-skelter, and they picked up the
pieces of a small hand mirror that had fallen off a chair. Was this
a sign of approaching death, as the women of the faubourg liked
to say?

That evening, after a mournful dinner in the bright dining room,
with its big floral bouquets, Pascal talked of going to bed early.
Clotilde was to leave the following morning, by the ten-fifteen train;
and he was worried about the length of the trip for her, twenty hours
cooped up in a railway carriage. When it came time to go to bed, he
embraced her, but insisted, from that very night, in going to bed on
his own, back in his old room. He was absolutely determined, he said,
that she get some rest. If they stayed together, neither of them would
shut an eye, it would mean a sleepless night of fathomless sadness. In
vain, she implored him with her big loving eyes, held out her exquisite arms to him: he found the superhuman strength to walk away, after
placing kisses on her eyelids as if she were a child, tucking her into
bed and enjoining her to be reasonable, to sleep well. Wasn't the separation already complete? It would have filled him with shame and
remorse if he'd slept with her again when she was no longer his. But
how awful it was to return to that damp, abandoned room, where the
cold bed of his bachelorhood awaited him! It seemed to him that
he was stepping back into his old age, which came down on him once
more, and forever, like the lead lid of a coffin. At first he blamed the

wind for his sleeplessness. The lifeless house filled with howling, imploring voices and angry voices, merging amid unending sobs. Twice he got up and went to listen at Clotilde's door, but heard nothing. He went downstairs to close a door that was banging, with muffled thuds, as if sorrow was knocking on the walls. Puffs of wind blew through the pitch-black rooms and he went back to bed frozen, shivering, haunted by ominous visions. Then he realized that the loud voice causing him such distress, taking away his sleep, was not coming from the raging mistral. It was Clotilde calling, the strange feeling that she was still there yet he'd deprived himself of her. After that, he thrashed around in a convulsion of wild desire, and appalling despair. Oh, God! Never to have her as his own again, when he could, with a word, have her still, have her forever more! It was like tearing off his own flesh, the youthful flesh they were removing from him. At thirty, you can find another woman. But what an effort it was, with all the passion of his waning virility, to give up this fresh body, with its wonderful smell of youth, this body that had given itself royally, that belonged to him as his possession, his own creature! A dozen times he was on the point of leaping out of bed and going in to her to take her again, and hold on to her. The alarming attack lasted until dawn, amid the furious assault of the wind from which the whole house shook.

It was six o'clock when Martine, thinking her master had tapped on the parquet floor to call her to his room, went upstairs. She turned up with the same sprightly and exalted air she'd had for the past two days, but stood there frozen to the spot with worry and shock when she saw him lying across the bed half dressed, ravaged, biting into his pillow to stifle his sobs. He had tried to get up and dress at once, but a fresh paroxysm had just felled him and he was dizzy and choking with palpitations.

He had only just recovered from a short fainting fit when he started stammering out his torment again.

'No, no! I can't, I'm in too much pain… I'd rather die, die now…'

Yet he recognized Martine, and he threw off all restraint and confessed his sins to her, worn-out, drowning and wallowing in pain.

'My poor girl, I'm in too much pain, my heart's breaking… She's taking my heart with her, taking all of me. And I can't live without her now… I nearly died during the night, I'd like to die before she goes so I don't have the heartache of seeing her leave me… Oh, God! She's going, and I won't have her any more, and I'll be alone, all alone…'

The servant, so cheerful coming up, had turned as pale as wax, her face hard and smarting. For a moment she watched him clutching at the sheets with clenched fists, in a rage of despair, his mouth glued to the quilt. Then she seemed to make up her mind with a sudden effort.

'But Monsieur, there's no sense upsetting yourself like this. It's ridiculous... Since that's how it is, and you can't do without Mademoiselle, I'll go and tell her what a state you've got yourself into...'

He suddenly shot up at that phrase, though still reeling and holding himself upright by the back of a chair.

'Don't you dare do that, Martine!'

'As if I'd listen to you! And find you half dead again, crying your eyes out!... Oh, no! I'm going straight to Mademoiselle and I'll tell her the truth and force her to stay with us, you see if I don't!'

But he grabbed her arm in fury and he would not let go.

'I order you to keep quiet, do you hear? Or you can leave with her... Why did you come in here? I was sick because of the wind. That's nobody else's business.'

Then, overcome with compassion and yielding to his normal goodness, he ended up smiling.

'My poor girl, see how angry you've made me! Let me do what I have to do, for everybody's sake. And not a word, you'd hurt me a great deal.'

Martine, in her turn, held back brimming tears. It was just as well they'd reached an understanding then, because Clotilde came in almost immediately, having risen early and being in a hurry to see Pascal again, no doubt hoping, till the last minute, that he would keep her. Her eyelids, too, were heavy with lack of sleep, and she stared at him at once, her eyes boring into his with that searching expression of hers. But he still looked so distraught she became worried.

'No, it's nothing, I assure you. I would have slept well, actually, if it hadn't been for the mistral... Isn't that so? Martine, I was just telling you.'

The servant gave a nod, backing him up. And Clotilde played along, too, didn't complain about her night of struggle and suffering, while he lay agonizing in the next room. The two women, docile now, merely yielded and helped him in his selflessness.

'Wait,' he went on, opening the secretaire, 'I've got something for you. Here! There's seven hundred francs in this envelope.'

And although she protested, resisted, he went through it all with her. Of the six thousand francs from the jewellery, barely two hundred had been spent, and he'd keep a hundred to go on with till the end of the month, sticking to the strict thrift, the bleak stinginess he'd shown lately. After that, he'd probably sell La Souleiade, he'd work, he'd find a way to get himself out of his troubles. But he didn't want to touch the remaining five thousand francs, since they were her property, hers alone, and she would find them there, still in the drawer.

'Maître, you're really distressing me—'

He cut her off.

'It's what I want, you're the one who's breaking my heart... Let's see, it's half past seven. I'll go and tie up your trunks now they're closed.'

When Clotilde and Martine found themselves alone, face to face, they gazed at one another for a moment in silence. Since the new situation had arisen, they had been well aware of their unspoken antagonism, the obvious triumph of the young mistress, the secret jealousy of the old servant, all over their adored master. Now, it seemed it was the servant who had won. But at the last minute, their shared emotion brought them together.

'Martine, you mustn't let him eat like a pauper. You will promise me that he'll have wine and meat every day?'

'Never fear, Mademoiselle.'

'And, you know, the five thousand francs lying there, they're his. The two of you won't, I don't think, die of hunger with that money sitting there. I want you to spoil him.'

'I'll make it my business, as I say, Mademoiselle, Monsieur will want for nothing.'

There was another silence. They held each other's gaze.

'And make sure he doesn't work too hard. I'm going away deeply worried, his health hasn't been so good lately. Look after him, won't you?'

'I'll look after him, don't worry, Mademoiselle.'

'Well, I leave him in your hands. He'll only have you now, and what reassures me a little is that you're fond of him. Love him with all your heart, love him for both of us.'

'Yes, Mademoiselle, as much as I can.'

Tears welled in their eyes and Clotilde spoke again:

'Will you give me a hug, Martine?'

'Oh, Mademoiselle, with pleasure!'

They were in one another's arms when Pascal came back. He pretended not to see them, no doubt to avoid becoming emotional. In a too-high voice he talked about the final preparations for Clotilde's departure, as though he were a busy man who didn't want anyone to miss their train. He had tied up the trunks, old father Durieu had just carted them away, and they would find them at the station. But it was scarcely eight o'clock, they still had two long hours ahead of them. Those two hours were deadly with vacant anguish, painful shuffling about, the bitter grief of the separation revolving constantly in their minds. Breakfast barely took a quarter of an hour. Afterwards they kept getting up, then sitting down again. They never took their eyes off the clock. The minutes seemed to drag on forever, like the pangs of a death, throughout the gloomy house.

'Ah, what a wind!' said Clotilde, as a blast of the mistral caused all the doors to groan.

Pascal went to the window, watched the trees frantically trying to break free of the storm.

'It's been getting worse all morning. I'll have to have a look at the roof later on, some tiles have gone.'

Already, they had stopped being together. They could hear nothing now but the furious wind, sweeping everything away, blowing their life away.

Finally, at eight-thirty, Pascal simply said:

'It's time, Clotilde.'

She rose from the chair she was sitting on. There had been moments when she'd forgotten she was going. All of a sudden, the appalling certainty came back to her. She looked at him for the last time, but he didn't open his arms to keep her. It was over. And her face drained of life, as though she'd been struck dead.

First they exchanged the standard words.

'You'll write to me, won't you?'

'Of course I will, and you let me know how you're going as often as you can.'

'Above all, if you get sick, call me back immediately.'

'I promise. But, have no fear, I'm pretty sound.'

Then, just as she was about to leave this house that was so dear to her, Clotilde took it all in with an unsteady gaze. And she fell against Pascal's chest, held him tightly in her arms, stammering.

'I want to hug you here, I want to thank you... You've made me what I am, Maître. As you've often said, you corrected my heredity. What would I have become, up there, in the environment Maxime grew up in? Yes, if I'm worth anything, I owe it to you alone, to you who uprooted me and set me down in this house, full of truth and goodness, where you raised me to be worthy of your love... Today, after taking me and heaping your blessings on me, you're sending me back. Your will be done, you're my master, and I obey you. I love you, no matter what, I'll always love you.'

He hugged her to his heart and replied:

'I only want what's good for you, I'm just putting the finishing touches to my work.'

And on the last kiss, the heart-rending kiss they exchanged, she sighed and said in a voice just above a whisper:

'Ah! If only the child had come!'

At that, she thought she heard him stammer a few indistinct words in an even lower voice, on a sob:

'Yes, the longed-for work, the only good and true work, the work I wasn't able to produce... Forgive me, and try to be happy.'

Old Madame Rougon was at the station, all very cheery, very animated, in spite of her eighty-odd years. She was gloating, she felt she now had her son Pascal at her mercy. When she saw that they were both in a daze, she took charge of everything, bought the ticket, booked the luggage, installed the traveller in a ladies-only compartment. Then she spoke at length about Maxime, gave instructions, and demanded to be kept up to date. But the train would not leave and another five excruciating minutes went by, during which they stood there face to face, not saying another word. Finally, everything went dim and there were hugs and kisses, a great clatter of churning wheels, waving handkerchiefs.

Suddenly, Pascal saw that he was alone on the platform, while, over there, the train had vanished behind a bend in the track. At that, he stopped listening to his mother and set off running at a young man's furious gallop; he raced up the slope, leapt over the tiered drystone walls and found himself on the terrace of La Souleiade in three minutes flat. The mistral was wreaking havoc there, an almighty squall was bending the hundred-year-old cypresses as if they were straws. In the ashen sky, the sun seemed weary of all this wind that had been scudding violently across its face for six days now. And, like the wildly

waving trees, Pascal stood firm, his clothes snapping like flags, his
beard and hair blown about, whipped by the storm. Breathing hard,
with both hands on his heart to stop it pounding, he watched the train
racing away in the distance, across the open plain, a tiny little train
that the mistral seemed to sweep along like a sprig of dead leaves.

12

THE very next day Pascal shut himself away in the bowels of the big empty house. He did not emerge again, completely stopped the rare house calls he had still been making, and lived there, doors and windows shut, in absolute solitude and silence. And the order given to Martine was categorical: she was not to let anyone in, under any circumstances.

'But Monsieur, what about your mother, Madame Félicité?'

'My mother is the last person I want to see. I have my reasons... You will tell her I'm working, that I need time to myself to think, and that I beg her pardon.'

Three times in a row, old Madame Rougon turned up. She stormed around downstairs, and he would hear her raising her voice, getting cross, trying to bypass her son's orders and force her way in. Then the noise would subside, and there would be only a whispering of complaint and plotting, between her and the servant. But not once did he yield, did he lean over the banister and shout at her to come up.

One day Martine ventured to say:

'It's rather harsh, all the same, Monsieur, for a person to refuse to let his own mother in. Especially as Madame Félicité comes with good intentions, since she knows how hard up Monsieur is, and she only insists because she wants to offer her assistance.'

Exasperated, he yelled:

'Money! I don't want any money, do you hear! I'll work, I'll earn enough to live on, for God's sake!'

But the issue of money was becoming pressing. He was determined not to take a sou out of the five thousand francs locked away in the secretaire. Now that he was on his own, he felt completely unconcerned about material life, he'd have been happy with bread and water; and every time the servant asked him for something to buy wine, meat, some sweets, he would shrug his shoulders: what was the point? There was a crust left over from yesterday, wasn't that enough? But in her affection for this master of hers who she knew was in pain, Martine despaired at a frugality even harsher than her own, at this pauper's deprivation to which he was surrendering, taking the whole household with him. They lived better in the homes of the workingmen of the faubourg. And so, for a whole day, she seemed to be in the throes of a terrible inner struggle. Her love, the love of a docile dog, fought against her passion for her money, accumulated sou by sou, and hidden somewhere, making babies, as she liked to say. She would have been happier giving some of her flesh. As long as her master had not been suffering on his own, the idea of drawing on her hoard had never even occurred to her. So it was nothing short of exceptional heroism, on the morning when, driven to extremes, seeing her kitchen without heat and the cupboard bare, she disappeared for an hour and came home with provisions and the change from a hundred-franc note.

At that very moment, Pascal came downstairs and was shocked, asked her where the money had come from, already beside himself and ready to throw the lot into the street, thinking she'd been to his mother's.

'No, no, no, Monsieur!' she stammered. 'That's not it at all…'

And she ended up speaking the lie that she'd prepared.

'You wouldn't credit it, but they're sorting out the accounts at Monsieur Grandguillot's, or at least that's what it looked like to me… I got the idea, this morning, to go and see, and they told me you'd surely get something back, that I could take a hundred francs… Yes, they were even happy just with a receipt from me. You can fix it up later.'

Pascal didn't seem remotely surprised. She had been madly hoping he wouldn't go and check the facts for himself. And so she was relieved to see with what casual nonchalance he accepted her story.

'Ah, good!' he cried. 'I said we must never despair. This will give me time to get my affairs in order.'

His affairs—that meant the sale of La Souleiade which he'd been vaguely entertaining. But what an appalling wrench it would be, to leave this house where Clotilde had grown up, where he had lived with her for nearly eighteen years! He'd given himself two or three weeks to think it over. But now that there was hope of getting back some of his money, he stopped thinking about it altogether. Once again, he threw off all restraint, ate whatever Martine dished up, didn't even notice the austere comfort she surrounded him with again, on her knees as she was, in adoration, torn in two to be digging into her little treasure-trove, but so happy to feed him now without his suspecting that he owed his continued existence to her.

What's more, Pascal didn't exactly repay her in kind. He would take pity on her afterwards, regret his violent outbursts. But in the state of febrile desperation in which he lived, that didn't stop him from starting again, from getting angry with her at the slightest cause of dissatisfaction. One evening when he'd heard his mother chatting away again, down in the kitchen, he flew into a fit of fury.

'You listen to me, Martine. I don't want that woman setting foot in La Souleiade ever again. If you let her in down there, even once, I'll send you packing!'

Dumbstruck, she stood there rooted to the spot. Never in the thirty-two years she'd been working for him had he threatened her with dismissal like this.

'Oh, Monsieur! You wouldn't have the heart! And anyway, I wouldn't go, I'd lie across the doorway.'

He was already ashamed of his outburst and spoke more gently.

'It's just that I know perfectly well what's going on. She comes to indoctrinate you, to set you against me, doesn't she? Yes, she's got her eye on my papers, she'd like to steal everything, destroy everything, up there in the cupboard. I know her, when she wants something, she'll stop at nothing to get it. Well, you can tell her that I'm watching, that I won't let her get anywhere near the cupboard, not while I'm alive. Anyway, the key's here, in my pocket.'

In fact, all his old terror as a scientist threatened and encircled had returned. Since he'd been living on his own, he had the feeling that a new danger lurked, that an ambush was being laid at all hours of the day in secret. The circle was closing in again, and if he acted so harshly in fighting the attempts at invasion, if he repelled his mother's assaults, it was because he was under no illusions about her real designs and he was afraid of being weak. Once she got inside, she would take him over little by little to the point where she destroyed him. So his torments started all over again, and he spent the days on the lookout, locked the doors himself in the evening, and often got up again, at night, to make sure no one was forcing the locks. What worried him most was that the servant, won over to the cause, believing she was securing his eternal salvation, would open up for his mother. He felt as if he could see the files blazing in the fireplace, and he mounted guard around them, once more a prey to a long-suffering passion, a heart-wrenching affection for that chilling mass of papers, those cold handwritten pages, for which he had sacrificed a woman, and which he now forced himself to love enough to forget everything else.

Without Clotilde there any more, Pascal threw himself into work, tried to lose himself, to drown himself in it. If he shut himself away, if he no longer set foot in the garden, if one day when Martine came up to tell him Doctor Ramond was downstairs, he had the strength to say he couldn't see him, the sole purpose of this whole austere quest for solitude was to disappear in unceasing toil. Poor Ramond, how gladly he'd have embraced him! Pascal easily guessed the exquisite sentiment that had made him come running to console his old master. But why waste an hour? Why risk emotional mayhem and tears from which he'd emerge diminished? From the crack of dawn he was up and at his table, would spend all morning and all afternoon there, often continuing by lamplight till very late. He wanted to put his old plan into action: to start his whole theory of heredity again from a different perspective, to use the files and documents furnished by his family to establish the laws according to which, within a set group of people, life is distributed and leads mathematically from one person to the next, taking the different environments into account: a vast Bible, a Genesis of families, of societies, of all humanity. He hoped the size of such a project, the effort needed to realize an idea so colossal, would consume him completely and give him back his health, his faith, his pride, through the nobler pleasure of finishing his life's work. But try as he might to take a passionate interest, to devote himself unstintingly, unsparingly, all he managed to do was to overexert his body and his mind, while still remaining distracted, his heart not on the job, sicker by the day and now without hope. Did this mean work was in the end a failure? He, whose existence had been consumed by work, who had regarded it as the sole mover, the saviour and consoler—would he now be forced to conclude that to love and be loved eclipses everything else in the world? He fell at times to exploring deep and complex ideas as he continued to sketch out his new theory of the balance of vital forces, a theory which laid down the generally applicable law that everything we take in as sensation must be given back in movement. How normal, how full and happy life would have been, if only a person had been able to live it all, working like a well-tuned machine, giving out in energy what it burns in fuel, maintaining itself in all its vigour and beauty through the logical, simultaneous interaction of all its component parts! He felt that there was as much physical labour involved in this as intellectual labour, as much feeling as reasoning, as big a role played by the reproductive function as by the intellectual function, with no overexertion, on either side, since overexertion simply spells imbalance and illness. Oh, yes! To start life over again and know how to really live it, to dig over the earth, study the world, love a woman, arrive at human perfection, the future city of universal happiness, by employing your whole being properly—what a beautiful last will and testament that would be for a philosopher-doctor to leave! But this distant dream, this half-glimpsed theory ended up filling him with bitterness at the thought that, from now on, he was just a wasted and spent force.

What lay at the very bottom of Pascal's grief was this overwhelming feeling that he was finished. Pining for Clotilde, the misery of not having her any more, the certainty he'd never have her again, engulfed him more with each passing hour in a tidal wave of pain that swept everything before it. Work was defeated, and he sometimes let his head drop on the page in progress, and he would cry for hours, without having the courage to take up his pen again. His relentless determination to work, his days of deliberate self-annihilation would end in terrible nights, sleepless nights of burning fever, during which he would bite into the sheets to stop himself from crying Clotilde's name. She was everywhere, in this mournful house, where he cloistered himself away. He found her once more walking through every room, sitting on all the chairs, standing behind every door. Downstairs in the dining room, he couldn't sit at the table without finding her seated across from him. In the workroom, upstairs, she continued to be his companion of every moment, she herself had lived so long shut away in there that her image seemed to emanate from things: without respite he felt her spirited up beside him, he saw her standing at her desk, straight-backed and slim, head bent over a pastel, with her fine profile showing. And if he didn't leave the house to escape from being haunted like this by the precious and torturous memory, it was only because he knew for certain that he would run into her all over the garden as well, daydreaming at the edge of the terrace, ambling slowly along the walkways in the pine grove, sitting under the plane trees coolly refreshed by the eternal song of the spring, lying on the threshing floor, at twilight, her eyes wandering, waiting for the stars. But for him there was one place especially that held desire and terror, a sacred shrine that he entered only in awe: the bedroom where she had given herself to him and where they had slept together. He kept the key on him always; he hadn't moved a single thing from its place since the calamitous morning she left, and a forgotten skirt still trailed over an armchair. There, he inhaled her very breath, the fresh youthful smell of her which lingered in the air like perfume. He would open his frantic arms and wrap them around her ghost, drifting in the soft half-light created by the closed shutters, rosy with the faded pink of the old printed calico, the colour of dawn, on the walls. He would sob before the furniture, he would kiss the spot on the bed outlined by her exquisitely willowy body. And his joy at being there, his heartache at not seeing Clotilde there any more, all this violent emotion would exhaust him so thoroughly that he didn't dare visit this daunting place every day, but went to bed in his own cold room, where his nightly insomnia didn't show her to him as quite so near and so alive.

In the middle of all his furious work, Pascal had another great but painful joy, Clotilde's letters. She wrote to him regularly twice a week, long letters of eight to ten pages, in which she told him all about her daily life. It didn't seem as if she was very happy in Paris. Maxime, who now never left his invalid's chair, was obviously torturing her with the demands of a spoilt brat who was also a sick man, for she talked as if she was a recluse, permanently on duty by his side, not even able to go near a window to cast a glance over the avenue where fashionable society out for a ride in the Bois streamed past; and, from certain things she said, it was clear that her brother, after clamouring for her so impatiently, was already suspicious of her, was beginning to distrust her and hate her, as he did everybody who waited on him, in his perpetual anxiety about being exploited and robbed. She had twice seen her father, gay as a lark as always, snowed under with business, converted to the Republic, and absolutely triumphant politically and financially. Saccard had taken her aside to say that poor Maxime really was unbearable, and that she must have spunk if she consented to be his victim. As she couldn't do everything, he had even been kind enough, the following day, to send over his hairdresser's niece, an eighteen-year-old slip of a girl called Rose, very blonde and innocent-looking, and Rose was now helping her with the patient. Clotilde wasn't complaining, though; on the contrary, she went out of her way to sound unruffled, contented, resigned to life. Her letters were full of grit, free of anger at their cruel separation, free of any desperate appeal to Pascal's tenderness designed to get him to call her home. But reading between the lines, how clearly he could feel her simmering with mutinous rage, soaring towards him in spirit, ready for the folly of coming home in an instant, at the slightest word!

But that was the word Pascal was determined not to write. Things would sort themselves out, Maxime would get used to his sister, the sacrifice must be carried out to the bitter end, now it had been made. A single line written by him, in a moment of weakness, and the whole point of the effort would be lost, the old misery would start all over again. Never had Pascal needed greater courage than when he replied to Clotilde. During his torrid nights he thrashed about, wildly called her name, got up to write and call her home immediately, by telegram. Then, in the light of day, after he had shed many tears, his fever would drop; and his reply was always very curt, almost cold. He carefully monitored every sentence, and began again if he felt he'd let himself get carried away. But what torture they were, these repulsive letters, so brief, so frosty, in which he went against his heart, solely to turn her away from him, to take all the blame and make her think she could forget him since he'd forgotten her! He would emerge from the ordeal in a lather of sweat, wrung out, as if he'd just performed a violent act of heroism.

It was coming to the end of October and Clotilde had been gone a month, when one morning Pascal suddenly had a choking fit. Several times before this he had had bouts of mild breathlessness which he'd put down to work. But this time the symptoms were so unmistakable that he couldn't deceive himself: a sharp pain in the region of the heart that spread to the whole of his chest and down his left arm, a horrible sensation of being crushed and of anxiety, while cold sweat poured out of him. It was an attack of angina pectoris. The spasm lasted barely a minute and at first he was more surprised than alarmed. With the blindness peculiar to doctors when it comes to the state of their own health, he had never suspected that his heart might be diseased.

Just as he was recovering, Martine came up to say that Doctor Ramond was downstairs, insisting once again on seeing him. And Pascal, perhaps yielding to an unconscious need to know, called out:

'Well, then, let him come up, since he's so keen. I'd be delighted.'

The two men embraced, and the only allusion to the absent woman, she whose departure had turned the house into an empty shell, was an energetic and sympathetic handshake.

'You don't know why I'm here?' Ramond asked right away. 'I've come about money... Yes, my father-in-law, Monsieur Lévêque, the solicitor whom you know, spoke to me again yesterday about the funds you invested with Grandguillot the notary. And he strongly advises you to get moving, since a few people, they say, have managed to get something back.'

'But,' said Pascal, 'I know that's being sorted. Martine's already recovered two hundred francs, I believe.'

Ramond looked utterly amazed.

'Martine! How? Without your intervention?... Well, what about authorizing my father-in-law to take up your cause? He'll get to the bottom of things, since you have neither the time nor the inclination for the job.'

'Of course, I hereby authorize Monsieur Lévêque, and give him my most grateful thanks.'

Then, that business settled, the young man, who had noticed the doctor's pallor, questioned him and Pascal answered with a smile:

'You won't believe it, my friend, but I've just had an attack of angina pectoris... Oh! It's not my imagination, all the symptoms were there. But, look, since you're here, you can listen to my chest!'

At first Ramond resisted, and gamely tried to turn the consultation into a joke. Would a conscript like him dare deliver a verdict on his general? But he examined him nevertheless and found his face drawn and anxious, with a strange look of bewilderment in his eyes. He ended by listening to Pascal's chest very carefully, his ear glued for a long while to his ribcage. Several minutes went by in profound silence.

'Well?' asked Pascal when the young doctor had straightened up again.

Ramond didn't say anything for a moment. He felt the eyes of the master boring straight into his. So he didn't look away, and in the face of the calm bravery of the question, he replied quite simply:

'Well, it's true, I think there is some sclerosis.'

'Ah, it's good of you not to lie to me!' the doctor said. 'I was afraid for a moment you would lie, and I'd have been hurt if you had.'

Ramond had gone back to listening, and spoke in a small voice.

'Yes, your pulse is strong, the first sound is faint, while the second is the opposite, it's thunderous. You can sense the tension dropping and being transferred towards your armpit. There is some sclerosis— at least, it's very likely.'

Straightening up again, he added:

'A person can live for twenty years with that.'

'Sometimes, no doubt,' said Pascal. 'Unless they drop dead at once.'

They talked a bit more, and expressed amazement at a strange case of coronary sclerosis that had been observed in the hospital in Plassans. And as the young doctor was leaving, he announced he would return as soon as he had any news of the Grandguillot affair.

When he was alone again, Pascal felt done for. Everything was becoming clear, his palpitations over the past few weeks, his dizzy spells, his breathlessness; and especially the wear and tear on that poor organ, his heart, overstrained by passion and work; that feeling of being tremendously tired and close to the end, an end about which he could now no longer deceive himself. But it wasn't fear that he felt just yet. His first thought was that he, too, in his turn, was paying for his heredity, that the sclerosis, this sort of degeneration, was his share of malnutrition, the inevitable legacy of his terrible ancestry. Others had seen neurosis, the original lesion, turn to vice or virtue, to genius, crime, drunkenness, or saintliness; others had died of consumption, epilepsy, or ataxia; he had lived on passion and was about to die of the heart. And he was no longer afraid of it, he was no longer angry about his manifest, inescapable, and no doubt necessary heredity. On the contrary, he was overcome by a kind of humility, the certainty that any revolt against the laws of nature is wrong. Why, then, had he once gloated, overjoyed at the idea that he wasn't one of the family, at the feeling that he was different, that he had absolutely nothing in common with them? Nothing could be less enlightened. Only monsters grew up in isolation. And being one of the family, God! It finally felt as good and as beautiful as being part of any other, for weren't all families alike, wasn't humanity the same everywhere, with the same sum of good and bad? And under the threat of suffering and death, being so modest and so gentle, he felt he had come to accept all that life might entail.

From then on, Pascal lived with the thought that he could die at any moment. And it only made him grow in stature, elevating him to the point where he completely forgot about himself. He never stopped working, but he had never before understood so clearly to what extent effort had to be its own reward, work being always ephemeral and remaining unfinished regardless. One evening, at dinner, Martine told him that Sarteur, the hatter, the ex-inmate of the asylum at Les Tulettes, had just hanged himself. For the rest of the evening, he thought about that strange case, about this man he thought he'd saved from homicidal mania by treating him with hypodermic shots and who, evidently in the grip of another fit, had had enough clarity of mind left to strangle himself instead of going for the throat of some passer-by. He could see him again, so perfectly sane, as he advised him to take up his old working life once more. What, then, was this destructive force, the need to murder that turned to suicide, death doing its job come what may? With that man, Pascal's last shred of his pride in himself as a healer disappeared; and every morning, when he settled down to work again, he felt he was nothing more than a schoolboy doing his spelling, still searching for the truth as it expands and recedes.

But in this new state of serenity, one thing still worried him: he was anxious to know what would become of Bonhomme, his old horse, if he died before him. The poor animal, now completely blind and para-lysed in the legs, no longer got up off his litter. He could still hear his master, though, when he came to see him, and would turn his head, aware of the two big kisses the doctor planted on his nostrils. All the neighbours shrugged their shoulders, joked about the old relative the doctor refused to have put down. Would he go first, then, knowing they'd call the knacker the very next day? But one morning, when he went into the stable, Bonhomme didn't hear him, didn't raise his head. He was dead, and he lay on the ground looking peaceful, as though relieved to have died at home, quietly. His master knelt down and kissed him one last time, in farewell, as two big tears rolled down his cheeks.

That same day Pascal took a greater interest in his neighbour, Monsieur Bellombre. Going to a window, he saw the man, over the garden wall, in the pale early November light, doing his usual circuit; and the sight of the old teacher, living in perfect contentment, at first struck him with wonder. It felt as though it had never occurred to him before—the fact that a man of seventy was living there next door, without a wife, without a child, without a dog, deriving all his self-centred happiness from the joy of living apart from life. Then he remembered his fits of rage at the man, his sarcastic remarks about his fear of living, the calamities he had wished upon him, his hope that punishment would be visited on him in the shape of some servant mistress, some kinswoman he'd never heard of, who would turn out to be his nemesis. But, no! He saw that the man was still as robust as ever, and sensed that he would go on for a long time yet ageing this way, unfeeling, tight-fisted, useless, and happy. And yet, he didn't loathe him any more, he could easily have pitied him, so ridiculous and pathetic he felt him to be, not being loved. He, who was dying because he'd been left on his own! He, whose heart was about to burst because it was too full of others! Well, he'd take suffering, and nothing but suffering, any day of the week over such selfishness, such a death of all that is alive and human in us!

The following night, Pascal had another attack of angina. It lasted close to five minutes, and he thought he'd choke to death without having the strength to call his servant. When he got his breath back, he didn't disturb her, preferring not to tell anyone about this turn for the worse his illness had taken; but he was now certain that he was finished, that he might not see out another month. His first thought was of Clotilde. Why didn't he write to tell her to come running? He had in fact just received a letter from her the day before, and he wanted to reply to her that very morning. Then, all of a sudden, he remembered his files. If he died suddenly, his mother would be in charge and she would destroy them; and not just the files, but his manuscripts and all his papers, thirty years' worth of thinking and hard work. And so the crime he had always dreaded, fear of which alone, during his nights of fever, had made him get out of bed shivering, ears pricked, listening to hear if someone was forcing the lock on the cupboard, would actually be perpetrated. He broke out in a sweat again as he saw himself dispossessed, outraged, the ashes of his works scattered to the four winds. And he immediately returned to Clotilde, telling himself that all he had to do was call her back: she would be there, she would close his eyes, she would defend his memory. Already, he had sat down in a rush to write to her, so that the letter would leave by the morning mail.

But as Pascal faced the blank page, pen in hand, he was filled with growing qualms, with self-disgust. Wasn't thinking about his files, the brilliant plan of giving them a custodian and saving them—wasn't this his weakness speaking, an excuse he'd dreamed up just to see Clotilde again? It was, basically, selfish. He was thinking of himself, not of her. He saw her coming back to this barren house, doomed to look after a sick old man; above all he saw her broken-hearted, horrified by the agony of his dying, when he would terrify her, one day finally dropping dead right in front of her. No! That was the awful moment he wanted to spare her, those few days of cruel farewells, and the misery that follows, a dismal gift he could not offer her without considering himself a criminal. Her peace and quiet, her own personal happiness, were all that counted, what did the rest matter! He would die in his hole, happy believing she was happy. As for saving his manuscripts, he would see if he had the strength to part with them by handing them over to Ramond. And even if all his papers were to perish—well, let them; he really wouldn't want anything of himself to remain in existence, not even his ideas, if it meant that nothing of him would afterwards trouble the existence of his darling wife!

So Pascal started on one of his usual replies, deliberately and with great difficulty making it trivial and almost cold. In her last letter, Clotilde hadn't exactly complained about Maxime, but had intimated that her brother was losing interest in her, being more diverted by Rose, Saccard's hairdresser's niece, the little slip of a girl who was so very blonde and innocent-looking. And he smelled some manoeuvre of the father's, a cunning snare set around the chair of the cripple, who was again captive to his once-so-precocious vices, at the approach of death. But his concern didn't stop him from giving Clotilde very sound advice, and he told her yet again that her duty was to see it through to the end. When he signed his name, tears were clouding his eyes. It was his own death as an old and solitary animal, a death without a kiss, without a friendly hand, that he was signing. But then he was assailed by doubt: was he right to leave her up there, in that foul environment, where he sensed all kinds of horrors happening around her?

At La Souleiade, the postman brought the letters and the papers every morning at around nine; and whenever Pascal wrote to Clotilde, he always watched after he handed his letter over to make absolutely sure his correspondence wasn't intercepted. Well, that particular morning, when he came down to give the postman the letter he'd just written, he was surprised to get another one from Clotilde, since it wasn't her day. Yet he still let his go. Then he went back upstairs and took his place at his table, ripping open the envelope.

At the very first lines he was completely dumbfounded, stunned. Clotilde wrote that she was two months' pregnant. She had hesitated so long to tell him the news because she wanted to be absolutely sure herself. Now, she could not be mistaken, she must have conceived back in the last week of August, that blissful night when she gave him the ultimate royal feast of youthfulness, the night that followed their miserable trail from door to door. Hadn't they felt, in one of their bouts of lovemaking, the exquisite and heightened sensual pleasure that meant a child was being created? After the first month, once she'd got to Paris, she wasn't sure and thought she might just be late, or unwell, which would have been perfectly understandable with the turmoil and heartache of their separation. But when she didn't see anything the second month either, she had waited a few days and was now certain of her pregnancy, which all the symptoms, what's more, confirmed. The letter was short, simply stating the fact, and yet it was full of a burning joy, a rush of infinite tenderness, in her longing to come home immediately.

Dazed, fearing he hadn't read it properly, Pascal started the letter again. A child! The child he'd attacked himself, the day she left amid the great desolate gusts of the mistral, for not being able to produce, but who was already there then, whom she had taken away with her, as he stood and watched the train racing away in the distance across the open plain! Ah! This was the true work, the only good, the only living work, the one work that filled him to the brim with happiness and pride. His research work and all his fears about heredity vanished. The child would come to be, what did it matter what it would become, as long as it meant continuation, life passed on and perpetuated, another self! He sat there stirred to the depths of his soul, his whole being thrilling with tenderness. He laughed, and talked out loud, and madly kissed the letter.

But the sound of footsteps made him collect himself a little. Turning his head, he saw Martine.

'Monsieur, Doctor Ramond's downstairs.'

'Ah! Send him up! Send him up!'

Still more happiness was coming. From the doorway, Ramond cried out cheerily: 'Victory! I bring you your money back, Maître, not all of it, but a good amount!'

And he told him the story, how there'd been a stroke of unexpected good luck, which his father-in-law, Monsieur Lévêque, had ferreted out. The receipts for the one hundred and twenty thousand francs that named Pascal as a private creditor of Grandguillot's were worthless, since the notary was insolvent. Salvation had come in the form of the power of attorney that the doctor had given him one day, at his request, to the effect that he could use all or part of the doctor's money in mortgage investments. As the name of the authorized agent had been left blank, the notary, as is sometimes done, had borrowed the name of one of his clerks; and, thanks to that, eighty thousand francs had just been recovered, invested in sound mortgages through the agency of a decent man in no way mixed up in his boss's affairs. If Pascal had taken action, had gone to the public prosecutor, he would have cleared the whole thing up long ago. Well, he was now about to pocket four thousand francs in solid interest.

Pascal grabbed the young man's hands and squeezed them excitedly.

'Ah, my friend, if you only knew how happy I am! This letter of Clotilde's brings me great bliss. Yes, I was about to call her back to me, but the thought of my destitution, of the hardships I'd be forcing on her, spoilt my joy at the whole idea of having her back. But now the money's rolling in again, enough of it at least to set up my little tribe!'

In his emotional exuberance, he handed Ramond the letter and made him read it. Then, when the young man gave it back to him smiling, touched to see him so deeply moved, he yielded to an overwhelming need for tenderness, and took Ramond in his open arms, like an equal, like a brother. The two men kissed each other on both cheeks, energetically.

'Since happiness has sent you, I'm going to ask you to do one more thing for me. You know I don't trust anyone here, not even my old housekeeper. So *you* can take my telegram to the post office for me.'

He sat down again at his table and wrote simply: 'I'm waiting for you, leave tonight.'

'Let's see,' he said, 'today's the sixth of November, isn't it? It's nearly ten o'clock, she'll get my telegram around noon. That gives her plenty of time to pack her bags and get on the eight o'clock express this evening, which will drop her in Marseilles in time for breakfast tomorrow morning. But since there's no connecting train for quite a while, she'll only be able to get here, tomorrow the seventh of November, by the train that gets in at five.'

He folded the telegram and rose to his feet.

'God! Five o'clock tomorrow! That's still so far away! What am I going to do till then?'

Then, filled with concern, he became grave:

'Ramond, my friend, will you do me the great kindness of being perfectly frank with me?'

'How do you mean, Maître?'

'Yes, you know exactly what I'm saying... The other day you examined me. Do you think I can keep going for another year?'

And he held the young man's gaze, preventing him from looking away. Yet Ramond tried to escape nevertheless by making a joke of it: surely a doctor couldn't seriously ask such a question?

'Please, Ramond, let's be serious.'

And so Ramond, in all sincerity, answered that, in his view, Pascal could very well cherish the hope of living another year. He gave his reasons: the relatively early stage of the sclerosis, the perfect health of his other organs. No doubt they needed to allow for unknown factors, things no one knew about, since a sudden attack was always possible. And the two of them ended up discussing the case as calmly as if they'd found themselves in consultation at the foot of a patient's bed, weighing up the pros and cons, each giving their arguments, predicting when the end would come in keeping with the most advanced and consistent symptoms.

As if it had nothing to do with him, Pascal regained his composure, his self-forgetfulness.

'Yes,' he murmured at last, 'you're right, another year of life is possible... Ah! You see, my friend, what I'd really like is two years, a mad hope, no doubt, an eternity of joy...'

And he abandoned himself to this dream of the future:

'The child will be born around the end of May... It would be so good to see him grow a bit, till he's eighteen months, twenty months, you know! No more than that! Just long enough for him to stand on his own and take his first steps... I don't ask for much, I'd just like to see him walking, and after that, God! After that...'

He completed his thought with a wave of the hand. Then, running away with the fantasy, he added:

'But two years isn't out of the question. I had a very interesting case once, a wheelwright from the faubourg who lived four years, much longer than my best guess... Two years, two years, I'll see them through! I must see them through!'

Ramond had hung his head, and stopped replying. He was distressed to think that he'd allowed himself to sound too optimistic; and his master's joyfulness worried him; it was becoming painful, as if this very excitement, unsettling a mind once so stable, alerted him to a hidden but imminent danger.

'Didn't you want me to send this telegram straight away?'

'Yes, yes! Off you go, quick, my dear Ramond. I'll expect you the day after tomorrow. She'll be here, and I want you to hurry over and embrace us.'

The day was long, and that night, at around four, as Pascal was finally dropping off to sleep after being kept awake for hours with happy hopes and reveries, he was woken up suddenly by an appalling attack. It felt as if an enormous weight, the whole house, had collapsed onto his chest, so that his breastbone, flattened, was touching his back; and he could no longer breathe, the pain spread to his shoulders and his neck, and paralysed his left arm. What's more, he remained fully conscious of what was happening: he had the sensation that his heart was shutting down, that his life was about to be snuffed out by this horrible crushing vice that was choking him. Before the attack reached its acute phase, he had the strength to get up and tap on the floor with a walking stick to get Martine to come up. Then he fell back on the bed, no longer able to move or speak, soaking in cold sweat.

Luckily, in the vast silence of the empty house, Martine heard him. She got dressed, wrapped herself in a shawl and sprinted upstairs with her candle. It was still dark, but it would soon be light. And when she saw her master lying there, with his jaws clenched, his tongue tied, his face ravaged with agony, and with only his eyes showing signs of life as they watched her, she was filled with terror and could only throw herself at the bed in alarm and cry:

'My God! My God, Monsieur! What's wrong? Tell me, Monsieur, you're frightening me!'

For a good minute, Pascal went on choking, unable to get his breath back. Then the vice of his ribs gradually loosened and he murmured very faintly:

'The five thousand francs in the desk drawer are Clotilde's... Tell her the other money's been sorted out at the notary's, with what's there she'll have enough to live on...'

At that point Martine, who'd heard him out with her mouth hanging open, despaired and confessed her lie, not knowing the good news Ramond had brought.

'Monsieur, you must forgive me, I lied. But it would be wrong to go on lying... When I saw you on your own, and so unhappy, I dipped into my own money...'

'My poor girl, you didn't!'

'Oh, I had hoped Monsieur would pay me back one day!'

The attack was easing off and he was able to turn his head and look at her. He was stunned and deeply moved. What on earth had gone on in the heart of this miserly old maid, who'd been grimly building up her hoard for thirty years, and who had never once pulled out a sou, either for herself or for others? He didn't yet understand, but simply wanted to show himself grateful and kind.

'You're a decent woman, Martine. You'll get it all back... I really do think I'm about to die...'

She didn't let him finish, her whole being rising up and rebelling in a cry of protest.

'Die! You, Monsieur! Die before I do! I won't have it, I'll do anything, I won't let you!'

And she threw herself on her knees by the bed and grabbed him frantically, probing to see where it hurt, restraining him as if she trusted no one would dare take him from her if she held him down.

'You must tell me what's wrong with you, I'll nurse you, I'll save you. If I have to give you some of my own life, I will, Monsieur... I can easily spend my days, my nights beside you. I'm still strong, I'll be stronger than the disease, you'll see... Die! Ah, no, you can't! The good Lord can't want such an injustice. I've prayed so hard to Him in my life, He has to listen to me a bit, and He'll hear my prayer, Monsieur, He'll save you!'

Pascal looked at her, listened to her, and suddenly it dawned on him. She loved him, this pitiable old maid, she had always loved him! He thought back over her thirty years of blind devotion, her mute adoration of bygone days, when she was young and she'd served him on her knees, then later her secret fits of jealousy over Clotilde, all that she must have suffered unconsciously at the time. And here she was, still on her knees today, at his deathbed, her hair turning grey and her eyes the colour of ash in a face as wan as that of a nun dulled by her single, celibate life. And he sensed that she knew nothing at all, not even what kind of love it was that she felt for him, loving only him in all the world for the sheer joy of loving him, of being with him and serving him.

Tears rolled over Pascal's cheeks. A painful compassion, infinite human tenderness overflowed his poor half-broken heart. He addressed her familiarly.

'My poor girl, you're the best girl there is... Here! Kiss me the way you love me, with all your might!'

She was sobbing now, too, as she dropped her grizzled head, her face worn by the long years of domestic service, on to her master's chest, and she kissed him, frantically, pouring her whole life into the kiss.

'Right, well! Let's not get too emotional, because, you see, no matter what we do, this is still the end... If you want me to be fond of you, you'll do as I say.'

First, he was determined not to stay in his room. It felt freezing to him, high-ceilinged, empty, dark. He had a sudden longing to die in the other room, Clotilde's room, the room they'd loved each other in, which he never entered now without a reverential shudder. And so Martine had to deny herself one last time, help him get up, support him and guide him, tottering, to the still sweet-smelling bed. He had taken the key to the cupboard from under his pillow, where he kept it safely with him every night; and now he put the key under the other pillow so he could watch over it while he was still alive. Day was only just breaking as the servant put the candle on the table.

'Now I'm lying down again and breathing a bit better, you can run and get Doctor Ramond for me. Wake him up and bring him back with you.'

She was just leaving, when he suddenly panicked.

'And whatever you do, don't you dare go and tell my mother—that's an order.'

Embarrassed, imploring, she turned back to him.

'Oh, Monsieur! Madame Félicité made me promise her so many times...'

But he was unbending. His whole life, he'd been deferential towards his mother, and he believed he'd earned the right to protect himself from her at the moment of his death. He absolutely refused to see her. The servant had to swear she'd keep quiet. Only then was he able to smile again.

'Off you go, then, quick... Oh! You'll see me again, it won't happen just yet.'

The day was finally dawning, a sad little dawn, breaking over a pale November morning. Pascal had had the shutters opened, and when he found himself alone, he watched the light growing, the light of the last day he would certainly ever see. The previous day, it had rained and the sun remained covered, yet still warm. From the nearby plane trees he heard a whole dawn chorus of birds streaming in, while far away, deep in the dozing countryside, a locomotive whistled with an unremitting wail. And he was alone, alone in the big mournful house, whose emptiness he could feel all around him, whose silence he could hear. The day was slowly coming on, and he continued to watch the splash of reflected light growing bigger and brighter over the window-panes. Then the candle flame was overpowered and the room appeared in its entirety. He had expected to find solace from it and he was not disappointed; consolation came to him from the wall covering, the colour of dawn, from each familiar piece of furniture, from the vast bed in which he had loved so intensely and where he had now lain down to die. Beneath the high ceiling, throughout the shimmering room, a pure smell of youth, love's infinite sweetness, still hung, enveloping him like a faithful caress and comforting him.

Yet, although the acute phase of the attack was over, Pascal was in terrible agony. He still had a sharp pain in his chest cavity, and his left arm, which was numb, hung from his shoulder like a lead weight. In the interminable wait for the help Martine would bring back with her, he ended up concentrating all his thoughts on this suffering with which his flesh was screaming. And he resigned himself to it, he no longer felt the outrage that the mere sight of physical pain once used to rouse in him. It used to exasperate him, as a monstrous and point-less cruelty. With all his doubts about himself as a healer, the only reason he had still treated his patients was to fight it. If he ended up accepting it now that he himself was being tortured by it, did this actually mean he was rising to a new height in his faith in life, to that pinnacle of serenity from which life seems wholly good, even with the fatal condition of suffering, which might well be life's wellspring? Yes! To live all of life, live and endure all of it, without rebelling, without thinking you could make it better by making it painless—this now stood out, blindingly obvious to his dying man's eyes, as true courage and true wisdom. And so to kill time while he waited and take his mind off his disease, he went back over his latest theories and dreamed of a way of using suffering, of converting it into action, into work. If man feels pain more acutely the higher up the ladder of civilization he climbs, it is quite certain that he also becomes stronger, better equipped and more resilient. That organ, the functioning brain, develops and stabilizes, as long as the balance between the sensations it takes in and the work it gives out is not upset. So could we not dream of a humanity in whom the sum of work would so exactly equal the sum of sensations that suffering itself would be put to use and, in a way, eliminated?

Now, the sun was rising and Pascal was vaguely turning these remote hopes over in his mind in the half-sleep induced by his pain when he felt a fresh attack starting to build deep in his chest. He had a moment of excruciating anxiety: was this the end? Would he die alone? But just then rapid footsteps came up the stairs and Ramond stepped in, followed by Martine. And before he choked, Pascal had time to say to Ramond:

'Inject me, inject me now, with pure distilled water! And do it twice, at least ten grams!'

Unfortunately, Ramond had to look for the tiny syringe, then get everything ready. That took several minutes, and the attack was frightening. He followed its progress anxiously, the face becoming distorted, the lips turning blue. Finally, when he'd done the two injections, he observed that these phenomena, after remaining stable for a moment, then diminished in intensity, slowly. This time too, disaster had been averted.

But the moment he stopped choking, Pascal threw a glance at the clock and said in a quiet, weak voice:

'My friend, it's seven o'clock… In twelve hours, at seven tonight, I'll be dead.'

As the young man started to protest, ready to argue, Pascal said:

'No, don't lie. You witnessed the attack, you're as well informed as I am… Everything will happen now with mathematical rigour; I could describe the phases of the disease to you, hour by hour.'

He broke off to gulp in air, then added:

'Besides, all is well, I'm happy… Clotilde will be here at five, all I ask now is to see her and die in her arms.'

Soon, however, he felt noticeably better. The effect of the injections really was miraculous, and he was able to sit up in bed with his back against the pillows. His voice became easy again and his mind had never felt clearer.

'You know, Maître,' said Ramond, 'I won't leave you. I told my wife we're going to spend the day together, and whatever you say, I do hope it won't be the last… All right? You won't mind if I make myself at home.'

Pascal smiled and gave Martine orders. He wanted her to get on with breakfast, for Ramond. If they needed her, they'd call her. And the two men stayed there on their own, chatting away cosily like close friends, the one lying down, with his great white beard, discoursing like a sage, the other sitting at the foot of the bed, listening with all the deference of a disciple.

'Actually,' the master murmured, as if he were talking to himself, 'it's extraordinary, the effect of those injections...'

Then he spoke up and said, almost gaily:

'My friend Ramond, it may not be much of a gift, but I'm going to leave you my manuscripts. Yes, Clotilde has been instructed to hand them over to you, when I'm no longer here. You can go through them and you may well find a few things in there that aren't too bad. If you get one good idea out of it all one day, well, all the better for everyone.'

And he went on from there, making his scientific will and testament. He was well aware that he himself had been no more than a lone pioneer, a trailblazer, tentatively putting forward theories, feeling his way through practice, and coming to grief because of his method, which was still relatively primitive. He recalled his excitement when he thought he'd discovered the universal panacea with his injections of nerve substance, and then his disappointments, his bouts of despair, Lafouasse's sudden death, consumption carrying off Valentin in spite of everything, victorious madness taking hold of Sarteur again and throttling him. And so he was going off now full of doubt, no longer having the faith a doctor healer needed, but so in love with life that he'd ended up putting all his faith in it, certain as he was that it had to derive its health and strength from itself alone. Yet he didn't want to close off the future; he was happy, on the contrary, to bequeath his hypothesis to the young. Theories changed every twenty years; only acquired truths, on which science continued to build, remained unassailable. Even if the only merit he had had was to provide a momentary hypothesis, his work would not have been wasted, for progress surely lay in effort, in human understanding forever moving forward. Then again, who knew? He might well die troubled and weary, not having realized his hopes for hypodermic injections; but other toilers would come along, young, keen, committed, and they would take up the idea, clarify it, expand on it. And perhaps a whole age, a whole new world, would begin there.

'Ah, my dear Ramond,' he went on, 'if only we came back in another life!... Yes, I'd start again, I'd take up my idea again, as I've been struck lately by the amazing results I've been getting just with hypodermic injections of pure water, which have been almost as effective... So it doesn't matter what liquid is used, the action is a straightforward mechanical one. I've written a lot about it over this past month. You'll find notes, curious observations. All in all, I've reached the point where I believe only in work, where I see health as lying in the balanced working of all the organs, a sort of dynamic therapeutics, if I may hazard the term.'

He was gradually becoming so impassioned he forgot that death was near, driven only by his burning curiosity about life. And he broadly outlined his latest theory. Man was immersed in a medium—nature—which constantly stimulated his sensitive nerve endings through contact. Hence the activation, not only of the senses, but of all the surfaces of the body, both external and internal. Well, it was these sensations which, resonating in the brain, the bone marrow, the nerve centres, were converted there into tone, movement, and ideas; and he was convinced that being well consisted in this work being performed at a normal pace: receiving sensations, and returning them as ideas and movement, fuelling the human machine through the regular interaction of the organs. Work thereby became the great law, the regulator of the living universe. Consequently, if the balance were upset, if the incoming stimuli ceased to be sufficient, it followed that therapeutics would create artificial stimuli so as to restore tone, which is the state of perfect health. And he dreamed of a whole new treatment regime using suggestion, the all-powerful authority of the doctor in relation to the senses; electric currents, friction, and massage for the skin and tendons; special diets for the stomach; nature cures, on high plateaus, for the lungs; and lastly, transfusions, hypodermic injections of distilled water for the circulatory system. It was the undeniable and purely mechanical action of the latter that had put him on the right track, and all he was doing now was extending the hypothesis out of a need he had to generalize, as he once again saw the world saved through this perfect balance of vital forces, with as much work going out as sensation coming in, the sway of the world in its eternal toil.

Suddenly he began to laugh openly.

'Ha! There I go again! When what I believe, basically, is that the only wise thing to do is not to intervene at all, to let nature take its course! Ah, what an incorrigible old madman I am!'

But Ramond had grabbed both his hands in a burst of affection and admiration.

'Maître, Maître! It's madness, it's passion like yours that genius is made of!.... Have no fear, I heard you, and I'll try to be worthy of your bequest, especially as I believe as you do that the great future that's coming may well lie there, in its entirety.'

In the tender and peaceful room, Pascal again began to talk, with the bold serenity of a dying philosopher giving his last lesson. Now, he went back over his personal observations, explained that he'd often cured himself by work, regular, methodical work, with no overexertion. As it struck eleven o'clock, he wanted Ramond to eat, and he continued the conversation, far away now on some higher plane, while Martine served lunch. The sun had finally pierced through the morning's grey clouds, a sun still half covered and very soft, whose wash of golden light took the chill off the vast room. Then, after drinking a few mouthfuls of milk, he fell silent.

At that moment, the young doctor was eating a pear.

'Are you in more pain?'

'No, no, keep eating.'

But he could not lie. It was an attack, and it was awful. Suffocation struck like a thunderbolt, knocked him back against the pillow, his face already blue. With both hands he clutched the sheet and clung on, as if seeking a fulcrum to lever off the frightening mass crushing his chest. Aghast, ashen, he kept his eyes wide open and fixed on the clock, with a dreadful expression of despair and grief. And for ten long minutes, he was close to breathing his last.

Ramond had immediately injected him again. The relief was long in coming, the effectiveness less marked.

Big tears appeared in Pascal's eyes as soon as life returned. He still didn't speak, but he wept. Then, still watching the clock through clouded eyes, he said:

'My friend, I'll die at four. I won't see her.'

When Ramond, hoping to distract him, asserted that the end was not so near, despite the evidence to the contrary, Pascal was seized again by his passion as a scientist, wanting to give his young colleague one last lesson, based on direct observation. He had treated several cases similar to his own, and remembered in particular having dissected, at the hospital, the heart of an old pauper who had died of sclerosis.

'I can see my heart... It's the colour of a dead leaf, the filaments are brittle, it looks reduced in size, even though it's slightly enlarged. The inflammatory activity must have hardened it, you'd have trouble cutting into it...'

He went on, his voice fainter. A moment ago, before the injection, he had indeed felt that his heart was flagging, its contractions becoming sluggish and slow. Instead of the normal jet of blood, all that was coming out of the aorta was red froth. On the other side, the veins were gorged with black blood, the level of asphyxiation was increasing, as the suction- and force-pump, which regulated the whole machine, slowed down. Then after the injection, despite his suffering, he had followed the organ's gradual revival; that boost had got it going again, clearing the black blood from the veins and once more pumping in energy with the red blood of the arteries. But there would be another attack as soon as the mechanical effect of the injection wore off. He could predict it to within a few minutes. Thanks to the injections keeping him going, there would be another three attacks. The third would carry him off. He would die at four.

Then, in a weaker and weaker voice, he went into raptures for the last time at the valour of the heart, that relentlessly determined labourer of life, endlessly at work, every second of our existence, even while we're asleep, when the other lazy organs take a rest.

'Ah, brave heart! How heroically you struggle!... What loyalty, what generosity, you never-weary muscle!... You've loved too much, you've beaten too hard, and that's why you're breaking, brave heart, you who don't want to die, and heave hard so you can go on beating.'

But the first of the predicted attacks occurred. Pascal only emerged, this time, to lie there panting, haggard, his speech wheezing and laboured. Barely audible moans escaped him, despite his greatness of soul: God! Would this torture never end? And yet, he had only one burning desire left and that was to prolong his agony, to live long enough to embrace Clotilde one last time. If only he were wrong, as Ramond kept telling him! If only he could stay alive till five! His eyes had gone back to the clock, and he no longer took them off the hands, giving every minute the weight of eternity. In days gone by, they'd often joked about this Empire clock, an ormolu mantel clock, on which smiling Love gazed on sleeping Time. It showed three. Then three-thirty. Two hours of life, another two hours of life, that's all, God! The sun was sinking on the horizon, a great calmness descended from the pale winter sky; and he heard, now and then, distant loco-motives whistling across the open plain. This particular train was the one that went past Les Tulettes. The other one, the one from Marseilles, would never get there!

At twenty to four, Pascal motioned to Ramond to come closer. He could no longer speak loudly enough, could not make himself heard.

'For me to live till six, my pulse would have to be much stronger. I still had hopes, but it's over...'

And in a whisper, he called Clotilde's name. It was a stammered and harrowing farewell, voicing the unbearable sorrow he felt at not seeing her again.

Then his concern for his manuscripts returned.

'Don't leave me... The key's under my pillow. Tell Clotilde to take it, she has instructions.'

At ten to four, a fresh injection had no effect. And four o'clock was about to strike when the second attack started. All of a sudden, after gasping for air, he flung himself out of bed and tried to stand, to walk, marshalling all his strength. A need for space, for light, for fresh air, propelled him forward, across the room. Next, it was the irresistible appeal of life, of his whole life, that he heard calling him from inside the workroom next door. And he ran there, faltering, choking, listing to the left, and clutching at the furniture.

Doctor Ramond rushed to hold him back.

'Maître! Maître! Get back to bed, please.'

But Pascal was quietly determined to die on his feet. His passionate longing to stay alive, the heroic notion of work, lived on in him, carrying him along like a felled tree in a stream. He groaned, he stammered.

'No, no... there, over there...'

With his friend having to support him, he made his way, stumbling and haggard, to the back of the workroom and dropped onto his chair, at his table, where a fresh page he'd started writing still lay among the riot of papers and books.

There, for a moment, he caught his breath, and his eyes closed. Soon he opened them again while he groped around for work he'd done. His fumbling hands came upon the Family Tree, lying among other scattered notes. Only two days before, he had corrected a few dates. And he recognized it, drew it towards him, spread it out.

'Maître! You're killing yourself!' Ramond told him again, shaking, overcome with pity and admiration.

Pascal wasn't listening, didn't hear. He felt a pencil roll under his fingers, and he held it and leant over the Tree, as if his failing eyes could barely see now. And then, for the last time, he went over the members of the family. The name Maxime gave him pause and he wrote: 'Dies ataxic, in 1873', in the certainty that his nephew would not see out the year. Then, next to that, Clotilde's name leapt up at him and he completed that note too: 'Has a son, in 1874, by her uncle Pascal.' But then he looked for himself, wearing himself out, getting lost. Finally, when he found himself, his hand recovered strength, and he finished himself off, in an erect and spirited script: 'Dies of heart disease, 7 November 1873.' That was the supreme effort, the death rattle grew louder and he was choking again when suddenly, above Clotilde, he spotted the blank leaf. His fingers could hardly hold the pencil any more. Yet, in wobbling letters, shot through with tortured tenderness, with the riotous distress of his poor heart, he added: 'The unknown child, to be born in 1874. What will he be?' And then he swooned, and Martine and Ramond were only able to carry him back to bed with great difficulty.

The third attack occurred at four-fifteen. In this final paroxysm of asphyxiation, Pascal's face conveyed terrible pain. Till the very end, he was forced to endure his martyrdom, both as a man and as a scientist. His blurry eyes seemed still to be trying to see the clock to take note of the time. And Ramond, seeing his lips move, bent down, glued his ear. Pascal was in fact murmuring words so faint they were no more than an exhalation.

'Four o'clock... The heart is going to sleep, no more red blood in the aorta... The valve is going slack and stops...'

He was shaken by an appalling death rattle, and his faint breath became very distant.

'It's all going too fast... Don't leave me, the key's under the pillow... Clotilde, Clotilde...'

At the foot of the bed, Martine fell to her knees, choking with sobs. She could see very well that Monsieur was dying. She hadn't dared run and get a priest, in spite of her strong urge to do so; and so she herself recited the prayers for the dying, praying ardently to the good

Lord, so that he would forgive Monsieur and Monsieur would go straight to heaven.

Pascal died. His face was quite blue. After a few seconds of complete immobility, he tried to breathe, pushed out his lips, and opened his poor mouth, the beak of a baby bird trying to take a last mouthful of air. And that was death, it was very straightforward.

13

IT was only after lunch, at around one, that Clotilde received Pascal's telegram. She had actually been shunned that particular day by her brother Maxime, who had generally been making her feel the brunt of his invalid's whims and rages with growing harshness. All in all, she hadn't been much of a success with him; he found her too unsophisticated, too serious to cheer him up; and now he had locked himself away with young Rose, the little blonde with the innocent look, who made him laugh. Ever since the disease had been keeping him immobile and weak, he had lost some of his rake's self-centred caginess, some of his long-held mistrust of man-eating gold-diggers. So when his sister went to tell him that their uncle was calling her home and she was leaving, she had some trouble getting them to open the door, as Rose was in the process of giving him a rubdown. He agreed with alacrity and, although he asked her to return as soon as possible, as soon as she'd finished her business down there, he did not insist, wanting only to sound caring.

Clotilde spent the afternoon packing her trunks. In her excitement, her head spinning with the suddenness of Pascal's directive, she didn't stop to think, she was so completely caught up in the great joy of going home. But after the rushed dinner, after the farewells to her brother and the interminable coach ride from the Avenue du Bois-de-Boulogne to the Gare de Lyon, when she found herself in a ladies-only compartment, having left the station at eight o'clock in the middle of an icy and rainy November night, and already rolling along out of Paris, she calmed down and was gradually assailed by questions, ended up feeling troubled by vague anxieties. Why the telegram, then, so sudden and so brief: 'I'm waiting for you, leave tonight'? Obviously it was his answer to the letter in which she'd told him she was pregnant. Except that she knew how much he wanted her to stay in Paris, where he imagined she was happy, and she now wondered at his haste in calling her back. She hadn't been expecting a telegram but a letter, and then making arrangements and going back in a few weeks' time. So, did this mean there was something else, an ailment perhaps, a longing, a need to see her again immediately? And from that point on, this fear sank in with the force of a premonition, grew, and soon possessed her completely.

All night long, torrential rain lashed the windows of the train, all the way across the plains of Burgundy. It only stopped pouring at Mâcon. After Lyons, light appeared. Clotilde had Pascal's letters on her, and she had been waiting impatiently for dawn to look at them again and study them, as the handwriting had seemed different to her. Indeed, she felt a little chill in her heart, seeing the way the words wavered and broke up as though there were cracks in them. He was sick, very sick: that, now, turned to certainty, thrust itself upon her as fact through a genuine revelation that had less to do with rational thought than with acute prescience. The rest of the trip was horribly long, for she felt her anguish growing the closer she got. The worst thing was that, getting out at Marseilles at half past twelve, she found she couldn't catch a train to Plassans until three-twenty. Three long hours of waiting. She had lunch in the station's buffet, eating frantic-ally as if nevertheless afraid of missing her train; then she dragged herself around the dusty garden, trailing from one bench to the next in the pale, still warm sunlight, amid the congestion of omnibuses and cabs. Finally, she was rolling along again, stopping every fifteen minutes at each little station. She stuck her head out of the carriage; it felt to her as if she'd set out over twenty years ago and that all the stops must have changed. The train was just pulling out of Sainte-Marthe when, craning her neck, she was deeply stirred to see La Souleiade, on the horizon, very far away, with the two centenarian cypresses on the terrace that could be seen for seven miles.

It was five o'clock and twilight was already falling. The turntables clanked, and Clotilde hopped down. But she had a shooting pain, a sharp pang, when she saw that Pascal wasn't on the platform waiting for her. She had been telling herself over and over since Lyons: 'If I don't see him straight away, when we arrive, it will be because he's sick.' But perhaps he'd stayed in the waiting room, or was seeing to a vehicle, outside. She rushed out but found only old father Durieu, the carter the doctor usually used. She promptly questioned him. The old man, a taciturn Provençal, was in no hurry to reply. He had his cart there, and asked for the luggage-ticket, wanting to see to the trunks first. In a trembling voice, she repeated her question:

'Everyone's well, Père Durieu?'

'Why, yes, Mademoiselle.'

She had to insist before he told her that it was Martine, the day before at around six, who had ordered him to turn up at the station, with his cart, to meet the train. He hadn't seen, no one had seen, the doctor for two months. It may well be, since he wasn't there, that he'd had to take to his bed, for there was a rumour going round the town that he wasn't holding too steady.

'Wait till I get the luggage, Mademoiselle. There's a place for you on the seat.'

'No, Père Durieu, that will take too long. I'll go on foot.'

She strode up the ramp. Her heart felt so tight, she could hardly breathe. The sun had disappeared behind the slopes of Sainte-Marthe, and a fine ash was falling from the grey sky, with the first November chill; and as she turned into the Chemin des Fenouillères, she caught a fresh sight of La Souleaide that chilled her to the bone, the facade forlorn in the gathering gloom, all the shutters closed, in a state of such melancholy sadness that it looked abandoned and in mourning.

But the most terrible blow of all hit Clotilde when she recognized Ramond, standing in the hall doorway, apparently waiting for her. He had in fact been looking out for her and had come downstairs, wanting to cushion the effect of the appalling catastrophe. She arrived winded, having come via the quincunx of plane trees, by the spring, to take the shortest route; and seeing the young man there instead of Pascal, whom she had still been hoping to find at the door, she had a sense of disintegration, of irreparable tragedy. Ramond was very pale, overcome, despite his struggle to be brave. He didn't utter a word, waiting for her to question him. She herself couldn't breathe, said nothing. And they stepped inside in silence and he led her to the dining room, where they stood for a few seconds more facing each other, speechless, in deafening anguish.

'He's sick, isn't he?' she stammered at last.

He simply repeated:

'Yes. Sick.'

'I realized when I saw you', she went on. 'For him not to be there, he'd have to be sick.'

Then, she pressed him further.

'He is sick, very sick, isn't he?'

He didn't answer this time, but went even paler, and she studied him. At that moment, she saw death all over him, over his still shaking hands, which had nursed the dying man, over his despairing face, in his dull eyes, which held a reflection of the final agony, in his whole rumpled appearance, that of a doctor who'd been there for twelve hours, fighting, powerless.

She screamed.

'He's dead!'

And she reeled, struck down, and collapsed into Ramond's arms; and like a brother, he hugged her to him, on a sob. With their arms around each other, they wept together.

Then, when he'd sat her on a chair and he could speak, he said:

'I was the one who took the telegram you received to the telegraph office yesterday, at around ten-thirty. He was so happy, so full of hope! He had dreams for the future, for living another year, two years... But this morning, at around four, he had the first attack and sent for me. He knew at once that he was gone. But he hoped to hold out till six o'clock, to live long enough to see you again... The disease moved too fast. He described its progress to me right till his last breath, minute by minute, like a professor doing a dissection in a lecture theatre. He died with your name on his lips, at peace and in despair, like a hero.'

Clotilde would have liked to run, to bolt upstairs to the bedroom in one bound, but she remained rooted to the spot, without the strength to get up from the chair. She had listened, her eyes swimming with tears that ran without respite. Every sentence in the tale of this stoical death resounded in her heart, and etched itself there deeply. She pieced together that dreadful day. For the rest of her life, she would relive it.

But her despair overflowed when Martine, who had come in a moment earlier, said in a harsh voice:

'Ah! Mademoiselle can cry, all right, for if Monsieur is dead, it's only because of Mademoiselle.'

The old servant stood there, to one side, by the kitchen door, heartsore and infuriated that her master had been taken from her and killed; and she made no attempt to offer the slightest word of welcome or solace to this child she had brought up. Without considering the effect of her tactlessness, the hurt or joy she might cause, she gave vent to her feelings, telling it as she saw it.

'Yes, if Monsieur is dead, it's only because Mademoiselle left.'

From out of the depths of her devastation, Clotilde protested.

'But he's the one who turned on me, who forced me to leave!'

'Oh, well! Mademoiselle must have been only too happy to go along, not to see through that... The night before she left, I found

Monsieur half dead, he was so broken-hearted; but when I decided to tell Mademoiselle, he stopped me... Then again, I've seen what's been going on, myself, since Mademoiselle's been gone. Every night, it'd start again, he'd tie himself in knots to stop himself writing and asking her to come home... Well, he died of it, and that's the honest truth.'

A light dawned in Clotilde's mind, crystal clear, and she felt both very glad and tortured. Oh, God! So it was true, what she'd suspected for a moment? But afterwards, in the face of Pascal's brutal relentlessness, she'd ended up believing he wasn't lying, that given the choice between her and work, he'd genuinely chosen work, as a man of science for whom love of work prevails over love of a woman. And yet he had been lying, he had taken devotion, selflessness, to the point of sacrificing himself for what he thought was her happiness. And what was so sad was that he'd got it wrong, he'd only compounded the unhappiness of them all.

Once again, Clotilde protested, despairingly.

'But how could I have known? I did what he said, I poured all my love into doing what he said.'

'Ah!' Martine cried out once more. 'I reckon I'd have worked it out, if it was me!'

Ramond intervened, speaking gently. He took his friend's hands again, and explained to her that grief may have hastened the end, but that, sadly, the doctor had been doomed for quite some time. The heart disease he was suffering from must have gone back a fairly long way already: given a lot of overexertion, the part played by heredity, and finally all his recent passion, his poor heart had broken.

'Let's go up,' said Clotilde. 'I want to see him.'

Upstairs, in the bedroom, the shutters had been closed, and the melancholy twilight had been kept out. Two church candles were burning, in candlesticks, on a small table at the foot of the bed. They shed a pale yellow glow over Pascal as he lay stretched out, legs together, hands placed half clasped over his chest. Someone had reverently closed his eyes. He looked as if he was sleeping, his face still bluish but already at peace, his white hair and beard spread out all around. He had been dead for barely an hour and a half. Infinite serenity had begun, eternal rest.

Seeing him again like this, telling herself he could no longer hear her, could no longer see her, that she was on her own from now on, that she would kiss him one last time then lose him forever, Clotilde felt a huge rush of pain, and threw herself on the bed, able only to stammer out this loving appeal:

'Oh, Maître, Maître, Maître...'

She pressed her lips to the dead man's forehead and, finding that he'd barely gone cold, that he was still warm with life, she was able to delude herself for a second, to believe that he could feel this last loving caress, so long awaited. Didn't he smile in his stillness, happy at last and able to get on with dying, now that he could feel them both there with him, she and the child she was carrying? Then, breaking down in front of the terrible reality, she began sobbing again, uncontrollably.

Martine came in with a lamp, which she put to one side on a corner of the mantelpiece. And she heard what Ramond said as he watched over Clotilde, worried to see her so shattered, in her condition.

'I'll take you away if you're not up to it. Remember that you're not alone, that there is this dear little creature he was already talking to me about with so much joy and love.'

Throughout the day, the housekeeper had been surprised at certain words she'd overheard by chance. Suddenly, she understood, and just as she was about to leave the room, she stopped, and continued listening.

Ramond lowered his voice.

'The key to the cupboard is under the pillow, he told me several times to tell you... You know what you have to do?'

Clotilde tried to recall and to reply.

'What I have to do? With the papers, you mean?... Oh, yes! I remember, I have to keep the files and give you the other manuscripts... Don't worry, I haven't lost my mind, I'll behave sensibly. But I won't leave him, I'll spend the night here—very quietly, I promise.'

She was so sad, and looked so determined to watch over Pascal, to stay with him until they carried him away, that the doctor let her be.

'Well, then, I'll leave you, they must be waiting for me at home. Then there are all sorts of formalities, the official registration of death at the town hall, the funeral, which I'd like to spare you having to deal with. Don't worry about anything. Tomorrow morning, when I come back, everything will be settled.'

He embraced her again and walked out. And it was only then that Martine in turn vanished, in his wake, locking the door downstairs and running through the darkening night.

Now Clotilde was alone in the room and around her, beneath her, in the great silence, she could feel how empty the house was. Clotilde was alone, with Pascal dead. She moved a chair over to the bed by the pillow and sat, motionless, alone. When she'd entered the room, she had simply taken off her hat; now she noticed that she was still wearing her gloves and removed them too. But she stayed in her travelling frock, dusty and rumpled as it was after the twenty-hour train trip. No doubt Père Durieu had long ago dropped the trunks off downstairs. But she had neither the intention nor the strength to wash her face or change her clothes; she just sat there annihilated at present, on this chair she had dropped on to. A single regret, an immense remorse, filled her being. Why had she obeyed him? Why had she finally agreed to go? She had the fierce conviction now that if she'd stayed, he would not have died. She would have loved him so much, made so much of him, she would have healed him. Every night she would have taken him in her arms and rocked him to sleep, she would have warmed him with all her youthfulness, she would have breathed her life into him with her kisses. When you didn't want death to take someone you held dear from you, you stayed and gave of your blood, you put death to flight. It was her fault if she'd lost him, if she could no longer embrace him and wake him from eternal rest. And she felt so stupid not to have realized, craven not to have given her life, guilty and forever punished now to have gone away when simple common sense, for want of heart, ought to have kept her here, at her task as a submissive and loving subject watching over her king.

The silence became such, so absolute, so large, that Clotilde took her eyes off Pascal's face for a moment to gaze around the room. She saw only vague shadows, as the lamp cast light obliquely on the mirror of the great cheval-glass that was like a plate of unpolished silver; and, below the high ceiling, the two candles only gave out two tawny circles of light. At that moment, she thought again of the letters he'd written to her, so short, so cold; and she understood how he'd tortured himself to smother his love. What strength he must have needed to put his plan for her happiness, his sublime and disastrous plan, into action! He'd been determined to bow out, to spare her his old age and his poverty; he dreamed she was rich, free to enjoy being twenty-six far away from him: it was total selflessness, self-annihilation in love for another. And she felt profound gratitude and peace, mixed with a sort of angry bitterness at such an accursed fate. Then, all of a sudden, the happy years sprang to mind, her youth, her adolescence spent by the side of that incredibly good, incredibly ebullient man. She remembered how he'd won her with his slow-burning passion, how she'd finally felt she was his, after the mutinies that had kept them apart for a brief moment, and in what transports of joy she had given herself to him, to be even more and completely his, because he wanted her! This room where he now lay growing cold still felt warm and shimmering from their nights of tender love.

The clock struck seven, and Clotilde started at the faint ringing sound in the vast silence. Who had spoken? She remembered and looked at the clock, whose bell had struck so many hours of joy. The antique clock had the tremulous voice of a very old lady friend, something that used to amuse them, in the dark, when they lay awake in each other's arms. And, from all the furniture, in that moment, memories came flooding back to her. Their two images seemed to rise again, from out of the pale silvery depths of the cheval-glass: they stepped forward, indistinct, almost merged, with a flickering smile, as they did on those days of rapture when he would bring her here, to deck her out with some piece of jewellery, a gift he'd have been hiding since the morning, in his mania for gift-giving. There was also the table where the two candles were burning, the little table on which they'd had their paupers' dinner, the night they ran out of bread and she had served him a royal feast. How many crumbs left over from their love she would find in the white marble chest of drawers, rimmed with beading! How they'd laughed, on the chaise longue with the stiff legs, when she'd be sitting there putting on her stockings and he'd come and tickle her! Even from the wall covering, from the old faded red printed calico that had gone the colour of dawn, a whisper reached her, everything sweet and tender they'd said to each other, the endless baby talk of their passion, and even the smell of her own hair, a smell of violets he'd adored. But then, as the seven strokes of the clock stopped vibrating deep in her heart, she brought her eyes back to Pascal's still face and she was once again overwhelmed.

It was in this state of growing prostration that, a few minutes later, Clotilde heard a sudden sound of sobbing. Someone had burst in, and she saw it was her grandmother Félicité. But she didn't move, didn't

speak, she was already so numb with pain. Martine, anticipating the
order she would surely have been given, had just run over to tell old
Madame Rougon the terrible news; and the latter, stunned at first by
the suddenness of the catastrophe, then profoundly distressed, had
come running, erupting into effusive grief. She sobbed before her
son, and embraced Clotilde, who returned the kiss as if in a dream.
From that moment on, without breaking out of the despair in which
she had isolated herself, Clotilde was acutely conscious that she was
not alone at the continual hushed-up bustle, the faint sounds of which
travelled through the room. It was Félicité crying, coming and going
on tiptoe, tidying up, ferreting around, whispering, dropping onto
a chair only to get up again immediately. And at around nine o'clock
the old woman absolutely insisted on getting her granddaughter to
eat something. Twice already she had lectured her, quietly. She now
returned to say in her ear:

'Clotilde, my darling, I tell you this isn't right. You must keep your
strength up, otherwise you'll never last the distance.'

But, with a shake of the head, the young woman once more stubbornly refused.

'Come now, you must have had something in Marseilles, at the
buffet, surely? But you haven't had anything since. Is that sensible?
I won't have you falling ill, too... Martine has some stock. I told her to
make a light soup and to add a chicken. Go down and have a mouthful,
just a mouthful, while I stay here.'

With the same pained shake of the head, Clotilde still refused. She
eventually stammered:

'Leave me alone, Grandmother, for pity's sake. I couldn't eat anything, it would stick in my throat.'

And she spoke no more. Yet she didn't sleep, her eyes were wide
open, stubbornly fixed on Pascal's face. For hours she didn't move
a muscle, sitting straight-backed and stiff, as though she wasn't there,
but somewhere far away, with the dead man. At ten o'clock, she heard
a noise: it was Martine winding up the wick in the lamp. At around
eleven, Félicité, who kept watch in an armchair, appeared to become
agitated, left the room, then came back. From then on, there were
comings and goings, impatient prowling around the young woman,
who was still wide awake, sitting there with her big staring eyes. The
clock chimed midnight, and only a single nagging thought remained
in her empty head, like a thorn stopping her from falling asleep: why

had she obeyed? If she'd stayed, she would have warmed him up with all her youthfulness, and he would not be dead! And it wasn't until just before one that she felt even that idea growing fuzzy and being swallowed in a nightmare. Exhausted with grief and weariness, she fell into a heavy sleep.

When Martine had gone to announce her son's unexpected death to her, old Madame Rougon, in her shock, had let out an initial cry of anger, mingled with her sorrow. What! Pascal had been dying and he hadn't wanted to see her, had made this servant swear not to let her know! That made her blood boil, as though the battle that had gone on between the two of them, all their lives, was set to continue beyond the grave. Then, after throwing on some clothes and running to La Souleaide, the thought of the terrible files, of all the manuscripts filling up the cupboard, overwhelmed her with a simmering passion. Now that Uncle Macquart and Aunt Dide were dead, she no longer dreaded what she called the abomination of Les Tulettes; and poor little Charles himself, in dying, had removed one of the defects that were the most humiliating for the family. Nothing remained now but the files, the abominable files, threatening the triumphal legend of the Rougons that she had spent her entire life creating, that was the sole concern of her old age, the work to whose victory she had doggedly devoted the last exertions of her energetic and crafty mind. For many a long year, she had kept her eye on them, never tiring, starting the battle all over again when she was thought to be beaten, always lying in ambush, and tenacious. Ah! If she could get hold of them at last and destroy them! That would mean the abysmal past wiped out, it would mean the glory of her people, so hard won, rid of every menace, flourishing freely at last, imposing its lie on history. And she saw herself parading through the three different districts of Plassans, hailed by all and sundry, bearing herself like a queen, nobly wearing mourning for the fallen regime. So, when Martine told her Clotilde was there, she stepped up the pace as she approached La Souleaide, spurred on by the fear of getting there too late.

As soon as she had installed herself in the house, however, Félicité promptly recovered herself. There was no hurry, she had the whole night ahead of her. However, she did want to get Martine on side without delay; and she knew only too well what would work on that simple-minded creature, set in the beliefs of a narrow religious faith. So the first thing she took care to do, downstairs amid the chaos of the kitchen, where she had gone to watch the chicken roasting, was to feign deep affliction at the thought that her son had died without having made his peace with the Church. She interrogated the servant, demanded details. But the woman shook her head, despairingly. No! No priest had come, Monsieur didn't even make the sign of the cross. She alone had gone down on her knees to recite the prayers for the dying, which, of course, was not enough for the salvation of a soul. Yet how fervently she had prayed to the good Lord, so that Monsieur went straight to heaven!

Her eyes on the chicken turning on the spit in front of a great bright fire, Félicité went on in a lower voice, apparently thinking aloud:

'Ah! My poor girl, the main thing stopping him from going straight to heaven is those abominable papers the unhappy man has left up there, in the cupboard. I don't know how it is that Divine Wrath hasn't yet come down on those papers and reduced them to ashes. If they're allowed to leave this place, it will mean pestilence, disgrace, and everlasting hell!'

Martine heard her out, quite pale.

'So, Madame thinks it would be doing a good deed to destroy them, a deed that would ensure the repose of Monsieur's soul?'

'Good God! Of course I do!... Oh, if we had them, those ghastly old scribblings, listen! I'd throw them straight on this fire! Ah! You wouldn't need to add any more vine-shoots. With nothing but those manuscripts from upstairs, there's enough to roast three chickens like this one here.'

The servant had grabbed a ladle to baste the bird. She too now seemed to be pondering.

'Only, we don't have them... I even heard a conversation about them that I can repeat to Madame word for word... It's when Mademoiselle Clotilde went up to the room. Doctor Ramond asked her if she remembered the orders she'd been given, before she went away, probably. And she said that she remembered, that she was supposed to keep the files and give him all the other manuscripts.'

Félicité, quivering, couldn't curb a gesture of panic. Already, she could see the papers escaping her; and it wasn't just the files she wanted, but all the pages with writing on them, the whole unknown, dubious, and dark work, from which only scandal could ensue, according to the obtuse and impetuous brain of this proud old bourgeoise.

'We must act,' she cried, 'this very night! Tomorrow it may well be too late.'

'I know where the key to the cupboard is,' Martine went on in a voice just above a whisper. 'The doctor told Mademoiselle.'

Félicité immediately pricked up her ears.

'Where is it, then, the key?'

'Under the pillow, under Monsieur's head.'

Despite the lively blaze of burning vine-shoots, a small icy current passed, and the two old women fell silent. All that could be heard was the sizzling of the juice falling from the roasting chicken into the dripping-pan.

But after Madame Rougon had dined, promptly and on her own, she went back upstairs with Martine. There and then, without any further talk, they knew they'd reached an understanding; it was decided that they would get hold of the papers before daybreak, by whatever means possible. The simplest thing would be just to take the key from under the pillow. Clotilde would have to fall asleep in the end: she looked too exhausted not to succumb to fatigue. All they had to do was wait. So they started spying, prowling from the workroom to the bedroom, watching like hawks to see whether the young woman's enormous eyes, widened and staring, hadn't at last shut. One of them would always go and check, while the other one cooled her heels in the workroom, where a lamp was burning black. This went on till close to midnight, at fifteen-minute intervals. But those eyes, fathomless, and full of darkness and immeasurable despair, remained wide open. Just before midnight, Félicité reinstalled herself in an armchair at the foot of the bed, determined not to leave the room while her granddaughter remained awake. She no longer took her eyes off the girl, annoyed to see that she scarcely batted an eyelid, staring with that inconsolable fixedness that defied sleep. And Félicité was the one, in this two-hander, who became drowsy and very nearly dropped off. Infuriated at this, she could stay there no longer. And she went to find Martine again.

'It's no use, she won't go to sleep!' she said, her voice strangled and shaky. 'We'll have to think of something else.'

Of course she'd already thought of breaking the cupboard open. But the old oak frames seemed to be rock solid and the old ironwork fittings held fast. What could they break the lock with? Not to mention the fact that they'd make a terrible racket and that the noise would certainly be heard in the room next door.

But she planted herself in front of the thick doors, nevertheless, and fumbled around, feeling for any weak points.

'If only I had a tool...'

Martine, less impetuous, interrupted her, protesting.

'Oh, no, no, Madame! We'd get caught!... Wait, perhaps Mademoiselle's sleeping.'

She tiptoed back to the bedroom and returned immediately.

'Yes, she is, she's sleeping! Her eyes are closed and she's not moving.'

They both went to check, holding their breaths and trying hard not to make the floorboards creak. Clotilde had in fact just fallen asleep and she looked to be so thoroughly annihilated that the two old women felt emboldened. But they were still worried they'd wake her if they brushed past her, for she had her chair set right against the bed. And it was also a sacrilegious and terrible act, whose horror struck terror into their hearts—slipping your hand under the dead man's pillow and stealing from him. Wouldn't they have to disturb him in his repose? Wouldn't he stir with the jolt? They paled with fear at the idea.

Félicité had already stepped forward with her arm out. But she drew back.

'I'm too short,' she stammered. 'You try, Martine, go on.'

The servant in her turn approached the bed. But she suddenly started shaking so badly that she also had to step back to stop herself from falling over.

'No, no, I can't! I feel as if Monsieur will open his eyes.'

And, shivering, appalled, they stood there a moment longer in this room filled with the great silence and majesty of death, in the presence of Pascal forever still and Clotilde annihilated under the crushing weight of her widowhood. The nobility of a lifetime's lofty endeavour may well have appeared to them in the trace it left over that silent head, which, with all its weight, guarded its life's work. The flame of the candles burned very pale. A sudden sense of sacred terror came over them and drove them out.

Félicité, usually so brave, a woman who once upon a time had never recoiled at anything, not even bloodshed, fled as if she were being pursued.

'Come away, Martine. We'll think of something else, we'll go and look for a tool.'

In the workroom, they drew breath. The servant suddenly remembered that the key to the secretaire ought to be on Monsieur's bedside table, where she'd spotted it the day before, when he was having his attack. They went to check. The mother had no scruples and opened the desk. But all she found were the five thousand francs, which she left at the back of the drawer, for money was the last thing she was worried about. In vain she looked for the Family Tree, which she knew was usually in there. She would so happily have started her work of destruction with that! It was still lying in plain sight on the doctor's desk in the workroom, but she didn't even see it there, in the feverish passion that made her ransack locked furniture, without leaving her the clear-headed calm needed to proceed methodically around her.

Her overwhelming desire brought her back to the cupboard, and she went and planted herself once more in front of it, sizing it up, taking it in with eyes burning with the fire of conquest. Notwithstanding her short stature, notwithstanding her eighty-odd years, she drew herself up with a nimbleness, an outlay of strength that was extraordinary.

'Ah!' she said again. 'If only I had a tool!'

And she looked once more for the chink in the colossus's armour, the crack that she could get her fingers into, to break it open. She devised plans of attack, dreamed up violent acts, then fell back on cunning, on some act of villainy that would open the cupboard doors to her just by her blowing on them.

Suddenly her eyes glinted, she'd hit on it.

'Tell me, Martine, isn't there a small latch that holds the inner door in place?'

'Yes, Madame, it hooks over a screw-ring just above the middle shelf... Here! It's level with that moulding there, more or less.'

Félicité gave a wave of certain victory.

'You do have a gimlet, a sizeable gimlet, don't you? Get me a gimlet!'

Martine swiftly ran down to her kitchen and brought back the required tool.

'This way, you see, we won't make any noise,' the old woman went on, setting to work.

With a peculiar power no one would have suspected of her little hands, withered with age, she drove in the gimlet and made a preliminary hole at the level Martine had indicated. But that was too low, and she could feel the point going into the shelf. A second drilled hole took her straight to the iron latch. This time it was too close. And so she went on drilling holes, right and left, until, using the gimlet itself, she could finally thrust the latch up and out of the screw-ring. The bolt of the lock slid across and both doors swung open.

'At last!' cried Félicité, beside herself.

Then she froze, anxious, and cocked an ear towards the bedroom, fearing she'd woken Clotilde. But the whole house was asleep in the vast black silence. Still the only thing emanating from the bedroom was the hallowed peace of death, and all she could hear was the clear chiming of the clock as it marked one in the morning with a single stroke. And the cupboard was wide open, yawning, displaying the heaps of papers with which its three shelves were crammed to overflowing. So, she threw herself at it, and the work of destruction began, in the middle of the sacred darkness, the infinite repose of the deathwatch.

'At last,' she repeated softly, 'for thirty years I've been wanting and waiting to do this!... Hurry, we must act fast, Martine! Help me!'

Already she had taken the tall chair from the desk and leapt onto it in a single bound, wanting to get the papers on the top shelf first, since she remembered that that's where the files were. But she was surprised not to see the blue cardboard folders; there was nothing there now but thick manuscripts, essays of the doctor's that were finished but not yet published, studies of inestimable value, all his investigations, all his discoveries, the monument of his future glory, which he had bequeathed to Ramond so that he would look after them. No doubt, some days before his death, thinking that only the files were under threat and that no one in the world would dare destroy his other works, he had done some housekeeping and reorganized everything, separating the files from the earlier research work.

'Oh, too bad!' muttered Félicité. 'There are so many of them, let's start wherever we like, if we want to get through them... While I'm up here, let's clear this lot out anyway... Here, Martine, catch!'

And she emptied the shelf, flung the manuscripts, one by one, into the arms of the servant, who set them on the table, making as little noise as possible. Soon the whole pile was lying there and Félicité jumped down from the chair.

'On the fire! On the fire!... We'll end up getting our hands on the others, the ones I'm looking for... On the fire! On the fire with them! These ones first! Right down to the tiniest fingernail-size scraps, right down to illegible notes! On the fire! On the fire with the lot, if we want to be sure of stopping the spread of evil!'

She herself, fanatical, fierce in her hatred of the truth, and crazily determined to eradicate the testimony of science, ripped out the first page of a manuscript, set it on fire at the lamp, then went and threw this flaming firebrand in the enormous fireplace, where there hadn't been a fire for perhaps twenty years; and she fed the flame, went on throwing on the rest of the manuscript, one chunk at a time. Just as determined, the servant came to lend her a hand, taking another thick notebook and tearing out the pages one by one. After that, the fire never went out, the tall fireplace filled with a flaring blaze, a bright burst of fire which slowed down from time to time only to leap up again with greater intensity, rekindled by fresh fuel. A burning mass spread out little by little, fine ash piled up, along with a thickening layer of black sheets of paper over which raced thousands of sparks. But it was a time-consuming, seemingly endless business, for if too many pages were thrown on at a time, they didn't burn and had to be prodded and turned over with tongs; it was best to crumple each page and wait till it was well and truly alight before adding others. They gradually got the knack and the work was proceeding at a great rate.

In her haste to go and get a fresh armful of papers, Félicité collided with an armchair.

'Oh, Madame, look out!' said Martine. 'What if someone comes!'

'Comes? Who? Clotilde? She's sleeping too soundly, poor girl!... And anyway, if she comes when it's all over, I couldn't care less! No, I'm not going to hide, I'll leave the cupboard bare and wide open, I'll say out loud that I'm the one who's purged the house... As long as there isn't a single line of writing left, ah God, I couldn't care less about anything else!'

For close to two hours, the fire in the grate blazed away. They had gone back to the cupboard and emptied the other two shelves, and now there was only the lower part to go, the bottom, which looked to be stuffed pell-mell with notes. Intoxicated by the heat of the bonfire, panting, perspiring, they surrendered to a savage fit of destruction. They squatted, blackened their hands poking back fragments only half burnt, so violent in their movements that stray locks of their grey hair hung down over their ruffled clothes. It was a gallopade of witches, stoking a diabolical stake for some abomination, the martyring of

a saint, the burning of written thought in the town square, the destroying of a whole world of truth and hope. And the intense light, which
at times dimmed the lamp, set the vast room aglow and made their
enormous shadows dance on the ceiling.

But just as she was about to empty out the very bottom of the cupboard, having already burnt, by the fistful, the notes piled up there
pell-mell, Félicité let out a strangled cry of triumph.

'Ah! Here they are!... On the fire! On you go!'

She had finally fallen upon the files. The doctor had concealed the
blue cardboard folders right at the very back, behind the rampart of
notes. And after this she went wild, completely carried away by the
madness of extermination, sheer rage, grabbing the files by the handful and hurling them into the flames, filling the fireplace with the roar
of a conflagration.

'They're burning, they're burning!... At last, they're actually
burning!... Martine, that one, too, that one there!... Ah! What a fire,
what a magnificent fire!'

But the servant was becoming uneasy.

'Madame, look out, you'll set the house on fire... Can't you hear
that rumbling?'

'Ah, so what? Let it all burn!... They're burning, God! They're
burning, it's so beautiful!... Three to go, two, and now the last one's
burning!'

She laughed for joy, beside herself, terrifying, as bits of flaming
soot came falling down. The roar was becoming alarming, the fire had
got up into the chimney, which was never swept. This only seemed to
excite her further, whereas the servant, losing her head, started shouting and running round the room.

Clotilde was sleeping beside the dead Pascal, in the supreme stillness of the bedroom. There had been no sound there other than the
faint vibration of the clock's bell chiming three in the morning. The
candles were burning with a long still flame, and not the faintest rus-
tle stirred the air. And yet, from the depths of her heavy dreamless
sleep, she heard something like an uproar, a nightmare gallopade,
growing louder. When she opened her eyes, she didn't realize what
was happening at first. Where was she? Why was there this enormous
weight crushing her chest? Reality came flooding back, filling her
with horror: she saw Pascal, she heard Martine's cries next door, and
she rushed out in great distress to see what was going on.

Already from the doorway, Clotilde took in the whole scene, in all its brutal clarity: the cupboard wide open and completely bare, Martine panic-stricken by fear of the fire, her grandmother Félicité, radiant, kicking the last fragments of the files into the flames. Smoke and flying soot filled the room, where the rumbling of the fire produced the throttling sound of a murder, the ravaging gallopade she'd just heard deep in her sleep.

And the cry that shot from her lips was the same cry Pascal himself had uttered the night of the storm, when he'd caught her in the act of stealing his papers.

'Thieves! Murderers!'

At once she raced to the fireplace and, despite the terrible roar, despite the flakes of red-hot soot that were falling, and at the risk of setting her hair alight and burning her hands, she grabbed fistfuls of pages not yet burned and bravely put them out by hugging them to her chest. But that was virtually nothing, barely a few scraps, not one complete page, not even a few crumbs of the colossal work, the enormous and patient undertaking of a lifetime which the fire had just destroyed in two hours. And her rage intensified, exploded in a burst of thunderous indignation.

'You are thieves, murderers! You have just committed the most abominable murder! You have desecrated death, you have killed thought, killed genius!'

Old Madame Rougon did not back away. Quite the opposite, she stepped forward, remorseless, her head high, defending the sentence of destruction she had handed down and executed.

'Are you talking to me, your grandmother? I did what I had to do, what you once wanted to do with us.'

'Once, you drove me to madness. But I've lived since then, I've loved, I've understood... And then, this was a sacred inheritance, left to me in honour of my courage, a dead man's last thoughts, all that remained of a great mind and which I was meant to make known to all... Yes, you are my grandmother! And it's as if you'd just burnt your son!'

'Burnt Pascal just because I burnt his papers!' cried Félicité. 'Well! I would've burned the whole town to the ground to save the glory of our family!'

And she kept advancing, combative, victorious; and Clotilde, who had placed on the table the blackened fragments she'd saved, shielded them with her body, fearing she'd throw them back in the flames. But the old woman disregarded them, she wasn't even worried about the fire in the chimney which was luckily going out of its own accord, while Martine was smothering the soot and the last flare-ups of burning embers.

'Yet you know full well', continued the old woman, who seemed to grow in height from her diminutive stature, 'that I've only ever had one ambition, one passion, and that's the power and prestige of our family. I've fought, I've been vigilant all my life, I've only lived as long as I have to erase the vile stories they tell about us and to leave behind a glorious legend... Yes, I've never given in to despair, I've never laid down my arms, I've always been ready to take advantage of the slightest opportunity... And all I've ever wanted to do, I've now done, because I knew how to bide my time.'

With a sweeping gesture, she indicated the bare cupboard and the fireplace where the last sparks were dying away.

'Now, it's over, our glory is safe, those abominable papers will no longer be there to accuse us, and I won't leave any threat behind when I go... The Rougons have triumphed.'

Distraught, Clotilde lifted her arm, as if to drive the woman away. But Félicité left the room of her own accord and went down to the kitchen to wash her black hands and pin her hair back up. The servant was about to follow her when, turning round, she saw her young mistress's gesture. She came back.

'Oh, Mademoiselle! I'll leave the day after tomorrow, when Monsieur is in the cemetery.'

There was a moment of silence.

'But I don't want to send you away, Martine, I know very well you're not the real culprit... You've been living in this house for thirty years. Stay, stay with me.'

The old maid shook her grizzled head, her face quite pale and seemingly worn out.

'No, I served Monsieur, I won't serve anyone after Monsieur.'

'But what about me!'

She raised her eyes and looked the young woman straight in the face, this loved little girl she had watched grow up.

'You, no!'

At that, Clotilde was at a loss, and wanted to tell her about the child she was carrying, her master's child, whom she might consent to serve. But Martine read her mind, recalling the conversation she had overheard, and she looked at the stomach of this fertile woman who wasn't yet showing her pregnancy. For a second, she seemed to be mulling it over. Then she said, flatly:

'The child, eh?... No!'

And she ended by giving her notice, and settling the matter like a practical old maid who knew the value of money.

'Since I've got the means, I'll go and eat up my money quietly somewhere... You, Mademoiselle, I can leave you on your own as you're not poor. Monsieur Ramond will tell you tomorrow how they salvaged four thousand francs in interest at the notary's. Here, meanwhile, is the key to the secretaire, where you'll find the five thousand francs Monsieur left there... Oh! I know very well there won't be any trouble between us. Monsieur hadn't paid me for three months, I've got documents from him to prove it. Besides that, just the other week I advanced about two hundred francs from my own pocket, without him knowing where the money came from. It's all written down, I'm not worried, I know Mademoiselle won't leave me a centime short... The day after tomorrow, when Monsieur's no longer here, I'll leave.'

She, too, went down to the kitchen and, despite the fact that this old maid's blind devotion had made her take part in a crime, Clotilde felt horribly sad at being abandoned by her. Yet, as she was gathering the remains of the files before going back to her room, she was overjoyed when she suddenly saw the Family Tree, quietly spread out on the table unnoticed by the two old women. This was the sole intact survivor of the wreck, a holy relic. She took it, and went and locked it in the chest of drawers in the bedroom, along with the half-burnt fragments.

But when she found herself back in this hallowed room, a great wave of emotion washed over her. What supreme stillness, what immortal peace, beside the destructive savagery that had filled the room next door with smoke and ash! A sacred serenity fell from the shadows, the two candles burned with a pure firm flame, without a flicker. And she saw then that Pascal's face had gone very white, with his white hair and beard flowing down around it. He slept on in the light, crowned with a halo, supremely beautiful. She bent down and kissed him once more, and felt the chill of this marble face on her lips, as he lay with his eyelids closed, dreaming his dream of eternity.

Her grief at not having been able to save the great work he'd
entrusted to her safekeeping was so acute that she fell to her knees,
sobbing. Genius had just been violated, and it felt to her that the
world would be destroyed, through this savage annihilation of a whole
life of work.

14

IN the workroom, Clotilde buttoned up her bodice, still holding her baby on her knees, having just given him her breast. It was after lunch, around three, on a sparkling day in late August, with an incandescent sky; and the shutters, carefully shut, let only thin shafts of sunlight through the cracks into the sleepy warm gloom of the vast room. The great lazy Sunday peacefulness seemed to seep in from outside, with a distant volley of bells, ringing out the last summons to vespers. Not a sound rose from the empty house, where mother and baby were to remain on their own until dinner, the servant having asked permission to go and see a cousin in the faubourg.

For a moment Clotilde looked at her son, a big boy already three months old. She had given birth in the last week of May. Soon it would be ten months since she had been wearing mourning for Pascal, a simple long black dress in which she looked divinely beautiful, so fine, so willowy, with her incredibly sad young face wreathed by her gorgeous blonde hair. She couldn't smile, but she felt a certain peacefulness seeing the beautiful baby, fat and rosy, with his mouth still wet with milk, and whose eyes had lit on one of the shafts of sunlight in which dust motes danced. He looked very surprised, couldn't take his eyes off this flash of gold, this dazzling miracle of light. Then sleep came and he let his little bare round head, already sprinkled with a few fair hairs, fall back on to his mother's arm.

At that, Clotilde gently stood and laid him down snugly in the cradle by the table. She leant over him for a second longer to be quite sure he was asleep; then she pulled down the muslin curtain, in the crepuscular gloom. Soundlessly, with supple movements, walking with a step so light her feet barely touched the parquet floor, she next busied herself putting away some linen that was on the table, and crossed the room twice looking for a tiny stray sock. She was very quiet, very gentle, and very active. And that particular day, in the seclusion of the house, she was reflecting, the year she had just lived through unfolding in her mind.

Firstly, after the dreadful shock of the funeral, there had been the immediate departure of Martine, who had been doggedly unyielding, not even wanting to serve out a week's notice, bringing in someone to replace her, the young cousin of a local baker's wife, a big dark-haired girl who happily turned out to be passably clean and dedicated. Martine herself now lived in Sainte-Marthe, in the back of beyond, so parsimoniously that she must still have been putting money away from the return on her little hoard. She was not known to have an heir, so who would this furious avarice benefit? In ten months, she had not once set foot back in La Souleaide: Monsieur was no longer there, and she didn't even give in to the desire to see Monsieur's son.

Next, into Clotilde's musings crept the figure of her grandmother Félicité. This one came to visit her from time to time, with the condescension of a powerful relative who is broad-minded enough to pardon all sins, when they have been cruelly expiated. She would show up without warning, kiss the baby, lecture her, and offer advice; to deal with her, the young mother had adopted the straightforwardly deferential stance Pascal had always maintained. Besides, Félicité was completely caught up in her triumph. She was at last about to realize an idea long cherished, and given close consideration, which would perpetuate the unalloyed glory of the family through an imperishable monument. The idea was to employ her now considerable fortune in the erection and endowment of a home for the aged, which would be called the Rougon Old People's Home. She had already bought the land, part of the old medieval Jeu de Mail* grounds, just out of town near the railway station; and in fact that very Sunday, at around five, when the heat would have dropped a little, the first stone was to be laid—a proper solemn occasion, to be honoured by the presence of the authorities, where she herself would be the acknowledged queen, at the centre of an enormous gathering of people.

Clotilde, moreover, felt some small gratitude to her grandmother, who had recently shown perfect disinterestedness at the reading of Pascal's will. He had made the young woman his sole legatee, although his mother still had a legal right to a quarter of the legacy; but she had declared herself respectful of her son's last wishes and simply renounced the succession. She was determined to disinherit everyone in her family, to leave them nothing but glory, by using up her large fortune building this Old People's Home that would carry the respected and hallowed name of the Rougons into future ages; and having been, for half a century, so utterly avid to acquire money, she now disdained it, chastened by a higher ambition. Thanks to this liberality, Clotilde had no further anxiety about the future: the four thousand francs' annual income would do them, her and her son. She would raise him, she would make a man of him. She had even invested the five thousand francs from the secretaire in a life annuity in her little boy's name; and she still owned La Souleaide, which everyone was advising her to sell. It was true, the upkeep wasn't costly, but what a sad and lonely life, in this rambling deserted house, much too big for her, where she was virtually swallowed up! So far, though, she hadn't been able to make up her mind to leave. Perhaps she never would.

Ah, La Souleaide! All her love lay there, all her life, all her memories! It felt to her, at times, as if Pascal was still living there, since she had not disturbed a thing from their old existence. The furniture was in the same place, the hours marked out the same routines. The only thing she had done was to close up his bedroom, which she alone entered, as though into a sanctuary, to cry whenever her heart felt too heavy. In the bedroom in which they had loved one other, in the bed in which he had died, she lay down every night as she had before, when she was a young girl; and the only new thing there, standing flush with the bed, was the cradle, which she carried in at night. It was the same old sweet room, with its old familiar furniture, and its wall covering softened by age to the colour of dawn, the very ancient room rejuvenated by the baby. Then, downstairs, although she felt very lonely, very lost, at each meal in the bright dining room, she could hear echoes of the laughter, the hearty appetites of her youth, when they both ate and drank together so gaily to health and to life. And the garden too, the whole estate was tethered to her being by the most intimate heartstrings, for she couldn't take a step in it without seeing the two of them closely united in her mind's eye: out on the terrace, in the thin shade of the great hundred-year-old cypresses, they had so often gazed on the valley of the Viorne, bordered by the rocky ridges of the Seille and the burnt slopes of Sainte-Marthe! They had dared each other so many times to race up over the drystone terraces, through the scrawny olive and almond trees, like schoolchildren playing truant! And then there was the pine grove, its shade hot and fragrant, where the pine needles crackled underfoot; the immense threshing floor, carpeted with grass that felt spongy under your shoulders and from where you could see the entire sky at night when the stars came out! And best of all there were the giant plane trees, whose delicious peace they'd go and savour every day in summer, listening to the refreshing song of the spring, the pure crystal note it had been drawing out for centuries! Right down to the old stones of the house, right down to the earth on the ground—there was not an atom of La Souleaide where she didn't feel the warm beating of a bit of their blood, of a bit of their life together spread out and mingled.

But she preferred to spend her days in the workroom, and it was here that she relived her happiest memories. In here, too, there was only one new piece of furniture, the cradle. The doctor's table was in its place, in front of the window on the left: he could have come in and sat down, as the chair hadn't even been shifted. On the long table in the centre, among the old piles of books and pamphlets, nothing new had been introduced but the bright note of tiny baby clothes, which she was in the process of going through. The bookcases displayed the same rows of books, the big oak cupboard, firmly closed, looked as though it still held the same hoard of treasure in its entrails. Beneath the smoke-stained ceiling, the lovely clean smell of work still hung, amid all the chairs trailing around helter-skelter in the genial chaos of this shared atelier, where they had so long staged her girlish flights of fancy and his scientific investigations. Yet these days what touched her most was seeing her old pastels, tacked to the walls, both the copies she had made of living flowers, minutely reproduced, and the imagined ones soaring off into completely fantastical realms, the dream flowers whose wildly imaginative power was sometimes overwhelming.

Clotilde had nearly finished putting away the tiny clothes on the table when she looked up and happened to see right there in front of her the pastel of old King David, with his hand on the bare shoulder of Abishag, the young Shunammite. And she who no longer laughed, felt a surge of joy rush to her face, she was so moved. How ardently they had loved one another, how ardently they had dreamed of eternity the day she'd amused herself creating this proud and loving emblem! The old king, dressed sumptuously in a completely straight robe, heavy with precious stones, wore the royal headband around his snowy hair; but she was even more sumptuous, with nothing but the lily-like silkiness of her skin, her slim-waisted willowy figure, her small round breasts, and her supple and exquisitely graceful arms. Now he had gone, he was lying in the ground, while she, dressed in black, dismal from head to toe, revealed nothing of her triumphant nakedness, and had only the infant now to embody the easy, absolute gift she had made of her person, before the assembled people, in the broad light of day.

With care, Clotilde at last sat down beside the cradle. Shafts of sunlight stretched all the way across the room, the heat of the torrid day was growing heavier in the sleepy gloom made by the closed shutters; and the silence of the house seemed to further expand. She had set aside some tiny baby's vests, and was sewing laces back on, plying the needle slowly, gradually caught up in another daydream, amid this great warm peace that enveloped her, within the conflagration outside. Her thoughts at first returned to her pastels, both the accurate ones and the fantastical ones, and she now said to herself that all the duality of her nature lay in this passion for truth that sometimes kept her standing for hours at a time in front of a flower to copy it exactly; but then also in her need for another world beyond appearances, a need that, in days gone by, had flung her outside reality and swept her up in mad dreams to a paradise of unreal flowers. She had always been this way, and she felt that deep down she remained the same today as she was yesterday, beneath the flow of new life that was endlessly transforming her. And her thoughts then skipped to the profound gratitude she continued to feel for Pascal for having made her what she was. Long ago, when she was still quite small and he had lifted her out of an abysmal environment and taken her to live with him, he had surely yielded to his good heart, but he probably also wanted to experiment on her and see how she would thrive in a different environment, one that was all truth and love. That had been a constant concern of his, a long-held theory that he would have liked to test on a grand scale: how the environment can promote culture, and even heal, improving and saving the individual, both physically and morally. She certainly owed what was best in her to him, and sensed what a whimsical and excessive creature she might otherwise have become, whereas he'd only ever given her passion and courage. In that time of blossoming out in the sun, life had even ended up throwing them into each other's arms, and wasn't this child really the final effort of goodness and joy, this child who had come along and who would have delighted them together, if death hadn't parted them?

Looking back like this, she had a clear sense of the long and painful labour that had gone on inside her. Pascal had corrected her heredity, and she relived her slow evolution, the contest between the realist and the fantasist. It had started with her rages as a child, with the stirrings of rebellion, with a loss of balance that used to launch her into the most dangerous dreams. Then came her great attacks of piety, her need for illusion and lies, for immediate happiness, at the thought that the iniquities and injustices of this evil world would be compensated by the eternal joys of a future paradise. Those were the days when she'd fought with Pascal, and tortured him with intense misery, while dreaming of murdering his genius. But she had turned back, at that bend in the road, and recognized her master again, when he won her over through the terrible lesson in life he gave her on the night of the storm. Since then, the environment had acted, and she had evolved at lightning speed: she had ended up becoming the well-balanced, level-headed woman she was, happy to live life as it should be lived, in the hope that the sum of human industry would one day free the world of evil and pain. She had loved, she was a mother, and she understood.

Suddenly she remembered that other night, the night they'd spent on the threshing floor. She once again heard her lamentation out under the stars: how nature was vile, humanity abominable, science bankrupt, how you had to lose yourself in God, in the mystery of revealed truth. Outside self-abnegation, there was no lasting happiness. Then, she heard *him*, taking up his creed again: how reason made progress through science, how the only possible good was that of truths acquired slowly and for ever, his belief being that the sum of those truths, always growing in number, would end up giving man incalculable power, and serenity if not happiness. It all amounted to a passionate faith in life. As he used to put it, we had to keep going, to move on, in step with life, which always moved on. No pause could be hoped for, no peace found in the paralysis of ignorance, no relief in taking backward steps into the past. You had to have a steady mind and the humility to tell yourself that the only reward in life is to have lived it courageously, accomplishing the task it sets. Then, evil became a mere accident as yet unexplained, and from high above humanity looked like a gigantic mechanism in operation, toiling away towards an ever-changing future. Why would the workman, who vanished after finishing his working day, curse the work because he couldn't see or judge the end result? Even if there was to be no end result, why not savour the joy of action, the bracing air of movement, the sweetness of sleep after long hard work? The children will carry on the job of the fathers, they're born and are loved for this alone, for this, the business of life, which is passed on to them and which they will then pass on in turn. And so there really was nothing left to do but to be brave and resign ourselves to our role in the great shared task, relinquishing the mutiny of the self that demands its own personal, absolute, happiness.

She examined her conscience and found she didn't feel the anguish she used to feel once upon a time when she thought of what happened immediately after you died. That preoccupation with the afterlife no longer haunted her to the point of torture. Once, she would have liked to wrest the secret of destiny from heaven with violence. She had felt infinite sadness at being alive without knowing why. What were we on earth to do? What was the meaning of this vile existence, without equality, without justice, a life that had seemed to her like a nightmare produced by a night of delirium? But her fever had abated, she could think about these things now unflinchingly. Perhaps it was the child, this continuation of herself, who now hid from her the horror of her end. But it also had a lot to do with the emotional balance in which she lived, this notion that you had to live life for the sheer effort of living and that the only possible peace, in this world, lay in the joy of making that effort. She repeated to herself one of the things the doctor often said, whenever he saw a peasant going home, looking peaceful, after his working day was done: 'There's a man who won't lose any sleep over the debate about the afterlife.' He meant that that debate only gets bogged down and becomes poisoned in the fevered brains of the idle. If everyone did their job, everyone would sleep soundly. She herself had felt the almighty healing power of work, throughout all her suffering and mourning. Ever since he'd taught her how to make use of every hour given to her, and especially since she'd become a mother, constantly busy with her child, she no longer felt the thrill of the unknown brushing the nape of her neck as it passed, with a chilly little breath. She cast off any disturbing daydreams now without a struggle; and if a fear still troubled her, if one of the daily griefs made her feel sick at heart, she found comfort, an invincible resilience, in the thought that her child had one more day, this day, that he would have another day, the following day, that day by day, page by page, his living work was being written. This gave her a delicious respite from all distresses. She had a purpose, a goal in life, and she could tell by the happy serenity she felt that she was surely doing what she'd come here to do.

Yet, at that very minute, she knew that the visionary in her was not yet completely laid to rest. A faint noise had just stolen into the profound silence, and she looked up: who was the divine mediator who was passing by? Perhaps it was the dear dead man she wept for and whom she believed she could sense all around her. Even now she must be a bit the child believer of old, curious about the mysterious other world, driven by an instinctive need for the unknown. She had given this need its due, she could even explain it scientifically. However far science rolls back the frontiers of human knowledge, there is probably a point it will never go beyond; and it was there, precisely, that Pascal set the sole interest of living, in the desire human beings had constantly to know more. She consequently allowed that there were unknown forces with which the world was flooded, an immense dark realm, ten times bigger than the realm already conquered, an unexplored infinity which future humanity would go on endlessly scaling. Most certainly that was a vast enough field for the imagination to be able to lose itself in. During these hours of musing, she was satisfying the compelling thirst human beings seem to have for what lies on the other side, a need to escape from the visible world and indulge in the illusion of the absolute justice and happiness to come. What was left of her past torment was assuaged by her latest flights of fancy, since suffering humanity cannot live without the consolation of falsehood. But everything merged happily in her. At the turn of a century weary of science, unnerved at all the destruction it has wrought, seized with terror at the prospect of the new age, and feeling a panicky desire not to go any further but to leap backwards, she represented the happy balance, the passion for truth broadened by equal interest in the unknown. If the sectarian scientists blocked the view so as to strictly adhere to observable phenomena, it was up to her, as a good ordinary person, to give what she didn't know, and would never know, its due. And if Pascal's creed was the logical conclusion to his whole *œuvre*, the eternal question of an afterlife which she nevertheless continued to ask the heavens, opened the door once again on the infinite, which lay ahead of a humanity forever on the move. Since we need to learn, always, while resigning ourselves to never knowing everything, wasn't preserving the mystery of faith, and balancing eternal doubt and eternal hope, the same thing as embracing progress, embracing life itself?

A new sound, a wing flapping past, brushing her hair with a kiss, this time made her smile. He was clearly there. And everything inside her exploded in boundless tenderness, rushing in from all sides, flooding her whole being. How good and happy he was, what great love for others gave him his zest for life! He himself may well have been just a dreamer, for he had had the most beautiful of dreams, this ultimate belief in a better world, when science will have invested man with incalculable power: the power of accepting everything, doing everything to create happiness, knowing everything and fore-seeing everything, reducing nature to being merely a servant, and living with the serenity of satisfied intellect! Till that time, work sought and regulated was enough to ensure the good health of all. Perhaps one day even suffering would be put to use. And, in the face of this enormous labour, before this sum total of the living, good and bad, admirable either way for their courage and toil, she now saw only a fraternal humanity, she now felt only limitless indul-gence, boundless compassion and fervent charity. Love, like the sun, bathes the earth, and goodness is the great wide river from which all hearts drink.

Clotilde had been sewing for nearly two hours by now, plying her needle with the same regular movement while her thoughts strayed. But the laces of the little baby's vests had been sewn back on, and she had also labelled some new nappies she'd bought the day before. And so she stood up, having finished her sewing and wanting to put the linen away. Outside, the sun was sinking and the golden shafts coming into the room through the cracks were now very thin and slanting. She could hardly see and had to go and open a shutter; then she forgot herself for a second before the vast scene suddenly spread out before her. The sweltering heat had dropped and a light breeze was blowing in the magnificent unblemished blue sky. On the left, you could make out even the tiniest clumps of pines, among the blood-red tumble-down rocks of the Seille; while to the right, past the slopes of Sainte-Marthe, the valley of the Viorne stretched out to infinity, in the powdery golden light of the setting sun. She looked for a second at the tower of Saint-Saturnin, all golden too, rising over the rose-pink town; and she was just about to move away again when a spectacle brought her back, and held her, leaning at the window, for a long while still.

There was a crowd swarming, beyond the railway line, squeezing into the old Jeu de Mail grounds. Clotilde immediately remembered the ceremony and realized that her grandmother Félicité was about to lay the first stone of the Rougon Old People's Home, the victory monument destined to carry the glory of the family into future ages. Enormous preparations had been under way for a week, there had been talk of a plasterer's hod and a silver trowel, which the old lady herself was to wield, keen as she was to play a part, to triumph, for all her eighty-two years. What made her swell with queenly pride was the fact that she would thereby be carrying off the conquest of Plassans for the third time; for she was forcing the entire town, all three of the districts, to fall in around her, to form an escort for her and to cheer and applaud her, as a benefactress. There were indeed to be lady patrons there, chosen from among the noblest of the Saint-Marc quarter, a delegation from workers' associations from the old quarter, and finally the most eminent residents of the new town—lawyers, notaries, doctors—not to mention the commoners, a stream of people dressed in their Sunday best, flocking there as if to a fete. And, in the middle of this supreme triumph, she was perhaps even prouder that it was she, as one of the queens of the Second Empire, the widow who wore mourning for the fallen regime in so dignified a fashion, who had vanquished the young Republic by forcing it, in the person of the sub-prefect, to come and hail her and thank her. Initially there was only going to be a speech by the mayor; but it had become clear, since the day before, that the sub-prefect, too, would speak. From so far away Clotilde could only make out a riot of black frock coats and light-coloured gowns, in the dazzling sunshine. Then there was a for-lorn blast of music, the music of the town's amateurs whose brassy resonances the wind now and again blew her way.

She left the window and went to open the big oak cupboard to put away her work, still lying on the table. It was in this cupboard, once so full of the doctor's manuscripts and now empty, that she had set the baby's layette. It seemed bottomless, huge, yawning; and on the enor-mous bare shelves, there was nothing now but the delicate swaddling clothes, the little baby's vests, the little bonnets, the little socks, the piles of nappies, all this fine linen, the fluffy plumage of a bird still in the nest. Where so many ideas had lain in a heap, where one man's relentless labour over thirty years had piled up in overflowing paper-work, all that now lay was the linen of one little being, things that could hardly be called garments, the first little cloths, which protected him for an hour and which he would soon outgrow. In its vastness the old-fashioned cupboard looked gay and completely revitalized.

As Clotilde put the nappies and vests away on a shelf, she spotted a large envelope with the remnants of the files she had put back there after saving them from the fire. And she remembered what Doctor Ramond had again asked her to do only the day before: to see whether, among these remnants, any remotely significant fragment remained, something of scientific interest. He was in despair at the loss of the priceless manuscripts the master had bequeathed to him. Straight after Pascal's death, he had done his very best to write up the final conversation he'd had with him, the whole suite of comprehensive theories set out in detail by the dying man with such heroic equanimity; but all he could retrieve were rudimentary summaries; he needed the complete studies, the observations made day by day, the results obtained and the laws formulated. The loss was irreparable, all that work would have to be done again, and he deplored the fact that he only had a few indications—he said that for science it meant a setback of twenty years or more, as it would be at least that long before anyone again took up and used the ideas of this lone pioneer, whose works had been destroyed in a barbarous and idiotic catastrophe.

The Family Tree, the only intact document, was attached to the envelope, and Clotilde brought everything over to the table, by the cradle. When she took out the remnants, one by one, she saw what she had always been more or less certain of: that not a single entire page of manuscript remained, not one complete note that made any sense. There were only fragments, scraps of paper half burnt and blackened, unrelated, disjointed. But as she examined them, her interest was piqued by these incomplete sentences, these words half consumed by fire which no one else could begin to understand. She cast her mind back to the night of the storm, and the sentences completed themselves, the beginning of a word brought back individuals, stories. Thus it was that the name Maxime fell under her gaze; and she relived the life of this brother of hers who had remained a stranger to her and whose death, two months earlier, had left her almost indifferent. Next, a truncated line containing her father's name made her feel uneasy, for she had reason to believe that the man had pocketed his son's fortune and mansion, thanks to the hairdresser's niece, the so very innocent Rose, who'd been given a generous cut as payment. Then she came across other names, the name of her uncle Eugène, the former vice-emperor, a doddering old man these days; the name of her cousin Serge, the curé of Saint-Eutrope, who, they'd told her only the day before, had consumption and was dying. And every remnant came alive, the whole hideous and yet fraternal family was reborn from these crumbs, these black ashes over which only incoherent syllables now ran.

And so Clotilde felt curious enough to unfold the Family Tree and spread it out on the table. Emotion got the better of her, she was moved to pity by these relics; then when she read the notes added in pencil by Pascal, a few minutes before breathing his last, tears sprang to her eyes. With what bravura he had written down the date of his own death! And how strongly you could feel his desperate longing to live, in the wobbly words announcing the birth of their child! The Tree rose up, branched out, unfurled its leaves, and she forgot herself for a long while contemplating it, telling herself that the master's whole *œuvre* was right here, in all this classified and documented foliage of their family. She could hear the words he'd used to comment on each hereditary case, she recalled his lessons. But the children especially interested her. The colleague the doctor had written to in Noumea for information about the child born of Étienne's marriage, in the convict prison, had decided to reply; but all he mentioned was the child's sex: it was a girl, and she seemed to be in good health. Octave Mouret had nearly lost his little girl, who was very frail, while his little boy continued to be superbly robust. However, the hub of rude good health, and extraordinary fecundity, still lay in Valqueyras, in the home of Jean, whose wife had had two children in three years and was pregnant with a third. The brood was thrusting up merrily out in the sun, in the middle of good rich earth, while the father worked the soil and the mother stayed at home, resolutely making soup and cleaning up after the kids. There was enough new sap and work there to begin a world anew. At that moment, Clotilde felt she could hear Pascal's cry: 'Ah! Our family! What will become of it? What being will it finally end in?' She herself lapsed back into reverie before the Tree stretching its latest little branches into the future. Who knew where the sound bough would spring from? Perhaps the almighty long-awaited sage would germinate there.

A faint cry drew Clotilde out of her reflections. The muslin on the cradle seemed to be stirring with a puff of air: the baby had woken up and was singing out and getting restless. She swiftly picked him up and lifted him gaily into the air, so he could bask in the golden light of the setting sun. But he wasn't responsive to this end to a beautiful day; his vacant little eyes swivelled away from the vast sky, while he opened wide his little pink beak like an ever-hungry bird. And he bawled so loudly, woke up so greedily, that she decided to give him the breast again. It was time, anyway, as it was now three hours since he'd last had a feed.

Clotilde went and sat back down by the table. She laid him on her knees, where he hardly quietened down, but bawled even louder, fretting; and she watched him with a smile while she unbuttoned her dress. Her breast appeared, her small round breast, scarcely swollen by the milk. A small tawny halo had merely blossomed at her nipple, out of the delicate whiteness of her naked body, so exquisitely willowy and young. Already the baby could smell it, raised his head, and groped with his lips. When she clamped his mouth on, he gave a little growl of satisfaction and threw himself at her with the hearty voracious appetite of a man keen to live. He sucked as hard as his gums would let him, ravenously. At first, with his little free hand, he seized a fistful of breast, as if to mark it as his property, and defend it and safeguard it. Then, in his joy, as the warm milk streamed abundantly down his throat, he began to lift his little arm in the air, quite straight, like a flag. And Clotilde kept up her unconscious smile, seeing him, so vigorous, feeding off her. In the first few weeks, she had suffered badly from a cracked nipple and her breast was still sensitive even now; but she smiled anyway, with that serene air mothers have, as happy to give their milk as they would be to give their blood.

When she had unbuttoned her bodice, and her breast, her motherly nakedness was on display, another of her mysteries had appeared, one of her most hidden and most delicious secrets: the fine necklace with the seven pearls, those milky stars, which the master had hung around her neck on a day of dire poverty, in his passionate mania for gift-giving. No one else but Pascal had seen it again after the day it arrived. The necklace seemed to be part of her modesty, it was of her flesh, so simple, so childlike. And the whole time the baby sucked at her breast, only she could see it, and she was deeply moved as she relived the memory of kisses whose warm scent it seemed to have kept.

A blast of music in the distance startled Clotilde. She turned her head and looked out at the countryside, all blond and golden in the slanting sun. Ah, yes! The ceremony, the laying of the stone, up there! Then she brought her eyes back to the baby, and she became absorbed once again in the pleasure of seeing what a good appetite he had. She

pulled over a small bench to raise one of her knees, and leant a shoulder against the table next to the Tree and the blackened fragments of
the files. Her thoughts drifted, soaring up into a realm of heavenly
calm, while she felt the best of herself, this pure milk, flow from her
with a soft little sound, binding her ever more closely to this dear
little being who had emerged from her womb. The child had come,
perhaps the redeemer. The bells had rung, the wise men had set out,
followed by the multitudes, by all nature in festive mood, smiling
upon the baby in his swaddling clothes. And while he was drinking
her life, she, his mother, was already dreaming of the future. What
would he be, when she had made him big and strong by giving herself
entirely? A scholar who would teach the world a bit of the eternal
truth? A captain who would bring his country glory? Or, better still,
one of those shepherds of men who quell passions and establish
the reign of justice? She saw him as extremely handsome, extremely
good, extremely powerful. And this was the dream of all mothers, the
certainty of having given birth to the long-awaited messiah; and, in
that hope, in this unassailable belief of every mother in the certain
triumph of her child, there was the very same hope that creates life,
the belief that gives humanity the endlessly renewed strength to go
on living.

What would he be, this baby? She looked at him and tried to
work out who he took after. His father, of course: he had Pascal's
forehead and eyes, something noble and strong in the square cut of
his head. She saw herself in him, too, with his fine mouth and his
delicate chin. Then, quietly anxious, she looked for the others, the
terrible forebears, all those who were there, entered on the Tree,
spreading out in its thrusting hereditary leaves. Would it be this one,
then, or that one, or this other one that he'd come to resemble? But
then she relaxed, she could not *not* hope, her heart was so full of the
hope that springs eternal. The faith in life that the master had sown in
her kept her fearless, upright, unshakeable. What did the woes, the
sufferings, the abominations matter! Health lay in universal toil, in
the power that impregnates and gives birth. The work was good when
lovemaking produced a child. Then hope surged back, in spite of the
wounds laid bare, the dismal catalogue of human shame. A child
meant life perpetuated, embarked on yet again, life which we never
tire of believing good, since we live it with such tenacity, for all its
injustice and pain.

Clotilde cast an involuntary glance at the Tree of her forebears, opened out next to her. Yes, the threat lay there: so many crimes, so much sordidness, amid so many tears and so much wounded goodness! Such an extraordinary mix of the best and the worst, humanity in a nutshell, with all its defects and all its struggles! It made you wonder if it wouldn't have been better for the whole miserable, rotten ants' nest to be blasted apart by a bolt of lightning. But after so many terrible Rougons, after so many abominable Macquarts, yet another one had been born. With the daring defiance of its eternity, life wasn't afraid of creating one more. It went on with its work, propagated itself according to its laws, indifferent to hypotheses, moving on in its unending labour. At the risk of making monsters, it was compelled to create since, in spite of the sick and the mad it creates, it never gets tired of creating, in the hope no doubt that the healthy and the wise will come along one day. Life, life, which flows in torrents, which continues on and starts again, ending we know not where! Life in which we are plunged, life with its infinite opposing currents, always surging and immense, like a boundless sea!

A rush of maternal fervour rose in Clotilde's heart, happy as she was to feel the voracious little mouth guzzling her non-stop. It was a prayer, an invocation. To the unknown child, as to the unknown god! To the child who was to be tomorrow, to the genius who had perhaps been born, to the messiah the next century awaited, who would lift the peoples of the world out of their doubt and their suffering! Since the nation was to be made anew, hadn't this one come for that very task? He would take up the experiment again, raise the walls back up, give men groping in the dark some kind of certainty again, build the city of justice, where the rule of labour would alone ensure happiness. In times of trouble, we look for prophets. Unless he was the Antichrist, the demon of destruction, the heralded beast who would purge the earth of foulness, it having become too widespread. But life would go on no matter what, we just had to be patient for thousands of years more before the other unknown child appeared, the saviour.

But by now the baby had drained her right breast dry and, since he was getting cranky, Clotilde turned him round and gave him her left breast. Then she started to smile again, tickled by the greedy little gums. In spite of everything, she was hope. Wasn't a nursing mother the very picture of the world redeemed and carrying on? She leant over and met his limpid eyes, which opened up in rapture, eager for the light. What was he saying, this little being, for her to feel his heart beating beneath the breast he was draining? What glad tidings was he announcing, with the gentle suction of his mouth? What cause would he give his blood for, when he was a grown man, strong from all this milk he'd drunk? Perhaps he wasn't saying anything, perhaps he was already lying, and yet she was so happy, so full of absolute confidence in him!

Once again, the distant brass instruments exploded in a fanfare. This must surely be the crescendo, the moment when Grandmother Félicité, with her silver trowel, laid the first stone of the monument erected to the glory of the Rougons. The great blue sky, gladdened by the Sunday frolics, was festive. And, in the warm silence, in the lonely peace of the workroom, Clotilde smiled at her baby boy, who was still feeding, his little arm in the air, quite straight, raised like a flag rallying the world to life.

EXPLANATORY NOTES

5 *heredity*: see *The Fortune of the Rougons*, chapters 2 and 3.

6 *twenty-five years old*: Jeanne Rozerot's age in 1892 (when Zola was fifty-two).

L'Époque: Saccard fled into exile after the collapse of the Banque universelle (see *Money*) and has returned to France, resuming his first occupation, that of journalist: in *The Fortune of the Rougons* (chapter 3) he is shown working for the Republican newspaper *L'Indépendant*.

Tuileries papers: in 1870 the Government of National Defence had published the *Papiers et correspondance de la famille impériale: Pièces saisies aux Tulieries* (Paris: Imprimerie nationale, 1870). These documents pertained to reports by Louis-Napoleon's secret police, endowments granted to the Emperor's family, money disbursed for propaganda for the regime, etc. The papers were published in the Parisian press in July 1872, thus allowing us to date the beginning of the novel's action.

7 '*SACCARD*': see *The Kill*, chapter 2. Aristide Rougon decides to change his name to Saccard: 'there's money in that name; it sounds as if you're counting five-franc pieces'.

8 *superb*: Clotilde's artistic creations recall the paintings of French Symbolism, especially the works of Gustave Moreau (1826–98).

9 *marry again*: see *The Kill*, chapter 2.

12 *Les Tulettes*: the lunatic asylum south-east of Plassans, on the road to Nice, where Aunt Dide is shut away (see *The Fortune of the Rougons*, chapter 7) and François Mouret is also committed (see *The Conquest of Plassans*, chapter 17).

Sedan: on 19 July 1870 France declared war on Prussia. On 2 September Napoleon III, surrounded with his army at Sedan, surrendered. This ignominious defeat resulted in the immediate fall of the Second Empire. The Third Republic was declared on 4 September.

plebiscite: on 8 May 1870 voters were asked whether they approved of the liberal reforms made to the constitution since 1860. The result was a great success for the Emperor, with seven and a half million in favour and only one and a half million against.

13 *triumphed*: see *The Fortune of the Rougons*, chapter 2.

sealed: for a description of the yellow salon, see *The Fortune of the Rougons*, chapter 2; for a description of the green salon, see *The Conquest of Plassans*, chapter 6.

twin exploits: see *The Fortune of the Rougons*, chapter 6. First, Pierre Rougon takes control of the town hall in Plassans after distributing rifles to a few cronies. A little later, he lures a band of Republicans into an ambush, with the connivance of his half-brother Antoine Macquart. Four of the Republicans are killed, thus turning Rougon into a hero in the eyes of the townspeople.

14 *almost emperor*: see *His Excellency Eugène Rougon*.

new city of Paris: an allusion to Aristide Saccard's activities as a speculator in the context of the remaking of Paris by Baron Haussmann (1809–91). See *The Kill*.

Octave Mouret: see *The Ladies' Paradise*.

Abbé Mouret: see *The Sin of Abbé Mouret*.

15 *Banque universelle*: the founding and collapse of this bank are described in *Money*.

left him: see *The Kill*, chapter 7, and *Money*, chapter 12.

Maxime . . . had had a child . . . with some maid: see *The Kill*, chapter 3.

16 *Family Tree*: Zola produced several versions of this tree. The first was sketched out in 1868–9. A second was sent to the publisher Lacroix in 1869. A third was published in *A Love Story* in 1878. A final version was included with the preparatory material for *Doctor Pascal*.

17 *Aunt Dide*: the eccentric Adélaïde Fouque, later known as 'Aunt Dide', who becomes the common ancestor for both the Rougon and Macquart families. According to *The Fortune of the Rougons*, she was born in 1768. She becomes mad on witnessing the execution of her grandson Silvère in 1851 (see *The Fortune of the Rougons*, chapter 7).

22 *sunset*: the descriptions of Plassans and the surrounding countryside are based on Aix-en-Provence and its environs.

25 *drill*: a tough twilled cotton or linen fabric.

32 *product*: the theories outlined in the foregoing passage are derived from the two-volume *Traité philosophique et physiologique de l'hérédité naturelle* (1847 and 1850) by Prosper Lucas (1808–99). Charles Darwin (1809–82), in his *The Origin of Species* (1859), described this work as 'the fullest and the best on this subject'.

pangenesis: in *The Descent of Man* (1871) Darwin put forward a developmental theory of heredity which he called 'Pangenesis'. He suggested that all cells in an organism are capable of shedding minute particles ('gemmules'), which are able to circulate throughout the body and finally congregate in the gonads. These particles are then transmitted to the next generation and are responsible for the transmission of characteristics from parent to offspring.

perigenesis: Ernest Haeckel (1834–1919) was a German biologist, a disciple of Darwin. Perigenesis was the name he gave to a theory of reproduction positing that dynamic life force is transmitted from one generation to the next.

stirps: Francis Galton (1822–1911), a half-cousin of Darwin, was a pioneer in eugenics, coining the term itself as well as the phrase 'nature versus nurture'. 'Stirps' denotes hereditary transmission.

Weismann: August Weismann (1834–1914) was a German biologist whose main contribution to evolutionary theory involved germ plasma theory, according to which inheritance only takes place by means of the germ (egg and sperm) cells.

34 *Sudra*: an inferior caste in Hinduism, a domestic servant as opposed to the Brahmin, a superior caste specializing as priests and teachers.

Pravaz: Charles Pravaz (1791–1853), inventor of the hypodermic syringe, was a French orthopaedic surgeon.

38 *Creed*: this 'Creed' was inspired by the obituary of Ernest Renan (1823–92) by Melchior de Vogüé, published in the *Revue des deux mondes* on 15 November 1892. In some of his writings (especially *The Future of Science/ L'Avenir de la science*, begun in 1848 and published in volume form in 1890), Renan expressed the view that science could replace religion in providing man with an ethical system.

42 *bastides*: country houses in Provence.

43 *sharecropper*: a tenant farmer who gives a part of each crop as rent.

44 *Le Paradou*: an allusion to the ruined eighteenth-century chateau, and its wild garden, that figures prominently in *The Sin of Abbé Mouret*.

ataxia: loss of the ability to control or coordinate one's movements.

54 *blood-streamed pavement*: these details allude to events recounted in chapter 6 of *The Fortune of the Rougons*. Félicité bribes Macquart to lead a band of Republicans into an ambush at the town hall in Plassans. Four Republicans are killed. Pierre Rougon is made to appear as the saviour of the town. The Rougons facilitate Macquart's escape to Italy. See note to p. 13 (*twin exploits*).

alive: an allusion to *The Conquest of Plassans*, in which François Mouret, become insane, escapes from the lunatic asylum at Les Tulettes and sets fire to his own house.

74 *bankrupt*: the opinions voiced here by Clotilde echo articles written by Ferdinand Brunetière (1849–1906) in the *Revue des deux mondes* between 1886 and 1890, in which he announced the 'bankruptcy' of science. See Introduction, p. xiii.

82 *Union universelle*: the bank founded by Aristide Saccard in *Money* is called the Banque universelle. It was modelled by Zola on the Union générale, founded by Eugène Bontoux (1820–1904). There is an inadvertent blend here of the two names.

90 *circumstances*: Zola is summarizing here the theory of heredity of Prosper Lucas. See note to p. 32 (*product*).

impregnated: promulgated by Prosper Lucas, and by Jules Michelet (1798–1874) in his treatise *L'Amour* (1859), the theory of 'impregnation' held that a woman retains the 'imprint' of her first lover even to the extent that her children by another man will inherit certain of his characteristics. The plot of Zola's early novel *Madeleine Férat* (1868) turns on this theory.

92 *They started at the beginning . . . hope against hope*: Pascal–Zola proceeds to summarize the whole of *Les Rougon-Macquart*, beginning with *The Fortune of the Rougons* (1870). He does not follow the chronological order of the novels' publication, but groups the novels by evoking the lives, first of the Rougons, then the Mourets, then the Macquarts.

Eugène Rougon . . . vice-emperor: see *His Excellency Eugène Rougon* (1876).

Aristide Saccard . . . making merry: see *The Kill* (1872).

93 *Saccard again . . . deplorable life*: see *Money* (1891).

Angélique . . . nuptials: see *The Dream* (1888).

Marthe Rougon . . . François Mouret . . . priest: see *The Conquest of Plassans* (1874).

Octave Mouret . . . cracking apart: see *Pot Luck* (1882).

94 *Octave Mouret . . . Denise . . . takings*: see *The Ladies' Paradise* (1883).

Serge Mouret . . . Désirée . . . Albine . . . farmyard: see *The Sin of Abbé Mouret* (1875).

Hélène Mouret . . . Jeanne . . . Paris everlasting: see *A Love Story* (1878).

Lisa Macquart . . . Les Halles . . . decent folk: see *The Belly of Paris* (1873).

95 *Pauline Quenu . . . Lazare . . . die*: see *The Bright Side of Life* (1884).

Gervaise Macquart . . . empty: see *L'Assommoir* (1877).

Claude . . . hanging himself: see *The Masterpiece* (1886).

96 *Jacques . . . distance*: see *La Bête humaine* (1890).

Étienne . . . earth: see *Germinal* (1885).

Nana . . . collapse of everything: see *Nana* (1880).

97 *Jean Macquart . . . abomination of human beings*: see *Earth* (1887).

Jean . . . making all France anew: see *La Débâcle* (1892).

98 *social body*: Zola is echoing here his preface to *The Fortune of the Rougons*.

100 *Louiset*: the son of Nana.

Jacques Louis: the son of the painter Claude Lantier (see *The Masterpiece*).

Victor: the son of Saccard (see *Money*).

103 *Favouring of the mother*: Angèle Rougon, née Sicardot, was the first wife of Aristide Rougon (Saccard), and the mother of Maxime and Clotilde. She figures in *The Fortune of the Rougons* and *The Kill*.

117 *Is it you? . . . rottenness*: the references in this paragraph to family members are, respectively, to Aunt Dide and Antoine Macquart (*The Fortune of the Rougons*), Maxime Rougon (*The Kill*), Serge Mouret and Désirée Mouret (*The Sin of Abbé Mouret*), Claude Lantier (*The Masterpiece*), Jacques Lantier (*La Bête humaine*), and Anna Coupeau (*Nana*).

Is it this one . . . malnutrition?: the references here are, repectively, to François Mouret, Marthe Rougon, and Pierre Rougon (*The Fortune of the Rougons*), and Jeanne Grandjean (*A Love Story*).

130 *ministered to him*: the biblical story of King David and Abishag is related in the first Book of Kings.

Abraham . . . Hagar: the references are to Genesis 16.

Ruth and Boaz . . . the law: see the Book of Ruth.

131 *make him the gift of her magnificent youth*: there is a verbal echo here of the dedicatory note Zola wrote in the copy of *Doctor Pascal* which he gave to Jeanne Rozerot: see Introduction, p. xviii.

167 *therapeutics*: the treatment and care of patients.

183 *'Gendarme! Gendarme!'*: Aunt Dide is remembering her lover, the poacher Macquart, killed by gendarmes, and her nephew Silvère, executed by a gendarme at the end of *The Fortune of the Rougons*.

184 *cerebral congestion*: a now obsolete term introduced in 1761 as a cause of apoplexy.

282 *Jeu de Mail*: a now-obsolete lawn game similar to croquet; it originated in the late Middle Ages.

The Oxford World's Classics Website

www.worldsclassics.co.uk

- Browse the full range of Oxford World's Classics online

- Sign up for our monthly e-alert to receive information on new titles

- Read extracts from the Introductions

- Listen to our editors and translators talk about the world's greatest literature with our Oxford World's Classics audio guides

- Join the conversation, follow us on Twitter at OWC_Oxford

- Teachers and lecturers can order inspection copies quickly and simply via our website

www.worldsclassics.co.uk

American Literature

British and Irish Literature

Children's Literature

Classics and Ancient Literature

Colonial Literature

Eastern Literature

European Literature

Gothic Literature

History

Medieval Literature

Oxford English Drama

Philosophy

Poetry

Politics

Religion

The Oxford Shakespeare

A complete list of Oxford World's Classics, including Authors in Context, Oxford English Drama, and the Oxford Shakespeare, is available in the UK from the Marketing Services Department, Oxford University Press, Great Clarendon Street, Oxford OX2 6DP, or visit the website at www.oup.com/uk/worldsclassics.

In the USA, visit www.oup.com/us/owc for a complete title list.

Oxford World's Classics are available from all good bookshops. In case of difficulty, customers in the UK should contact Oxford University Press Bookshop, 116 High Street, Oxford OX1 4BR.

	French Decadent Tales
	Six French Poets of the Nineteenth Century
HONORÉ DE BALZAC	Cousin Bette
	Eugénie Grandet
	Père Goriot
	The Wild Ass's Skin
CHARLES BAUDELAIRE	The Flowers of Evil
	The Prose Poems and Fanfarlo
DENIS DIDEROT	Jacques the Fatalist
	The Nun
ALEXANDRE DUMAS (PÈRE)	The Black Tulip
	The Count of Monte Cristo
	Louise de la Vallière
	The Man in the Iron Mask
	La Reine Margot
	The Three Musketeers
	Twenty Years After
	The Vicomte de Bragelonne
ALEXANDRE DUMAS (FILS)	La Dame aux Camélias
GUSTAVE FLAUBERT	Madame Bovary
	A Sentimental Education
	Three Tales
VICTOR HUGO	Notre-Dame de Paris
J.-K. HUYSMANS	Against Nature
PIERRE CHODERLOS DE LACLOS	Les Liaisons dangereuses
MME DE LAFAYETTE	The Princesse de Clèves
GUILLAUME DU LORRIS and JEAN DE MEUN	The Romance of the Rose

GUY DE MAUPASSANT	**A Day in the Country and Other Stories** **A Life** **Bel-Ami**
PROSPER MÉRIMÉE	**Carmen and Other Stories**
MOLIÈRE	**Don Juan and Other Plays** **The Misanthrope, Tartuffe, and Other** **Plays**
BLAISE PASCAL	**Pensées and Other Writings**
ABBÉ PRÉVOST	**Manon Lescaut**
JEAN RACINE	**Britannicus, Phaedra, and Athaliah**
ARTHUR RIMBAUD	**Collected Poems**
EDMOND ROSTAND	**Cyrano de Bergerac**
MARQUIS DE SADE	**The Crimes of Love** **Justine** **The Misfortunes of Virtue and Other** **Early Tales**
GEORGE SAND	**Indiana**
MME DE STAËL	**Corinne**
STENDHAL	**The Red and the Black** **The Charterhouse of Parma**
PAUL VERLAINE	**Selected Poems**
JULES VERNE	**Around the World in Eighty Days** **Journey to the Centre of the Earth** **Twenty Thousand Leagues under the Seas**
VOLTAIRE	**Candide and Other Stories** **Letters concerning the English Nation** **A Pocket Philosophical Dictionary**